Men Cry In The Dark

Men Cry In The Dark

MICHAEL BAISDEN

A novel by the author of the best seller

NEVER SATISFIED
HOW & WHY MEN CHEAT

Copyright © Michael Baisden, 1997
All rights reserved

Fourth printing

Cover illustration: Albert Chacon
Book design: Stacy Hagstrom
Editor: Carolyn Bullard

Published by LEGACY PUBLISHING
P.O. Box 168685
Irving, Texas 75016-8685

Library of Congress Catalog Card No.: 97-072737
ISBN: 0-9643675-0-5

Printed in the United States of America

To all of the responsible fathers, husbands, and nice guys out there who don't get half the credit they deserve. This one's for you.

ACKNOWLEDGMENTS

I'd like to begin by giving thanks to God for once again blessing me with the vision and creativity to write a book that will have a positive impact on people's lives. My goal is to educate as well as entertain my readers. I'd also like to thank my best friend, Sam Jones, for sticking by me through thick and thin. He knew me back in the day before all the talk shows and best sellers' lists. I remember when I was so broke I had to borrow luggage to go out of town. But you always had my back, offering words of encouragement and constructive criticism. Thanks for being real!

To my brother, Tony, who is doing one hell of a job as a single parent, supporting and raising three daughters. Thanks for being such a positive example of a responsible black man. You have really been an inspiration for me while I was writing this book. And to my beautiful and energetic sister, Theresa, who seems more like the youngest than the eldest. Thanks for having faith in me and for being so enthusiastic about what I was trying to accomplish (She was so proud that she went back to her maiden name of Baisden after my first book was released). I hope to make you even more proud with this book. And I must send out a very special thanks to my hard working publicist, Yvonne Gilliam. Ever since we met back in 1995 you have been there hustling right along side me. Thanks for doing such a great job of promoting my work. And thanks for being more than just a publicist. You are truly one of my best friends.

I also must give much thanks to the countless radio stations, producers, and personalities who helped promote my books and seminars. And a special thanks to those individuals who supported me on numerous occasions and treated me like family. Robert Wilkins, Cliff Winston, and Janine Haydel at 102.3 KJLH in Los Angeles. Derrick Harper, and Mike and Carol on V103 in Atlanta. Ryan Cameron on HOT 97.5 also in Atlanta. My new family here in Dallas on K104, Skip Murphy, Nannette Lee, Sam Putney, Chris Arnold, and The Wig. We always have lots of fun when we hook up. Probably because we're all crazy.

And of course I can't forget to shout out to my hometown of Chicago. Crazy Howard McGee on WGCI. And of course V103 for giving me my first opportunity to be heard on the air. George Wilborn, John Monds, and my homegirl Bonnie Deshong.

Thanks for giving me the opportunity to pursue my dreams.

— Michael Baisden

CONTENTS

Men Cry In The Dark

HAPPILY SINGLE

Right now, I'm in Atlanta gazing out at the sunset from my hotel room window on the 42nd floor. What a view! As I listen to my Sade CD and sip on a glass of Hennessy, I'm wondering how I ever made it this far. A little over a year ago I quit my job at IBM and invested my life savings into a publishing company that was on the verge of bankruptcy. Everybody thought I was crazy. But it had always been my dream to publish my own magazine ever since I worked as editor of my college newspaper. So when I saw the opportunity I went for it.

"No guts, no glory," I always say. And that attitude paid off! Today *Happily Single* magazine is one of the top-selling publications in the country, maybe not as popular as *Ebony* and *Jet*, but we're getting there. And I owe much of my success to my editor, Monica, and my production manager, Tiffany, two women who offered me words of encouragement and support throughout this whole ordeal. They invested their creative talents and ten thousand dollars of their own money to make my dreams into their dreams. In fact, I was so moved by their faith in me that I named the company after them: Motif Publishing. Monica and Tiffany, get it?

However, what motivated me most was all those jealous and narrow-minded losers at my job who told me I couldn't do it. Whenever things got rough and I didn't think I would make it, I just replayed all their negative comments in my head and I was instantly rejuvenated. I'll never forget their reaction when I came into the office that Monday morning to submit my letter of resignation. The news of my leaving spread quickly throughout the company, and the calls began pouring in. Not calls of support, but of skepticism. "You're blowing a great opportunity," one of the VPs said. "Not many blacks make it up to this level." Then my pessimistic secretary offered her two cents' worth of advice saying she thought I should think it over for another year or so. I knew she was just trying to keep me around long enough to get into my pants. She has been trying to seduce me ever since she started working for me, but I told her I don't mix business with pleasure.

But the comment I'll never forget was from this asshole named Jeffery who worked in personnel. He was one of those back-stabbing Uncle Tom negroes who always had something negative to say. You know the type, always sees the glass as half empty instead of half full. Anyway, I was in the cafeteria saying goodbye to the cooks when he strolls in talking smack. "You're a damn fool," he said. "You'll be back in six months begging for your job back. And I'll be right here waiting to laugh in your face." Well, that was fourteen months and

500,000 issues ago and he's still waiting. Guess who's laughing now?

However, breaking the news to my father, Derrick Sr., was no laughing matter. For 25 years he had slaved out in the hot sun working construction to afford to send me to Morehouse College and then to grad school. And he took great pride in telling his friends that his son was a regional manager for a major corporation like IBM. Needless to say, he was furious when I told him I quit. "Are you crazy!?" he shouted. "How can you throw away $70,000 a year salary, a good pension, and ten years of seniority on a pipe dream? You must be on drugs." I was shocked by his angry response. That was the first time he ever shut me out without at least listening to what my reasons were, and it hurt. It hurt deeply.

I tried my best to understand his position. After all, I was his only son. He only wanted me to have all of the things in life he never had, money, security, and most important of all, choices. "Education is the key," he drilled into me. "Those who fail to plan, plan to fail." Yeah, he used that old line on me, and it worked. By the time I was 25 I had my BA in marketing and my MBA in business administration. Not bad for a poor boy who grew up in the projects eating government cheese.

But I wanted to explain to him that academic degrees, pension plans, and corporate seniority don't necessarily guarantee you security. And they damn sure don't guarantee you a promotion. I don't care how hard you work. If you're a female or another minority in corporate America, the glass ceiling is real. My supervisor was right; I was fortunate to have gotten as far as I did. And I knew I wasn't going any further. The most valuable lesson I took away from ten years in that concentration camp was that true security can only come from controlling your own destiny. And that means setting your own hours and making your own money. Universities should spend more time teaching students how to think creatively and take risks. The way the current educational system is set up, young people are only learning how to become more efficient employees, not entrepreneurs.

My dad was from the old school and couldn't understand my frustration with punching a clock every day. He was so upset that he didn't speak to me for two weeks. And although we've gotten back to talking on the phone on a regular basis, he's still disappointed with me. I can hear it in his voice. But this is my life and I've got to do what I feel is in my best interest. I don't want to be one of those bitter old men you see sitting around the neighborhood barber shops talking about what they should've and could've done. I can't go out like that. Maybe one of these days he'll see that the world is a very different place from when he was a young man and understand that I made the right choice, for me.

As for now, I'm going to finish sipping on my glass of cognac, take in this fantastic view of downtown Atlanta, and enjoy my success. God knows I've earned it. This year I traveled to over 40 cities and secured more than $200,000 in advertising contracts. As soon as I'm finished with my radio interview tomorrow morning, I'm going to relax, get some exercise, and then head out to one of these night clubs to celebrate. There's no way in hell I'm going back home without getting my groove on. Who knows, maybe I'll get lucky. They say southern girls are the best and I'm always looking for a few good women, just like the Marines. And besides, who wants to rush home to Chicago, anyway? It's freezing up there! My dad told me the high today was five degrees, fifteen below with the wind chill. Damn, that's cold!

At 6:00 a.m. the phone rang. It was my wake-up call. The radio interview wasn't until 7:30, but I wanted to give myself plenty of time to take a shower and get dressed. Making a good first impression is important in this business; it can be the difference between success and failure. People are very image-conscious. I decided not to wear a suit, "That's too damned formal," I

thought. So, I laid out my black long-sleeved Zanella shirt and a pair of tan Sartori slacks with matching socks. After taking a quick shower I shaved with my last disposable razor, sprayed my neck with Herrera cologne, and oiled my scalp with TCB. By 6:30 I was dressed to impress. On the way out the door, I grabbed my briefcase and a stack of magazines to give away at the station.

While I rode the glass elevator down to the lobby, I found myself feeling worried about the interview. Normally I have an opportunity to talk to the DJ prior to going on the air. That way I can get a feel for what he or she is like. I didn't know what to expect from the jock who was doing the interview that morning. All I knew about him was that he was around my age and single. I just crossed my fingers and prayed he wasn't one of those unattractive player haters who kisses up to women to get good ratings.

The radio station was only supposed to be 20 minutes away, according to the valet at the hotel. But I had driven for over a half hour and still didn't see any of the landmarks that he told me to look out for. After driving around for another ten minutes I started getting pissed. I hate being lost, especially when I'm in a hurry. Around another corner I turned, and then down a dead end street, and still no sign of the studio. I pulled over at a gas station to ask directions from a freckle-faced white kid who was sitting inside a bulletproof booth eating Cheese Puffs, but he had just moved from a small town in Utah and didn't know shit.

I could practically feel the steam rising from the top of my head as I drove back down the same street, for the fifth time. I started cursing out loud to myself, calling the valet all kinds of dumb sons of bitches, and stupid MFs. I even thought about pulling over and calling the hotel to curse him out. But at the next light I turned left and drove right into the radio station parking lot. I couldn't help laughing at myself for stressing out so bad. Oh well, I was thinking, he's still a stupid son of a bitch for not giving better directions.

After parking my car, I pulled the stack of magazines out the trunk and walked toward the front door. I followed the instructions I had scribbled down on the hotel stationery to ring the illuminated door bell and then wait for someone to come to escort me upstairs. Two seconds later a young lady, who I later found out was the morning show producer, came flying down the stairs screaming for me to hurry up.

"Come on!" she shouted. "We've been waiting for you! The phones are ringing off the hook."

According to my watch and the digital clock in my Nissan Maxima rental car it was only 7:15. We rushed down a dark hall, then through an office area and finally came to the sound-proof studio. The On Air sign was lit, so we paused outside the door until it went off. When it finally did, she led me into the room and introduced me to Justin, the morning jock. One look at him and I knew it was going to be a great interview. He was a tall, light-skinned, smooth-looking brother with womanizing eyes. He was a dog if I ever saw one. And you know what they say — A player knows another player.

"Look, Derrick, we've only got 30 seconds before we come out of this commercial break, so let me tell you what's going on," Justin said. "We were supposed to have a relationship expert on this morning to talk about why men cheat. But she canceled on us at the last minute. We decided to run with the topic anyway and tie it into the discussion about your magazine. Now, if you can make this interesting, we can promote your magazine for the next two segments. Can you handle that?"

"Without a doubt," I said slapping him five. "If Dr. Ruth can do it, so can I."

"Okay, go sit over there and get ready. I'm going to introduce you and then we're going right back to the phone lines to take callers."

The producer guided me over to the stool, slapped a set of headphones on my ears, and shoved the microphone in my face. Two seconds later, the On Air light came on and we were live. I smiled and tried to look cool, but the truth was I was nervous as hell.

"Joining us now is Mr. Derrick Reed, owner and promotions director for *Happily Single* magazine, one of the hottest publications in the country today," Justin said. "So, Derrick, tell us in your own words, why do you think men cheat?"

I sat there looking stupid trying to figure out what to say. As cocky as I was, I didn't want to say anything that would jeopardize my image or the image of the magazine. But when Justin began frantically signaling me with his hands, I had to say something. So I figured, "What the hell?" and said what I honestly thought.

"I think men cheat because women allow them to."

"What do you mean they allow men to cheat?" the producer said, playing devil's advocate. "Women don't go around telling their husbands and boyfriends that it's okay to screw other women. You're talkin' crazy!"

"I didn't say they promoted cheating, I said they allowed it. And you know **dog gone** well that women know when they're dealing with a dog. They just ignore the obvious signs because they are either too whipped or too comfortable in the relationship to do anything about it. Now, tell me I'm wrong."

"Only stupid uneducated women put up with that mess. I have a college degree, my own house, and my own money. My man would **never** cheat on me!"

Bam! The phone lines lit up like a Christmas tree. Even the private studio line was ringing off the hook. A few seconds later every female employee in the building came looking through the studio glass window nodding their heads in agreement to my comment.

"Okay, let's go to the phone lines and see what the listeners have to say. Shanika, you're on the air."

"I want to speak to that woman who said her man would never cheat on her," Shanika said, sounding frantic. "Where is she!?"

"I'm right here," the producer said with an attitude.

"Sister girl, you need to wake up and smell the coffee! Your man could be laying up with some skeezer right now while he's listening to you on the radio and you'd never know it. Like my mama always told me, never say never. And one more thing, about that comment you made about educated women not being cheated on, Yeah right! Let me tell you something, I know just as many doctors, lawyers, and engineers who are getting their heads bumped as women who work in McDonald's. All a degree does is make you a educated fool. That's all I have to say, bye."

"All righty then," Justin said. "Let's take the next caller for Derrick. Hi, Karen, you're on the air."

"First of all let me say that I agree with what Derrick said one hundred percent. Women do know when they're dating a dog. But my question to you is, why don't men come right out and tell you they want to see other women and avoid all the lies and game playing?"

"Let me answer that question with a question," I said. "If the man you were dating told you he wanted to have sex with other women, would you still date him?"

"I probably would!" Karen said confidently. "At this point in my life I'm too busy working and going to school for a full-time relationship. A booty call every now and then would be fine with me."

"Okay, then here's another question for you. Would you reserve the right to sleep with other men?"

"You damn right I would! Sorry, I didn't mean to curse," Karen said. "But, yes, I want the same freedom in the relationship that he has."

"Well, Karen, you just answered your own question."

"And how is that?"

"One of the main reasons that men lie to women about

being committed is to keep them from having sex with other men. Let's face it, men are too greedy and too insecure to share."

The women in the office were clapping and nodding in agreement. "That's right, that's right!" they were shouting. The phone lines continued to light up, but we had to take another break for commercials. During that time out Justin and I got better acquainted and talked about hooking up later that evening. It was obvious that we had a lot in common, particularly in regard to our philosophy on women. We exchanged phone numbers, gave each other that player's nod, and got back into position to take more callers.

"Okay, we're back with Derrick Reed from *Happily Single* magazine, and it's hotter than July in the studio. Today's topic is 'why do men cheat?' And before we go back to the phone lines, I just want to say that men aren't the only ones guilty of infidelity. Right Derrick?"

Again, I was dumbfounded. I wanted to reach across that counter and choke the shit out of him for throwing that bomb at me. I was hoping we would move on and talk about the magazine, but I guess controversy sells. So, once again I cleared my throat and tried my best not to step over the line.

"That's right! Women cheat too! And they're a lot better at it than we are. A man will cheat with the next-door neighbor who's broke as hell and on welfare. But a woman, she will make sure to have an affair with a man who has more money than the man she's cheating on. And she'll go to the Bahamas to do it."

"Having said that, let's move on," Justin said trying to keep from laughing. "What's your name, caller?"

"I don't want to give my real name," a woman with a sultry voice said. "Just call me Ms. Westside."

"All right Ms. Westside, what's your question for Derrick?"

"I'd like to know what makes you such an authority on relationships. From what I've heard you're not a Ph.D. or a certified therapist. And I'm willing to bet that you don't even have a woman."

"Now, come on, baby," Justin said. "Why you wanna go off on the brother like that? He's only trying to participate in a discussion. And I think he's doing a pretty good job."

"That's quite all right, Justin," I said. "Let me answer the lady's question. First of all, I wasn't asked my professional opinion, I was asked my personal opinion, which is what I gave. I'm sure you have taken advice from your girlfriends and your mother at one time or another, haven't you?"

"My mother is dead."

"I'm sorry to hear that, but my point is that good or bad advice can come from anybody, even a stranger. And speaking of advice, my advice to you is to chill out and stop taking things so seriously. We're just trying to have a little fun."

"So, do you have a woman or not?" she asked.

"No, I don't. Do you have a man?"

"Not at the moment."

"But I bet that doesn't stop you from giving your girlfriends advice, now does it?"

"You got that right! I counsel more women than Oprah Winfrey, Ricki Lake, and Montel Williams put together."

"Now, see? That's exactly what I'm talking about. You got the nerve to call up here giving me grief and you're out there doing the exact same thing. You must be from the west side of Mississippi."

"For your information I'm from the West Side of Chicago."

"Aw! I should have known!" I shouted "You West Side women are always trying to loud talk a brother. No wonder you don't have a man."

"I can have any man I want. I'm single by choice, and I'm perfectly fine with that. What you need to be doing is advising these women on how to be content with being alone."

I couldn't have agreed with her more. In fact that's exactly the point I was going to make before she got me off the subject. Now she had me on the defensive. Meanwhile all of this arguing back and forth had the station buzzing. The lines were blowing up like crazy and the window outside the studio started to resemble a talk show audience. The producer signaled that we only had 30 seconds left before the segment was over, so I wrapped it up.

"Before I let you go Ms. Westside, or whatever your name is, I just want to say that I agree with you about being alone. In fact, that's what *Happily Single* magazine is all about, learning how to be happy as a single man or woman. Society puts too much pressure on us to settle down and get married. Personally, I think you can be settled living by yourself."

"I think both of you made very good points," Justin said. "Maybe we can get you two Chi-town folks together to discuss this off the air. How about it Derrick?"

"That's fine with me."

"What about you Ms. Westside, you wanna make a love connection?"

"I don't think so. Derrick sounds a bit too cocky for my taste, but thanks anyway."

"Well, thank you for your comments and we hope you keep listening."

After the interview Justin and I gave each other one of those brotherly hugs and he walked me out to the office area to meet the program director and the rest of the staff. On my way out the door the operator gave me a hug for keeping it real and then cursing me out because the phones were still ringing off the hook. Women from age 15 to 55 were trying to find out where they could buy the magazine and what hotel I was staying at. Justin arranged to have all the other DJs announce the names of the stores where the magazine was available and that he and I would be hanging out at Harriston's night club in Stone Mountain that evening giving away free copies. I couldn't wait to get out there to meet all the beautiful southern women and to promote the magazine.

This was one of those rare occasions when I was looking forward to mixing business with pleasure.

Justin and I agreed to meet at Harriston's at 9:00 o'clock. He warned me that the Friday night crowd is sometimes snobbish and that parking was terrible, if you got there late. Which is exactly why I left my hotel at 8:15. I'm not one of those prissy men who have to make a grand entrance. In fact, I prefer to arrive as early as possible so I can get acquainted with the ladies before the club gets too crowded. By the time Mr. Debonair shows up at 11:00 or 12:00 o'clock looking all fresh and cool, I've already got the finest woman in the club hemmed up in the corner telling me her life story.

As I drove south on Highway 285 headed toward the club, I tuned the radio to V103 to hear some upbeat music to get myself in the party mood. Just my luck, they were in the middle of an Erykah Badu mix. The cut "On & On" off of her *Baduizm* CD was playing. I pressed the volume button and turned it up as loud as it would go. The bass was thumping so hard the dashboard was vibrating. Damn, it sounded good! I couldn't help smiling as I sang along and thought about how much fun I had at the radio station that morning. The response from the interview was so overwhelming that the magazine sold out all over town. The manager at one of the bookstores told me she sold 200 that afternoon. I personally signed 50 copies while I was there. Monica and Tiffany cracked up when I called and told them I had become a local celebrity. "We might have to promote a special centerfold edition with you sporting a pair of leopard print draws," Monica said. "I'll come down there and pimp you myself if it will sell more magazines."

But there was something else on my mind. Something that I just couldn't stop thinking about all day. The comment that Ms. Westside made about me not having a woman. Yes, I was single and sometimes not by choice. All three of my best friends had someone special in their lives. Mark was dating another white woman, I believe her name is Christie. Tony was engaged to marry his girlfriend Tracie. And Ben, well, Ben was trying to rob the cradle again with a 25-year-old hair stylist who worked at the beauty salon next door to his shop downtown. But at least he had someone he was interested in.

For the last 14 months I have tried to remain completely focused on my goal of making *Happily Single* magazine number one. And my success to this point has been based on my policy of not getting too seriously involved in a relationship. That meant absolutely positively no commitment! And every time I ignored this self-imposed restriction, I found myself in very stressful and emotionally draining relationships. First there was Patricia, whom I met right after I quit IBM. Her resume made her appear to be the ideal mate. She was a corporate lawyer with no kids, no debt, and a pair of breasts that made you want to revert back to breast feeding. She even knew how to cook. And you know how hard it is to find that quality in a professional woman. But Patricia had two bad habits. One, she kept changing the radio station in my car without asking. And two, she had a superiority complex, especially when it came to inner-city blacks, referring to them as, "Those People." Keep in mind that I am straight from the ghetto, so you know she had to be dismissed.

Then there was Theresa, my first and last young woman experience. She was a 23-year-old single parent struggling to make ends meet. When we met she was living at home with her mother while working her way through nursing school. And although she was broke as hell, I admired her for staying off welfare while raising her two kids. Sure, her language was a little on the rough side for my taste, but she had a good heart, and she never asked me for money. Not one thin dime. But what little we had established came to an abrupt end when her youngest daughter's father came back on the scene after two years in prison. Call me a coward if you want, but that was one crazy motherfucker. And besides the sex wasn't all that good anyway. Not good enough to die for. With a name like Killer, I knew he wasn't locked up for jaywalking.

Finally, there was sweet and innocent Samone. Yeah right! She went from Hazel the maid to hell raiser in four months. In the beginning of the relationship she appeared to have it going on. Samone was well-educated, childless, a great cook, a fitness freak, a super freak, and most importantly, no ex-boyfriends were stalking her. But as it turned out, she was nuttier than a bag of Snickers. For the first two months of the relationship everything was fine. I did my thing and she did hers. She never asked any questions about who else I was seeing or came by my apartment unannounced. That's something I don't tolerate! But when I began flying out of town more often on business she did a three-sixty. Samone expected me to call her twice a day from each city. Once when my plane landed and again after I made it to my hotel room safely. If that wasn't bad enough, she also insisted that I call her every night before going to bed. "I want my voice to be the last thing you hear before you close your eyes," she would say.

The one time I neglected to follow her instructions, she showed up at my hotel room in the middle of the night looking like Glenn Close in *Fatal Attraction*. She was crying and carrying on about how much she was worried about me. For the next two days she stuck to me like super glue, never letting me out of her sight except to go to the bathroom. In the middle of the night she would wake up sweating and screaming, talking crazy about how she dreamt that somebody took me away from her. I'm not ashamed to admit it, I was scared as hell. Luckily for me, her job transferred her to Alaska. Last I heard she was stalking some other poor soul, probably an Eskimo.

It took me all of two seconds to adjust my attitude and appreciate my bachelor lifestyle. "Ms. Westside can kiss my ass," I thought to myself. I was content, no, happy, being single. Any man would love to be in my shoes. I had a lavish condo on Lake Shore Drive, a new convertible Jaguar, and a fat bank account. All I needed out of a relationship at this point in my life was interesting conversation and occasional sex. If I could find a woman who could satisfy those needs without giving me drama, we could spend time together and have a little fun. Besides, the way I saw it women didn't have any leverage to be demanding a monogamous relationship, especially in a city like Atlanta where the ratio was ten to one. Whether they want to accept it or not, it's a man's world!

I was so pumped up that I almost missed the Covington Highway exit. After coming off the ramp, I drove straight for another mile then turned left on Harriston Road. Ten minutes later I saw Harriston's on the left side of the street. Justin was right, the club was packed. Brothers were swaggering through the parking lot in their conservative business suits and the sistahs looked like they had just stepped out of *Fashion Fair* magazine. I pulled up to valet parking and popped open the trunk. That's when I spotted Justin standing at the front door smoking a cigarette and talking to a group of women.

"Hey, Justin!" I shouted, "Can I tear you away from your adoring fans for a minute? I need a hand."

"Well, it's about time. People have been bugging me about you all night. I hope you brought plenty of magazines."

"I've got about a hundred."

"A hundred? Shit, we'll go through those in half an hour."

"Good," I said. "Then I can spend the rest of the night getting my groove on."

"Oh, and by the way. I've got a surprise for you," Justin said, handing me an envelope.

"What is this?"

"It's a letter from Ms. Westside. She's in the house tonight."

"Is that right? Where is she? And what does she look like?"

"I don't know. The manager told me the card was left at the door, anonymously. Open it up and see what it says."

After we got the box of magazines out the trunk, I used

Justin's car keys to tear the red and white envelope open. It read:

Dear Derrick,

I'm sorry I couldn't appear more interested than I really was this morning. I am a very private lady who doesn't like her business in the streets. I came out tonight with my sorority sisters to enjoy myself while I'm visiting Atlanta. But I also came to meet you face-to-face to tell you how much I admire you for your honesty. I've seen your picture in the magazine and I've read a few of the articles that you've written. Needless to say, I'm impressed with your perspective and your frankness. It's not often you meet a man who is brave enough to say what's really on his mind. I'm looking forward to buying you a drink and picking your brain. And by the way, don't keep looking over your shoulder trying to figure out which one is me, I'll find you when the time is right.

Yours truly,

Ms. Westside
Delta Sigma Theta - Forever!

P.S. I know you're wondering what I look like. Don't worry, you won't be disappointed!

I had to hand it to her, that letter was a smooth approach. And the red and white envelope was a nice touch too. Sorority women are always trying to represent, especially Deltas and AKAs. I blushed as Justin and I walked inside and sat down at a reserved table in the back. The club was wall-to-wall with well-dressed black folks drinking cocktails and chatting, mostly in their own little cliques. I couldn't help being amused by the way everybody was carrying themselves. The women were dressed provocatively but acting all stuck up like they didn't want anybody to talk to them. And the men were standing around trying to look cool, like they were posing for the cover of *GQ*. Instead of trying to meet the attractive women who were walking right past them, they stood around holding their drinks acting like the women were supposed to choose them. Fuck that! Growing up in Chicago you learn at a very young age that you've got to take charge, be aggressive. When I used to hang out at clubs like Chic Ricks and The Nimbus, I walked into the room like I owned the place and proceeded to mack down every woman in sight. And I didn't stop mackin' until I got a pocket full of numbers. Watching those brothers trying to run game was comical. I looked over at Justin, who was from Brooklyn, and said, "If these brothers were in Chicago trying to run this weak game, they would all be virgins." Justin gave me high five and replied, "And they damn sure wouldn't get any play in New York."

For the next two hours I greeted customers at the table, shaking hands and giving away copies of the magazine. But all the while I kept wondering, "Which one is she?" The room was full of so many fine women that I figured I couldn't go wrong no matter which one she was. But I suspected that Ms. Westside was going to be something special. I knew she would somehow stand out from the crowd. A woman with such a high level of confidence and style normally does. No sooner than I had that thought, the waitress came over with a refill on my glass of cognac. "This is from Ms. Westside," she said with a wide grin on her face. "She said to meet her at the DJ booth in ten minutes."

I immediately excused myself from the table and went to the bathroom to freshen up. I hated the idea that she was probably watching my every move. Her anonymity kept me from flirting with the other beautiful women who were trying to get my number. "She better be the finest thing in here," I was thinking as I washed my face. "If she's a dog I'm going to shake her hand, give her a copy of the magazine, and run." Once I was all spruced up, I went back to my table and shook as many hands as I could in five minutes. When that time was up, I told Justin where I was going and asked him to watch my back.

As I made my way over to the DJ booth, women were waving their hands in the air trying to get my attention but I kept my eyes fixed on my destination. Toni Braxton could have been standing right next to me and I wouldn't have known it. Once I'm locked in on something or someone, forget it! I'm like a hawk. As I got closer, I could see three attractive-looking women standing in the general area. One was tall and light-skinned, another was short and heavy-chested. "Not bad," I thought. But then there was number three, who was standing with perfect posture. I knew she had to be the one. She was about 5'9", wearing a short black dress, and her hair was pulled back in a long ponytail. I swear she looked just like a black *I Dream of Jeannie*. And you know how beautiful Barbara Eden is. Sure enough it was her. Before I even got over to where she was, we both started blushing. Our eyes never left one another as I forced my way through the crowded aisle. I know that's sounds kinda corny, but hey, that's how it was. When I finally made it over to her, I could see her legs were just as flawless as the rest of her body. I never saw a woman so well put together.

"So, Mr. Reed, we finally meet," she said in a soft and seductive tone.

"Well, it's about time!" I said, keeping the mood light. "How could you torture me like this?"

"Wasn't it worth the wait?"

I looked her up and down, slowly. Trying not to give too much attention to her chest area, which wasn't easy, let me tell you. Either she had on the world's best push-up bra or those were the perkiest set of breasts I ever saw.

"I think you know the answer to that question, Ms. Westside. By the way, what **is** your real name?"

"Angela, Angela Williams."

"Well, let me say, Ms. Williams, that you are without a

doubt **the** most stunning woman I've ever had the pleasure of meeting."

"Why thank you, Mr. Reed. You're not chopped liver yourself."

"Does that mean you'll have this next dance with me?"

"I don't know if I want to dance with one of you stuffy South Side brothers."

"How did you know I was from the South Side?"

"Because South Siders are all stuck up and bourgeois. That tight suit you have on was a dead giveaway."

"Don't let this so-called tight suit fool you, baby, I can still dance circles around you. I'm from the old school."

"All I hear is a bunch of talk," she said while looking around for someone she could trust to watch her purse. "Let's see what you got."

The bartender, who just happened to be dippin' in on our conversation, offered to watch her purse and my jacket. I took her by the hand and proudly escorted her onto the floor, and for the next hour we danced up a storm. Angela had very impressive moves for a woman of her age, which I accurately estimated to be 35. Even the younger women were checking her out as she swayed with grace and ground with intensity. And it was just my luck that the DJ was into a serious reggae mix; she couldn't help dancing nasty off of that funky beat. It was obvious that - back in the day - she was a real dance machine. It took all the control I had to keep from getting an erection. When she pressed her firm butt against me and began to pump, I thought I was going to explode. She damn near lifted me off the floor. As awkward as it was, I was loving every minute of it. The men were trying to hit on her by making eye contact but she played them off and moved in closer, sending them a clear message that she was taken. That's one of the qualities I like in an older woman; they know how to handle that kind of attention.

When we finally left the dance floor, she had me hot as hell. I had to put my hand in my pocket to keep from exposing myself. For the rest of the night we sat at the bar drinking Long Island Ice Teas and cracked jokes on couples who couldn't dance; people from Chicago love to do that. I was having so much fun that I almost forgot that I was there to do business. Angela had my undivided attention with her quick wit and her great sense of humor. By the end of the night, it seemed like we had known one another for years, or as the expression goes, "We clicked."

At 3:00 a.m. the club closed and I escorted her out to her car. We exchanged phone numbers and made tentative plans to get together when we got back to Chicago. For a minute I thought she was going to give me a kiss but her girlfriends started blowing the horn, yelling, "Hurry up!" Oh, I hate it when other women block just because they didn't get chosen. But she did give me a peck on the cheek and a firm hug. Not one of those non-booty hugs that women give you when they just want to be friends. But a tight squeeze that left no doubt that she wanted to get closer.

HOMECOMING

Why do plane rides have to be so stressful? I'm sitting here minding my own business trying to read *Think and Grow Rich* by Dennis Kimbrough and the guy next to me insists on making conversation. I know damn well he can read this expression on my face saying, "Leave me alone!" I swear if he asks me one more stupid question about Chicago, I'm going to curse him out. What I should do is give him directions to Cabrini Green projects; that'll fix him. Luckily we were on our final approach into O'Hare airport. Thank God, I was thinking.

Get me away from this psychopath.

As the plane made a smooth 180-degree turn on its final approach, I leaned forward in my seat to see if I could get a good look at Chicago's skyline. My window was on the left side of the plane, which briefly pointed toward the blue waters of Lake Michigan. But as we flew inland, I could see the Sears Tower, John Hancock Building, and the big ferris wheel on Navy Pier. What a spectacular view.

It was 12:30 by the time I made it to my car in the remote parking lot. I loaded my bags into the trunk, paid the attendant, and headed east on the Kennedy. As I pulled out into the congested freeway, it felt good to be home again. The reckless drivers, salted white asphalt, and the loud CTA trains which ran parallel to the expressway were a welcome sight. Sweet home Chicago! When I got closer to downtown I plugged my cellular phone into the cigarette lighter and called home to check my messages. I only had two. I was hoping one of them was from Angela.

"Hello son, I tried to catch you at your hotel in Atlanta but you had already checked out," my father said in his unmistakably deep voice. "I just wanted to let you know that Monica called me today and told me the news about the magazine reaching 500,000 in sales. That's wonderful son! It looks like you're well on your way to making it. Your mother and I are very proud of you. Just keep up the good work and...."

Right in the middle of his sentence, he abruptly stopped. I didn't know if he was trying to decide whether to hang up or finish what he had to say. After about thirty seconds or so, he continued his message.

"Look, son, what I really called to say was, I was wrong. You had a dream to do something special with your life and I should have supported you one hundred percent. I hope you can forgive me for being so stubborn. I was only trying to protect you from making what I thought was a big mistake. Maybe I'm the one who still has a lot to learn. Anyway, I just wanted to get that off my chest. Give me a call when you get settled in."

He paused again, this time for only a couple of seconds. "And one more thing, I love you, son."

I was so shocked that I swerved and almost hit the car in the next lane. My father was a very stubborn man who hated admitting he was wrong. I knew that was extremely difficult for him to admit. And that was the first time since I graduated college that he said he loved me. Even then he said, **we** love you, referring to him and my mother. I couldn't help getting choked up. It's very awkward hearing those words coming from such a strong and obstinate man. After I pulled myself together, I pushed the button to retrieve the next message.

"What's up Mr. Big Time Magazine Executive? This is Tony. It's eleven o'clock and I'm about to head out to the gym to meet up with Big Ben and Mark. I was hoping you might be back in town so I could slam dunk on you. Oh, well. Maybe next time. Give me a call when you get in. I've got some great news to tell you."

I looked down at my watch and I thought about driving to the South Side to meet up with them. My gym shoes and sweats were in my luggage and I didn't have any other plans. Besides, this was our regular weekend to shoot ball and have breakfast together. I guess you could call it our male bonding day. Why not? I thought. When I came to the Loop where all of the expressways connect, I kept straight onto the Dan Ryan and pressed down on the accelerator. We'll see who slam dunks on who.

When I arrived at the gym I could hear the familiar sounds of screeching rubber against the hardwood floor. On the east side of the gym four kids were playing two-on-two and talking plenty of smack.

"Pass me the rock, baby!" one kid yelled.

"Go to the hole and post up!" his teammate yelled back. "You've got the little man on you."

"Post up? Who do I look like, Karl Malone. Just throw me the damn ball!"

I couldn't help smiling as I watched them play. They reminded me so much of my friends and me when we were kids. Back in those days we would wake up at the crack of dawn and lace up our $12 PF Flyers and Converse All Stars and play until the street lights came on. Kids nowadays spend $200 for a pair of sneakers and play until one o'clock in the morning in the Midnight League.

My adrenaline was pumping and I was ready to post somebody up myself. I quickly ran downstairs and laced up my sneakers and put on my #33 Scottie Pippen Chicago Bulls sweats. When I came back upstairs I went straight over to the west side of the gym where Mark, Tony and Ben were playing full court against four young boys who looked to be between the ages of 19 and 21. As Tony passed the ball into play I stepped out onto the court and yelled, "I've got next!"

"Well, I'll be damned," Ben shouted. "Look who's here!"

"If it isn't Mr. Frequent Flyer himself," Tony said.

"I thought you weren't flying in until tomorrow," Mark said. "How long have you been back?"

"All I want to know is did you meet any honeys down in Atlanta?" Ben asked. "I heard they outnumber the men ten to one."

"What's with the hundred questions?" I said. "The only thing that matters is that I'm here, so stop talkin' and play ball."

Our conversation was taken as disrespect by the opposing team. They were already getting spanked 14 to 6, and the game was only up to 15, by ones. The youngest, who was guarding Mark, was the first to open his big mouth.

"Hey, old man. Who do you think you are, coming in here disrupting our game?"

"Old man?" I asked while sarcastically looking around to see who he was talking to. "Are you talking to me, junior?"

"Yeah, I'm talking to you, with those Buster Brown, imitation Nikes you're wearing. Where did you get those sneakers, at a flea market?"

Everybody was on the ground crackin' up. I wanted to laugh too, but my pride was bruised. And to make matters worse the gym was full of attractive young women who were watching closely. So, you know I had to show off. I got right in his face and challenged him to put up or shut up.

"Why don't you put your money where your mouth is, junior?" I said. "I'll bet you fifty bucks that I can score a basket on you with my first possession."

"You're on!" he said as he aggressively flung the ball toward me. "This will be like taking candy from a baby."

This was the type of challenge we live for in the hood, old versus young, poise against athleticism. The fact that he was 6' 3", faster, and could dunk with both hands, didn't matter. I had time on my side. The four of us had been playing ball together since we were ten years old. That's 25 years of experience. They didn't stand a snowball's chance in hell. All we had to do was run one of our patented plays and breakfast was going to be on me.

"Are you sure you don't want to warm up first, grandpa?" he joked. "I don't want you to throw your back out."

"Keep on talkin' youngster," I said. "In a minute you're going to be as humble as a blade of grass at a lawn mower convention."

What happened next could be best described as a Harlem Globetrotter routine. Mark threw the ball in bounds off the back of his defender, dribbled it through his legs and passed it up court to Tony. Tony bounced the ball into Big Ben, who had his man behind him at the free throw line. When I made my move to the hoop, he stepped out with that wide 260-pound body of his and set a vicious pick on my man. Once I was clear, he threw the ball over his head and off the backboard and I dunked it. Swish! The gymnasium erupted with cheers and high fives. Meanwhile the opposing team began criticizing each other for failing to stop me.

"Why didn't you call out that he was setting a pick on me!?" the guy who made the bet yelled.

"Man, who you hollering at?" his teammate replied. "You're the one who didn't play any D. Now, stop whining and pay the man."

After collecting my hard-earned money, we played a few more games and then hit the showers. It was one o'clock and everybody was starved to death and ready for breakfast. Mark insisted on acting as chauffeur so he could show off his new Mercedes S500.

"I can't believe you drove this car down here," I said as I got inside the Benz. "You must have Allstate's Platinum Ghetto insurance."

"I'm not worried about my car getting stolen. These are *my people*."

"Well, could you tell *your people* to give me back the AM radio they stole out of my old Chevy last month?"

"They stole an AM radio?" Ben asked.

"Yep, they sure did. And my eight-track tape player too."

"Damn. These crack-heads will steal anything."

"I wish somebody would touch my Benz. I'd make them wish they were never born."

"Yeah, right, like the thief is going to leave you an address and phone number where you can reach him," I said. "What you need to do is leave this car at home and drive your old Buick like you've been doing for the last five years. Besides, you shouldn't be flaunting your money in these people's faces."

"Don't be such a party pooper!" Mark said. "I'm just a hard-working young brother trying to make a dollar out of fifteen cents."

"That's exactly your problem junior," Tony said. "You're young!"

"I bet I'm not too young to drive your asses to breakfast. Now shut up and get in."

Tony was right. Mark had just turned 32 and was still going through that *car thing.* Over the last four years he had bought several expensive cars, a Ford Bronco, a Porshe 911, a Nissan Maxima, and now this Mercedes. Although he did trade in the Porshe and the Maxima, he needed to stop putting so much emphasis on materialistic things. Ben and I were 35 and Tony was 36. We had already gone through that phase. Sure, we all owned expensive cars too, but we kept our success on the down low.

But aside from making bad decisions about cars, Mark had his life together. In fact, he's probably the smartest out of the bunch. He graduated magna cum laude from DePaul University majoring in law. However, he chose to help run the family business instead of going to law school. Mark's family owned a strip mall out in the south suburbs. They rented out five spaces and operated three businesses in the other three: a video store, a liquor store, and a beauty supply wholesale shop, which is one of the largest in the country.

Five years ago, Mark and his older sister Yvonne moved out to the burbs to be closer to the businesses. Yvonne enjoyed being closer to the large shopping mall and Mark liked the convenience of being closer to his white girlfriends. Oh yeah, Mark loves those blond-headed, blue-eyed white girls with a passion. Over the past five years he's dated two white women, one Hispanic, an Asian, and zero black women. His mother thinks he's lost his mind. She can't understand how her son could grow up in the heart of the ghetto, watch her struggle to raise two kids on her own, then have the audacity to exclude black women. The key word for me is exclude, because I'm not a racist. I simply don't think it's healthy when a person refuses to date someone of their own race. That goes for whites, Asians, Hispanics, as well as for blacks.

Ever since we were kids Mark has been bitter toward black girls. I guess that was because he was always the odd man out when it came to playing spin-the-bottle and catch-a-girl-kiss-a-girl. Although he was one of the more attractive boys in the school, he was very skinny and suffered from a speech impediment. He stuttered in school and everybody made fun of him.

You know how cruel kids can be. But during his late teen years he changed dramatically! He learned to control his condition and started lifting weights and taking up karate. By the time he graduated high school he was 5' 11" and weighed 200 pounds. But despite the fact that he could have any woman he wanted, he chose to focus on all of his negative past experiences with black women. It still amazes me how long he kept all that animosity pinned up inside. I guess you never can tell what's going on inside a person's mind, even when that person is one of your best friends.

Big Ben was just as confused as Mark, but his issues were about age. He had a weakness for beautiful young women. And when I say young, I mean **young**! The last woman he dated was 21 years old. That's a baby. When I asked him why he was still robbing the cradle, he said, "I can't help it, I'm addicted to those firm young bodies." And just like any other junkie, he paid for his drug. Those young girls were taking him to the cleaners. Every time I turned around he was buying them gifts and taking them on expensive vacations. Which would have been fine, if they deserved it. But most of them were nothing but money-hungry tramps. If Ben were to drop dead tomorrow, they'd wipe their feet on his corpse and move on to the next sucker.

You would think a guy his size must have played football or some other of sport. Not Ben. After graduating high school he decided to study horticulture. We were all shocked by his choice of majors. He had occasionally joked about becoming a florist, but we never took him seriously. Turns out he was serious as a heart attack. Today, Ben owns ten stores in the Chicago area and has a fleet of twelve delivery trucks. Not bad for a poor black boy from the ghetto who started working out of his basement with two hundred and fifty dollars to his name. He is the classic example of a man who followed his dream and kept his eyes on the prize. No excuses about growing up without a father. And no pointing the finger at the man.

Too bad his smart business sense didn't transfer into his personal life. Sure, he was drug-free, self-employed, and hadn't fathered any children in or out of wedlock. But Ben was a hopeless romantic, or as Rick James would say, "He was a sucker for love." Those young girls were playing him like lotto. I tried to tell him that it's all a big game and that he had to stop being so damned trusting. But Ben was hard-headed. On a number of occasions, I tried to make him see that he was being taken advantage of. But once Ben decided he liked a particular woman, it was over. Next thing you know he was paying rent and loaning money that he would never see again. I guess some guys are just natural born Sugar Daddys.

Tony was without a doubt the most debonair of my friends. We nicknamed him pretty Tony because he was tall, light-skinned, and had what some women called good hair. You know, thin and wavy. The women were crazy about Tony. He had all the charm and charisma in the world. And he had smooth conversation. He could talk the panties off a nun. I guess that's why he and I grew somewhat closer than the others. We both had a way with women.

But Tony's playing days have been over ever since he met Tracie four years ago. After spending one afternoon watching them together, we knew his bachelor days were numbered. Tracie was everything you could ever ask for in a lifelong mate. She was energetic, educated, funny, mature, supportive, self-employed, and to top it off she played cards, serious cards! Like bid whist and poker. That's my kind of woman!

But like everyone else, Tony had drama too. The kind of drama that lasts a lifetime. Eight years ago, when he was preparing to go back to school to complete his engineering degree, his girlfriend Valarie came up pregnant. Which wasn't cause for celebration, since they had only been dating for six months. And what made it so bad is that he was just about to dump her. As it turned out, Valarie had been scheming from the very beginning to have his baby. Tony didn't realize what she was up to until he started adding up a lot of strange coincidences.

First he discovered that she stopped taking her birth control pills. When he confronted her with a box of unused pills he found in her medicine cabinet, she claimed the pills were making her ill and that she had an appointment to see her doctor for a new prescription. "I was going to tell you about it," she told him. "but it slipped my mind," Yeah right! Then she did something really desperate, punching holes in his condoms. The first time he noticed that his Trojan was punctured, he dismissed it as being defective. When it happened again, he knew something was up.

But by then it was too late. I'll never forget how distraught he was when he came by my apartment and told me the bad news. The expression on his face was depressing, one of total defeat and utter powerlessness. I'll never forget that look for as long as I live.

This is the drama I've had to live with for the last 25 years, but I wouldn't trade my boys for all the tea in China. We've been the best of friends since grammar school, and through it all we've managed to grow together in a positive direction. No drugs, no serious gambling habits, and up until this point, no wives. I say up until this point because I knew exactly what Tony's surprise was. He and Tracie had set a date to get married. That's great, **for him.** I just hope that insanity doesn't rub off on me. No offense to Tony, but I think marriage is for suckers.

When we arrived at IHOP the parking lot was full. I tried to tell Mark to stop at the Denny's restaurant down the street but Ben and Tony were still boycotting since those black FBI agents were denied service a few years ago. We went along with their protest just so long as we could feed our faces. Besides, the food at Denny's wasn't all that great anyway. After waiting 30 minutes for our favorite corner booth, we were seated. Ben wasted no time in getting into my business about my trip to

Atlanta. He was always eager to find out every intimate detail, like a little kid all excited about being told a bedtime story.

"So, let's get right down to business," Ben said. "How many women did you bone on <u>this</u> trip?"

"Why do you think that every time I go out of town I've got to be sleeping around?" I replied.

"Who said anything about sleeping, I just want to know if you got some pussy or not."

"You've got to excuse him," Tony said. "He hasn't had sex in so long he needs to hear stories about it. What I want to know is where did you go, and most importantly, how was business?"

"I went to Nashville, Memphis, and then down to Atlanta. And business went well, very well."

"How was Nashville and Memphis?" Mark asked. "I've never been down south before."

"Nashville was pretty cool. Everybody treated me with that good old southern hospitality. But Memphis was a trip. I've never seen so many black folks with gold-plated teeth in my entire life. Every time somebody smiled at me I had to put my sunglasses on."

They were all laughing, but I was dead serious. Why anybody would put so much damned metal in their mouth is beyond me. I hope they don't catch some kind of fatal mouth disease or get struck by lightning.

When the waitress finally made it over to our table to take orders, Tony ordered a western omelet and milk. And Mark and I had grits, toast, and hash browns, the usual. Meanwhile, Ben was staring her up and down checking out her body. When it was his turn to order, he tried to get fresh.

"And what can I get you?" she asked.

"How about those seven digits," Ben replied.

"Excuse me? I think you better stick with what's on the menu, sir."

"Aw, baby. Don't get an attitude, I'm just trying to make your day. Aren't you allowed to mingle with the customers?"

I was so embarrassed I had to cover my face with my napkin. All we wanted to do was eat, talk, and go home to watch the basketball game. But Ben was in one of his wannabe mack modes and there was no controlling him.

"Look, for the last time," she repeated, sounding upset, "do you want to order or not? I have other customers waiting."

"Okay!" he said, pushing the menu at her. "Just give me an omelet with onions, peppers, tomatoes, sausage, mushrooms, and cheese. And a side order of hash browns and pancakes."

"Anything to drink?"

"A large milk and orange juice."

"Thank you very much," she said while collecting all the menus.

As she walked away, Ben put his napkin up to his mouth and muffled a smart remark. "And while you're at it, tell the manager you need time off to adjust your attitude."

"Why do you always approach women with those tired lines?" I asked. "How about saying hello, how are you doing? No wonder you can't get a date."

"I'm just having fun, Derrick. Cool out!"

"One day one of these waitresses is going to pour a pot of hot grits on your big ass, like Al Green," Mark joked.

"Let's get back to your trip," Tony insisted. "What's up with Atlanta? I haven't been down there since I was a kid. I heard there's a lot of attractive, educated women down there who have it going on."

"Yeah, there's a few professional types with degrees who don't have a house full of kids," I admitted. "But most of them are broke as hell, especially the young ones. But they know how to perpetrate, big time! That's the one thing about Atlanta that turns me off. Black folks down there are too bourgeois."

"Let's get back to the women," Ben interrupted. "Is it true that there's ten women to every one man?"

"You better give Ben some information before he gets excited and comes all over himself." Mark laughed.

"Ben, even if the ratio was a hundred to one, you still

wouldn't get any pussy," I said.

We all laughed and slapped five while Ben pouted like a big baby. I couldn't help cracking on him. He had a bad habit of setting himself up.

"What's up with all those gay brothers down there?" Mark asked, changing the subject.

"What about them?"

"Is it true that they have the largest population of homosexual men in the country?"

"Man, I don't know!" I said. "Why in the hell are you asking me? It's not like I went down there to take a survey."

"Damn, what's your problem?" Mark said. "It was only a question."

I don't know why I snapped. I'm not homophobic, at least I don't think I am. Back in my college days I use to sit back and listen while the other guys degraded the gays and lesbians on campus. It was really interesting to observe how defensive they became whenever the subject of homosexuality came up. They would get all worked up and overly macho trying to downplay their choice of lifestyle. If you ask me, I believe that a lot of men are simply insecure with their own sexuality and need to lash out verbally and sometimes physically to reinforce their own fragile egos. Sure, I saw many black and white male couples holding hands in the restaurants and malls, but I didn't want to talk about it. "To each his own," I always say. As long as they respect my space, we will never have a problem.

"Moving right along," Mark said trying to break the ice. "Did you meet any ladies worth talking about?"

"I'm glad somebody finally asked. As a matter of fact I did. Her name is Angela and she's from the West Side."

"And?"

"And she's got it going on!"

"Yeah right. That's exactly what you said about old crazy-ass Samone, remember?"

"I remember, all right. But Angela is different. She's very independent and seems to keep herself very busy. There's nothing worse than a woman with too much time on her hands."

"So, what does this busy woman do for a living?"

"She's a P.E. instructor at a high school."

"Which high school"?

"Damn, Mark!" I said. "You're all in my business. Stop being so nosy!"

"I don't know about these two knuckleheads, Derrick. But I'm impressed," Tony said. "Anybody who can put up with these kids nowadays is a saint in my book. You've got to have a lot of patience and love to do that job. I always said that the two hardest occupations in the world are parenting and teaching."

"If I didn't know any better, I'd think you were the one trying to get with Angela," Mark said.

"That's not a bad idea," Tony said. "Why don't you give me her phone number and address and I'll check her out. You know, make sure she's your type."

We all busted out laughing. Tony has one hell of a sense of humor. If there's one thing I love most about hanging out with my friends is that we always have lots of laughs. Every one of them is a born comedian. We know each other like brothers and stand by one another through thick and thin, never letting anything or anybody come between us. Our motto is "Women and money will come and go, but friends are forever."

When the food arrived we all bowed our heads and said grace. While we ate I filled them in on the rest of the details of the trip and on Angela's wonderful personality and her incredible legs. As usual they were skeptical about how long this particular relationship would last. Not because they didn't think she was my type. But my recent track record wasn't all that good. Over the last year I had gone through three semi-serious relationships and a number of one-night stands. Nothing I said was going to change their attitude. They would have to meet her to understand and share my optimism.

After the waitress came to clear away our plates, Tony tapped on his glass with a fork to get everyone's attention.

"I have a very important announcement to make."

"What is it now," Ben interrupted. "Are you going through with that sex change?"

"Very funny bullethead, just pay attention."

"Stop cutting the man off and let him speak," I said.

"The big date has been set for June 7."

"Don't do it man, don't do it!" Mark joked.

"So, you're finally going through with it, huh?" I asked. "Another good man bites the dust."

"Stop being so dramatic. I'm getting married, not going away to prison."

"What's the difference?"

"I expected you to understand, Derrick. You know how much I love Tracie."

"I'm only kidding, you poor sap. Damn, you can't even take a joke. I'll show you how much I understand."

I stood up in the middle of the restaurant and screamed to get the customers' attention.

"Excuse me everybody. I'm sorry to interrupt your meal but my buddy is about to jump the broom. And I want him to know how much we all support a man trying to live right in the '90s. So, why don't we you all stand up and give him a hand. Come on, stand up!"

It wasn't long before everybody was applauding. He was so embarrassed he turned bright red. And that's not easy for a black man to do.

"Well, well, well, so you're finally gonna jump the broom?" Ben said.

"Yep, it's time to make that move," Tony replied. "But don't worry, things aren't going to change. I'll still be around once a month to play basketball."

"Now that's a big change right there," Mark said. "You haven't been playing ball worth shit over the last few weekends."

"He's right. Your game ain't what it used to be," I said. "You can't even touch the rim without a running start."

"So now everybody wants to gang up on me, huh?" Tony yelled as he got up from the table and put up his dukes. "Come on, I'll take on all of you young boys. Starting with you, Ben. Get your big ass up! After I knock you out, these two wimps will run like sissies."

Ben got up from his seat and put Tony in a serious bear hug. Then Mark and I grabbed his feet and carried him outside the restaurant onto the lawn where we slapped and punched him around. We must have looked like a bunch of overgrown kids out there in the snow with no coats on. Ben was on top, pinning down his arms and Mark and I were kicking and thumping his forehead. This lasted for about five minutes before we realized that the ground was wet and the temperature outside was about 20 degrees. Ben let Tony up off the ground and brushed him off. Then we put our arms around him and gathered in a close huddle to congratulate him.

"I wish you the best," Mark said.

"That goes for me too," I added.

Ben, who always had a flare for the dramatic, waited to have the last word. Doing a bad imitation of that guy on the Budweiser beer commercial, he put his arm around Tony.

"*I love you man.* Now can we please get the hell out of the cold? I'm freezing my ass off."

MY STEPDAUGHTER'S KEEPER

If that bitch calls my house one more time asking to speak to Tony without being courteous enough to say "Hello," I'm going to curse her out. I mean it! I don't give a damn if she gave birth to ten of his kids, she's got to realize that I'm his family now and this is my house she's calling. It's all about respect. For the last four years I've had to put up with Valarie's insecurities and ignorance, but lately she has been exceptionally nasty. Last month, on the day after Thanksgiving, she had Tony and me sitting in the car outside of her apartment for almost an hour waiting for his daughter, Erikah. We called two hours ahead of time to make sure she had all of her things together to spend the weekend, but she still wasn't dressed. Valarie promised that Erikah would be ready to go. But when we got there, she was still in the tub and her clothes hadn't even been ironed.

I was so pissed Tony had to stop me from marching up those stairs and pulling all the weave out her head. Then there was the stunt she pulled last week. Valarie practically held Erikah for ransom, demanding an additional hundred dollars in child support before allowing Tony to take her to see the movie *Pocahontas*. Erikah had been waiting all week and Tony didn't want to disappoint her. Besides, she made him promise they were going, and you know how kids are about having promises kept. So, he broke down and gave Valarie the money just to avoid arguing in front of his Erikah. Of course, I was furious when he told me about it later that evening.

"She has gone too far this time!" I yelled.

"Calm down, Tracie, I'll handle it."

"Baby, you know I don't like to get involved in your business where your daughter is concerned, but you can't allow Valarie to manipulate you this way."

"Don't you think I realize that?" he replied. "I just didn't want to upset Erikah. She's been looking forward to seeing this movie for weeks. And besides, it was only a hundred dollars."

I tried my best to remain calm, cool, and collected. My mother, who was from the South, always taught me to be submissive to my man. "There will be times when you want to speak out and get your point across," she advised "But hold your tongue and wait until things settle down." I took those words of wisdom to heart before I walked over to the couch where Tony was sitting and popped him upside the head.

"Ouch! That hurt! What did you do that for?"

"To wake you up!" I shouted. "Don't you see that she is setting you up. All she's doing is testing to see how far she can go."

"What did you expect me to do, just forget about Erikah? Why should she have to suffer?"

"Listen to me sweetheart," I said while rubbing his head where I thumped it. "If you don't take a stand right now on this issue, Erikah is going to suffer a lot more in the long run. And although it may only be $100 now, who's to say it won't be $200 the next time or maybe even $300. You're already paying $1500 a month, plus you spend nearly 300 additional dollars when you two hang out together. How much is enough?"

"You've got a good point, baby," he agreed. "I'll just have to explain to Erikah what's going on if this happens again."

"**If** it happens again?" I sarcastically responded. "You mean when!"

Any woman who is entertaining the thought of marrying a man with kids better think twice. Being a stepmother is without a doubt the most aggravating and stressful job in the world, especially when you're dealing with an ignorant, less attractive, and insecure ex-wife or girlfriend. Right away she starts sizing you up by scoping out your wardrobe, inquiring about your occupation, and peeking out the window to see what kind of car you're driving. And no matter how polite and cordial you try to be, she'll always find something negative to say about you. The last guy I dated was the father of two young boys. The six months I spent trying to get along in that situation was pure hell. When he would bring those little devils over to my house to visit, I had to put away all my nice crystal and cover up my glass dining room table. A person shouldn't have to do that.

The way I was raised was entirely different. When somebody told you not to touch something, you didn't touch it. And if you did, you got the snot beat out of you with either a leather belt, extension cord, or anything they could get their hands on. Well, this wimp refused to spank his sons, citing studies claiming that whipping young children can contribute to violent behavior as adults. "We believe in practicing time out," he said. "Physical punishment is unnecessary if you have good communication." Now, you know I gave him one of those looks, right? I'm standing there listening to this man thinking to myself, "You must be out of your freakin' mind." Don't get me wrong, I have seen time outs work effectively in many cases, but if my child continues to run around the house raising hell, that ass is mine! And if he or she wants to get slick and call child abuse hotline or DCSF, I'll tell them like my mama used to tell us: "If they come up in this house, I'll whip their asses too."

Another problem you have dealing with men with children is that they often feel obliged to have sex with their ex-mates just because they share parental responsibilities. On a couple of occasions I suspected my last boyfriend of getting a quickie when we would go by his ex-wife's apartment to drop off his kids. Sometimes he came downstairs all exhausted with a stupid-looking grin on his face. I'm almost certain that she was giving him a blow job on his way out the door. What's up with that? Why can't men simply learn to cut their sexual and emotional ties to their ex-lovers and move on? And to make matters worse, they don't even see it as being unfaithful. They feel as if they have ownership of a woman just because she bore their offspring. Now that's sick. But I guess the men can't be held solely to blame. After all, there has to be a stupid and desperate woman willing to go along with it too.

When Tony and I met, his situation appeared to be different. First of all, he had only one child, Erikah, who was three years old at the time. And unlike my former boyfriends, Tony was very stern, the type of man who would whip his child's butt in the middle of the parade at Walt Disney World. His relationship with Valarie was non-sexual, strictly platonic. The only time he ever saw her was when he was either picking Erikah up or dropping her off. There were no lengthy conversations or secretive whispering over the phone. That's when you know something's up. Tony was all business with Valarie. He wanted as little contact with her as humanly possible. In fact, Tony could hardly stand to be in the same room with her for more than a few minutes at a time. It was as if she made him ill. After we had been dating for a couple of months, I felt compelled to ask him why he had such an awkward relationship with the mother of his only child.

"I was waiting for you to ask me about my attitude toward Valarie," he said. "And I guess it's about time we talked about it."

"Is it that deep?" I asked.

"Oh, it's deep all right. Deep enough to drown in."

"So, tell me what's the deal between you two."

He propped himself up in his seat and took another sip of the Miller Draft he had been drinking.

"Valarie and I had only been knowing one another for nine months before she got pregnant. And out of that nine months we were only seriously dating for six months."

"Ok, and?"

"At the very beginning of the relationship, I made it perfectly clear to her that I was not interested in having any children. There was no way she could have misinterpreted my position. I made sure it was emphasized, *no kids!* She expressed to me that she felt the exact same way and from that point on we took the necessary precautions."

"I'm still waiting for you to get to the point," I said.

"Well, come to find out that she had never taken the birth control pills that she was prescribed. Hell, I don't even know if she ever went to her doctor to ask for a prescription."

"Now that's scandalous!" I yelled out. "But weren't you wearing protection?"

"I'm getting to that part, if you would stop interrupting," he continued. "On at least two occasions she punched holes in the tip of my condoms. She did it real slick too, always insisting on putting it on herself, saying it added a little spice to the process."

"What did you do after you discovered what she was up to?"

"I did what any sane person would do, I cursed her out,

gathered my belongings, and told her never to contact me again. But three months later, when it was too late for her to have a legal abortion, she called to tell me that she was pregnant. The rest is history, as they say."

At first I didn't buy a word of what he was saying. I had never heard of anything so ridiculous. A woman lying about taking the pill was nothing new, but punching holes in rubbers, now that's straight up trifling. He's just another brother making excuses, I remember thinking to myself. But the better I got to know Valarie, the less far-fetched it all seemed. When they met, she was 22 years old with no formal education, no marketable skills, and basically no future. What did she have to lose? Tony walked right into that trap. Back then, and even now on occasion, I find myself looking at him wondering, "What in the hell were you thinking about when you got involved with her?"

And he's not the only successful man out there making poor judgments. I can't begin to tell you how many handsome and affluent men I've met who have fathered children with some of the worst women you can imagine. In many of these instances the women aren't very attractive, don't make much money, and come from lazy and obnoxious families. One gentleman I met, who is a consultant for a Fortune 500 company, confessed to me that he met his daughter's mother at a wet T-shirt contest. She was 26 years old, living with her younger sister and aunt, both of whom had two kids and were on welfare. Now, is there something wrong with this picture, or is it just me?

But there comes a time when you have to chalk your mistakes up to experience and move on. And that's exactly what I've been trying to get across to Tony. All that anger and resentment he has toward Valarie is counter-productive and unhealthy. "Dealing with so much hate can affect your ability to think creatively," I told him. "Not only are you allowing her to diminish the quality of our life together, but of Erikah's too." I begged him, "Just let it go!" He took what I said to heart and has tried to work at being less irritated and more forgiving. If not for us, I knew he would do it for his "sweet little princess," as he called her. She was the only bright spot in an otherwise bleak situation. Make no mistake about it, he loved Erikah with all his heart and would do anything to make sure she was happy.

When Tony and I officially announced our engagement earlier this month, I was hoping that maybe, just maybe, Valarie will stop trippin' and accept the inevitable. We have been together for nearly four years now, and you would think that the message is clear that I'm here for the long haul. But it seems that the closer the wedding date gets, the more difficult she becomes. As I said, this telephone situation is getting way out of hand and I'm having a hard time following my own advice to stay cool. Sometimes she calls first thing in the morning and hangs up when she hears my voice, which is pretty stupid because she knows that we have caller ID. If I didn't know any better, I'd think she had some kind of drug or alcohol problem. I mean, look at how drastically she's changed. She can't keep a steady job, lately she's been asking for extra money, and her behavior is irrational. Ok, maybe that's only one out of three changes.

The point is that she needs to find something to do with her life, like taking up a harmless sport such as bungee jumping or alligator wrestling. Or maybe what she really needs is a man of her own. Yeah, that's what she needs, a good hard dick to relieve some of that self-hate and animosity she has all built up inside her. Valarie hasn't been involved in a serious relationship since I've known her. All she does is go back and forth with one loser after another. One guy she introduced me to was a stripper who promoted himself as Hurricane, a name he insisted on being called even in social settings. Talk about conceited. Despite the fact that he had a body that any woman would <u>drool</u> over, he didn't have much to offer in the intellectual department. In other words, he was one dumb son of a bitch. I guess all the high winds from that hurricane must have blown all the sense out of his head.

There's nothing more irritating and unattractive than a grown man who can't articulate himself. Here you have a 30-

something-year-old man trying to present himself as a professional, but his complete vocabulary revolves around street slang and curse words.

Don't get me wrong, I'm no saint, but when I'm in the company of strangers or in the process of doing business, I communicate in an appropriate manner. You can call it "talking white" if you want to, but I'm all about getting paid.

Then there was David, the wannabe musician. He still comes around every now and then to get himself a piece. He is in and out of her apartment so regularly that Erikah thought he was a relative. She even started calling him Uncle Dave. It's truly amazing to me how prematurely she brings strange men around her daughter. That is so dangerous nowadays. Tony made me wait a whole six months before ever meeting Erikah, which I thought was an excessive length of time, but that was his prerogative. He was the parent and that was his child, end of discussion. I could understand his position because I was raised with two older brothers down south in a single-parent household, and none of us ever saw our mother hugged up with strange men in our home.

On the rare occasions when Mom did bring a man home, you had better believe he was going to be around on a regular basis and for a long period of time. There was none of that wham bam thank you ma'am stuff under our roof. At least, we didn't see it. Which is the point I've tried to convey to Valarie. We all have gone through that dry spell in our lives and needed a quick visit from the maintenance man, but keep it on the down low. Kids should be sent over to a relative's house or the baby sitter's, at least until you determine that you are in a long-term relationship. Valarie has been careless and indiscreet. Erikah has seen things that a six-year-old just shouldn't see. And over the past six months, things have only gotten worse. Tony has called Valarie several times to plead with her not to expose Erikah to this kind of environment. He has even threatened to take her to court, charging her with child abuse. Recently, I decided to call Valarie myself, hoping to relate to her on a woman-to-woman level.

"Hello, Valarie? This is Tracie, do you have a minute?"

"I'm watching *Star Trek, The Next Generation*," she said with an attitude.

"And?"

"And, it's my favorite show. Can't you call me back later?"

"It's very important, and I won't take up much of your time, I promise."

She took a deep breath, then told me to hold on. I knew she was waiting for the commercial break.

"Ok, I've got a quick minute," she said. "What do you want?"

"Well, it's about Erikah."

"What about her?"

"Well, lately she's been very upset about some of the things that have been going on at your place."

"Things like what?"

"I was hoping you could tell me."

"Look, I don't have time for riddles. If you have something to say, then come right out with it."

"Okay, if that's the way you want it. Erikah has seen you engaging in intimate acts with the men that you bring home. Now, I don't know exactly what she saw, or how many times she saw it, but it has her very upset."

"Did she say that she saw me do something besides kissing?"

"Actually, she hasn't said anything. But I can tell when she is not herself."

"So now you're a damn child psychologist, huh?"

"Calm down, Valarie, I'm only trying to help."

The conversation hadn't even gotten off the ground and I could sense that she was ready to explode. I held the phone a few inches away from my ear and braced myself for her usual mean-spirited response.

"Look, Tracie!" she yelled. "Just because you've been around for a few years and you *think* you're getting married to

Tony, don't fool yourself into believing you have the right to call my house whenever you feel like it and criticize me on how I raise my child."

"Hold on for a minute, Valarie," I interrupted, trying to get a word in edgewise. "It's my responsibility as an adult and as someone who cares about Erikah to communicate to you when I think something is wrong. And I'm telling you that when she visits on the weekends she's all upset and crying over what she saw at home. All I'm calling to ask you is to be more careful about what you do with your men friends in front of her. It's becoming a serious problem."

That did it!

"Let, me tell you something, you uppity countrified heifer. Don't you ever call my house again trying to counsel me on how to be a good parent. If you want to play mother so bad, have your own damn kids."

I wanted to jump through the phone and choke the shit out of her. All I was trying to do was act like a concerned adult, and her reaction was to start a fight. It took all the control I had to keep from blowing up, but she kept on picking.

"By the way, Tracie, why is it that you don't have kids, anyway?" she asked in an evil tone. "Is there something wrong with your insides?"

"Excuse me?"

"You heard what I said. Tony and I already have a baby together, and I think you're jealous because you can't have one."

"Any dumb slut can lay down and have a baby. You should know that."

"I may be a dumb slut to you, but at least I have something you don't, Tony's baby."

"You know what?" I replied in a very assertive but calm fashion. "You are one disturbed young lady. I can't believe I even wasted my time trying to talk sense into your ignorant ass. My only hope is that Erikah will learn the appropriate way to conduct herself as a young lady from watching me, and not you."

"I beg your pardon?"

"Aw, don't beg, sweetheart, I'm not finished. And if you really want to know why I don't have kids, it's because I was raised by a strong-minded and spiritual woman who taught me never to bring a child into this world without a husband. Not a boyfriend, not a lover, but a husband. A man who loves me enough to commit himself to me before God."

By the time I stopped talking, the dial tone was ringing in my ear. "That skank hung up on me!" I yelled. My blood pressure was up and my heart was pounding. I pulled back the curtains of my living room window and looked out into the street, praying she was upset enough to drive over. I began throwing a few warm-up kicks and shadow punches just in case. Then, I remembered, She doesn't even own a car.

AROUND THE WAY GIRL

"**G**ood morning, Motif Publishing. How may I direct your call?" the receptionist asked.

"I'd like to speak to Mr. Derrick Reed, please."

"May I ask who's calling?"

"This is Angela Williams."

"Please hold."

The smooth sounds of jazz station 95.5 WNUA played over the speaker while Angela waited to be connected. She immediately recognized the song. It was the old cut by Bobby

Caldwell "What you won't do, you'll do for love." She was unable to hold back a wide grin as she reflected back on the days when she used to hang out at basement parties with her girlfriends talking about boys and drinking Pink Champales. Back in those days life was much simpler and less violent. Kids could play out in the streets without worrying about drive-bys or stray bullets. And her mother used to cook a big pot of collard greens and barbecue chicken out on the back porch for the whole neighborhood. "Those were the days," she reminisced.

Several minutes passed and still Derrick hadn't answered. She thought about hanging up and calling back, but the music was sounding too good. A song off of Paul Hardcastle's *Jazz Masters II* CD came on next. She listened to it almost every day, but for some strange reason she never could remember the titles to those songs. But the unique rhythm was unmistakable. While she sat on the phone snappin' her fingers getting into the groove, the receptionist picked up.

"Sorry, for the wait, Ms. Williams," she apologized. "He's at Ext.100. I'll put you through. Have a nice day."

"Hello, Angela!" Derrick said sounding genuinely excited. "How are you doing?"

"I was doing fine until you answered the phone. I was having a good time listening to Paul Hardcastle before you ruined my groove."

"Would you like for me to put you back on hold so you can finish listening to your song?"

"Ha ha, very funny."

"Well, you really sounded disappointed. I just want to do whatever makes you happy."

"Is that right?"

"Did you hear me stutter?" he confidently replied. "You heard what I said."

"In that case, you won't mind meeting me for lunch this afternoon. School is out until after New Year's."

"Fine with me. Just tell me when and where you want to meet."

"How about meeting me at 1:00 downtown at the Bennigan's on Michigan Ave?"

"Which one?" he asked. "There's two different locations, you know."

"Not the one on Adams, the other one, further down near Lake Street."

"You've got a date. I'll see you around 1:00. But if I'm late, don't leave. I have a meeting with a client at 12:00 in the south suburbs, out near River Oaks Mall. I might not make it exactly on time."

"No problem!" Angela said. "I'm going to do some shopping at The Water Tower, so I might be a bit late myself. Just call me on my cell phone if your plans change. Let me give you the number."

"Hold on, let me get a pen," he said while searching inside his desk for something to write with. "Ok, I'm ready, fire away."

"My number is area code 708."

"Wait a second," he interrupted. "This damn pen isn't writing. Why does that always happen?"

"Maybe God's trying to tell you something."

"He's trying to tell me something, all right. To stop buying these cheap-ass pens."

They both let out hearty laughs and were reminded of why they found one another so appealing when they met in Atlanta. Derrick finally found a pen that would write and took down Angela's cell phone number.

"Ok, I've got your information. I'll see you for lunch," Derrick said. "I'm really looking forward to seeing you again."

"Is that your manly way of saying you miss me?"

"I guess you could say that," Derrick answered reluctantly.

"Well if you miss me so much, why didn't you call me over the weekend?"

"Hey, baby, you had my number too, so don't try to put it all on me. But why don't we finish this investigation over lunch. My staff is waiting for me down the hall for our morning meeting."

"I'm sorry," she apologized. "I didn't mean to hold you, I'll see you downtown around 1:00."

It was 11:00 when Derrick wrapped up his meeting with the production department, staff writers, and assistant editors. As usual, Monica and Tiffany came up with all the new ideas. They discussed plans to add more articles on the impact of AIDS and bisexuality in the black community. Tiffany got the idea from reading the books, *Just As I Am*, and *Invisible Life* by E. Lynn Harris. His books had raised questions in the minds of many women about the sexual practices of prospective male partners. She felt the magazine should address these issues and not simply sweep them under the rug. But Derrick's attention was concentrated on the marketing strategy for the first quarter. He already had plans to begin the year with a trip to four major East Coast cities, including New York and Washington DC. Sales in that region were down. Derrick felt it was essential to get as much exposure in that part of the country as possible to generate interest in the February Valentine's Day issue, which was expected to be one of the year's most popular. Not to mention the fact that most of the major media and advertisers had headquarters in New York City.

Once the meeting was over, Derrick grabbed his portfolio and cell phone and rushed out the door for his twelve o'clock meeting with Caravan Productions. The business of attracting advertisers was his number-one priority, and he made sure everyone knew it. His motto was typed in bold letters and tacked to the walls of every room in the office, including the bathrooms: "No ads, no income, no business." But his mind was also on getting together with Angela. Ever since they met in Atlanta, he couldn't stop thinking about her. He was falling for her in a big way. But like most men, he wouldn't admit it. "She's all right," he told Tiffany and Monica. "Nuthin' to write home about." But he had already bragged on her to his friends.

Something he never did until after he experienced a woman sexually. He even mentioned her to his father. An honor reserved strictly for potential wives, or at the very least, serious girlfriends.

The more Derrick thought about it, the more uncomfortable it made him. Not because he didn't want to care, but because he wasn't sure if she cared more. His experience as a lady's man taught him one extremely valuable lesson: always keep the upper hand in the relationship. Translation, "Make sure the woman cares more for you than you do for her." As he drove south on Lake Shore Drive, he decided that the best plan of action was to deal with Angela like any other woman, give her ultimatums and demand to have things his way. If she went along, fine. If not, well, he was too arrogant to consider that possibility. After all, the game had worked on all of the other women.

After Angela got off the phone with Derrick, she headed straight for the health club on North Avenue. She couldn't pass up the opportunity to go to the gym during off hours. Normally she was right there sweating and grunting with all the rest of the nine-to-fivers at 7:00 in the morning. But today she didn't have to stand in line for equipment or run around the fat people on the track. After stretching to warm up she put on her gloves and went inside the free weight room. Starting with the squat machine, she did four sets of twelve with 150 lbs, then three sets on the leg curl machine. She finished up with a three-mile run on the track and 100 inclined situps, five sets of twenty. Her stomach had to be extra tight for Derrick that afternoon. Angela was a very strong and energetic 35-year-old-woman. On Saturdays she would go down to the YMCA and hit the punching bag for an hour and sometimes go a few rounds with the female boxers. She could give the average man a run for the money inside and outside the ring. Growing up on the tough streets of the West Side of Chicago made it necessary that she learn how to take care of herself. She knew how to box and wrestle before she could sew on a button or French- braid hair.

Like most of the kids in her neighborhood, she was raised in a single-parent household. For many years she and her younger brother Andre watched their mother struggle to make ends meet. Angela never forgot how determined her mother Faye was to break the cycle of poverty for her family, working two and sometimes three jobs to save enough money to afford college. In the end, her hard work and dedication paid off.

In December 1978 Faye graduated from City College and received her associate's degree in law enforcement. The following spring she passed the police exam and was hired as a Chicago police officer. A profession which was obviously very dangerous but provided a good salary, job security, and much-needed medical benefits for the family. Four paychecks later, they loaded their few belongings into a 19-foot U-Haul truck and moved into a better neighborhood and much larger home. For the first time in their lives, they had a patio and back yard to play in. There was even a nice park down the street with swings and monkey bars. The world seemed a much brighter place, filled with greater opportunities. Angela received an academic scholarship to Clark University in Atlanta, and her brother Andre had a 3.5 GPA going into his first year of high school. The American dream had finally come true for the Williams family. But like so many happy stories, there are often sad endings.

On March 25, 1984, one day before Angela's 24th birthday, her mother was gunned down while investigating a domestic dispute in her old neighborhood; not more than three doors down from the very apartment where she raised her children for 16 years. The investigation was handled incompetently and the details about what happened were sketchy. According to the police report, officers Williams and Heinson arrived on the scene and found the couple fighting on the front porch. Officer Heinson ordered them to stop and to put their hands up. The man ran inside. Officer Williams pursued, and shots were fired. The next thing you know, she had two bullets in her chest and lay dead on the living room floor.

But witnesses had a different story. They said that officer Williams had defused the whole situation by talking calmly to the couple. In fact, she knew the woman who was involved in the dispute. She was the eldest daughter of one of her former next-door neighbors. But officer Heinson, who was a well-known racist, began getting physically and verbally abusive, shouting racial slurs. The man broke away and ran inside the house. Officer Heinson told officer Williams to cover the front door while he ran around back. "Bring your black ass out here right now," he shouted. "If I have to come in after you, I'll kill your black ass." Not a wise thing to say in a community where it was well-known that some people had guns for personal protection. Five minutes into this altercation sirens could be heard in the distance. Nobody wanted to see a simple domestic dispute turn into a 1960s Black Panther shoot out. So, according to witnesses, Ms. Williams went inside the front door and pleaded with the man to give himself up. "Young man, you haven't broken any serious laws, yet. Please come out before things get out of hand." At that moment, the white officer came storming through the back door and fired at least one shot. The man, who was noticeably under the influence, returned fire. Angela's mother died on the scene.

Devastated and confused, Angela cried herself to sleep many nights trying to get over the loss of the only person who truly understood her. But what hurt most was that she never got the opportunity to say goodbye or to tell her mother how much she respected and admired her for raising two kids with little or no help from relatives, so-called friends, or a man. Not a simple task in the treacherous inner-city streets of Chicago where many teenaged girls become pregnant before finishing high school, and young men join violent gangs for protection and companionship. Somehow Faye Williams shielded her children from all of the negatives the streets had to offer and instilled in them a sense of pride and responsibility. "No children before marriage," she constantly drilled into Angela's mind. "Kids are not toys, they are a serious lifelong responsibility."

Her message for Andre was no less direct. "Don't go lying up with any little girl who's willing to open her legs. It takes a real man to exercise self control." These were the words of a woman who learned life's lessons the hard way. By the time she was 18 years old she was pregnant with her second child, and their father had run off, unable or unwilling to handle the responsibility of supporting two young children. But never once did she talk down about him to her children or deny him the opportunity to visit at any time. The door was always open for him to walk in and be a part of his children's lives. And although he never took advantage of that opportunity, she went to bed with a clear conscience every night, knowing she did the right thing. Unlike so many mothers nowadays who brainwash their kids with negative one-sided stories and use them as pawns to get revenge.

Then there were the strong examples of how to walk, talk and carry oneself like a lady. What Faye said was always backed up by how she lived. If she said don't smoke, it was because she didn't smoke. If she advised Angela not to stay out late, it was because she kept respectable hours, even as an adult. And when it was time to talk about the birds and the bees, Faye gave her the adult version, not that fantasy, white-picket-fence jive that mothers give their daughters trying to protect them from reality. She always told her to follow four basic rules when it came to dating. One, never have sex unless it's what you want. Two, always use protection. Three, never respond to a man blowing his horn for you to come out for a date. And four, never depend on a man to provide 100% of your living expenses, not even your own husband. "Boyfriends, husbands, and lovers may go away," she would preach, "but bills are forever."

These were the fond memories and lessons Angela took to the grave-site with her every single day for a week after the

funeral. She would stand over her mother's grave and read letters aloud to express how much she missed her dear mother.
Each message was filled with deep emotion and heartache. It
was Angela's way of dealing with the anxiety and pain of losing her number-one role model and her best friend. But the
time was nearing for her to go back to Atlanta to prepare for
finals and graduation. She knew her mother would have wanted her to finish what she had begun. There was nothing to be
gained by dropping out of school at this point. On the last night
before she was preparing to leave, Angela locked herself in her
mother's bedroom and prayed to God for guidance. Bright and
early the following morning, she wrote her final letter and went
to the grave-site to deliver it to her mother.

Dear Mama,

I know you're tired of listening to all these sad letters. I've
been out here every day in the cold and rain just to read to you
and have you all to myself. If I know you, you're probably
looking down from heaven thinking, "That child has lost her
mind." But the fact is that I miss you, Mama. I miss you so
much that sometimes I don't think I'm going to be able to make
it. Every day I wake up hoping that all of this is just some kind
of horrible dream and that you're going to come into my room
and tell me to get my lazy behind out of bed so we can go shopping. And for a brief moment I'm happy and everything is the
way it used to be. But after I get up and go into your empty
bedroom, reality sets in and my whole world comes tumbling
down around me. When that happens, nothing matters to me,
not school, not my career, not even food. Look at me, I've lost
nearly 15 pounds in the last two weeks and I'm as thin as a rail.
I guess I can finally be a super model after all.

I'm making fun because I woke up this morning with God's
comforting arms wrapped around me. He told me everything
was going to be all right and that it was time for me to get on
with my life. That's when I sprung out of bed and took inven-

tory of myself. I realized that I am the daughter of Ms. Faye Williams, a strong black woman who went through hell and high water to give her children a chance to make something of themselves in this cold world. I had to check myself, Mama, because you had to endure trials and tribulations ten times worse then death and you made it. I was first embarrassed and then ashamed of myself for not being stronger for you and for Andre. But I want you to know that I'm ok now, and with God's help I'm ready to move forward with my life and honor your name. My only wish is that I will grow up to be half the woman that you were. I love you, Mama. Rest in peace.

Your loving daughter,

Angela

Angela graduated with her class that May and returned home to sell the house and settle all of her mother's affairs. The money from the life insurance policy, her pension fund, and the profits from the sale of the house were put away in a trust fund for Andre, to go to college. Angela used some of the money to start a business in Atlanta and to purchase a used Cutlass Supreme for Andre, who was living with his aunt out in the suburbs. Buses didn't run after ten o'clock and she didn't want him to be isolated from his friends in the city, especially during this traumatic period in his life.

Besides, Andre didn't care for his aunt much and couldn't bear to be in her presence any longer than he had to. He remembered how cold-hearted and inconsiderate she was. Even though she was his mother's eldest sister, she was never there when they needed small favors, like a ride to the grocery store when the weather was unbearably cold. Or the time when the heat went out in their apartment building over the Christmas holiday, and she didn't even offer to put them up for a couple of days until it was repaired. Some kind of sister she was. The only reason she allowed Andre to stay with her in the first place was because of all the guilt she had built up. Not to mention the $300 a month she was getting to cover his expenses.

Angela sat down with Andre a few days after his high school graduation and talked with him about her plans to get him down to Atlanta and enrolled in Morehouse College, where he had been accepted.

"So, what are we going to do now, Sis?" Andre asked.

"Well, you could come down to Atlanta next week and move in with me and my sorority sister Denise until I find us a place to stay."

"Ugh!" he cringed. "I don't want to live with two women. What's my other option?"

"Look Andre, don't be difficult."

"I'm not trying to be difficult, Sis," Andre said as he put his arms around her neck. "You know I love you, but orientation isn't until mid August. I won't have nuthin' to do."

"Ok, then, Mr. Smarty Pants, what do you suggest?"

"How about I stay here with Aunt Frances until the end of the summer and then come down?"

"You've got to be kidding me!" Angela said. "I thought you couldn't stand being around her."

"I can't, but I'd rather be here with my friends over the summer than down there with nobody to talk to."

"I don't know, Andre."

"Please, Sis," he begged. "This is best for both of us. I can get a job and make a little pocket change and you can take more time to get situated in your new job and find us a place to stay."

Angela was stuck between a rock and a hard place. On one hand, she didn't want to leave him in Chicago for two long months with no one to closely look after him. He was still a reckless 18-year-old boy filled with a lot of pain and unresolved issues. And the fact that he had a new car to get around in didn't help to make her any more comfortable. On the other hand, she knew she could use the additional time to properly arrange for his arrival. The idea of living with both him and Denise was not all that appealing an idea anyway. She loved her brother to death, but just like any other little brother, he could get on her last nerve. After several minutes of thinking it over, she decided to let Andre stay until August. A decision she would regret for the rest of her life.

By mid July Andre had already begun staying out overnight without checking in. Aunt Frances, who was just waiting for an excuse, threatened to put him out. Angela called everyone she knew trying to locate him to get to the bottom of what was going on. She made it a habit to stay in touch with a few of the brothers from the hood just in case, and it paid off. She tracked him down at Rosco's apartment, a place in the old neighborhood where many of the thugs and dope dealers hung out.

"Andre, what in the hell do you think you're doing?" she shouted. "I've been worried sick about you."

"Chill out baby," he slurred. "Everything is cool."

"What did you call me?"

"I mean, I'm ok, Sis."

"Have you been drinkin', boy?"

"No, I haven't. I'm just a little tired."

"Tired?" she asked. "How in the hell can you be tired at 1:00 in the afternoon? That's it! Go over to Aunt Frances's house and start packing all of your belongings. I'm coming up there this weekend to get you. No, better yet, I'm coming tomorrow, and you better be ready!"

It was 3:20 p.m. when Angela's Southwest Airlines flight arrived at Midway Airport. She grabbed her suitcase at baggage claim and walked over the enclosed bridge to get to the CTA trains where she paid $1.50 to ride downtown. There she connected to the Congress train and rode it to the end of the line, where she had arranged to meet Aunt Frances and her hardheaded young brother. As the train approached the last stop,

Angela was shaking uncontrollably. She was trying her best to stay cool. Andre had really disappointed her when she needed him to be on his best behavior. They made an agreement and he broke it. And Angela hated for anyone to tell her they were going to do something and not follow through.

As the train pulled into the Des Plaines station, the conductor made the final announcement, "This is Des Plaines Avenue, end of the line, far as this train goes. Check to make sure you have all of your belongings." As the train came to a complete stop, he courteously concluded. "Thanks for riding the CTA, watch your step as you leave the train." Those words were very familiar to Angela, who briefly relaxed and paused to reminisce on when she used to ride the trains to and from downtown as a little girl. She and Andre use to grab the sides of the trains and ride them until the platform ran out. Like most kids, they never thought about how dangerous a game that truly was. But her flashback only lasted momentarily. The frantic crowds rushing off the train to catch their buses quickly woke her up to the reality of where she was and why she was there.

Her hands began to tremble once again as she stepped onto the escalator going down to ground level. She could see Aunt Frances waiting at the foot of the escalator with a distressful look on her face, but Andre was nowhere to be seen. Angela sensed something was wrong, terribly wrong! Before Aunt Frances could even get a word out of her mouth, Angela burst into tears.

"Where is Andre, Auntie?" she cried. "Where is my baby brother?"

"Come on, baby, let's go. I'll tell you all about it on the way home."

"No, no, no, tell me now!" she shouted, becoming hysterical. "Where is he?"

"Angela, please, not here."

"Oh God, no!" Angela screamed. "Not Andre, please God don't take him away from me too!"

Angela's intuition was uncanny when it came to those close

to her. Andre had been killed in a drive-by shooting the night before by gang members looking for revenge. When the police apprehended the shooters, they said the whole incident was provoked by one teenager stepping on another's foot at a nightclub. Another promising young teenager killed in America over dumb shit!

The experience of losing the two most important people in her life was very traumatizing for Angela. For many years she only spoke to her therapist and her close sorority sisters about how she felt. And even those conversations were limited. She dealt with her loss the way many women do: She threw herself into her books and her career. Within two years of her brother's death, she had earned a master's degree in physical education and opened her own private health spa for women, specializing in personal fitness training and physical therapy. As for relationships and marriage, Angela never saw them as much of a priority. All the men she met were either too insecure or too stuffy. She was a homegirl from the streets with an education, a successful business, and a strong sense of self, a combination which was proving difficult for most men to handle, especially Southern men. She eventually got homesick, sold her business, and moved back to Chicago, taking a job as a P.E. instructor. Not that she needed the money; she just wanted to keep busy while making up her mind about her future. However, after only two years of the harsh Midwest winters, Angela was considering a move back to the South. She could handle the snow; that was ok. But that Chicago Hawk was kickin' her ass.

But Angela's moving plans had been put on hold since Derrick came into her life. She wasn't going to Atlanta or anywhere else until after she found out where their relationship was going. She knew that finding a good man wasn't easy, especially one who could handle her strong personality. Derrick was the type of man she needed, aggressive! A take-charge kind of guy. When he talked to her, he looked her straight in the eyes without blinking. Angela was easily turned off by men who were intimidated by her education and her good looks. She couldn't stand it when guys would nervously stutter and run off at the mouth about how much money they had and what they could do for her. Not Derrick. His charming personality and handsome face were impressive enough. He stood an even six feet and had shoulders broad enough to build a house on. And what an ass. Angela loved tight buns. For the first time in her life, she had met her match. Never before had she encountered a man who was so brash and confident, borderline arrogant. During her workout, she had to admit to herself that he was everything she ever wanted in a man. Good-looking, bold as hell, and most important of all, he presented a challenge.

At 12:30 sharp, Derrick concluded his meeting with his clients from Caravan Productions. He was relieved to have done business with black folks who came into a meeting with money on the table. No contract alterations and no haggling. By 12:40 he was rolling smoothly down the Calumet Expressway listening to the sexy voice of Irene Mojica on WGCI. She was stirring up trouble and having fun with the listeners as always. Irene always brightened up his afternoons with her seductive voice and wonderful personality. Derrick had tried on a number of occasions to get through to the station to tell her how much he enjoyed her show, but the lines were always busy. As the songs played, Derrick turned up the volume and sang along, trying his best to sound like the soul artist D' Angelo. He couldn't sing worth shit, but you couldn't tell him that.

And for a minute it looked as if he might actually make it on time for his one o'clock lunch date with Angela. But traffic on the Dan Ryan Expressway did not cooperate. Cars were backed up all the way from 95th to 63rd Street. There was nothing in the world that drove Derrick crazier than being stuck in traffic. He tried his best to get over into the right lane so he could exit, but nobody would let him cut in. "Ya stubborn son of a bitches, let me over!" he shouted. But nobody could hear him. They were all screaming too. There was nothing left to do but try to relax and enjoy the ride. He called Angela on her cell phone to inform her he would be late. She was leaving Bloomingdales when he reached her.

"Hello, Angela, this is Derrick."

"Hi Derrick, are you already at the restaurant?"

"No, as a matter of fact I'm stuck in traffic on the Ryan."

"Where are you exactly?"

"Right now I'm approaching 79th street."

"Just how bad is it out?"

"It's pretty bad, baby. Do you want to cancel?"

"Absolutely not!" Angela shouted. "I'm starving and besides, I just bought an outfit to wear especially for you."

"In that case, never mind. I'll see you when I get there!"

Derrick was so excited that he drove on the shoulder of the expressway from 76th to just past 63rd, where the congestion ended. And as usual there were no visible signs of any road construction, car accidents, or anything else that justified why traffic was so backed up. "Why in the hell are these cars moving so slow?" he thought to himself as he accelerated to make up time. "These people in Chicago can't drive worth shit!"

The restaurant was unusually busy for a Monday afternoon, as if there was a convention in town. Derrick stood by the entrance and looked around to see if he saw anyone who resembled Angela. There were two very attractive black women sitting at the bar, but neither of them was his girl so he decided to made a quick pit stop in the men's room to freshen up. Once he relieved himself of the two cups of coffee he had drunk earlier, he went over to the sink and opened up his leather briefcase, which doubled as a traveling medicine cabinet. Inside he had several brands of colognes, lotions, a wash towel, toothbrush, dental floss, pocket mirror, nail clipper, deodorant, mouthwash, multi-vitamins, and a shaving kit. Derrick always carried an ample supply of hygienic equipment with him wherever he went, a habit he developed back in his womanizing days. "Always be prepared," he jokingly whispered to himself as he sprayed his neck and wrist with Anucci cologne. He stroked his hair a couple of times with his brush and admired himself in the mirror one last time before putting away his portable beauty shop. "Damn, I look good!"

Derrick was ready to lay on the old charm as he jacked his slacks and headed for the restroom exit. As he grabbed the handle to opened the door, a group of men rushed past him childishly racing to the urinals. They were sloppy drunk and talking wildly about a woman who had just arrived.

"Did you see that black broad?" a white redneck asked his buddies.

"Hell, yeah, I did!" one guy enthusiastically replied with an annoying Southern accent. "She was gorgeous!"

"What a set of legs!" the first man added. "I damn near tripped down the stairs trying to get a peek."

"I wonder if she's here with anybody," the man who was the most intoxicated asked while slightly pissing on the floor.

"I don't think so," the first guy responded. "Larry and Steve are over there right now hounding her for her phone number."

Derrick knew exactly who they were boasting about: his girl Angela. She had the same effect on him in Atlanta. Of course, he was a lot more discreet and respectful about his admiration. He calmly walked out into the bar area and looked around to see where she was seated. Finding her was not difficult. All he had to do was look in the direction of all the men's attention. And there was Angela sitting at the end of the bar looking sexy and poised. Men were hovering over her like vultures waiting for a wounded animal to die. Most were casual admirers, while others were scavengers plotting to make their move. Derrick noticed that she was somewhat preoccupied, occasionally looking over her shoulder toward the door, obviously looking out for him. But instead of rushing over to rescue her, he played it cool and took a seat at the opposite side of the bar, making sure to leave a vacant stool next to him.

He gestured to the bartender for service and ordered his usual, a shot of Hennessy, no ice. After receiving his drink he leaned forward, resting his forearms on the bar, and watched the parade of men going over to Angela trying to get their mack on. She was talking skillfully with two and three men at a time, always making sure not to give one more attention than the other. She was quite the conversationalist. Over a fifteen-minute period she greeted and dismissed more than ten different men, both white and black. But it was obvious by the frustrated look on her face that she was becoming very annoyed with all the attention, especially from the two knuckleheads who were doing the most blocking. Derrick figured they were the two guys that the men from the restroom were talking about, Larry and Steve. Both happened to be black.

The shorter of the two had his wallet out flashing money and credit cards offering to buy drinks. Meanwhile his slick buddy was inching his way closer to Angela every time she turned her head. Big mistake! He broke the cardinal rule of dealing with a classy sistah: don't ever invade her space. Angela slowly stood up from her stool and pressed her hand firmly against his chest, in a sort of stiff-arm position. And just as she looked like she was about to smack the shit out of him, Derrick interrupted with his usual charm.

"Excuse me Ms., can I please have a moment of your time?"

"Well, certainly, sir," Angela replied with a wide grin, "Just let me gather my things and you can have all the time you want."

The entire room seemed completely silent; all eyes were on them. Larry and Steve just stood there totally stunned and helpless. Derrick was taller and wider than both of them, not to mention better looking. Angela mockingly drank the last sip of her cocktail, grabbed her bags, and strutted behind Derrick, feeling like a rescued princess. She wanted badly to stick out her tongue in retaliation, but she didn't. Once they exchanged cordial hugs and got situated, Derrick ordered himself another drink, this time a glass of white Zinfandel. Angela had the same.

"How long have you been here, Derrick?"

"Long enough." Derrick laughed. "I thought I'd have to save you from that big brute. I'm glad I stepped in when I did."

"He's the one who needed saving," Angela said, sounding cocky. "I've knocked out bigger guys than him. He's a lightweight."

"Is that right?"

"That's right. I'm not one of those docile females who needs to call for a man to help her every time she's in trouble. I know how to take care of myself."

"All right, Cleopatra Jones, calm down, I'll take your word for it. Now can we please change the subject?"

"Ok, let's do that. Why don't we talk about why you didn't call me this weekend."

"The same reason you didn't call me, baby. Like I told you this morning, you had my number too. So, what's your excuse?"

"My excuse is that I'm a woman."

"And?"

"And the man should initiate the phone call."

Derrick sarcastically picked up Angela's drink, sniffed it, and then took a hit.

"Hey! What did you do that for?" Angela asked. "That's mine!"

"I just figured there must be something else in that glass besides wine to make you give me such a stupid answer."

Angela hopped up from her stool and began playfully slapping Derrick upside the head. Once again all eyes were on them, but they didn't care. This was their way of getting reacquainted and an excuse to touch one another. Friendly punches became love taps. Although they had been apart for only four days, they missed being together. She couldn't stop thinking about him, and he couldn't get his mind off of her. It was the kind of feeling they remembered getting in high school as teenagers. And neither of them had experienced it since.

"So where do we go from here?" Derrick asked.

"Why don't we just take our time and have fun getting to know one another. People rush into things so fast that they don't get an opportunity to really get to know one another. I don't want that to happen between us."

"Yeah, you have a point there, baby. We men do have a tendency of rushing into relationships just to get next to That Thang!"

"Well, thanks for being so honest."

"I'm just telling it to you straight up. Men will tell you anything to get into those pants."

"What about you Derrick? Have you ever told a woman a lie to get next to her?

"Ok, that's enough with all the questions."

"What's wrong, baby? Can't you take a little heat?"

"A little heat, yes, but you're turning the thermostat up to HELL!"

"You are so crazy, Derrick." Angela laughed while holding her stomach. "Let me go to the bathroom before you make me pee on myself."

"Wait, before I forget to ask you. Would you like to come over to my place for New Year's Eve? I throw a party every year and I would love to have you over to meet my friends."

"Can we talk about that when I get back from the little girl's room? I'm about to burst."

"Ok, but don't take all day. You women know how to get lost in the bathroom."

"You just hold on to that invitation for a quick second and I'll be right back."

The ladies' rest room was located in the back of the restaurant, right across from the men's. Angela finished off her drink, grabbed her purse, and took off around the corner out of Derrick's sight.

By this time Larry and his buddies had put down several shots of rum and tequila, obviously trying to build up the courage to confront Angela again. Their opportunity came when she passed by their table on the way to the restroom.

"Hey baby," Steve shouted. "Hold up a minute!"

"Yeah, wait a second, sweetheart," Larry added as he grabbed his crotch. "I've got something for ya."

Angela paused briefly as if to contemplate whether to react or not. Then she took a deep breath and went inside the restroom. The whole situation should have ended right then and there, but Larry was persistent. He had to show off in front of his white co-workers, trying to play the hip black dude in the group. He enlisted the help of Steve, another Uncle Tom, to play a trick on Angela.

"Come with me, Steve," Larry directed as he stood up, barely able to keep his balance. "I've got an idea."

"What are you up to?" Steve asked, while gulping down the last of his drink for added courage.

"Ok, this is what I want you to do. Stand outside the ladies' room and watch out for me while I go inside. If anybody comes along, just tell them the bathroom is out of order."

"I think you guys might be going a bit too far," an older white man said. "She doesn't look like the type of woman you want to mess around with."

"Don't be such a party pooper," Larry replied. "I know how to handle black women."

After the coast was clear and Angela was alone in the ladies' room, Steve waited outside, blocking the door while Larry snuck inside.

"I'll be back in a minute," Larry chuckled. "I just need a minute to charm the pants off of her."

"Do me a favor and palm that big ass one time for me," Steve said as they slapped five.

Once Larry got inside, he turned on the water in one of the sinks and began washing his hands and face as if preparing for a hot date. Angela was just getting off the toilet when she heard whistling.

"You sure are in a happy mood."

"I sure am," Larry replied in a deep male voice.

"Who in the hell is that?" Angela asked in a curious but troubled tone.

"Come out and see."

Angela picked up her purse off the floor and opened the stall door. And standing there leaning against the door with his shirt halfway unbuttoned and a silly-ass grin on his face, was Larry.

"Here's Johnny!"

"What in the hell are you doing in here? Don't you know you're in the ladies' room, you drunk bastard?"

"Look, I just wanted to apologize for disrespecting you earlier," Larry said as he blocked her way to the door.

"So, you thought this was the ideal place to tell me that? Get out of my face, Lenny."

"My name is Larry."

"Larry, Lenny, whatever your name is. Just get the hell out of my way."

"Aw baby, don't be like that. I just want a minute of your time. Your boyfriend isn't going to miss you."

"I'm going to count to 10, and if you don't move your big dumb ass from in front of that door, I'm going to move it for you."

"Just relax Angie, I just want to get to know you better."

Angela began to take off her earrings and rings as she slowly started to count.

"1, 2, 3, 4."

"Hey, baby. I don't want to hurt you."

"5, 6,7, 8."

"Ok, stop counting. Why don't you just tell me how much it's going to cost to get better acquainted," Larry said as he pulled out his wallet.

"Excuse me?" Angela said.

"Look, I know a high-maintenance woman when I see one. Just tell me how much. I've got plenty of money."

"You think I'm some kind of prostitute?"

"No, not a professional. But you've got your price just like everyone else."

Angela's face turned as red as a black person's could. She tried to control her temper but couldn't. In one quick motion she gave Larry a roundhouse kick to the groin that Kung Fu would've been proud of. Bam! He flew right out the door and landed on top of Steve. By this time the hallway was filled with women waiting to get into the restroom. They all started yelling for security. The commotion got everyone's attention, including Derrick's, who rushed right over to find out what was going on. He was unable to get through the crowd, but he could see Angela standing in the hallway yelling obscenities at Larry.

"And don't you ever disrespect another woman like that again, you pig. I hope they take your sick ass to jail."

"Fuck you, bitch!"

"What did you call me?"

"I called you a bitch; a bitch and a ho!"

Larry had broken the number-one rule of dealing with black women. Never, ever call them a bitch. Angela took off her high heels and walked over to Larry and punched him right in the jaw. Smack! And she didn't stop punching him until he was on the floor covered with blood. Derrick finally managed to get through the crowd to pull her off of him.

"Let me go! Let me go goddammit!" Angela yelled.

"Hold on, baby, it's me!" Derrick shouted. "Let's go, I think you made your point."

After the security guards moved in to take Larry away, Angela calmly straightened out her dress and put her shoes back on. Within seconds she was completely composed. Derrick couldn't help being turned on as he helped Angela on with her coat. That was the first time he ever saw a grown woman beat a man the way she did. There was none of that sissy kicking and scratching. Angela gave Larry an industrial-strength ass whipping that any man would've been proud of.

Derrick escorted Angela to her car, hoping he would at least get a kiss. But when she didn't volunteer one, he did what he had to do. He took it. After kissing for what seemed like an eternity, they finally came up for air.

"Umm!" Angela sighed. "I love a man who takes charge."

"And I love a woman who knows how to take care of herself."

"So, does that mean you still want me to be your date on New Year's Eve?" Angela joked.

Derrick paused for a moment. Then he smiled as took Angela's swollen knuckles into his hands.

"As long as you promise not to punch out any of my friends, you're still invited."

WHITE CHRISTMAS

It was three o'clock in the afternoon on Christmas Eve and all three of my stores were jam-packed. The video store was out of new releases, the shelves with the V.S.O.P cognac were emptied out in the liquor store, and the beauty supply shop was down to the last jar of TCB hair oil. It never ceases to amaze me how much money people spend during the holidays. Even the lottery machine was working overtime. Some customers dished out as much as a hundred bucks on Lotto, Little Lotto, and the Pick Three, hoping to strike it rich so they could pay off all those credit card bills they ran up buying all kinds of unnecessary junk for their spoiled kids and ungrateful relatives. They swear they're in complete control and playing for the fun of it, but the majority of them are gambling addicts who couldn't quit if they wanted to. But who am I to argue? If they want to spend their hard-earned money on a pipe dream that's their business. In fact, I encourage them. "Hang in there," I say enthusiastically. "You're bound to hit sooner or later!" The odds are a million to one, but they keep playing.

Then you have the holiday alcoholics who wait around all year for an excuse to get drunk and make fools of themselves. They come into the store with a pocket full of cash, which is often their rent money, and buy as much booze as they can afford. And if there's any change left, they'll buy a cheap bottle of wine, Richard's Wild Irish Rose and Thunderbird are the most popular. All in the name of friendly holiday fun. Yeah right! Christmas and New Year's Eve are simply excuses to drink more heavily. That's exactly why the liquor companies are so filthy rich. No matter what time of the year, winter or summer, spring or fall, rain or shine, people want to get their drink on. Teenagers do it because of peer pressure and adults drink to be sociable and to escape the reality of their pitiful lives. I know that sounds cruel, but it's true. Every weekend I sell thousands of dollars worth of liquor to men and women who frequent the cheap motels down the street, most of them married or shacking. They come in every Friday night and buy a pint of Tanqueray Gin or Bacardi Rum, then hurry off to their cozy little room to screw each other's brains out. I just look into their pathetic faces thinking to myself, "Why don't you get a divorce?"

Sometimes I think they can read what's on my mind. I've really got to learn to check myself and remember that it's about the business. Money is green no matter where it comes from. My sister Yvonne is much better at dealing with social and domestic problems while conducting business. That's exactly why she works full-time at the beauty supply store. I've never seen a woman who could talk about pedicures, hair weaves, and relationships all in the same conversation. She should seriously consider hosting her own television talk show. I think she could give Oprah Winfrey and Ricki Lake a run for the money.

When traffic finally lightened up, I told the manager to hold down the fort while I went next door to see if Yvonne needed change. When I walked in I could see she was engaged in one of her daily male-bashing sessions with her two bitter girlfriends, Carol and Wanda. I stooped down behind the magazine stand to listen to what they were gossiping about this time.

"Yeah, girl, these men out here are good for nothing," Yvonne said. "This guy I met last week had the nerve to invite me out to an expensive restaurant and then claimed he left his wallet at home."

"No he didn't!" Wanda replied.

"Yes he did. And we were at the cash register with a long line of people behind us when he decided to tell me. I've never been so embarrassed."

"That just goes to show you, once a man finds out that you have money, they start playing games," Carol added. "I bet you told him your family owns these stores, didn't you?"

"I think I might have mentioned it to him once."

"See, what did I tell you? These men out here are looking for a woman to take care of them. They start out doing nice things to butter you up, but once you're caught up, they start clowning."

"Most of the men I meet don't even bother to wine and dine you," Wanda said. "The last guy I dated had the nerve to send me flowers COD. What kind of shit is that?"

I had to put my hand over my mouth to keep from busting out laughing. I fell back against one of the display tables but luckily they didn't hear me.

"At this point, I just wish I could find a man who has a steady job, keeps himself clean, and knows how to fuck," Yvonne said. "And to be perfectly honest with you, I don't care if he's married or not. In fact, I prefer a man who has a woman to go home to. That way he won't be laying his butt around my house flicking the remote control like a lunatic and keeping me up all night with his snoring and farting."

"I heard that, girl," Wanda said co-signing as they gave each other high fives. "There's nothing like getting your groove on and sending them back home to their wives and girlfriends with the drama."

Yvonne and her conniving girlfriends made a sport out of screwing around with other women's men. Sometimes they were so bold they would approach the man while his wife was in the same room. "One day you're going to fuck with the wrong woman," I told her. But she didn't care. The way she looked at it was, the man was the one who took the vows to be faithful, not her. My back was beginning to ache from bending over. I decided it was time to show myself. But before I could spring up to surprise them, I heard Wanda mention my name. Without having to guess, I knew she was about to touch on her most favorite topic.

"Yvonne, I hate to say this about your brother," Wanda said as she began to gather her merchandise. "But I've got to get this off my chest before I go."

"Go ahead girl, don't be shy, say what's on your mind."

"Your brother Mark is nothin' but a sellout! I haven't seen him with a black woman since I've known him."

"Yeah, Yvonne, what's up with that?" Carol asked. "Did he forget where he came from?"

"Look, I've been trying to figure out what's up with him since he first brought home this light-skinned Hispanic girl from high school," Yvonne said as they all began to walk slowly toward the door. "That was 13 years and 100 white women ago. Now he's dating some blond bimbo named Christie who lives in Country Club Hills. To be honest with you, I don't know what the deal is with him. I guess he's got a case of jungle fever."

"Jungle fever, my ass," Wanda asserted. "He's got the plague!"

"Most of these brainwashed negroes feel that a white woman is some kind of status symbol," Carol said. "Once they start making a little money they head straight for the North Side and the suburbs to find little Ms. Barbie."

"I think they're just looking for a freak in the bedroom, someone who will do whatever they tell them to," Yvonne said, getting in the last word before escorting them outside to their cars. "And you know how easy these stupid white girls are to manipulate and control."

When the door closed behind them I stood up and stretched my back. I thought about running outside and cursing them out, but I knew it wouldn't make any difference. They were lonely and bitter women who didn't have one healthy relationship between them. But I couldn't help being upset. All my life I've had to listen to black women criticize me for dating outside my race. They called me every dirty name under the sun from Honky Lover to Uncle Tom. On a few occasions I've gotten into serious fights over some of their nasty comments. But no matter what they say, I'm going to continue to date whoever I choose to. If I meet a woman who is fun to be with and makes me happy, then that's who I'm going to be with. I don't give a damn if she's Hispanic, Asian, white, or even blue. Life is too short to be waiting around for the perfect woman of your own race to come along.

Besides, I've given the so-called African American women an opportunity to get with me, but it hasn't worked out. Everything with them is money, money, money. How much you make, and how much you're willing to spend. Which is exactly what all this animosity seems to boil down to is the dollars, because I don't hear any of the so-called sistahs making a big deal out of broke or blue-collar black men who date outside their race. The focus is always on famous athletes, entertainers, or any other brothers who have big bucks. Take my situation for example. On a number of occasions I've tried to get acquainted with the attractive and well-educated black women who come into my stores. But because I was working behind the counter wearing an apron or mopping the floor, they didn't give me the time of day. I guess they assumed I was just a lowly store clerk with no future and, most importantly, no money. But when I had my Benz parked out front and they found out I was the owner of the store, their whole attitude changed. That's what they get for assuming!

When Christie and I met, she didn't exhibit that kind of materialistic mentality. In fact, I was hard at work sweeping out the front of the store in my dingy blue jeans when she came into the video store looking for a movie to rent. I still remember the title. It was *Imitation of Life* made back in 1959. Unfortunately, I didn't have it in stock, but I told her I would order it if she was willing to wait a few days. She agreed. And when it finally arrived a week later, she invited me over to watch it at her place. What a night that turned out to be! We stayed up until two o'clock in the morning talking about everything from world politics to the latest music. Christie had an impressive collection of R&B and Hip Hop music. I almost fell out when she broke out The Fugees' new CD and Barry White's greatest hits. "What were you expecting?" she asked sarcastically, "Led Zeppelin and Pink Floyd?"

But despite the fact that Christie was down-to-earth and very polite, Yvonne couldn't stand her. When I asked her to give me one good reason why she didn't like Christie, the only answer she could come up with was, "Because she's white, that's why!" I just looked at her and told her that she was nothing but a damned racist. It is exactly this kind of hostile attitude that turned me off to dating black women. I'm sick and tired of dealing with their gold diggin' and male bashing attitude because they've watched too much TV and read too many books written by other angry and manless females.

For whatever reason, black women can't seem to exist in a peaceful relationship. They need to have their daily dose of drama in order to be content. It seems like the only time they're happy is when a man is either running game or going upside their heads. But I don't have time for all that mess. I'm out there seven days a week, sixteen hours a day, busting my ass trying to get ahead in this dog-eat-dog world. The last thing I need is a smart-mouthed woman with an attitude waiting to greet me at the door when I come home. And the more educated and financially well off black women are, the more lip they give you. "I'm independent," they say. "I don't need a man." Well, if that's the case then why don't they get the hell out of the way of the white women who openly admit to needing a man, a black man?

When I try to talk to Tony and Derrick about how I feel, they make up all kinds of excuses for why black women act the way they do, especially Derrick. If I say black women are materialistic, he says it's because they were raised by mothers who taught them to pursue men with money. If I say black women are disrespectful and too flip-mouthed, he says it's because they were raised in female-dominated households with no father figure to discipline them. Then, when I say black women are combative and argumentative, he comes up with the stupid excuse of slavery. "Black women have had to endure a lot of pain over the last three hundred years," he says. "Separation from their families, racial and sexual discrimination in the work place, and rape."

Although I do understand the point he's trying to make from a historical perspective, I've got to look at the reality of my personal and present situation. When I get home from a hard day's work, I have a right to have someone there I can share my dreams and aspirations with. A woman who will listen to my problems and love me for who and what I am. I don't give a damn about slavery. I need a supportive woman in my life, and Christie is filling that void. She's a caring and supportive woman who cares about what my goals are and how my day went. Derrick can take his slavery philosophy and shove it! It's all about being happy. And besides, he should take a long hard look at his own past experiences with black women. They haven't exactly been all that positive. I mean, he hasn't had a decent relationship since I've known him. All the women he has dealt with were either stuck up, mentally ill, too ghetto, or broke as hell. He has a lot of damn nerve trying to act like Les

Brown giving motivational speeches on dating black women. He needs to look in the mirror.

And let's not forget about poor Tony, who has been taken through pure hell over the last seven years dealing with Erikah's ignorant mother, Valarie. Here's a classic case of a good man getting caught up with a good-for-nothing tramp who was out for money. Sure, he was at fault for not using protection, no doubt. But Valarie has been tearing this man down for years despite the fact that he has lived up to his responsibilities. He calls his daughter every day, picks her up every other weekend, and has never missed a month of child support. Still she tries to hurt him every chance she gets. What's up with that? Tony is probably one of the most positive and responsible men I know. He paid his way through college, is very active in the community, and avoided all the pitfalls of growing up in the ghetto, such as drugs and gangs. But in the end it was a woman that brought him down, a **black woman**!

So, as far as I'm concerned, Yvonne, her girlfriends, and Tony and Derrick could all kiss my ass. It's Christmas Eve, business is booming, and Christie's coming over to spend the night. The more I think about it, the more I realize that I'm happier than all of them put together.

On Christmas morning Christie and I got up bright and early and ran into the living room to open our gifts. We looked like two overgrown kids as we tore off the wrapping paper and flung it into the air, making a big mess. I already knew what I was getting, a laptop computer and a bottle of Herrera cologne. Christie thought she was getting a necklace and a VCR, but I had a big surprise for her.

"This box feels awfully light for a VCR, Mark," Christie said as she lifted the box from beneath the tree.

"Hum, I hope they didn't deliver the wrong box," I said, playing dumb. "Open it up and let's see."

Christie removed the paper slowly, with a look of utter disappointment on her face, convinced her VCR was not inside.

"Well, on the outside of the box it says Sharp VCR, but the box feels empty," she said.

"Those damn fools must have made a mistake." I continued with my charade. "Let me give them a call right now and see if they're open. I'm really pissed off that they spoiled your Christmas."

I got up from the floor, grabbed the phone, and pretended to call the store.

"Why don't you open it up and see if there's some kind of paperwork inside," I instructed her.

While I faked as if I was talking to the store manager, she used a pair of scissors to open the side of the box. When she finally got all the tape off she turned it upside down and shook it.

"What is this?" She smiled as a sexy lingerie top fell out first. "Mark I'm going to kill you."

Then the lace panties dropped out along with a thick white envelope. I hung up the phone and watched her as she opened it.

"Is this what I think it is?" she asked.

"Just open it and see."

Her eyes opened wide and her hands were slightly trembling when she pulled out the contents. Inside were two plane tickets to Miami and two passes for a five-day Carnival cruise.

"Oh, thank you sweetheart, thank you, thank you, thank you!" she screamed as she ran over and jumped into my arms like a big kid. "You remembered."

"Of course I remembered," I said while looking into her beautiful eyes. "Like I told you in the beginning, you take care of me and I'll take care of you."

"I can't believe you played such a dirty trick on me," she said while playfully hitting me on the chest. "You should have stopped kidding around when you saw how upset I was."

"So what are you trying to say? Would you prefer the

VCR instead?" I laughed.

Christie picked up the empty box and began chasing me around the house, hitting me on the back of the head when she got in close enough. After letting her get in a few good whacks, I turned on her and wrestled her to the floor. We tussled back and forth childishly rolling around on the carpet. I pinned her arms down with my knees and made her declare me the winner.

"Do you give?" I asked her while tickling her underneath her arms.

"No, never!" she chuckled.

I intensified the tickling and focused on her neck, which I knew to be her most sensitive spot.

"Do you give now?"

"Yes!" Christie laughed. "I give!"

"First tell me, who's the man?" I demanded.

"Not you!" she laughed hysterically. "I'm the man."

"Oh yeah, take this." I said as I went all out, tickling her all over.

"Ok, Mark, I give up," she said, turning red in the face. "You're the man."

"Say it louder, I can't hear you."

"You're the man, I said!"

After lifting Christie up off the floor I immediately threw my hands in the air declaring myself the champion.

"Winner and still undefeated champion of the world, Marvelous Mark."

"You mean, Miniature Mark, don't you?" Christie cracked, "after that weak ten minutes of sex you put in last night."

Before you knew it we were on the floor again, wrestling and knocking furniture around. But this time I let Christie win. She flipped me onto my back and jumped on top of my chest.

"I guess you want me to say that you're the man, huh?" I asked.

"No, I want you to say something else, something special," she said, as her expression turned serious.

"Like what?"

"Tell me that you really care about me and that you'll always be a part of my life." Her eyes began to fill with tears.

The moment of truth had finally come, after months of sharing our thoughts, our dreams, and our beds together, Christie was laying her feelings on the table. The holidays somehow have a way of bringing out pent-up emotions.

"I do care about you Christie, I care about you very much," I said while lifting my back off the floor and sliding her down onto my lap.

"But do you love me?" she asked, as the tears began to fall. "Because there is no doubt in my mind that I love you."

"Damn, that's deep, baby! Are you're sure you know what you're saying?"

"Yes, I'm sure. I've been sure ever since the day you came over to my house to watch the movie. Since then I've grown closer to you than any man in my whole life."

"But Christie, what about your family, what are they going to say about you falling in love with, or even dating a black man? You know as well as I do that they're racist as hell."

"My family?" she said in an angry tone as she got up off of me. "I don't give a damn about what my family thinks. This is my life, goddamit. Do you think I give a shit about what my family or anybody else thinks? Huh, do you!?"

"Sweetheart, I'm just trying to make sure you know what you're getting yourself into. This isn't the movies where we ride off happily ever after into the sunset."

Christie slapped me right in the face. Smack! Her face turned red and her hands began to tremble.

"All my life I've had to listen to people warn me about getting involved with black men! My uppity college friends, my racist parents who try to pass themselves off as Christians, and white female co-workers who are just jealous because they don't have the courage to date anyone outside their own race. Now, you think that you have to advise me on what the negative consequences are of dating an African American male in this society. Well, let me tell you something, Mr. Oppressed Black

Man, I have been cursed out, spit on, and called every hateful name under the sun: white trash, race trader, honky bitch, and nigga lover just to name a few. So don't waste your breath trying to warn me about what I'm getting myself into, because believe me Mark, I know!"

I sat there speechless with my mouth wide open. It was as if all of her frustration and pain was released in that one short speech. I knew at that moment that I was in love with her too. The only problem with this romantic moment was the thought of dealing with my mother's reaction. Sure, she knew I occasionally dated white women. But how was she going to take the news that her grandchildren will be yellow, not brown. Thank goodness she and my stepfather were vacationing in Boca Raton, Florida. At least that gave me another week to practice my speech.

It was 5:00 p.m., Christie and I had just finished eating dinner and were sitting on the floor in front of the fireplace sipping Mums champagne when the phone rang. It was my mother.

"Hello, sweetheart, Merry Christmas!"

"Merry Christmas Mom," I happily responded. "How's the weather down there in sunny Florida?"

"It's absolutely beautiful son, the temperature is in the mid 70s and there isn't a cloud in the sky. Eat your heart out!"

"Aw, you know you're wrong for that Mama. You didn't have to rub it in."

"Well, I figure that after 32 years of raising two devil children that I deserve as much spoiling as I can get."

"What do you mean **two** devil children? Yvonne was the problem child, I was a complete saint."

"You were a saint all right, a Saint Bernard," she laughed.

My mother was a real trip. We were almost like brother and sister in the way we related to one another. She and I never went to bed mad at one another in my 29 years on this planet.

Okay, maybe once or twice when I was a kid, but for the most part we were the best of friends.

"So, how is Dad doing," I asked. "Is he enjoying himself?"

"You know Raymond, he's off somewhere fishing."

"Tell him I said to watch out for those crocodiles or alligators, whichever it is. He can't help me work on my car with a stub for a hand."

"Boy, you are so crazy," she laughed.

"Mark, tell your mother I said Merry Christmas," Christie said in the background.

"Mom, Christie is here with me. She wants to say hello."

"I didn't want to talk to her," Christie nervously whispered. "Just tell her I said Merry Christmas."

"Go ahead and say hello," I whispered while picking up the phone in the kitchen to listen in. "She's not going to jump through the phone and bite you."

"Hello, Mrs. Wilson," Christie said while giving me the evil eye. "Merry Christmas."

"Merry Christmas to you too, Christie. Are you enjoying your holiday?"

"Yes ma'am."

"Well, just don't let Mark get on your nerves. He can be a real pain in the butt sometimes.

"You can say that again. As a matter of fact I'm going to strangle him as soon as I get off this phone."

"I'm sure he deserves it. Let me speak back to him before I go. And Christie,"

"Yes ma'am?"

"I'm looking forward to meeting you when I arrive back home to Chicago. Maybe we can all get together for dinner."

Christie paused. She couldn't believe her ears. My mother had never shown any interest in meeting any of the women I ever dated, at least not the white ones. I came back into the living room and Christie handed me the cordless phone.

"What did you say to Christie, Mom? She's as pale as a ghost."

"I just told her I would like to meet her when I came home, that's all."

"When did you all of a sudden become interested in meeting my girlfriends?"

"Since I realized that the most important thing in the world is for you to be happy," she replied in that motherly tone. "Maybe it's the Christmas spirit or maybe it's just the good Lord working on my heart. All I know is that while flying down here all I could think about was how much I would have regretted not spending more time with you if my plane were to crash."

"That's really sweet of you to say. But I think our relationship is great!"

"No, Mark, let's be honest with one another. You know as well as I do that I never approved of your dating white girls, and I have allowed my prejudice to keep us apart. We used to see each other every weekend until you met Christie. I should have been there for you especially after I realized that you were in love with her. You do love her, don't you?"

"Yes I do, But how did you know how I felt?"

"Boy, I raised your nappy-headed behind from diapers. Don't you think I know when my child is in love?"

"I'm glad you understand how I feel. It's important for me to be able to share this part of my life with you. I don't care about what the rest of the world thinks, but it means everything to me to have your blessing."

"Oh baby, you do," she said getting choked up. "Look, I've got to go now. But I'll see you and Christie when I get home. You take care and have a Happy New Year's."

"You do the same Mama, and remember you will always be my number-one girl. I love you more than ever."

"I love you too son, bye."

Immediately after hanging up the phone, I excused myself to go to the bathroom. Once inside I leaned over the sink, looked at myself in the mirror, and broke down. It was like a heavy burden was lifted off my chest. Some people may think that's weak, but the stress from dealing with this interracial dating situation has been building up inside of me for years. It had taken my mother and me over 30 years to reach this point in our relationship. Any tears that were shed were well-earned.

I remember when I was in high school and how nervous I used to get asking her if I could bring a lady friend home. The first thing out of her mouth was, "Is it a black girl this time?" That really made me upset because I felt she was being hypocritical, being sanctified and all. But as I grew older I realized she was only trying to protect me from a racist society that sometimes reacts violently to mixed couples, especially if that couple happens to be a black male and a white female. And the fact that she grew up in Mississippi back in the early '50s didn't help matters much. In those days a black man could get lynched just for looking in the direction of a white woman. But things are different now, and I can date whomever I please. If people don't like it, that's their problem. The only person's opinion I ever cared about anyway was my mother's. And it looks like I've finally got her blessings.

As for Christie's parents, well, let's just say they are less than enthused about inviting me out to their lily white neighborhood for a cozy dinner and chit chat. And that prejudiced attitude has cost them quality time with their daughter. She hasn't been home to visit in six months. When her controlling father called and demanded that she come home for Christmas, she told him. "If Mark's not invited, then I'm not invited!" He was beside himself. That was the first time she ever stood up to him. Christie was his only child and he hated the idea of her being away from home during the holidays. It was a family tradition.

But that was the price he was willing to pay. He hated everything about me, my nappy hair, my chocolate skin, my deep voice, my pierced ear, and my small businesses. Although I earned well over $200,000 a year, it wasn't good enough for their Ivy League daughter. They wanted her to marry a hotshot divorce lawyer or a world-renowned cardiologist. Someone they could show off to their snooty friends at the country club.

But I bet you if I was some dumb jock with a multimillion-dollar contract they would welcome me into their home with open arms. Some white people are funny that way. For whatever reason, they don't see rich celebrities as niggers.

COMPATIBILITY

My mother is going to kill me when I tell her that I've decided to move in with Tony before our wedding in June. It
was a tough call, but I really need to know if I can deal with living with a man on a day-to-day basis. Sure, we spend lots of
time at each other's apartments and we're truly in love, but as
Tina Turner would say, "What's love got to do with it?" Over
the years I have watched too many of my desperate girlfriends
and co-workers allow their emotions to get the best of them.
They rush off blindly into marriage just for the sake of being

able to say, "Look everybody, I found someone who loved me enough to marry me!" They swear to God they've found Mr. Right and will live happily ever after. But after only a few months, or in some cases only a few weeks, reality comes crashing down on them like a ton of bricks. Next thing you know they're calling me up at all hours of the night asking for relationship advice or for the phone number of a good divorce lawyer.

What they failed to realize before frantically jumping over the broom was that a successful marriage is not based solely on how much you love a person, but equally as important, how compatible two people are together. Living harmoniously with a man 24 hours a day, 7 days a week, 365 days a year is a hell of a lot more complicated than dating, especially if you're a woman who has lived on her own most of her adult life. My Aunt Catherine, who is my mother's younger and only sister, didn't get married for the first time until she was 35, the same age I am now. She was the one person I could turn to for advice when there were issues I was unable to work out on my own. As always, she had all the angles worked out when I asked her about shacking up with Tony.

"Let me tell you what you do. First, rent your condo out on a six-month lease, just in case," she advised. "Then, take only your clothes and hygiene items over to his place. No furniture, and no expensive electronics like TVs and VCRs. Everything else goes into storage."

"Isn't that kinda like expecting things not to work out?" I asked naively.

She paused for a moment, obviously irritated by my comment. I knew she was about to let me have it.

"Look, baby girl," a nickname she only used when I got on her nerves, "you can love a man's dirty drawers and still not be able to live with him, Trust me, I know what I'm talking about."

And she was definitely an expert; she's been married four times in fifteen years. Her first husband, who was a gynecologist, lasted the longest, almost five years. The next two were successful businessmen. Both marriages fizzled out after only two years. And her current husband, John, who is my favorite, is a retired electrician. They've been happily married for about three and a half years now. He looks like a keeper. In each of her marriages she was the one who filed for divorce. Aunt Catherine had little patience for men who didn't keep their promise to love, honor, and cherish. What I respected most about her was the way she handled her three divorces; none of that legal quarreling over money and property. All she wanted was out!

Aunt Catherine was the ultimate role model. She symbolized everything I felt a real woman should be: educated but street smart, very demanding but extremely generous, classy but down-to-earth. And what a sense of humor! Just thinking about some of her antics makes me burst out laughing, like the performance she put on three years ago at her birthday party, which also happened to be the first time she met Tony. As usual she was sitting at the kitchen table teamed up with my mom playing her favorite card game, bid whist. In my 35 years I hardly remember seeing them lose. Personally I think they're just good at cheating. When Tony and I arrived she sprung up from the table and greeted him like he was family, hugging him tight and giving him a big wet kiss on the cheek. She offered to make his drink and fix his plate. But all that warm Southern hospitality quickly turned to a big chill when Tony and Uncle John insisted on playing cards. Talk about an ass-whipping, Aunt Catherine and my mom must have won ten straight games. Twice they ran Bostons, winning every book.

You should have seen the looks on their faces. Uncle John was so humiliated I thought he was going to cry. For some strange reason, men think they're inherently better at playing cards just because they have testicles. Where they get that dumb idea I'll never know. To add insult to injury, Aunt Catherine signified on Tony for the rest of the night about everything from his mismatched socks to his uneven hair cut. I warned him that night about waiting till the last minute to get ready and then rushing to give himself one of those uneven house cuts. Men are forever trying to play barber.

By 1:00 a.m. everyone was tired and ready to go. Mom made leftover plates to take home, and I went upstairs to get the coats. Finally, after four hours of drinking, dancing, and shouting it was time to go home. Tony was clearly relieved that his torturous evening was coming to an end, or so he thought. As he headed for the door, bidding everyone a goodnight, Aunt Catherine stopped him and playfully threw him against the wall and began frisking him like he was a criminal. "Wait just a minute," she said while feeling up and down his pant legs. "Let me see if you stole any of my valuables. I don't trust anybody from Chicago." What made it so funny is that Tony actually thought she was serious. I was laughing so hard I almost peed on myself, especially after she planted one of her diamond rings in his pocket and shouted, "Ah huh, call the police!"

Everybody was on the ground holding their stomachs trying to keep from passing out. That was a night I'll never forget. And believe it or not after all the hell she put Tony through, they are the best of friends. As a matter of fact, he seems even more anxious to see her at the wedding than I am. It's too bad she had to move so far away. Last April Uncle John's mom passed away, and they decided to move to Pittsburgh to live in the family house. Since she's been gone I've really missed being able to stop by her place every now and then to discuss my problems. In many ways she was my very best friend and my psychotherapist. My long-distance phone bill was over $200 last month, all calls to her in Pittsburgh, but she's worth every dime.

My mother, on the other hand, was from the old school. She absolutely positively did not believe in a woman shacking up with a man. "Why buy the cow when you can get the milk for free?" she preached. "Once a man has a woman under his roof, he has no incentive to marry her. He's got a live-in maid, a live-in cook, and live-in pussy. Why should he commit himself to anything?" My mother was a woman who believed in speaking her mind and I respected her for that. However, this is my life and I have to decide what's best for me. As far as I'm concerned, Tony and I are already committed. We're committed to supporting one another, we're committed to raising his daughter, Erikah, and we're committed to being each other's best friend. Now, if you take all that and include the fact that we are also committed to praying together every single night, I believe we have a real chance of making it.

My attitude has always been to do whatever it takes to make my man happy and then put the rest in the Lord's hands. That's all any woman can do. There's no sense in stressing out over things you can't control. If a relationship doesn't work out, chalk it up to experience and move on. It simply wasn't meant to be. Women need to be more realistic and accept the fact that every man they lay down with is not necessarily going to be their next fiancee or husband. The sistahs out there who are cooking, cleaning, and fucking some guy just to get him to marry them are making a big mistake. A man will settle down when he's ready to, not before.

Which brings me back to the compatibility issue. Some men I've dated got on my last nerve with their annoying and barbaric habits, such as leaving the toilet seat up and drinking juice out of the container; that's so uncivilized. Lucky for me, I've got a man who doesn't have those aggravating habits. Tony washes dishes, cooks gourmet meals, and puts the toilet seat down. As a matter of fact, he keeps house better than I do. Not bad for a 35-year-old bachelor. My only complaint is his obsession with clothes and toiletries. He takes up almost as much closet and counter space as a woman, and you know that takes some doing. His closets are completely full with sport coats, suits, dress shirts, sweaters and ties. The closet in the hallway is reserved for jeans, gym shoes, and other manly sportswear.

But what really tripped me out is how orderly everything is arranged. All of the jackets are facing the same direction with the dark colors and heavy wool fabrics in the back and the lighter colored Versaces and Armanis toward the front. As for his shirts, they're mostly white business styles and expensive Italian designs by Lorenzini. All arranged according to how recently they were worn. Is that sick or what? To be honest with you, I didn't think I could handle dating a man who is so damned neat. And his bosom buddy Derrick is just as meticulous. Birds of a feather truly do flock together. When I first saw this fashion extravaganza, my mind flashed back to the movie *Waiting to Exhale* and Bernadine's husband's closet. Now that was one anal-retentive brother. I was determined not to get involved with that type.

But then I thought about it for while and I began to realize the benefits of having a man who knows how to dress. At least I wouldn't have to teach him how to match his socks or tie his necktie. Tony is one of those rare men who know how to put a sharp outfit together. Unlike so many fashion misfits I've dated, who still wear gold chains outside their shirts and black socks with gym shoes. Now that's country!

Meeting the ideal mate is no easy task, especially if you're a woman bent on dating only those men who fit into a specific category: highly educated, large bank account, and wears a suit and tie to work every day. For 30 years, that was me. And although it was painful to finally admit, this mentality was probably the reason why I was still single, and yes, very lonely. Sure, I had money, a sharp Corvette, and a nice investment portfolio. But what I didn't have was a man, at least not a quality one. Not that I was looking for one to make me happy, you understand, but I thought it would be nice to have someone in my life to share my dreams and aspirations with. You know, someone to enhance what I already had going on. I figured the best thing for me to do was to take time out and reevaluate myself before jumping into another relationship, and that's exactly what I did.

For the next two long years I chilled. No serious dating, no empty promises, and no casual sex. Which wasn't much of a sacrifice considering the few men that I had sex with never satisfied me anyway. Big dicks, long tongues, incredible stamina and all, they never gave me what I needed most: love, romance, and most importantly, the feeling that I was learning and growing as a human being.

The day I met Tony, getting involved in a serious relationship was the furthest thing from my mind. My attentions were focused on one very important goal, to close the deal on a rental property in the South Shore area. One of my regular clients, Ginger, a moderately attractive 40-something snob, wanted to look it over early that afternoon. So, at 1:30 p.m. we met at my office and headed out. We were making good time too, until we turned onto 79th and Stony Island, an intersection custom-made for traffic accidents. There had been a three-car collision earlier and, as usual, people were slowing down and being nosy. Now I had to listen to Ginger's obnoxious conversation about the stock market and the O.J. Simpson trial. "I think he did it," she said. "What do you think?" I just looked at her and kinda shrugged my shoulders indicating that I didn't have a position. What I really wanted to say was, "Who cares? He's not putting any food on my table." As far as I was concerned, he was just another rich man in America who could afford to buy justice, or injustice.

Ginger had a terrible habit of trying to discuss major issues with little or no information. The topics were mostly about celebrities who were in the news, or her other favorite topic, money. I guess she saw herself as some kind of high roller since she had recently inherited a few thousand dollars from her dead husband's insurance policy. Every chance she got, she would flash her clothes and jewelry in my face while casually mentioning how much it cost. Needless to say, I wasn't impressed. In my eyes she was nothing more than a tacky bimbo wrapped in an expensive fur coat. How does the saying go: "You can put perfume and pearls on a pig, but it's still a pig." All I wanted was to take her for a quick look at the property and get rid of her, and what made it really annoying was that her cheap perfume was beginning to make my eyes water.

Tony and another man were finishing up on remodeling the inside of the third-story apartment when we drove up. They were scraping and painting in the 90-degree heat, while a favorite song of mine by Earth, Wind, & Fire, called "Reasons" played loudly from inside the three-flat. You should have heard them trying to hit those high Phillip Bailey notes. They sounded terrible. I blew the horn to get their attention.

"Excuse me, is it ok if I bring a client up to look over the inside of the building?" I shouted. "I'm the agent responsible for selling this property."

"Sure, come on in, the door is open," the older man shouted from the first-story window. "Just be careful, the paint hasn't completely dried in the hallway yet."

While I parked the car, Tony played it off, pretending not to be impressed by either me or my fire-engine-red Vette. He nonchalantly went back to work scraping and painting while singing along to the music, but I could tell he was checking me out from behind those smeared goggles. Men think they're so slick.

"Tracie, are you sure it's safe to go inside?" Ginger asked while looking at herself in the passenger side mirror with conceit. "I have on high heels and I don't want to get any dust in my hair. I just spent $80 at the salon this morning getting it laid."

"You'll be fine, Ginger," I assured her. "I just want you to get a quick peek inside. We'll be in and out in no time."

Boy, the people you have to put up with in this business. And it's always the ones without any money or the ones who have just recently come into a little cash that are the biggest pains in the ass. I just want to hurry up and make this sale and drop her wannabe-Ivana-Trump ass off at the bank.

By the time I finally managed to get **Ms. Thang** out of the mirror, Tony was gone. I figured he was either trying to make an escape out onto the back porch or washing up to make himself more presentable. Pretty boys hate being seen when they are less than perfect, and Tony was a real cutie. I tactfully began Ginger's tour of the property with a look at the back yard. After seeing that the coast was clear, I took her inside and walked her through the basement apartment and then the first and second floor. Still no sign of Tony. Judging by the look on Ginger's face, she was in love with the building. When I asked if she needed to see the third floor before making up her mind, she said, "Sure we can take a look if it's safe to go up, but I can tell you right now, I'm sold!"

At that very moment guess who comes strolling into the room acting like he needed something out the tool box? That's right, Mr. Pretty Boy himself. I could tell that he had been working hard to get the paint spots off his face. The strong smell of turpentine was unmistakable. However, I must admit he looked damn good in those worn out jeans he had on. And that tight T-shirt showed off his muscular back and broad shoulders.

I wanted to jump his bones right then and there, but of course I played it cool.

"Excuse me, are you the same contractor who did the work on the property on 74th and Colfax?" I asked, trying to make conversation before he got away.

"As a matter of fact, I am," Tony replied in a deep smooth tone. "Why do you ask?"

"Because I'm also the agent who sold that property. My name is Tracie Johnson," I said, extending my hand nervously. "Nice to meet you."

"Nice to meet you too, Mrs. Johnson. My name is Tony, Tony Page."

"Please, Mr. Page, call me Tracie, I don't like formalities. And by the way it's Ms., not Mrs. Johnson."

"Ok, Tracie," Tony replied with a cute grin. "You can call me Tony."

"Well, Tony, I'm glad we had this opportunity to meet in person so I could tell you how much I admire your work.

You're very talented."

"Why thank you Ms. Johnson, I mean Tracie," he corrected himself. "It's always a pleasure to meet someone who appreciates quality work, but I can't take all the credit. My partner Mitch is responsible for most of the plumbing and electrical work in that building. Would you like to meet him?"

"Sure, it would be my pleasure."

"Hey Mitch, can you stop doing whatever it is you're doing and come down here for a second?" Tony shouted up the dusty stairway. "There's someone down here I'd like for you to meet."

"Uh hum, excuse me," Ginger said after sarcastically clearing her throat. "I hope I'm not interrupting your little get-together here."

"Oh, I'm sorry Ginger, forgive my rudeness. Tony, this is my favorite client, Mrs. Ginger Walker."

"Please to meet you Mrs. Walker," Tony responded with a flirtatious grin. "I hope we left you enough room to get around in. We'll have all this stuff cleaned up and out the way by the end of the week."

"No, it's not a problem at all. And by the way, it's Ms. Walker," she replied as she anxiously extended her hand. "My husband recently passed away."

"I'm sorry to hear that. I can only imagine how difficult an adjustment that must be for you."

"Oh, I'm doing just fine!" Ginger replied with spirit. "What about you, are you married?"

I couldn't believe she asked him such a bold and personal question. Talk about tacky. But I must admit I was just as interested in the answer as she was. And just as he was about to respond, Mitch comes into the room, calming the moment and our female hormones.

"Ladies, this is my partner, Mitch Taylor. Mitch, this is Ms. Tracie Johnson and Ms. Ginger Walker."

"Pleasure to meet you ladies. So what do you think about the building?"

"I think it looks great. You've both done a wonderful job," I replied. "In fact Ms. Walker has just decided to purchase it."

"That's great news!" Tony said. "Maybe you could put in a good word for us with your clients and toss a little business our way. I don't have another contract until late next month."

"I think your work speaks for itself. But I'll be sure to strongly recommend your company to anyone looking to rehab properties. As a matter of fact, let me give you one of my cards." I said whipping it out of my pocket like a switch blade. "Why don't you give me a call at my office every week or so, and I'll let you know if I need your services."

Yeah, that's right, I meant it just the way it came out and I suspect everybody knew it. My only hope was that he wasn't married. I didn't go that route under any circumstances. Been there, done that.

"Well, ladies," Tony interrupted, "if you will excuse us, we've got to get back to work. I promised to have this apartment ready by this weekend."

"Don't you get more money if the work takes longer?" Ginger asked, sounding conniving. "I'm sure whoever hired you can afford another day's pay. Why not milk it for a few more bucks. It probably belongs to a white company anyway."

"First of all, Mrs. Walker," Tony replied in an irritated and unpleasant tone, "we don't get paid by the hour, we get paid by the job. And although I could easily create all kinds of structural complications and overcharges for materials that could make me thousands of additional dollars, in the end it wouldn't be worth the trouble. Sooner or later doing bad business will catch up with you. But what it really boils down to is being able to sleep at night knowing you cheated someone out of their hard-earned money, no matter what color they are. Now if you ladies will excuse us, we have work to do."

At that moment I never felt more proud to be a black woman. It's not often you find a brother who takes pride in his work and has that rare characteristic called integrity. What also impressed me was his anti-racist attitude. Regardless of who was signing his check, he was determined to do what was right, a quality that was made more significant because of the fact that I was the owner of the building and also the one he remodeled on 74th Street. Meanwhile Ginger's reaction was expectedly ignorant and hostile. Instead of respecting his honesty, she began name-calling and putting him down.

"What's his problem?" she said with an attitude. "He ain't nothin' but an old Uncle Tom. I was simply suggesting a way for him to put a few dollars in his pockets. God knows he needs it, as broke as he is."

"How do you know he's broke?" I said defending him.

"Just look at him! He's filthy, walking around in this dirty mess with paint and dust all over himself. Only a man with no education and no future would do this kind of degrading work for a living"

She had a lot of goddamn nerve putting him down. I just ignored her narrow-minded comment and headed for the car, trying to explain the economics of the labor industry to a dizzy broad who never worked a day in her life would have been a complete waste of time. Little did she know, Tony was the owner of a small but very successful landscaping and construction company that had an impeccable reputation. The last two jobs alone, which took less than two months to complete, paid more than $7,500 each. I know because I personally signed the checks. But regardless of how much he was worth, I was determined to get better acquainted with this attractive and positive human being. My only concern was that he was either married with children, or even worse, gay. Sometimes you never can tell. I waited for his call impatiently, checking my voice mail every hour, but after three days, still no message. At first I thought about going back over to the building and confronting him with my true feelings, but that was too bold and out of character for me, so I kept my faith and put it in God's hands like I always do. Just to help the process along a bit, I added Tony in my prayers every night.

"Lord, you know I don't ask for much, only good health and

continued prosperity for myself and my family. But now I'm callin' in a favor. You know, just a little sumth'in, sumth'in. Now I've been staying away from other women's husbands and working extremely hard to keep my thoughts pure, but I ain't lying, I've got a lot of lust in my heart at this moment. I know you know that. But please Lord, pretty please, let this man be the one for me. If you answer this one prayer for me, just this one, I **promise** to put a little more money in the collection plate on Sunday and to stop talking about people so bad behind their backs, Amen."

By the end of the week my prayers were answered. Tony called Friday afternoon looking for another job. I gave him the name of an associate of mine who was interested in hiring him to remodel a 20-unit building. The contract was for $100,000, half up front and the other half when the job was done. Tony was elated! He invited me out that evening to celebrate. Over dinner, he said he was very attracted to me and was interested in pursuing both a personal and business relationship. Since that date four years ago, I've been giving him more work than he can handle. And by the way, I've added 20 dollars to the collecting basket every Sunday since. But I'm still working on trying to keep that other promise. Hey, nobody's perfect.

It's 6:00 p.m. on New Year's Eve and I can't make up my mind about what to wear to Derrick's party tonight. Pants, or skirt, heels, or flats, black or red? How in the world can any mortal woman make such complex decisions in only three hours, especially with all of the distractions going on around here? Erikah and those twins from next door are driving me up the wall. Kevin and Tevin are as cute as they can be, but those are two bad-ass little boys. I'm talking *Children-of-the-Corn*, bad. They're so bad that eight kindergartens on the South Side have refused to take them in. Their mother, Karen, has had to move numerous times in order to find a school that hadn't heard about their reputation.

Over the last six months those little heathens have terrorized two baby sitters and been kicked out of four schools. At one school, Kevin stopped up the tub and sink with toilet tissue and practically flooded the entire first floor. When she tried to enroll them into a more strict program out in the suburbs, Tevin smuggled a box of matches into his backpack and gave one of the teachers a hotfoot. When asked why he did it, Tevin said he got the idea from watching Bugs Bunny and Road Runner cartoons.

But Erikah loves those little monsters to death, always hugging and kissing them like they are her own brothers. And believe it or not, they listen to her when she tells them to do something. If she says sit, they sit. If she puts on a video cassette and says be quiet, they will sit in front of the TV without making a sound, at least most of the time. Which is why I'm surprised by how much noise they're keeping up in the living room.

"Erikah!" I shouted. Come here, right now!"

Suddenly, everything got quiet. I could hear one of the boys teasing Erikah as she headed back to the bedroom.

"Ooh, you gonna get it."

"Now see what you did," Erikah whispered back. "You got me in trouble. Here I come, Tracie!"

When I turned around ready to call her again, she was standing in the doorway with this pitiful look on her face. You know, that innocent look kids give you to keep from getting their behinds whipped.

"Young lady, you know Tony and I don't stand for all that nonsense, don't you?"

"Yes, ma'am," Erikah humbly replied while looking down at her feet.

"Look at me when I'm talking to you," I insisted. "Do you want me to tell your daddy that you haven't been a good girl when he comes back from the grocery store?"

"No."

"Well, I suggest that you go back in there and settle down, understand? And keep an eye on Kevin and Tevin. Karen should be over in a minute to pick them up."

"Yes ma'am," Erikah answered. "But is it ok if we make peanut butter and jelly sandwiches? We're hungry."

"No you can't. Your father called and said he was stopping at Kentucky Fried Chicken to pick up something for dinner. I don't want you to spoil your appetite."

"Please Tracie, can we make just one sandwich and split it?"

"What did I just tell you, Erikah? Don't make me repeat myself again. Now go back in the living room with the boys and let me finish doing what I'm doing, and remember, no more running and jumping."

I could kill Tony for leaving me here for so long with all three of them, especially when I'm trying to pick out clothes to wear. He left out of here at 4:30 to get gas, go to the grocery store, and pick up a bucket of chicken. Now here it is almost 6:30 and he hasn't made it back yet. Leave it to a man to make a journey out of a simple task.

"I'll get it!" Erikah yelled when the telephone started to ring.

"Let me know if that's your father, I want to talk to him."

"Hello, Page residence," Erikah cordially announced. "Hi, Uncle Derrick, Happy New Year's to you too. No my daddy isn't here right now, would you like to leave a message?"

"Who is it, Erikah?" I shouted from the bedroom.

"It's Uncle Derrick. He's looking for Daddy."

"Bring me the phone sweetheart, I want to talk to your favorite uncle."

"Hold on Uncle Derrick, Tracie wants to talk to you."

I decided to take a break from my stressful task of fashion coordinator. After looking over five pants suits, seven dresses, and five boxes of shoes I don't even remember purchasing, I was thoroughly frustrated.

"Derrick what in the world are you callin' here to bug us

about now? You must need your weekly tip on how to dress."

"Oh, so you wanna start signifying, huh? You better save those tired jokes for tonight."

"Don't worry, Junior. I've got a million of 'em."

"Look, I didn't call to talk to you anyway, you big kick-stand-head, especially not to get tips on how to dress from a woman who takes an hour just to decide on which pair of shoes to wear. You've probably got half your wardrobe lying out on the bed right now."

He knew me all too well.

"Oh, wait till I see you," I threatened. "I'm going to pop you right upside your big head."

"We'll see who pops who first. In the meantime where is your old man?"

"Your shadow went to the store two hours ago and should be returning any minute now. Do you have another one of those important manly type messages you'd like for me to deliver."

"As a matter of fact I do, Ms. Smarty Pants. Tell him not to worry about picking up that bottle of Bacardi. Mark said he'd bring everything we need from his liquor store. Oh yeah, there's one more thing, don't forget to bring those Parliament and Funkadelic albums."

"Why do you want him to bring those old records?"

"Don't tell me you forgot," Derrick said.

"Forgot what?"

"That the theme for this year's party is, 'Bringing in the *New* Year with *Old* school', get it?"

"Oh yeah, that's right! Thanks for reminding me. I've got the perfect outfit."

"Perfect outfit my butt. All you gonna do is put away the 20 new dresses you pulled out and go pull out twenty old ones," Derrick laughed.

"You got that right," I said proudly. "Like my momma always told me: Baby, don't throw away nuth'in. In 20 years it'll be back in style."

"Look, I've got to finish getting things ready over here.

Don't forget to give him my message."

"Don't worry, I won't forget. Oh, by the way, how many people are you expecting tonight?"

"Let's see, there's you and Tony, Mark and Christie, me and Angela, and Benjamin is bringing some woman named Nikki who he's been trying to date for the last two months."

"Where did he met this one?"

"She works at the salon next door to his downtown shop on Wabash."

"I swear, between the three of you, I don't know who's the most pathetic, Mark and his white women, Ben and his gold diggin' hoochies, or you and your little harem."

"Now wait just a minute, Trace," an affectionate nickname only he calls me, "Angela is the only woman I'm seeing, **right now**," Derrick said in his defense.

"If she's the only one you're seeing, who was that short, long-nosed, big-breasted woman you came by here with on Christmas Eve?"

"Aw, you mean Lisa? She's just a friend I promised to take out that particular weekend. I really wanted to be with Angela but she had commitments too. As of tonight, we are exclusively dating."

"Listen to you, Mr. Playboy. I've never heard you give a woman so much props, she must be the bomb!"

"I'm telling you Trace, this woman is something special. She might even be the one."

"Yeah right, Derrick, you said the exact same thing about that crazy sistah named Samone who showed up at your hotel room in the middle of the night, remember?"

"Hey, how was I supposed to know she was a few cans short of a six-pack?"

"Any woman who goes over to a man's house and starts cooking and cleaning on the first date should be suspect, don't you think?"

"I guess you've got a point there," Derrick admitted. "That's why I need you to check Angela out for me. I trust your judgment."

"Well, the first thing I need to know is what is her zodiac sign?"

"She's an Aries."

"And you're a Cancer, right?"

"Right."

"Aries woman and Cancer man, huh? Let me see," I said, thumbing through the pages of *Black Erotica*.

"Perfect!" I shouted. "According to the book, you make great business partners."

"Thanks for the psychic reading, Dionne Warwick. I'll have you read my palm next time," Derrick joked.

"Laugh if you want, but I'm telling you, there are signs that just don't get along. Tony and I are both Geminis and we get along like ice cream and cake, but put two Cancers together and you can forget it. Too many emotions."

"Hum," Derrick said sounding thoughtful. "When I think about it, you're right."

"I should start charging you for my dating services," I said. "Now, let me go so I can get myself together. I'll give Tony your message."

"Hold up a minute, what time should I be expecting you?" Derrick asked. "You know how I am about promptness."

"What time is everyone else coming?"

"I told them 9:00 p.m., which of course means 9:30 to 10:00 CP time."

"We should be there at least by 9:00, if Valarie comes by to pick Erikah up at 7:00 like she promised. But you know how unpredictable she can be."

"All right Trace, I'll see you later. Tell Erikah I love her and give her a big kiss for me."

After I hung up, my instincts told me to call Valarie right away to make sure she didn't forget her agreement to pick up Erikah on time. After four rings, the answering machine picked up. Needless to say I was furious. Tony specifically told her to contact him before leaving the house. He made it perfectly clear that Erikah had to go home that evening, no ifs, ands, or buts. I took a deep breath to calm myself down before leaving a brief and cordial message asking her to call us as soon as possible. Of course I left out the part about going to Derrick's party, knowing it would only encourage her not to show up on time or at all. She is such a juvenile young heifer.

"Daddy, Daddy, Daddy!" Erikah yelled as Tony's car drove up in front of the building. "Tracie, Daddy's back."

"Thank God," I said in relief. "It's about time. Go and open the front door, I know his hands are full."

Just like a man. Tony tried to carry in two bags of groceries, three bags of KFC, and two large pops all in one trip. One of the pops fell out of his hand coming up the stairs and he lost his grip on the KFC bag with the extra crispy just as he walked in the front door, what a mess.

"Hurry up baby," Tony gasped, "the bag with the milk in it is about to burst!"

"Why do you have to be so lazy trying to bring all these bags in at once?" I said while grabbing the torn bag.

"Shit, it's cold out there!"

"Tony, watch your mouth around the kids!"

"Sorry kids," Tony apologized, making sure to direct most of what he had to say at the evil twins. "I said a bad word, and I don't ever want to hear you use it, ok?

Tevin and Kevin nodded their heads up and down in agreement, but I could tell by the way they glanced over at one another that they had just put another curse word in their arsenal, as if they needed encouragement. Tony set the bags on the kitchen counter, hung his coat up in the closet, and began shouting directions like a drill sergeant.

"Erikah, you and the boys go wash your hands and get ready for dinner. Tracie, get out the paper plates and cups for the kids and bring the cranberry juice over to the table."

"And what are you going to do, your majesty?" I asked sarcastically.

"I'm going to kick back and allow you to serve your king."

The box of tampons I pulled out of the bag went flying right at his head. Unfortunately, I missed.

"Oh, so you want to play rough, huh?"

Tony ran over and put me in a bear hug and playfully carried me into the dining room and threw me onto floor.

"Fight, fight, fight!" the twins yelled as they ran toward us with their little hands still soaked with water.

"Get off, you big bully!" Erikah shouted as she jumped onto Tony's back.

Next thing you know we were all tumbling around on the floor wrestling and tickling each other. Tevin had one of Tony's legs and Kevin had the other. Erikah, meanwhile had him in a semi head lock trying to pull him off of me. But it wasn't long before our playful tussle turned into a tender moment. With the kids screaming, scratching, and choking, Tony paused and passionately looked into my eyes as I hopelessly struggled.

"Stop fighting me baby," he whispered. "I have something for you."

"Wha, wha, what is it?" I gasped, knowing exactly what it was."

As if in slow motion, like in the movies, he leaned downward toward my anxiously waiting lips. His strong hands, which had been firmly pinning my arms down, were now gently stroking my face and neck in that unmistakable way that says, "I love you." We kissed for what seemed like several minutes, our tongues dancing around in each other's mouths, interrupted only by occasional lip smacking. Uum, it felt so —— good. Of course, the twins were shocked and made somewhat uncomfortable by our actions. All of a sudden the playing stopped, and all eyes were on us.

"Ooh, they're doing the nasty," Kevin said, breaking the silence.

"No they're not," Erikah said, correcting him. "They're just kissing. Let's go eat and leave these two lovebirds alone."

"I wanna watch," Tevin insisted as Erikah pulled him into the kitchen.

"Boy, come on here and get out of grown folk's business."

Tony busted out laughing and rolled off me onto the floor. He had never heard Erikah say that before. Of course, he said it to her all the time, but hearing it come out of her mouth really cracked him up. After wiping the tears out of his eyes, Tony and I got up off the floor, served dinner and then dropped the twins off next door. At 8:00, an hour later than planned, Valarie pulls up in front of the house blowing the horn and screaming for Erikah to come out. It took everything I had to keep from running at there and dragging her silly ass out the car, but I promised myself earlier that this was one night she wasn't going to ruin.

"Erikah, let's go!" Valarie yelled from inside the car.

"I'm coming, Mommy."

"Have a Happy New Year's, princess," Tony said to Erikah giving her a hug and kiss on the forehead. "I'll call you first thing in the morning, ok?"

"Ok, Daddy, I love you."

"I love you too, baby."

Once Erikah was gone, we finished getting dressed for Derrick's party. By 8:15 we were dressed to kill. I finally decided on a sexy one-piece bell-bottom jumpsuit with thick four-inch pumps. You know, something to remind Tony of how lucky he is. Every now and then I think a woman should wear something provocative to get her man's attention. Tony decided to go all out and dress like a pimp. He sported a leisure suit that a friend of his found at a Goodwill store. The pants were tight in the crotch and the collar on the jacket was wide as hell. He looked just like Goldie in the movie "The Mack," especially after he put on this afro wig I borrowed from my hairdresser. All he needed was one of those hair picks with the peace sign and soul fist to set it off.

"You look delicious tonight, baby," I said while we stood in the full-length mirror admiring ourselves. "Good enough to eat."

"You want a taste before we go?" he said with that look in his eyes. "You know what they say, the blacker the berry, the sweeter the juice."

"Oh no you don't," I said, pulling away. "Let's go!"

"Aw, baby, come on. Let's have a little quickie. This is the first time we've been alone all day."

"The last time we called ourselves having a little quickie, we were in the bedroom for two hours, remember? Now can we please get going? Derrick is expecting us at nine o'clock and you know how he is about you showing up late. If we leave now we can make it right on time."

"Are you sure that's the only reason why you don't want to do *the nasty?*" he said in a childish tone, mocking Kevin.

"What in the world are you talking about?"

"I'm talking about those tampons you had me pick up at the store. Did you get your period early this month?"

"That would just ruin your little sex plans for tonight, wouldn't it?" I laughed.

"Hell naw!" he said while reaching into the linen closet and pulling out the infamous red towel. "It's New Year's Eve. I'm going to get mine, one way or the other!"

"Well don't worry, sweetheart, I'm not expecting my friend from out of town until later this week, so you can put away **Big Red**."

After pawing me for another ten minutes or so, he gave up and helped me on with my coat. Don't get me wrong, I wanted some too, but not at the expense of messing up my hair. It had taken me entirely too long to get it just right and nothing was going to make me go back in the bathroom and do battle with that curling iron again. Now later on that night would be an entirely different story. I had something very special planned for pretty Tony, something that would bring his New Year in with a bang! Early that week I bought candles, whipped cream, a sexy garter belt, and even a rope, just in case I got into one of my real freaky moods.

NEW YEAR'S RESOLUTION

When he arrived at Nikki's apartment, Ben was upset to find that she wasn't dressed. When he talked with her earlier, she promised to be ready by 8:30. It was 9:35 and she hadn't even finished doing her hair, and the baby sitter for her eight-year-old son Jason hadn't arrived yet.

"Women!" he mumbled while sitting impatiently on the living room sofa. "I knew I shouldn't have gotten involved with a female with kids."

To make matters worse, Nikki's loud girlfriend Jackie,

who didn't have a date, was in the bedroom running her mouth and slowing down the process.

"If she's not ready by ten o'clock, I'm outta here," Ben decided.

When the clock on the living room wall read 9:58, Ben got up from the sofa and went to announce he was leaving. But before he could knock on the bedroom door, it swung open and out walked a vision of beauty. Nikki was decked out in a pair of tight, bell-bottom blue jeans that laced up in the front and a red long-sleeve blouse that cut off in the middle of her stomach, just above her belly button. Her trim 24-inch waist and firm young breasts had Ben speechless.

"Well, how do I look?"

"Huh, what? Ben stuttered, unable to take his eyes off her chest area.

"I said, how do I look? Do you like my outfit?"

"Yes, I love it! It's very, uh, '70s."

"Girl you *know* you look good!" Jackie co-signed.

"Can we go know?" Ben asked while reaching for her coat.

"I'm still waiting for Jason's father to come pick him up. He was supposed to be here by eight o'clock."

"I've got your back," Jackie said. "Just leave your keys with me and I'll wait for Eric to show up. Hell, I don't have nuthin' else to do."

"I would really appreciate that," Nikki said, sounding genuinely grateful.

"No problem, girl. What are friends for? You've watched my three brats many a time when I wanted to go out and get my groove on. I owe you."

"But what if Eric doesn't show up?"

"Would you stop worrying and take your ass on before I change my mind. It's New Year's Eve, go out and enjoy yourself. God knows you deserve it."

"Thanks Jackie. I'll give you a call to let you know what time I'll be back."

"I hope you're not thinking about callin' me anytime tonight. I'll be dead to the world by one o'clock. And besides, why would you be in a hurry to come home to an empty house? If I had a fine brother like Ben picking me up in a sharp Lexus, I wouldn't come home for at least a week."

"Girl you need to quit."

Ben helped Nikki on with her coat, picked up his leather gloves and car keys from the cocktail table, and headed for the door.

"Come here, Jason, and give mommy a kiss goodnight."

"Have a good time, Mama," Jason said. "And have a Happy New Year. You too Mr. Woods."

"Why thank you, little fellah," Ben replied as he stooped down to shake hands. "You have a happy New Year's too."

"Don't think because I'm being friendly that you can keep my mother out all night," Jason said, sounding like the man of the house. "I want her back by midnight."

Yes sir," Ben said standing up and saluting. "Is there anything else."

"Yeah, don't drink and drive."

"Boy, you're a mess," Jackie said and gently pushed him toward his room. "Go to your bedroom and play Nintendo until your daddy gets here. I'll be back there in a minute to challenge you to a game of Mortal Combat."

After a few refresher instructions on how to activate the burglar alarm system, they were finally on there way. Nikki waved goodbye to Jackie and Jason, who were staring out of the window as if she was going on prom. Ben escorted her around to the passenger side of his Lexus and helped her in, closing the door behind her in a gentlemanly manner. Although he was every bit of six-foot-five and 260 pounds, Ben was smooth as silk. Once he was inside he turned on the heat and slid in his favorite Isley Brothers tape. The one with "Footsteps" and "Voyage to Atlantis."

"Before we go," Ben said. "I just want to tell you how incredible you look."

"Thanks for the compliment, Ben. And thanks for not leaving. I really needed to be around some positive people for a change. I've been spending entirely too much time with people who only talk about who they slept with last and which new club they went out to."

"I can guarantee you the conversation will be much broader than that tonight. All of my friends own businesses."

"Now that's what I need!" Nikki said enthusiastically. "To be associated with people who have goals!"

"What about your other needs?" Ben asked, changing the subject and the mood. "Don't you need someone to satisfy your emotional and physical needs?"

The answer to that question was apparent in the way she looked at him with her light brown eyes. Nikki was a 23-year-old single parent who was fed up with dating immature boys her own age. Although she was very independent, working full time at a salon and taking college classes three days a week, she needed someone she could learn from and someone she could count on. Ben was exactly what she needed, an experienced man with good manners, stable lifestyle, and a large bank account. Not that she was a gold digger, but if she was going to get sexually involved with another man, she swore it would be with one who had money.

Nikki leaned over, gently holding the back of Ben's thick neck, and kissed him.

"I hope that wasn't a charity kiss," Ben said.

"Would you like another just to make sure?"

"I'll take as many as you're willing to give."

Just as Ben was about to reach over and kiss Nikki again, a car rushed up behind them with its bright lights on.

"What the hell?" Ben exclaimed as he grabbed for the door handle.

"Hold on a second, don't go," Nikki said while holding Ben to keep him from getting out.

"Why not?"

"Because I know who that is."

"Who is it?"

"It's my baby's daddy, Eric."

"I suggest that you tell Eric to get those bright lights out of my face before I get out of this car and bust his ass."

"Calm down, Ben, don't curse at me. I'm on your side."

"You're right, baby. I'm sorry. Go take care of your business. I'll be right here if you need me."

Once Nikki stepped out of the car, Eric turned off his lights. Through the rear view mirror, Ben counted two other men in the late-model Buick. Both were drinking beer and smokin' weed. Smoke was gushing out of the side windows like a chimney. Ben reached in his glove compartment for his 9 millimeter pistol, just in case, and placed it between his legs. Eric and Nikki stood by the car talking for few minutes and then went inside the house. When they came out five minutes later, Eric was talking loud and trying to grab Nikki as she walked toward the Lexus. Ben stuffed the gun into his coat pocket and slowly got out of the car.

"Hey, my man," Ben said calmly, "chill out for a second!"

"Who in the hell are you?" Eric shouted. "You better mind your own damned business."

His boys put a cap on their beer and jumped out the Buick.

"Look, young brother. I don't want any trouble. Just let her go and we can work this thing out like civilized black folks."

"First of all, I ain't your brother. Second of all, I ain't got shit to talk to you about. So, why don't you get in your fancy little car and take your proper-talkin' black ass back to the white suburbs where you came from."

Ben's face turned to stone and his eyes widened. He wasn't used to being disrespected. Coming up on the low end of town, he was one of the most intimidating men on the South Side, even the hard-core gang bangers didn't want to tangle with him. But now he was standing out in the snow in his brand new Ferragamo shoes being dissed by some 25-year-old punk who didn't weigh more than a buck-0-5. He tried to compose, but his instincts took over. Ben lunged forward, grabbing Eric by the neck and then tossing him to the ground like a wet paper bag.

"Let me show you where I'm from, you little punk."

One of his boys ran toward Ben gesturing like he was reaching under his jacket for a pistol.

"Freeze motherfucker!" Ben shouted as he pulled his gun out of his coat pocket."

"Don't shoot! Please don't shoot!"

"Calm down brother," Eric said, sounding like a sissy. "I just came by to pick up my kid."

"Don't make the mistake of thinking that because you have a child with a woman that you own her."

"Ok, brother, whatever you say. Just put the gun away."

"Stop callin' me brother," Ben said, stepping away. "You said we weren't related, remember? Now get up and get out of my sight."

"Let's go, Eric," one of his boys said. "I told you not to come over here starting shit on New Year's Eve. You're blowing my high."

Ben kept his gun drawn until all three of them were inside the car. "And just in case you're thinking about revenge," he said, slipping him a business card, "I advise you to ask around about me. You'll find out that we know a lot of the same people." Ben was very popular with many of the gang bangers on the South Side. A former member himself, he employed many ex-cons at his stores and regularly donated flower arrangements for the funerals of gang members who seemed to be getting younger and younger.

While all of this excitement was going on, Nikki stood silently in the frigid December air staring at Ben like he was a knight in shining armor, come to defend her honor. Ben walked over casually, like it was all no big deal, and put his arms around her.

"Are you all right?"

"I'm fine," she said, staring up at him. "Do you do this kind of thing often?"

"Only on New Year's Eve."

Christie was shaking like a leaf by the time she and Mark arrived at Derrick's apartment building. This was her first time meeting his friends, her coming out party. Mark could see the tension on her face and paused to comfort her after pushing the button for the elevator.

"Are you going to be all right?"

"I'll be fine," Christie said after taking a deep breath.

"I don't know why I'm so nervous. It's not like I'm meeting your parents."

"You're right, it's much worse." Mark laughed.

"Thanks, I needed that."

While they waited for the elevator, they set the bag of records on the floor and checked to make sure Mark hadn't forgotten the Teena Marie and Rick James albums. A moment later two black women and an older white couple walked up and stood silent, watching their every move. When the elevator arrived everyone piled in and pushed the buttons for their respective floors. The black women pushed 15, the white couple 22, and Mark pressed the button for the 25th floor. Immediately after the doors closed, the staring and disapproving facial expressions began. Mark paid little attention to the attitudes of his fellow passengers, hugging Christie tight and kissing her on the cheek. But Christie was unable to relax with all the tension in the air and gently pushed Mark away.

"Mark," she said in a tone that made it clear that she was uncomfortable.

"What's the matter, baby?" Mark asked in a soft whisper. "It's New Year's Eve, we should be having fun."

"I know, but."

"But what?" he asked defiantly, while making eye contact with the white couple, and then the two black women. "I don't give a damn about what these people think."

Right on cue the elevator stopped on the 15th floor and the door slowly opened. The taller black woman walked off, giving Mark the finger. The other woman, who had a weave that was way too long, decided that wasn't enough and got into a nasty verbal exchange with Christie.

"You ain't nuthin' but white trash," the black woman said while holding open the door with her foot. "If it wasn't for the fact that I just got my nails done I'd wipe the floor with your pale ass."

"Who are you callin' white trash, you black bitch?" Christie retaliated.

Mark lunged forward, forcing the woman to back up and move her foot out of the way. But before the door could completely shut, she was able to get close enough to spit in his face.

"That's for sellin' out, **brother**!" she said angrily.

While the elevator made its way up to the next stop, Christie reached inside her purse and pulled out a handkerchief and wiped the saliva off Mark's cheek. The old white couple, who were still on the elevator, were pressed as far back against the wall as they could get, both looking scared out of their minds. When the door opened onto the 22nd floor, the white couple paused, as if expecting to be attacked, and then ran off down the hallway. Mark and Christie just looked at one another for a second and then started laughing; not in a cheerful way, but in a way that relieves tension.

By the time they arrived at Derrick's apartment, both had managed to gain their composure and look normal. "There's no point in spoiling the holiday mood for everyone," they agreed. Mark double-checked himself in Christie's compact mirror, took a deep breath, and rang the doorbell.

"Something smells good," he said

The distinct smell of fried chicken and macaroni and

cheese penetrated the thick oak door, and the familiar thumping bass to the song, "Flashlight," was causing the walls to vibrate.

"I know those fools can't hear the bell with that music blasting," Mark said as he knocked hard on the door and rang the bell again.

"I'm coming, hold your horses," a woman's voice shouted. "Who is it?"

"It's me, Mark."

When the door swung open, Tracie jumped right into Mark's arms like a big kid, almost knocking him down.

"Happy New Year's, little brother."

"If I didn't know any better I'd think you missed me."

"You know I miss you, Marky,"

"I hate when you call me that." Mark laughed as he lifted her up with one arm and carried her into the apartment.

"Hi, you must be Christie," Tracie said while reaching over Mark's shoulder to shake her hand. "I'm Tracie, pleased to meet you."

"Pleased to meet you too," Christie replied with a wide grin on her face.

Derrick and Tony were in the kitchen frying chicken and mixing drinks when Mark walked in, still carrying Tracie over his shoulder.

"What's up fellahs?" Mark shouted as he gave Derrick a high five with his free hand.

"Would you mind putting my woman down?" Tony said laughing. "Go pick up your own woman; that one belongs to me."

"Oh, I love it when two handsome men fight over me."

Mark dropped Tracie abruptly, and all three men begin to hug. It had been a whole week since either had seen the other and more than two weeks since they had all been together at once.

"So much for chivalry," Tracie said while comically fixing her hair and brushing herself off.

"By the way, where is this woman I've been hearing so much about?" asked Tony.

"She was right behind us," Mark replied, looking around. "Christie, where are you?"

At the very moment Christie came around the corner, the record ended and the needle on the Pioneer stereo returned to drop the next LP. For a brief moment the apartment was absolutely silent as all eyes fell on Christie.

"Christie, these are two of my best friends in the whole wide world, Mr. Derrick Reed and Mr. Tony Page."

"Hi, guys. It's a pleasure to finally meet you," Christie said while reaching out and shaking both their hands. "Mark has told me so much about you."

Both stood there speechless, completely caught off guard by how attractive she was. Mark had a history of dating white women who were marginal at best.

"Well, he didn't tell us enough about you!" Tony said as he and Derrick slapped five.

"You have to excuse them, Christie, they're stupid," Tracie said, grabbing her by the hand and escorting her to the living room to take her coat.

"You hit the jackpot with this one," Tony said, loud enough for Tracie to hear. "Hell, I might even go out and get a white woman myself."

"I heard that!" Tracie shouted.

"Just kidding honey."

Moments later the doorbell rang again. This time it was Ben and Nikki. After making formal introductions, everyone settled into the living room for drinks and conversation. It was 10:30 and everyone was there, everyone except the guest of honor, Angela. Tony and especially Tracie were anxious to meet the woman who had Mr. American Gigolo himself talking commitment.

"So Derrick, where is this mystery woman of yours?" Tony asked.

"Yeah, Derrick, where is Sugar Ray Angela?" Mark

joked, referring to the fight Derrick told him about at Bennigan's.

"Why do you call her Sugar Ray?" Christie asked.

"It's a long story. I'll let Derrick tell you about it one of these days."

"She had some volunteer work to do over at the mission on State Street," Derrick replied. "She called a little while ago and said she would try her best to be here before eleven."

"We're not going to wait until she gets here before we eat, are we?" Ben asked, looking toward the platter of chicken steaming on the dining room table. "I'm starvin' like Marvin."

"Gone and take your big ass in the kitchen and make yourself a plate," Derrick said laughing. "And while you're at it, make a pitcher of Kool-Aid, the sugar is in the pantry."

"If Ben's going to eat, so am I," Tony said, rushing to get a plate.

There was a domino effect once Tony decided to eat. One by one, everybody went into the kitchen to fix their plate. Even Nikki, who was the smallest out of the bunch, nudged people out of the way to get the last wing. Derrick was noticeably let down by the fact that Angela had not made it. He had arranged everything so that his old friends and his new woman would sit down at the dinner table and eat together.

"Oh well, what the hell, dig in," he announced as he reached for a plate himself. "No sense in starving to death."

But before he could get situated at the table, the phone rang. It was Angela.

"Hi baby, sorry I'm late."

"Angela, where are you?"

"I'm right outside your front door," she said in a seductive tone. "Are you going to let me in or what?"

"Hold up, everybody!" Derrick instructed. "Don't start eating yet."

"Why, what's up?" Ben asked after sneaking in a fork full

of macaroni and cheese.

"Angela's here."

"How do you know? I didn't hear any doorbell."

"She's right outside the door; that was her calling me on her cell phone."

Derrick played it cool, walking calmly to the door, but deep down inside he was nervous. His palms were sweaty and his heart was racing. He hadn't seen Angela in over two weeks because of business deadlines and other commitments. This reunion was anxiously anticipated. He looked through the peephole to confirm that she was there, then turned to check himself in the hallway mirror. Once satisfied that he was *together,* he adjusted his posture and opened the door.

"Well, hello stranger," Angela said, looking very happy to see him. "Happy New Year's."

"Happy New Year's to you too. Come on in."

She was as fine as he remembered, maybe even finer. He played the gentlemanly host and offered to take her coat, knowing damn well he really wanted to give her a big hug and kiss. Not being a man who is used to forcing the issue, he played it cool and watched impatiently as Angela unwrapped herself like a piece of caramel candy from her full-length leather coat. He knew he was in for an eyeful and Angela did not disappoint. The snugly fitted mini dress she had on was made of authentic kente cloth. It had a short split on the side and the back was out. Her accessories were perfect, from her multi-colored earrings, down to her matching three-inch kente-cloth pumps. She was sharp.

"You look absolutely beautiful," Derrick said. "I hope you wore that outfit for me."

"You know I did."

"Let me introduce you to everybody. They're all in the dining room getting ready to eat."

"I'm ready when you are," Angela said confidently. "But first, don't I get a New Year's Eve hug, or something?"

"I thought you'd never ask."

This was the moment they had been waiting on for ten days. Another chance to press up against one another and hold on tight. Their long conversations on the telephone had them quite comfortable and familiar with one another. Sometimes they would talk on the phone for hours, joking about their experiences growing up and how, as children, they never realized how poor they were. They also talked about personal things. Derrick was open about his womanizing past, admitting he was a dog amongst dogs. "But that was back in the day," as he put it.

This wasn't a news flash to Angela. She knew what she was getting into with Derrick. Not that she didn't trust him, but like any other man he was **booty motivated.** Angela revealed a very private side of herself too. For the first time she discussed the death of her brother and mother with someone other than family and her best friend, Denise. On one occasion she broke down in tears, releasing a waterfall of pent up emotions and unresolved pain. Derrick stood fast, like a man should, encouraging her to vent and afterwards making her laugh to feel better. It was as if they had known one another forever.

"I can't believe how much I've missed you," Angela confessed as she laid her head against his chest.

"I missed you too."

"I miss both of you!" Ben interrupted. "Now get your behinds in here so we can eat."

"The natives are getting restless," Derrick said. "Let me hurry up and introduce you to everyone before a riot breaks out."

"I'm right behind you, baby," Angela replied, holding him by the hand. "Lead the way."

Introductions were short and sweet. Formalities aren't very important when black folks are hungry. The Kool-Aid was turning warm and the chicken was getting cold. Angela quickly made herself a plate and sat down next to Derrick at the table.

"Let's all join hands," Derrick instructed as everyone bowed their heads in prayer.

"Lord, we want to thank you for allowing us to be here in good health to celebrate a new year. We also want to thank you for blessing us with successful businesses and also for blessing us with families who love and support us and who keep us from getting too materialistic and big-headed, especially my egotistical friends."

Tony, Ben, and Mark briefly looked up and give Derrick a look as if to say, "Look who's talking."

"As I was saying, Lord, we're all very thankful for being here together and ask that you bless this food we're about to receive. Amen."

"Wait a minute!" Tony interrupted. "I'd like to add something."

"Now what?" Ben asked, looking frustrated. "Are we going to eat, or what?"

"Go ahead, man," Derrick said. "Forget him."

"Well, I just want to give thanks for my beautiful fiancee Tracie, who has stood by me through thick and thin for the last four years. And I think all of the men here should be very thankful to have such beautiful and intelligent woman by their side to bring in this New Year."

"Amen, to that!" all the ladies echoed as they stood from the table and toasted with their glasses of Kool-Aid."

"Now can we eat?" Ben asked.

"Go ahead, you big baby," Derrick said. "But remember, first one to finish eating has to wash dishes."

"Since when did we start that tradition?"

"Since today."

It was a little past eleven by the time everyone finished eating. Ben and Derrick started cleaning up the kitchen, Angela went downstairs with Mark to get the rest of the liquor out of his car, and Tony took the other ladies into the living room and began giving lessons on how to step.

"Mark has been trying to teach me how to do this dance for months," Christie said. "But I told him white people don't have enough rhythm to move that quick and smoothly."

"Aw, that's just nonsense," Tracie said. "I was watching the country network on cable the other night and those white people were jammin'. As a matter of fact I learned a couple of new moves."

"Why don't you and Tony dance off a record and I'll watch. Maybe I can get a better idea about how I should be moving my feet."

"That's not a bad idea," Tony agreed. "Hey, Ben, do me a favor and find a good song to step off of. I know you brought those James Brown CDs."

"I knew I forgot something," Ben said in disgust, slapping himself on the forehead with his soapy hand. "Man, I rushed out the house and left those on my kitchen counter."

"Don't worry," Christie said. "I have something that would be perfect,"

By this time Mark and Angela had made it back and were unpacking the bags. Meanwhile Christie was digging deep into a sack of albums and CDs trying to find a song for Tony. Everybody stood silently with a puzzled look on their face, wondering what in the world is this blonde-headed, blue-eyed white girl from the suburbs going to pull out of this bag. Tony didn't hesitate to make light of the situation.

"Look, Christie, don't take this personal, but we can't step off of The Smashing Pumpkins or Hootie And The Blowfish."

Tracie and Nikki turned away totally embarrassed, while Derrick and Ben covered their mouths to keep from bursting out in laughter, but the last laugh was going to be on them. Christie wasn't your typical white girl. Although she may have been raised in a conservative household, she rejected that lifestyle and did her own thing. While her parents were listening to Frank Sinatra and Lawrence Welk records, Christie would be in her bedroom with headphones on, groovin' to songs by Prince and The O'Jays. "For the love of money," was one of her favorites.

"Tony, I think you're going to be in for a bit of a surprise." Mark said laughing.

"Ok, let's see what you got."

"How about this one?" Christie asked as she pulled out the first album. "The original 1975 version of "Summer Madness" by Kool and the Gang. Can you step to that?"

Tony was speechless. Derrick and Ben slapped five and walked over to see what other goodies she had.

"How about "School Boy Crush" by The Average White Band, or maybe the cut by Randy Crawford, "Give me the night."

"Please stop!" Tony yelled "I think you've made your point."

"I thought so," Christie replied as she turned to slap five with the ladies.

"That'll teach you men never to underestimate a woman," Angela co-signed, "Even a white one from the suburbs."

Derrick looked over at the digital clock on the microwave, it read 11:55.

"Hey, everybody, it's almost that time."

He rushed over to the television and turned on Channel 7 to see the Chicago countdown. Tony, Mark, and Ben hurried to pour everyone a drink so that they could toast in the new year. As the one-minute countdown began, everybody gathered around the television set.

"Ben, can you reach over and turn off that lamp, please?" Derrick asked. "Everybody stay clear of the window. You never know when these fools around here will start shooting."

"But we're all the way up on the 25th floor," Christie said naively.

"Bullets can travel up 25 stories, believe me."

Now the countdown was at 10 and everybody joined in. 9-8-7-6-5-4-3-2-1.

"Happy New Year!" they yelled together and then toasted.

As always they tried to sing along with that New Year's song that nobody knows the words to.

"May old acquaintance be forgot, and la, la, la, la, hum."

No matter what the words, they were having a ball. Angela pulled Derrick into the kitchen and put her arms around him.

"This is the best New Year's Eve I've ever had," she whispered as she looked deep into his eyes. "Thanks for inviting me."

"If I have things my way we'll be together on every New Year's Eve to come."

"Is that a promise?"

"Cross my heart and hope to die," Derrick said as he slowly moved toward her lips, waiting for an invitation.

Angela met him halfway, leaning her head slightly to the side for a perfect angle, and for the second time they kissed. Taking the cue from the host, Tony pulled Tracie into his arms and they kissed too, then Mark and Christie got into the act.

"Well, what are **you** waiting for, you big teddy bear?" Nikki said. "Come over here and sweep me off my feet."

Lips were smackin' and spit was flying everywhere. The mood went from festive to sexual.

"Okay, that's enough of that, for now," Derrick said, interrupting the orgy. "Let's all take a chill pill and try to get through the rest of this evening without exchanging any more bodily fluids."

"What do you suggest we do to take our minds off of, you know what?" Tony asked while Tracie was still nibbling on his ear. "I'm ready to take my woman home right now and body slam her!"

"Wait right here, I've got a surprise," Derrick said as he walked toward the hallway closet.

When he came back into the living room, his arms were filled with board games. He set them down on the dining room table and took a vote on which one they should play.

"Ok, this is what we're going to do, raise your hand when

I call out a game you want to play. Let's start with Monopoly."

"That takes too damn long to play," Tony said. "What else you got?"

"How about Taboo?"

"Hey, that sounds like fun, let's play!" Nikki said.

"Aw, no you don't," Tracie said, shaking her finger at Derrick. "Tony already told me about how you and Ben used to cheat at this game."

"Are you serious?" Nikki said, looking at Ben with her hand on her hip.

"Yeah, girl, they use to make bets with their little hoochie girlfriends, and whoever lost a game had to take their clothes off. You know, kind of like strip poker."

"You talk too damn much, Tony," Ben said.

"My fault fellahs, I must have been drunk," Tony said, defending himself.

"Yeah, right."

"Look, why don't we just play a game of cards instead," Derrick suggested. "Everybody knows how to play spades, right?"

"Spades?" Tony, Tracie, and Angela asked at the same time.

"That's a kid's game," Tracie said. "Whoever is lucky enough to get the most spades wins. Let's play bid whist. At least that involves a little skill."

"I don't think playing cards is such a good idea," Ben said.

"Why not?" Tracie asked.

"Because every time we play cards, there's always a fight, especially between couples. If you play against one another, then somebody gets mad if the other is kickin' their ass. If you play together, then somebody gets upset when the other makes a mistake. It's a no win situation. Tracie, you and Tony should know that better than anybody. Every time you guys play, Tony ends up sleeping on the sofa."

"Moving right along," Tracie said, being in total agreement. "What else you got?"

"Here's one from way back in the day, Twister!"

"Twister?" Angela said jumping up all excited. "I haven't played that game since I was in the fifth grade. Let's play!"

While Derrick and Angela cleared away space to lay down the mat, Christie, Mark, Tony, and Tracie took off their shoes, anxious to play the first game. Once everybody was ready, Ben popped the spinner with his big finger and the game was on!

"Left foot, red!" he shouted.

"Something tells me this is a bad idea," Tony said, looking over at Tracie.

"Don't worry, baby. I've got your back," Tracie replied. "Just don't step on my foot with those size thirteens."

"Right hand, blue!" Ben shouted

"What is the object of the stupid game, anyway?" Tony asked.

"To keep from fallin' on your ass," Ben replied. "Now stop talking and pay attention. Right foot, yellow!"

In only three moves they were tangled like a ball of rubber bands. Mark had his head in Tracie's chest, and Christie's butt was in Tony's face.

"Man, this game could have you in divorce court," Ben said.

"Just hurry up and call out the next move," Tony replied.

"All right grumpy. Left hand, green!"

What had started out as a harmless child's game began to resemble an advanced yoga class. Christie and Tracie were grunting and straining to put their left hands on the big green dot. But old age and lack of balance did them all in. The pile came crashing down with Tony on the bottom.

"I'm getting too old for this shit!" he moaned.

"Are you all right, sweetheart?" Tracie ask looking concerned.

"I'm fine, baby, just get your elbow out my back."

"Ok, rookies. Let a pro show you how it's done," Derrick boasted, as he took off his shoes.

Angela, Ben, and Nikki took their shoes off too, and stood

ready as Tony made the first spin of the wheel.

"Left foot, red!"

"This is a piece of cake," Ben said.

"Left hand, yellow!"

"Angela, are you fully insured?" Derrick asked.

"Yes, I am. But what made you ask that?"

"Because if Big Ben falls on top of you, you're going to need an ambulance."

"And you're going to need a parachute when I throw your ass out this 25-story window." Ben laughed. "Now keep talking."

Tony spun the wheel again and Nikki fell flat on her stomach. She moved over to the side, and the game continued for another turn. Then it happened. Ben let out a loud and nasty-sounding fart.

"What in the hell was that?" Mark asked.

"That was buffalo Ben releasing one of his terminators," Tony said, laughing with all the others.

"You see, that's why I didn't cook baked beans this year," Derrick said while waving his hands to try to clear the air. "Somebody open a window, quick!"

After the games were put away and the apartment was thoroughly ventilated, the women gathered in the kitchen to get better acquainted while the men huddled in the living room with a bottle of champagne for their traditional Men's Only, New Year's Eve toast. A ceremony that began over 20 years ago when they were bright-eyed, runny-nosed, nappy-headed little boys full of hopes and dreams for the future. Back then they use to sneak a bottle of Richard's Wild Irish Rose and a six-pack of Old English 800 malt liquor into Derrick's basement to bring in the New Year. Now they were successful businessmen sipping on Dom Perignon, looking down from the 25th story of a luxury apartment, with a spectacular view of downtown Chicago. Life had been good to them, and they acknowledged it as they joined hands and bowed their heads to give thanks. It was Tony's year to do the honors.

"Lord we thank you for bringing us together in good health and prosperity for another year. Please continue to guide our lives and help us to become better businessmen and better human beings. And last but not least, thank you once again for rescuing all of us from that burnt-out roach-invested hell hole called the ghetto. We have truly been blessed."

"Amen to that," they all said.

"Now that we have that out the way," Mark said, "let's move on to our annual New Year's resolutions, starting with you, Tony."

"I'm resolved to doing 50 situps every night, drinking less coffee, and most importantly, I'm resolved to doing my best not to lose my temper and kill Valarie this year."

"That's not a resolution," Mark said. "You're asking for a damn miracle."

"Very funny, Eddie Murphy. Let's get back to resolutions. You're next, Ben."

"I'm resolved to losing ten pounds and to stop eating pork."

"Get the fuck outta here," Derrick said. "You know damn well you can't stop eating that swine. If I put a plate of greasy bacon in front of your big ass right now, you'd eat it."

"One of my clients is a Muslim. And he says that since he stopped eating pork he lost ten pounds and his face cleared up."

"Are you trying to tell me there are no fat Muslims with bad skin?"

"No, that not's what I meant."

"I didn't think so," Derrick said. "I'm not giving up my pork chops and pork ribs for anybody."

"Would you please get off of Ben's case so we can get this over with?" Tony said. "Go ahead, Mark, it's your turn."

"I only have one resolution and that is to stop allowing people to upset me about dating a white woman. All my life I've had to deal with dirty looks, verbal abuse, and sometimes, physical violence. And it really used to bother me. But I think it's time that I accept that this society will never be completely color blind and move on with my life. That's all I have to say."

They sat there speechless, looking at each other and wondering what to say behind that bombshell. Mark routinely experienced problems when going out in public with his white girlfriends. Once he got hit upside the head with a bottle while walking downtown on Rush Street. But what did he expect living in **the** most segregated metropolitan city in the nation. Although Chicago had areas such as Oak Park and Hyde Park where blacks and whites lived together, they still kept to themselves and did their own thing.

Derrick knew that Mark's comments were directed in part at him. He was the only one who spoke out against interracial dating. Ben supported him no matter who he dated. And Tony didn't give a damn one way or the other. He had Tracie. Derrick was the odd man out. This was his chance to resolve some of his own issues and reaffirm his friendship with Mark. He took a long sip of champagne, and then cleared his throat.

"I guess it's my turn," he said, looking right into Mark's eyes. "I'm resolved to stop allowing my social and racial beliefs to get in the way of my friendships. And although I know this doesn't have a damned thing to do with resolutions, I want to apologize to you, Mark, for not being there for you. We have been friends for over 25 years, and my main concern should have been your happiness. And it's obvious that Christie makes you happy. I hope you will forgive me for being so selfish and narrow-minded. My attitude has affected our relationship and I want us to get back to where we were."

Mark was shocked, and so were Tony and Ben. That was the first time they ever heard Derrick apologize for anything, least of all his attitude toward interracial dating. It was a turning point in his life and in their friendship. Derrick walked over to Mark and shook his hand, and then they hugged; not in a masculine fashion, but in an emotional way that said, you're my brother and I love you.

THE WAITING GAME

The clock on my nightstand read 7:00 a.m. when I felt Angela get out of bed. She went into the bathroom for a few minutes, then came tiptoeing out and slipped into her matching royal blue Victoria's Secret underwear. I lay there motionless with one eye squinted open, pretending to be asleep while enjoying the magnificent view of her perfectly shaped body. Damn she looked good. After putting on the rest of her clothes, she gave me a kiss on the forehead and strutted off down the hallway. When I heard the door close I rolled onto the floor, got on my knees, and thanked God she was gone.

For two and a half hours Angela used my body as a sexual punching bag, stopping only once to get a glass of water and use the bathroom. I have never experienced a woman with so much energy and stamina. She matched me stroke for stroke and round for round. I lost count of how many condoms I went through. But as good as it was, I was happy to see her go. My testicles and back were aching so bad I had to get up and soak in the tub for an hour and rub myself down with BenGay ointment before I could go back to sleep.

When I woke up, it was a little past one o'clock, the latest I had slept in years. I got out of bed slowly, expecting to still have pain in my lower back, but surprisingly it felt fine. My testicles on the other hand needed to be admitted to intensive care. Angela had completely drained me! I mean every drop. "This is a goddamned shame!" I thought to myself while gingerly walking to the bathroom. "I should call the police and have her arrested for sexual abuse." Right away I went into recovery mode, preparing a high-protein breakfast and popping multivitamins like a junkie. I even drank a bottle of that Chinese Ginseng powder. It had been sitting in my cabinet for years, but in my condition I was willing to try anything. After resting up a while, I forced down another bowl of whole grain cereal with a sliced banana this time, determined to generate enough energy to get in a light workout. And just as I was about to limp out the door, the telephone rang. I knew it could only be nosy Tony calling to find out if I got some.

"So tell me, did you hit it last night?" Tony asked, without even saying hello.

"I hit it all right? But this time <u>it</u> hit back."

"She rode the wave, huh?"

"It was more like she mastered the wave," I said. "Angela thoroughly convinced me that women reach their sexual peak after 35."

"It was that good, huh?"

"It was the bomb! I must have come at least three times."

"Three times? You must think you're 21 years old. At your age, you've got to ration out those orgasms."

"I tried, Tony. I swear did," I said, sounding whipped. "But Angela was jumping up and down on me like a possessed woman. She stroked me so hard, I hit my head on the headboard."

"Isn't that supposed to be the other way around?" Tony said, laughing.

Although I was laughing too, I felt sexually defeated. Angela had gotten the best of me and my manly ego couldn't handle it. I was accustomed to being the one putting the hurt on, not the other way around. The biggest mistake I made was letting her get on top. Women can make you come easily in that position, especially if you allow yourself to get carried away, which was exactly what happened. Angela's body felt so firm and soft that I broke the most important rule of the lovemaking game, "Ladies first," which simply means, always make sure the woman comes before you do. Most men are too selfish to understand that. Climaxing is never my number-one goal. I see it more as compensation for a job well done. But I didn't practice what I preached and Angela got the best of me. And I knew Tony was never going to let me hear the end of it.

"So you finally met your match?" Tony laughed. "I guess there's a new sheriff in town."

"Do me a favor, Tony."

"What's that?"

"Shut the fuck up and put Trace on the phone."

"Don't get mad at me because your dick is all beat up."

"Ha ha, very funny."

"Tracie, telephone!" Tony yelled. "It's Mr. Limp Dick."

As annoying as he was, I had to laugh myself. After all, it wasn't the end of the world. And besides, I would have cracked on him too if the shoe was on the other foot. It happens to the best of us, I thought to myself. When Tracie finally picked up the phone, I was anxious to change the subject and get the scoop on what she thought about Angela. Her opinion, above anyone else's, meant a lot to me.

"So, Tracie, what did you think about Angela? Is she cool or what?"

"You want me to be honest with you?" she said, sounding as if she had something negative to say.

"No, lie to me," I said sarcastically. "Of course I want you to be honest with me. Tell me what you think."

"I think she is without a doubt **the** most interesting, funny, and down-to-earth sistah you've ever introduced me to."

"Didn't I tell you she was all that?"

"Yes you did. Now I know why you're so excited about this lady. She's really got her stuff together."

"You sound like a fan, Tracie."

"Let's not get carried away. I just believe in giving credit when it's due. Even Christie is pretty sharp. Being a partner at a law firm is very impressive."

"What about Ben's girlfriend Nikki? I know he called for your report card on her."

"You know he did, first thing this morning. And I told him that I thought she was cute and very nice, but."

"But what?"

"But, I didn't think she was the type of woman he needed at this point in his life and in his career."

"Oh brother! I know he didn't want to hear that."

"Well, he asked me what I thought and I told him. I mean really, Derrick, what is he going to do with a 23-year-old woman, with no education, a young child, and a crazy-ass father in the picture? He told me about what happened when he went to pick her up. He doesn't need to be involved in that kind of unstable situation."

"Come on Tracie, you know Ben's not the type to judge a woman by how much money or formal education she has. If he's happy with her, why not just support him? Besides, she is going to school trying to better herself."

"Ok, let me ask you this. If the situation was reversed, do you think she would be dating Ben?"

"What do you mean exactly?"

"What I'm asking you is, do you think Nikki would be interested in Ben if she was an educated and successful 35-year-old businesswoman and he was a broke, uneducated, father of a child whose mother was a hoodlum?"

Derrick paused and the phone went silent.

"Hell no!" Tracie said before Derrick could respond. "And that's exactly the point I'm trying to make. Successful men, and men in general, are clueless when it comes to deciding who to get involved with. All they care about is how large a woman's ass and breasts are and how freaky she is in the bedroom. What they should be concerned about is her family upbringing and how stable she is emotionally and financially. And besides, Nikki is a Scorpio and Ben's a Libra. They're not even compatible."

"There you go with that zodiac matchmaking, again. Next thing you know you'll be taking over Omar's astrology column in the *Chicago Sun Times*."

"Mark my words, Derrick," Tracie warned. "Ben is setting himself up for a year of serious drama with that young lady. Scorpio women are evil, stubborn, and hot to trot, especially the young ones."

"Ben is a grown man, Trace. If she's not right for him, he'll figure it out for himself. Now that's enough about his problems. Let's get back to Angela for a second."

"What's left to say. I told you I think she's great!"

"Did she mention anything to you about marriage or settling down?"

"No, why do you ask?"

"Because she stayed with me last night and I don't want her to start trippin' after what happened."

"What happened?" Tracie asked.

"You know, I hit it."

"Hit it?"

"You know we knocked boots, bumped flesh, did the wild thang."

"And?"

"And, women sometimes have a tendency to start trippin' after sex."

"Oh, really?" Tracie said with an attitude. "And what kind of trippin' do you expect Angela to do?"

"Ok, for example, she might become possessive and start calling me at all hours of the night, interrogating me about where I've been."

"I don't think you'll have to worry about that with Angela. She seems pretty well balanced."

"They all **seem** pretty well balanced in the beginning, but then they start showing up at your apartment at one o'clock in the morning claiming they just happened to be in the neighborhood. I've seen it happen a thousand times."

"Look, you egomaniac, Angela isn't one those naive young girls from the suburbs who falls in love after a few orgasms. If she had sex with you, it's because she liked you. Or maybe she just needed a little maintenance. Women use men too, you know? So, if I were you I wouldn't worry about her going through any changes. Angela is a mature woman who knows the rules of the game. In fact, she knows the game so well that I think you'll end up trippin' long before she does."

It had been three days since I heard from Angela and I was starting to get upset. Not because she didn't call but because she didn't call after we had sex. I'm not used to that. Women always called me back after I gave them some of this good lovin'. Angela is just playing hard to get, I thought. Well two can play at that game. With my ego thoroughly shattered, I did what most men do in this situation. I pulled out my little black book and made a few calls to prove I was still **The Man**. It was a bit dusty, but all the pages were still intact. I started with the A's and worked my way forward. My first call was to Adrienne, a tall, exotic-looking sistah who I had a one-night stand with about three months ago.

"Hello?" a woman's voice said.

"Hello, how are you doing? Is Adrienne in?"

"Who's calling?"

"This is Derrick."

"Hold on. Adrienne, it's for you!" she yelled.

"Who is it?" a distant voice asked.

"Some guy named Darrin, Derrick, or something!"

"Hi baby!" Adrienne said sounding excited. "I was expecting to hear from you sooner. Where have you been?"

"I've been busy, you know, taking care of business."

"So what's up for tonight?" she asked. "Do you have a party or something lined up for me, or what?"

"Huh?" I asked, not knowing what she was taking about.

"You know, like the one I did last month. But this time I want $200 if I have to strip naked and at least $100 for blow jobs."

"What did you say?"

"Hold up, is this Darrin Green?"

"Uh, I think I've got the wrong number baby," I said, and quickly hung up.

I should have known she was a pro by the way she freaked me. Thank God I used a rubber. Luckily I blocked the call so she couldn't redial my number using *69. After remembering that I had been tested for AIDS a month ago I relaxed, made myself a stiff drink, and went straight to the B's. Belinda was next. A 31-year-old accountant who lived in the building down the street. We met back in early November while jogging on the lakefront. She told me she was recently divorced from her psychopathic husband who used to follow her out to clubs and slash her car tires. According to her he had been out of the picture for over a year. I dialed her number, hoping she would be as enthusiastic as she was back then.

"Hello, may I speak to Belinda?"

"This is Belinda, who is this?"

"This is Derrick Reed, remember me?"

"Who in the fuck is that callin' here this time of night?" an angry man's voice shouted from the background.

"It's nobody baby, go back to sleep," she said, sounding frightened. "Sorry you have the wrong number." She hung up.

I couldn't believe she got back with that crazy bastard. Or maybe it was another lunatic. Some women are attracted to men who abuse them. I guess they think love has to hurt. Before throwing in the towel, I decided to give it one last shot. This time I started near the back of the book in the P section. The first name I saw was Patricia. In my mind this was a sure thing. She was always flirting with me when I came into the library, asking me if I needed any special help. At the time I was too busy traveling to follow up. Maybe the time is right. I thought. When I dialed her number, I had a good feeling that we would hit it off.

"Hello?" a soft and sweet voice said.

"May I speak to Patricia?"

"This is Patricia."

"Hello Patricia, this is Derrick Reed. How are you doing?"

"Praise God, how are you doing Derrick? The Lord truly works in mysterious ways. I was just praying about you yesterday."

"Oh really," I said, a little uncomfortable with all the religious language.

"Yes indeed," she replied. "I saw a copy of your magazine at the African American bookstore in Hyde Park the other day. It reminded me of you. How is business?"

"Business is great. How are things at the library?"

"Oh, I quit that job over a month ago so that I could concentrate on getting my master's degree. I'm just going to class every day and trying to live right. You know what I mean?"

I hesitated to answer, afraid that I might be setting myself up for a long church sermon.

"Yeah, sure."

"It's not easy trying to do the right thing when you live in a world filled with so many nonbelievers and devils."

"Excuse me?"

"What I'm trying to say is, the devil is always working on people's minds trying to make them do bad things like commit adultery and fornication."

I did my best to back out of that conversation as quickly as possible, telling her my beliefs were somewhat different than hers but she had a lot of valid points. I even let her slide on the issue of why Jesus Christ is always portrayed as blond-haired and blue-eyed, and trust me, that was a first. But she kept on preaching for another half hour trying to convince me to go to church with her on Sunday and get saved. So, I lied and told her I would be there just to get off the phone. After that little chat I made myself another drink, went into the living room, and watched the last quarter of the basketball game on TBS. There's was no sense of fighting it, God was definitely trying to tell me something.

Early Sunday afternoon I got a head start on cleaning up my apartment and packing my clothes for the East Coast trip. I was determined not to wait to the last minute and forget something important as I always seemed to do. Like the time I went to New Orleans in April and left my new business cards. It was embarrassing as hell writing down my number on scratch paper and apologizing for not being better prepared. Sometimes business decisions are based on details even more trivial than that. I should know since I have discarded hundreds of business cards simply because the number on the card was scratched out and penciled in. That may sound minor to some people, but my attitude is this: If you can't invest a few dollars in a halfway decent card, you shouldn't be doing business. But what really burns me up is when somebody gives me a professional-looking card with only a pager number on it. I hate that! You better believe those suckers go right in the garbage.

All bases had to be covered on this trip, especially the New

York stop. My meeting with Mr. Starks was an important step in moving forward with *Happily Single* magazine. In fact, it was critical. A contract with an established corporation such as Starks Enterprise would signal to corporations and investors across the country that we were serious players in the magazine market. Right up there with *Ebony*, *Jet*, *Emerge*, and *Essence*. But the window of opportunity was closing fast. There were a number of copycats coming on the scene trying to take advantage of our ideas. If we didn't move fast, the magazine would lose pace and be reduced to nothing more than a quality local publication. This trip was all or nothing as far as I was concerned, and I wasn't about to come up short. At least not because of being unprepared.

By 6:00 p.m. I was finished packing and the apartment was spotless. Even my presentation was revised and ready to go. Now all I had was time on my hands, time to relax, time to reflect, and time to think about Angela again. Why hasn't she called! Then I realized that not only had she not called but my phone hadn't rung all day. When I went to check my answering machine to see if the volume was turned down, the counter read 0 messages. Not even a call from my best friends! Then I remembered, Tony told me the night before that everybody was getting together for dinner that evening. When he asked me if I wanted to join them I said no, giving him the excuse of having work to do. Which wasn't exactly a lie, since I did have that important presentation to prepare. But the presentation was not the real reason why I didn't want to go. The truth was I didn't have a date. Sure, there were women I could have called if all I wanted was a body next to me, but there was no one special in my life. At least not special enough to take out to a nice restaurant. Unlike some men, I don't take just any old body out to dinner, not even to McDonald's.

The truth of the matter was, I was lonely. Most men would never admit that, not even to themselves. But as I looked at my reflection in the bedroom mirror I saw a man who was just that. But instead of cutting my wrists or doing something really drastic like calling Psychic Friends Network, I did what I always do when I need insightful advice, I called my dad. If anybody could help me deal with what I was going through, it was Derrick Sr., my mentor, and my best friend. When he picked up the phone I could tell he was feeding his face on Mom's great cooking.

"Hello, Reed residence," he said with a mouth full of food.

"What's up Dad? Did I catch you at a bad time?"

"Junior, you've been catching me at a bad time ever since the day you were born. I swear, every time I get a hot plate in front of me, you call," he said, chuckling. "What is it this time, money or women?"

"A little of both, Dad. Can you call me back when you're finished eating? I really need to talk."

"Hold on for a minute and let me go wrap this plate of chicken and dumplings up in aluminum foil and I'll be right with you, ok?"

"Okay, Dad."

I could tell by the length of time that passed that he was setting up his little counseling office downstairs in the basement. That's where he always went to talk on the phone when he wanted absolute privacy. His fatherly instinct must have told him this conversation was going to get really deep.

"All right, Junior, I'm back. What's on your mind?"

"There's so much going on right now, Dad, I don't even know where to begin."

"Why don't you start with what's bothering you most?"

"That would have to be the trip to New York tomorrow," I said.

"You're talking about your meeting with the advertisers, right?"

"That's the one. I really feel like this is it for me, Dad. If I can't secure this contract I don't know what I'm going to do."

"What do you mean, you don't know what you're going to do? You're going to do what you've always done when things got tough — make adjustments."

"This is different situation, Dad. The time factor is working heavily against me on this deal. Competition is coming out the woodwork and my current sponsors are looking for some kind of sign that we're moving forward. Starks Enterprise could be that big break that we need to get over the hump. If we get them to come aboard, all the other companies will follow suit."

"What's so special about this contract with Starks Enterprise, anyway?" he asked.

"First of all, they represent many of the major record companies. Right there we're looking at thousands of advertising dollars for new releases for their recording artists. They also handle the marketing for several fragrance and clothing manufacturers. And I don't need to tell you how profitable those contracts can be."

"As important as all that sounds, son, I honestly believe you will succeed regardless of the outcome of that meeting. There are always other opportunities, even when we think there aren't. But if it's meant to be, then this deal will happen for you. So, relax and stop worrying about circumstances you can't control. Like I've always taught you, things happen in God's time, not yours."

"I guess you're right."

"I know I'm right. Now stop beating around the bush and tell me why you really called," he said.

"What are you talking about, Pops?" I said trying not to sound too guilty. "I'm telling you what's on my mind!"

"You must think you're talking to one of your friends," he said. "Don't you think that after raising you for 35 years I should know when something's bothering you?"

"If you want to be technical, you only raised me until I graduated high school. I've been out of the house since I was 18."

"You can fool yourself into believing that nonsense if you want to," he said laughing. "I'm still raising your butt today."

I had to laugh too, because I knew he was right. All my life he's been there for me when I needed help. Through all the fights in grammar school, the awards in high school, and all the confusion and distractions of college. Dad was the one constant that kept me focused. If anybody deserved an award for being a good parent, it was definitely him.

"You're right, Dad, there is something else on my mind. Remember that woman I told you about named Angela, the one I met in Atlanta?"

"Yeah, I remember. She's the one who punched that guy out at Bennigan's, right?"

"That's the one."

"So, what about her?" he asked. "Did she hit you in the jaw or give you a black eye?"

"None of the above. She did something even worse. She didn't call me back after we had sex on New Year's Eve."

"I see," he said sounding thoughtful. "And you're too proud to give her a call? Am I correct?"

"It's not a matter of being proud," I said. "I look at it simply as an act of courtesy. After all, I did invite her over to my home for food, drinks, and whatever. The least she could have done was call to say thank you."

"Did you want her to thank you for the food, the drink, or for the sex?"

"In this case, all of the above."

"Son, can I tell you something without you getting upset?"

"Sure Dad, fire away."

"These women out here have you spoiled rotten! You are so used to having things your way that you can't handle it when a woman reacts in a way you don't approve of. What you need to do is stop being so selfish and childish."

"Dag, Pops. I thought you were on my side."

"I'm on your side, Junior. Which is why I'm telling you the truth about yourself. What kind of father would I be if all I did was agree with you, even when you're wrong?"

"How am I wrong?"

"First of all, you didn't even call to see if she made it home safely, did you?"

"No I didn't!"

"Which means she could be laying in a hospital bed some-where in critical condition, or even dead, and you wouldn't even know, would you?"

"I guess I wouldn't," I said in a depressed tone.

"Look, son. I'm not trying to make you feel bad, but as a man, it's your responsibility to take the initiative in a relationship, not to act childishly by playing some kind of waiting game."

I was speechless. Everything he said was right. The uncon-ditional love and blind devotion of so many women throughout my life had spoiled me rotten. I had become a manipulating player who was interested in only one thing, control. Control over a woman's body and her actions. And because Angela didn't allow me that, I was off balance. So I reverted back to doing what I did best, burying my emotions. In fact, I had become such an expert at it, that I could sometimes bury them so deep they would cease to exist. But it didn't work this time. Whatever it was that I felt for Angela would not stay under. The more dirt I tried to throw over it, the deeper the hole became. I was hopelessly hooked.

"What can I say, Dad? You're one hundred percent right. I need to stop playing all these unnecessary games and start act-ing my age."

"Not only that, son, but you can miss out on a good thing if you continue to approach your relationships with this kind of manipulating mentality. And based on what you told me about this young lady, she seems to have a lot to offer."

"She really does," I admitted. "Not only is Angela beauti-ful, but she's also very funny, intelligent, down-to-earth, street smart, considerate, provocative, financially well off, and damn good in bed."

"Hell, if you don't want her, I'll take her!" Dad said. "A woman like that is hard to find."

"Tell me about it. All the women that I've met over the last few years have either been broke, crazy, or had a house full of kids."

"But can she cook?" Dad asked. "A man can't live off of love and fast food, you know."

"That's not really important to me at this point. I can cook for myself."

"You're saying that now, but I guarantee you that in a few years you'll be crying like a baby to have your woman cook you a good meal, at least twice a week, and especially on Sunday. Why do you think I've been with your mother for 35 years?"

"I thought it was because you loved her."

"Well, that's one reason, but the other is that she can throw down in the kitchen. Her pot roast melts in your mouth, and she can put her foot in some collard greens."

"Can we please try to stay on the subject? I thought we were discussing my situation with Angela."

"Oh yeah, that's right. Sorry Junior. I just get carried away when it comes to your mama's cookin'. But getting back to what I was saying. This woman sounds like someone who you have a lot in common with. Why don't you stop stalling and give her a call? She's probably just as anxious to hear from you."

"I think I'll do that. Maybe she's home right now."

"And don't forget what I said about this meeting in New York. It will all happen for you if it's meant to be. So, do your best and stop stressing out over things you have no control over."

"Thanks for the pep talk, Dad. You always come through when I need you. Give Mom my love and tell her I'll try to stop by when I get back in town."

Angela's telephone number was right next to the phone on the nightstand but I didn't need it. I knew the number by heart. As her phone rang, I felt myself getting nervous. It had been six long days since we last talked. But instead of talking to Angela I got her answering machine. Needless to say I was disappointed. My first impulse was to hang up, but I didn't. As the recording played I cleared my throat and prepared to leave a brief message.

"Hello and Happy Holidays!" Angela's energetic voice announced. "You've reached the Williams residence. Sorry there's no one here to take your call at this time. At the tone please leave a brief message and I will return your call at my earliest convenience. Oh, if this is you, Derrick, I hope you like your Christmas gift. I put it inside the hallway closet on the top shelf, just in case you forgot to look. Call me when you get time. Bye."

Boy, did I ever feel stupid. Here I was sitting around pouting like a big baby for the last six days and Angela was waiting to hear from me all along. Tracie was right, I was the one who ended up **trippin'**. The time had come for me to take serious inventory of myself. If I was going to take another step toward getting involved with this unique lady, I had to come correct.

After splashing a handful of cold water on my face to help me snap out of my foolishness, I went to the closet to get my gift. Inside the box was a wind-up Mickey Mouse clock, a pack of Jockey brand underwear, size 32 inch waist, and a red and white envelope addressed to Mr. Lover. I carried the letter back to my bedroom, took a long sip of my drink, and leaned back against the pillow to read the letter.

Dear Lover,

Last night was very special for me. It was the first time in years that someone made me feel comfortable enough to truly let myself go. When you held me in your arms I felt relaxed, safe, and wanted. Those are the feelings that every woman is searching for, regardless of how educated or independent she claims to be. It just takes the right kind of man to allow you to let down your defenses and be vulnerable.

I hope I'm not scaring you away by sharing how I feel. I'm not trying to obligate you or tie you down. I only wanted you to know how much I enjoyed the time we spent together and hope we can get together sometime soon. And just in case you're wondering if I do this sort of thing all the time, the answer is, hell no! There's not a woman in this world who cherishes her body more than I do. So, please don't misinterpret my passion and aggressiveness for being loose. I chose you because I trust you.

I'm off to Atlanta to visit my friend Denise. You can reach me at her place. The number is on the back of this letter. I'll be there until Monday afternoon, so call me if you're not too busy working on that presentation. If I don't hear from you, I'll understand.

Hugs and Kisses,

Angela Williams

P.S. You are the most tender and considerate man I've ever met. I loved the way you kept covering me up with the blanket and asking me if I was all right. Most men don't give a damn how the woman is doing. Thanks for being a real gentleman.

After reading her letter for the fifth time I picked up the phone and dialed the number on the back of the letter. After three long rings, the phone picked up. I cleared my throat and tried my best to sound cool.

"Hello, how are you doing? This is Derrick, is Angela there?"

"Well hello, Derrick, this is Denise," she said, sounding genuinely excited. "I've heard a lot about you."

"I hope it was all positive."

"As a matter of fact, it was very positive. Hold on, I'll get Angela for you. Oh, by the way," she said coming back to the phone. "I've seen your magazine around town in some of the book stores. You've got a real winner there."

"Thanks Denise. I appreciate the compliment."

"You're welcome. Now hold on for just a second. Let me get off the other line and then I'll put Angela on."

A few minutes later she clicked back over and yelled for Angela to pick up the other phone. I could hear the smooth sounds of Ronny Jordan playing in the background and the voices of what sounded like several women yapping. I couldn't make out exactly what was being said, but there was no doubt that the topic was men.

"Hello, who is this?" an unfamiliar and intoxicated voice asked.

"This is Derrick, who is this?"

"Don't worry about who this is, just answer me one thing."

"Ok, shoot!"

"Why would a man cheat on his wife if she's giving him everything he wants at home?"

"To be perfectly honest with you, most men are greedy and they know they can get away with it."

"Girl, get your drunk ass off the phone." Angela laughed as she grabbed the phone out of her hand. "He didn't call here to provide you with free marriage counseling. Hello, Derrick? Please excuse my crazy soror Debbie. She just found out her husband spent New Year's Eve at a hotel with her next-door neighbor. Now she's over here auditioning for the Ricki Lake Show."

"Which sorority did you say you belonged to?"

"Delta, of course. What else?"

"You Greek sistahs kill me with that I'm the best attitude. Deltas, AKAs, Zetas, you're all the same, conceited."

"Hey, if you don't believe your organization is the best, who will?"

"I guess you've got a point there," I said. "But let's get back to you. How are you doing?"

"I'm doing fine now that I'm talking to you," she said, sounding sincere. "I was beginning to think you had forgotten about me."

"I don't think anybody could forget a woman who is as

beautiful and sweet as you."

"Oooh, listen to you. Have you been drinking?"

"The only thing I'm intoxicated off of is you, baby."

"You keep talking' like that, I'll be on the next plane back to Chicago."

"I dare you!" I said boldly.

"All right now." Angela warned. "I'm already packed and ready to go. And Denise lives in College Park, only a hop skip and a jump away from the airport."

"Well, hop, skip, and jump your behind on home to me."

"You're serious aren't you?"

"You damn right, I'm serious. I really miss you, baby."

"Aren't you leaving for New York first thing in the morning?" she asked.

"Yes, I am. But I still want to see you."

Angela paused for a moment.

"Tell you what, why don't we meet in New York instead?"

"I thought you had to be back at work tomorrow. And what about the airfare? Those last-minute tickets are expensive."

"Would you stop worrying so much, I'll take care of my end," she said confidently. "All I want to know is whether or not you want me to come. Yes, or no?"

"Of course I do, but."

"But nothing. Just give me the name and address of the hotel you'll be staying at and what time you want me to meet you. I'll take it from there."

"Sounds like a plan," I said. "I'm really looking forward to seeing you again."

"That goes ditto for me," Angela said. "And don't forget to bring the Mickey Mouse clock and underwear I brought you for Christmas."

"Thanks for reminding me. I meant to ask you, how did you decide on those two gifts?"

"Well, I bought the wind-up clock because you complained about the hotels not giving you your wake-up calls."

"And what about the underwear?"

"What else do you buy the man who has everything? If there's one thing I've learned in my 35 years it's that a man could have a million dollars in the bank and he still won't go buy himself a new pair of drawers."

I couldn't help but burst out laughing because I looked in the mirror at the drawers I had on and they were dingy as hell. Even the elastic was beginning to wear out.

STRICTLY BUSINESS

It was 7:45 Monday morning. Derrick hurried out the door with his garment bag over one shoulder, a laptop computer over the other, and a suitcase on wheels. The drive to O'Hare during rush hour was going to take at least an hour. He knew he was cutting it way too close. After struggling to get off the crowded elevator and through the revolving door in the lobby, he flagged down a taxi, threw his bags in the trunk, and hopped in.

"Where you goin' mister?" the driver asked in a foreign accent.

Derrick just looked at him thinking to himself, where in the hell do you think I'm going dressed in a business suit and carrying three pieces of luggage, to a barbecue, you idiot?

But instead of getting smart, he politely told him O'Hare airport was his destination and that he was in a big hurry.

"No problem, mister," he said. "What time is your flight?"

"It leaves at 9:15."

"Don't worry, I'll get you there in plenty of time."

Taking his word for it, Derrick relaxed and pulled out his cell phone to call Monica and Tiffany at the office. They were both very nervous about the East Coast trip, realizing as he did that it was the moment of truth, make it or break it time. If *Happily Single* was going to compete with other national publications they had to secure long-term advertising contracts with major companies.

"Well, ladies, this is it!" Derrick said. "This is what we've sacrificed and worked so hard for."

"Did you remember to take the layouts for the February and March issues?" Monica asked.

"Yep, I'm looking at them now."

"What about those story ideas I left on your desk last week?" Tiffany asked.

"I've got them right here in my portfolio. Everything you gave me will be included in my presentation."

"I hope they're impressed enough to invest serious money." Monica added. "I've put my heart and soul into this magazine."

"I know you have, and I want you both to know how much I appreciate all of your hard work and that I couldn't have made it this far without you."

"Are you trying to get mushy, Derrick?"

"You damn right I am. Now shut the hell up so I can finish giving you this compliment. As I was saying, I've never been associated with two more talented and dedicated individuals. You have worked day and night busting your butts to put together an attractive and professional-looking product that anyone with an ounce of sense would die to be a part of. So, relax, and let me do what I do best, wheel and deal!"

As cool and confident as Derrick tried to appear he under a tremendous amount of pressure, Monica and Tiffany had invested every dime of their savings into the magazine, including money they borrowed from family and friends. But Derrick had already taken it upon himself to do the accounting, just in case, and estimated that there was more than enough money to pay off Monica and Tiffany's debt, regardless of what happened. As for him, it wasn't about the money. It had more to do with having freedom from corporate America. There was no way in hell he was going to accept failure and go back to punching a clock nine to five, no way! In Derrick's mind that was nothing but slavery. He had worked too hard and come too far to be denied. And besides, he could never face going back to work for IBM, not after all the negative comments from his co-workers. The thought of facing them again was too humiliating for him to imagine. He would sell incense and key chains on the streets before he went back begging for his job back. It was that serious.

By 8:30 the taxi had only gotten as far as California Avenue, which was barely halfway to the airport. When Derrick looked over the front seat at the speedometer, it read 50 mph. At that rate of speed he was definitely not going to make it. He called TWA from his cell phone, praying his flight would be delayed, but it was scheduled to leave on time. Why is it that flights never leave on time until you're running late trying to catch them? he thought. The urgency of his predicament began to sink in. He was about to miss the most important flight of his professional life. All of his hard work was about to be washed down the drain because of some sorry-ass cab driver. He had to do something.

"Excuse me, driver," he said, "but didn't I tell you that my flight departs at 9:15?"

"9:15?" the driver asked, sounding confused. "I thought you said 9:50."

Derrick's blood pressure jumped 100 degrees. He tried his

best to stay cool, but the stress from possibly missing his flight was too overwhelming. He snapped!

"Man, I told you 9:15! Can't you understand fuckin' English?"

"Look, mister, don't get upset," he said nervously.

"Don't tell me not to get upset. I specifically told your dumb ass 9:15! Now, I'm screwed!"

"I'm sorry mister, my mistake. But if you calm down I promise I can get you there on time."

"You damn well better!" Derrick shouted. "Your life may depend on it!"

The driver pressed his foot down firmly on the accelerator and the car lunged forward. The speedometer went from 50 to 75 in five seconds.

"Now, that's what I'm talkin' about, Muhammad," Derrick said. "Drive this taxi like Speed Racer."

By 8:55 they arrived at the TWA terminal. The driver quickly got out and opened the trunk. "It's amazing how motivated a person can get with an angry black man in the back seat," Derrick said as he to reached into his pocket for the fare. "Let's get together and do this again sometime soon, shall we?" He gave the driver an extra five-dollar tip, snatched his bags from the truck, and took off running through the airport like O.J. Simpson.

"Excuse me, pardon me, coming through!" Derrick yelled.

"Slow down buddy!" an airport employee shouted while pushing a passenger in a wheel chair. "You're going to kill yourself."

"If I don't catch this plane on time, I'll be as good as dead."

His only chance of making it in time was going straight to the gate. The metal detectors were the only obstacles that stood between him and the friendly skies. "Lord, please don't let these lines be long," he prayed. But as he turned the corner to the security check point, he saw that his prayer was unanswered. Not only were the lines long, but they were moving slowly. Derrick was pulling his hair out as he watched the same stupid people go through the metal detectors two and three times because they forgot to take all the change out of their pockets. And to make matters worse, passengers carrying camcorders and laptop computers were being asked to turn them on for security purposes. That added another eight minutes. When Derrick finally made it through the line, he checked the TWA monitor for his flight. It read **Final Boarding**. He looked at his watch, took a deep breath, and broke out in a full sprint. His flight was departing from gate 32 at the very end of the concourse. But he maneuvered his way through the thick crowd and managed to get there just as the flight attendant was about to close the outer door.

"Hold up!" he shouted while waving his ticket in the air. "Don't even think about leaving without me. Not after all the hell I've gone through!"

The temperature in Atlanta was a pleasant 68 degrees. Denise and Angela were cruisin' down I 85 in Denise's red BMW with the convertible top down and the music thumbing. Angela was pushing the buttons on the radio like a maniac, switching back and forward from V-103 to hot 97.5.

"Leave it on 97," Denise said. "That's my jam!"

"You love that rap music, don't you?"

"Tupac is one of my favorite artists!" she said as she sang along with the song. "Or should I say, he was. Too bad he got himself killed. He was a talented young brother."

"Girl, you don't even know what those lyrics mean with your 35-year-old, Alabama countrified self."

"I know I don't," Denise said. "But nobody knows that except you."

"Let me turn back to V-103 so I can hear the end of that Kenny Lattimore song."

"Go ahead. I've got his *Makaveli* CD at home, anyway. But don't you hate it when they wait until you get in your car to play all your favorite jams?"

"Yeah, I noticed that. Somebody needs to invent a car radio that records."

As they approached the exit for the airport, Angela double-checked to make sure she had her confirmation number and the information that Derrick gave her.

"You got everything?" Denise asked.

"I think so. But I can't seem to find that piece of paper that I wrote Derrick's hotel address on."

"I thought you had all that stuff memorized."

"I did. But all I can remember now is that I'm supposed to meet him at four o'clock in the lobby of the Marriott Hotel."

"Well, I'm sure there's more than one Marriott hotel in New York City."

"No shit Sherlock," Angela said grinning. "Tell me something I don't know."

"Okay, smart-ass. That piece of paper you're looking for is right there between your legs."

They were still laughing when they pulled up to the Delta Airlines curbside ticket counter. Denise blotted her face with a piece of tissue, then popped the trunk while Angela put on a fresh coat of lipstick. All eyes were on them as they rose out of the plush leather interior. Denise had on a pair of shorts and a tight t- shirt that showed off her well-rounded breasts. And Angela, who was appropriately dressed for the New York cold, had on a pair of black leather pants, black boots, a leather cowboy hat, and a black turtle neck sweater. The skycaps damn near broke their necks trying to be the first one over to check her luggage.

"Look out, fellahs!" the younger one shouted. "I've got this one."

"Wait a minute, junior," the older one said. "I outrank you. Now step aside so I can take care of this beautiful young lady's bags."

"Outrank me? What do you think this is, the damn military? You step aside!"

"Now boys, ya'll don't have to fight over little old me," Angela said, doing a bad imitation of a Southern belle. "There's plenty of luggage to go round."

"Girl, you know you need to quit," Denise said. "The furthest south you've ever been is the South Side of Chicago."

They exchanged hugs and kisses and Denise got in her car and turned the station back to 97.5.

"Now I can listen to my kind of music," she said while turning up the volume. "Tell Derrick I wish him luck and don't forget to check out the soul food at the Shark Bar in Manhattan. It's the bomb!"

"I won't forget. And thanks for taking me for a quick drive downtown. I needed that last dose of warm weather before I go back north to freeze my buns off."

After checking her bags, Angela gave both skycaps two-dollar tips, and hurried into the terminal. She was not in the mood to be bothered with their unsophisticated come-ons. But their childish advances did remind her to do one very important thing, put on the phony wedding ring she kept in her purse. Although it never prevented the stubborn and aggressive types from approaching her, it was effective at keeping the more timid hounds at bay. And the airports were full of German shepherds and poodles. Most of them being middle-aged white businessmen looking to cheat on their wives or girlfriends.

Angela's contact with black men in airports was usually limited to baggage checkers, concession workers, and other airline employees. Rarely did she meet any attractive men on her flights and only twice in the last three years had she sat next to a black man in first class. And wouldn't you know it, one was married and the other, who was fine as wine, turned out to be gay. She just looked at him thinking to herself, What a damn shame! As she rode up the escalator coming from the underground Trans she looked around and saw that this trip would be just as colorless as all the rest. The terminal was crowded with white business travelers and vacationers standing around at the bars getting drunk or sitting on the floor working with their laptop computers. The only black people she saw were a young female airport employee pushing a wheel chair and an attractive hazel-eyed flight attendant sitting at her gate. After checking in at the ticket counter, she took the seat next to the flight attendant and tried to make conversation.

"Hi, how are you doing?" Angela asked.

"I'm fine," the flight attendant replied. "But I'll be doing much better if I can get aboard this flight."

"So, you're on standby, huh?"

"Yes, I am, but it's looking pretty good. This flight doesn't seem to be overbooked. By the way my name is Vanessa."

"I'm Angela. Pleased to meet you."

"So where are you from, Angela?"

"Chicago."

"Oh, I love Chicago. When I was there last year a friend of mine took me out to a restaurant called Home Run Inn for deep dish pizza. That was the best I ever had. I'm from Detroit, myself. Have you ever been there?"

"Several times. One of my girlfriends from college got a job there about three years ago. I go up to visit her a couple of times a year. She's a real party animal. We went downtown to Floods for drinks. Then we went to party at a club in the Southfield Plaza Hotel. But I can't remember the name."

"You're talking about Nickels. That's one of my favorite hangouts on Fridays. But you've got to get there early to avoid the teenyboppers."

"So, are you working on a flight out of New York today?"

"No, I'm off duty for the next few days. I'm going to New York to help my sister look after her new baby. She had some complications during surgery and needs a helping hand."

"Do you have any crumbsnatchers?"

"I hope this doesn't sound too selfish, but children are not a requirement in my life! I don't have the time or patience for them. I've been on my own for more than 18 years, traveling the world, and coming and going as I please. I couldn't even imagine what it would be like to have to find a baby sitter before making plans to leave town. And besides, I've worked entirely too hard on this figure to let it go now." Vanessa stood up and proudly put her hands around her tiny waistline. "At 37 years old your body doesn't snap back like it did at 21."

"I heard that, girl!" Angela said slapping Vanessa five. "I'm with you. I love children to death, but after a few hours of chasing them around the house and changing diapers, you're ready for them to go home."

"Could you please call my old-fashion mother and explain to her that nothing is wrong with me. She swears that I have some kind of a psychological problem. In her mind every woman has a responsibility to contribute to the population of this already overcrowded planet."

"Let me add this while we're on a roll," Angela said. "Kids cost money! And I like spending money on myself. When I eat, my whole family eats."

"Angie, you're my kind of sistah. Let's exchange phone numbers and stay in touch." Vanessa passed her a business card. "Are you in Atlanta often?

"All the time. It's my second home."

"Good. Maybe we can get together sometime and hang out. A close friend of mine manages a club downtown called Jazzmin's. We can drink free and party all night. That is, if your husband will let you go out of the house," Vanessa said, while looking down at Angela's wedding ring.

"Look who's talking," Angela said, pointing at the rock on Vanessa's hand. "What about your warden?"

"Well, just between you and me," Vanessa whispered. "I'm not married. This is my blocking ring."

"Mine too!" Angela said as they laughed and slapped five again.

The flight was beginning to board. The agent called Vanessa up to the counter to give her a seat assignment. With a little maneuvering they managed to get seated next to one another. Angela was elated. For the first time in years she was sitting next to another black person. Someone with a great sense of humor and someone who she seemed to have a lot in common with. As the plane lifted off the runway, they picked up the conversation right where they left off.

"So, are you going to New York on business or pleasure?" Vanessa asked.

"It's pleasure for me and business for my friend."

"When you say friend, do you mean friend or **friend**?"

"I mean friend as in, I couldn't sleep last night."

"What exactly does your friend do, if you don't mind me asking?"

"Have you heard of Motif Publishing or *Happily Single* magazine?"

"Of course I have! Who hasn't? It's the most provocative magazine to come out in years. As a matter of fact, I have the December issue on my cocktail table."

"Well, I'm going to New York to have dinner with the publisher."

"You're kidding me, right?"

"No, I'm serious."

"You're going to have dinner with Derrick Reed?"

"How did you know his name?"

"Girl, every woman in Atlanta knows who Derrick Reed is. He was in town back in early August speaking at a reception given by the alumni at Spellman College and turned it out! Then he was on the radio doing an interview where he talked about how he got started in the publishing business and what type of woman he would be interested in settling down with. Women were breaking their necks trying to meet him when he came out to sign copies of the magazine at the bookstore downtown. I was one of the first in line to get an autograph. He's one of the most interesting and intelligent men I've ever met. And fine too!"

Angela couldn't help feeling proud to hear someone speak so highly of her man. She blushed slightly but kept her composure.

"I'll make sure to tell him that he has a fan."

"I'm sorry Angela. I didn't mean to be disrespectful, but it's not often you meet a brother who is doing something positive. What he's accomplished with that magazine in only one year is pretty impressive. Don't you think?"

"Yes I do, Vanessa. And I'm just as excited about it as you are. In fact, he's meeting with an important client this afternoon that could help make the magazine one of the top publications in the country. Hopefully he'll have good news when I meet him at the hotel this afternoon and we can celebrate."

"There are a lot of women who wish they were in your shoes. It's hard to find progressive-minded men these days who have a dream and the discipline and courage to follow through with it!"

"You know, I never really thought about it quite like that before," Angela said, placing her hand on her chin. "I guess he did gamble big-time when he quit his job at IBM. There aren't many men who would give up the security of a $70,000-a-year job, especially growing up as poor as he did."

"Like I said, it took a lot of courage to step out there the way he did. Men like that are hard to find. If I ever get my hands on one, you better believe I'm gonna hold on tight and never let go."

For the remainder of the flight Angela thought long and hard about everything that was said. Although she already had a great deal of respect and admiration for what Derrick had accomplished, it took a beautiful and intelligent woman like Vanessa to make her appreciate him just a little bit more.

It was 4:10 p.m. when Derrick's limo dropped him off in front of the east side Marriott. While the valet put his bags on the cart, he went inside to the front desk to check in.

"May I help you sir?" the clerk asked.

"Yes you can, reservation for Derrick Reed, please."

"Yes, Mr. Reed we have you confirmed with us for two

nights, is that correct?"

"That's correct."

"Will you need one key or two?"

"I think you better make it two. And could you please check to see if I have any messages."

"You have two messages," she said while punching the keys of her computer. "Would you like to retrieve them when you get to your room?"

"Can you give them to me now?"

"Sure, that's not a problem. One is from a Ms. Williams. She says good luck with your meeting and she should make it here to the hotel on time. The second message is also from Ms. Williams," the clerk said with a smirk on her face, as if she was holding back a smile. "It reads, Don't look now but there's a woman behind you with a rose."

When Derrick turned around Angela was right behind him holding a single red rose and smiling like she just hit the lottery.

"You're incredible!" Derrick said as he grabbed her by the waist and lifted her off the floor. "How did you get here before me?"

"Let's just say I took a few shortcuts," Angela said. "Now put me down before I have to call security."

"I should embarrass you by carrying you all the way upstairs after that trick you played on me."

"Now, I'm daring you!"

Derrick turned to the clerk and thanked her for the messages and then instructed the valet to follow him upstairs to his room.

"Could you please get my briefcase off the counter?" Derrick asked the valet. "I'm going to need both hands for this job."

"Derrick, you have completely lost your mind. I was just kidding. Now put me down!"

"Oh no, you dared me, remember? So you may as well relax and enjoy the ride."

Angela was totally embarrassed. The lobby was full of

people watching and applauding as they walked onto the elevator. It was a scene right out of *Officer and a Gentleman* when Richard Gere walked out of the factory carrying his girlfriend at the end of the movie. As awkward as it was, Angela was loving every minute of it.

When they finally made it to their room, Derrick set her gently on the bed, tipped the valet five dollars, and went into the bathroom.

"Derrick, I'm going to call Denise real quick to let her know I made it here safely, ok?"

"No problem. Feel free to call whomever you need to."

After leaving a brief message on Denise's answering machine, Angela began unpacking her clothes.

"So, how was your trip?" she asked Derrick, who was still in the bathroom.

When he didn't answer. She knocked on the door to see if he was ok.

"Derrick, are you all right in there?"

"I'm fine, baby." he said as he opened the door. "I was just saying a short prayer."

"You don't have to be shy about praying around me. Why don't you include me next time?"

"Actually I didn't go into the bathroom to pray, I went to wash my hands. But when I thought about my meeting this evening, I felt the immediate need."

"This evening? I thought your meeting was early this afternoon."

"So did I, but something important came up at his office and he had to reschedule. He was very apologetic and insisted on buying me dinner this evening to make it up to me."

"What about the meeting?"

"The meeting is tonight, after dinner. Mr. Starks has arranged to have a small area in the hotel restaurant partitioned off."

"This guy must have serious pull," Angela said. "I can see why you're so nervous about meeting with him."

"He's the man, all right."

"So what have you been doing all afternoon?"

"Well, you know me. I found a way to make lemonade out of lemons," Derrick joked. "I've been riding around town talking with magazine stand owners, bookstore managers, and anybody else that can help me with distribution."

"You ain't nothin' but a Chicago hustler, Derrick."

"Thank you very much. I take that as a compliment."

"So, what time are you going to meet with him for dinner?"

"We are going to meet him for dinner at 7:00. I already told him I had plans with you for tonight and he insisted that you join us. Of course, if it was left up to me I would have sent you down the street to McDonald's or for takeout Chinese."

Angela picked up a pillow and hit him right upside the head and then threw him down on the bed.

"Take it back!" she yelled while continuing to beat him with the pillow. "Say you didn't mean what you said."

"Ok, I didn't mean it! I apologize!

"Now kiss me and let me feel how much you miss me," Angela said in a more serious tone.

"I do miss you, baby. More than you can imagine," Derrick whispered as their lips met.

He slowly maneuvered his hand down her back and pulled her sweater out of her pants and then unsnapped her belt. Their kisses became more passionate and their breathing deepened. Derrick reached for his briefcase at the foot of the bed where he had his condoms stashed, but Angela grabbed his hand. She wasn't ready to go there, not yet.

"What's wrong?" Derrick asked.

"Nothing is wrong. I just want to wait until tonight."

"Are you sure? I don't know if I can wait that long. I might be compelled to attack you in the middle of dessert."

"You are a real nutcase Derrick. I swear. Yes I can wait and so can you. Besides, I've got a big surprise for you tonight."

"What surprise?" Derrick asked sounding like a little kid. "I hope you're not going to tie my hands to the headboard and whip me with a leather strap."

"No, I'm saving that kinky bit for next time, you comedian. You'll just have to wait and see."

"So what are **we** supposed to do until then?" he said while looking down at the bulge in his pants. "You can't just leave us like this."

"Why don't you both go downstairs to the health club and get in a quick workout before your meeting. As a matter of fact, why don't we all go down together. I think we could use the stress release."

By the time they returned from the health club it was six o'clock. Angela grabbed her cosmetic case off the bed and quickly jumped into the shower. Derrick set up his portable CD player and miniature speakers, then put up the ironing board to press the wrinkles out of his Armani suit. While he listened to the CD by Groove Theory, he tried to relax and think about what he was going to say to Mr. Starks over dinner. This was his big chance, the opportunity of his professional life. He didn't want to blow it.

Angela could feel the tension in the air when she came out of the bathroom. She didn't say a word while she slipped out of her towel and into her black Bob Mackie cocktail dress. It was obvious that Derrick was into deep thought because he didn't even try to sneak a peek while she was naked.

"Are you finished in the bathroom, sweetheart?" Derrick asked in a serious but warm tone.

"Just let me put on my makeup and I'll be out of your way."

While Angela went back into the bathroom to put on her blush and lipstick, Derrick pulled the notes out of his briefcase and looked over his presentation one final time. He was determined not let Monica and Tiffany down. They were counting on him.

"This is really it," he mumbled.

"Derrick, did you say something?"

"No, I was just talking to myself."

Angela felt helpless. She wanted badly to put her arms around him and tell him everything was going to be all right, but she knew how men could get in these kinds of situations. Sometimes the best thing to do is to leave them alone and let them work it out for themselves. Maybe if she knew him better she would have taken the initiative, but in reality she was still a stranger. While Derrick took his shower Angela took a peek at his presentation, which was left out on the bed. The graphics and artwork for the upcoming issues were very colorful and the story ideas were provocative and humorous. The title for one article, "Who's makin' love to your old lady?" cracked her up.

What she found most impressive was the clarity of his notes. Derrick was very organized and had excellent handwriting for a man. Angela worked with many so-called educated men who wrote worse than ten-year-old children. One guy she dated wrote so badly that she used to send his love letters back because she couldn't decipher them. She called it "doctor's handwriting."

By 6:45 they were both dressed and ready to go. Angela put on her diamond necklace, Rolex wristwatch and a light spray of Boucheron perfume to set it off. Derrick turned off the music and called downstairs to see if Mr. Starks had arrived. The clerk at the front desk said that he had just called and left a message that he was in route and should be in the lobby no later than 7:15.

"Well, I guess it's showtime!" Derrick said.

"I guess so."

Derrick walked to the door, grasped the knob, then paused.

"Before we go, let me say that you look absolutely gorgeous tonight, Ms. Williams."

"You don't look too bad yourself, Mr. Reed."

"I also want you to know that I appreciate you giving me my space tonight. It's very important for me to have time out to concentrate before doing business. Also, I want to tell you how much it means to me to have you here on such a historic occasion, probably the most important day of my adult life."

"Can I say something now?"

"There's just one more thing," Derrick promised. "Regardless if I get this contract or not, I'm going to celebrate tonight. You know why? Because no matter what happens, I'll have your warm arms to hold me and your beautiful face to sooth me."

"Damn, baby, that was deep," Angela said, trying to hold back the tears. "That's the sweetest thing anybody has ever said to me. Come here and give me a hug, boy!"

Angela hugged him as tight as she could, trying not to get lipstick on his suit. She had been aching to hold him in her arms all night, hoping to relieve him of whatever small amount of stress she could.

"Derrick I know how important this meeting is for you, but baby you've got to have faith in yourself. You have come a long way from the ghettos on the South Side of Chicago and from IBM. Who else could have come this far with virtually no experience in this business? Not many people, I'm telling you. Everybody who comes in contact with you believes in what you're doing, your friends, your family, perfect strangers, and me. I believe in you too. So if rich Mr. Starks doesn't share in that believe, fuck him! You can make it without him. I've got your back!"

Derrick looked her right in the eyes, held her face in his hands, and placed a gentle kiss on her cheek.

"Angela, you could make a garbage man feel like the president of the United States. Sometimes even someone who is as motivated as myself can use a little reassurance every now and then. Thanks for being so sweet and supportive. Now, let's go get paid."

By the time Derrick and Angela made it down to the lobby, Mr Starks and his two associates were waiting at the bar, having drinks. Although Derrick had never met him personally, he recognized his face from several television commercials and an article they did on him in *Black Enterprise* magazine. According to his biography he was in his mid fifties, but he was in excellent shape and could easily past for early forties or even late thirties.

"Excuse me, Mr. Stark?" Derrick said. "How are you. I'm Derrick Reed."

"Mr. Reed. It's a pleasure to finally meet you face to face!" he said enthusiastically. "And who is this beautiful young lady?"

"This is my very special friend, Ms. Angela Williams."

"Ms. Williams, you look very lovely tonight."

"Thank you Mr. Starks. But please call me Angela, I hate formalities."

"That makes two of us. You can call me Calvin."

"Well, Calvin, you're looking mighty dapper yourself this evening."

"Why, thank you. My wife has great taste in men's clothing. Personally I wouldn't know Sax Fifth Avenue from JC Penny. If it were left up to me my entire wardrobe would consist of stone-washed blue jeans and tennis shoes."

After introducing his two associates, one being his accountant and the other his marketing director, they were escorted to the reserved area of the restaurant to be seated. The layout was first class. Two bottles of champagne were chilling on the table, and all the glassware was authentic crystal. Mr. Starks even went so far as to request special waiters for the occasion. Derrick was thoroughly impressed and flattered. After putting in their orders for appetizers and drinks they relaxed and got better acquainted.

"Derrick, allow me to apologize again for canceling our meeting this afternoon. Mondays are always full of surprises. Something always needs my immediate attention."

"That's quite all right sir. I managed to make a productive day out of it."

"And, how was your flight from Chicago?"

"My experience with flying has always been pretty bad. Today I had a restless seven-year-old boy behind me who insisted on using the back of my seat as a football."

"I bet you wanted to turn around and pop that rascal right upside the head, didn't you?"

Derrick was caught off guard by Mr. Stark's sense of humor, but he liked it.

"Yes I did. As a matter of fact, I wanted to pop his father too for allowing him to continue to do it."

Except for the stony faces of his associates the mood was incredibly relaxed. It seemed more like a friendly get-together than a business meeting worth millions of dollars. For the next hour they drank and discussed everything except their business deal. Mr. Starks talked about his experiences growing up very poor in Mississippi back in the late '40s and early '50s. Recalling the horrible memories of lynching and Jim Crow laws. Sometimes he became very emotional about the stories. Derrick and Angela sat there like two children listening to their grandfather tell fairytales. Never once did they blink or even take a sip of water. But after dinner was finished, the atmosphere and the conversation turned to business. The waiters cleared the table and Derrick asked to have his material brought in. A screen was set up at the back of the room with an overhead projector, along with an easel for Derrick's charts.

"Ok, Derrick, let's get down to business," Mr. Starks said. "As you know, Starks Enterprise has strong ties with the entertainment and clothing manufacturing industries. We represent athletes, singers, actors, etc. What we're looking for is a media that we can utilize to reach the 25-to-40-year-old market. Mainly, but not exclusively, African Americans. So tell me, what can we expect your magazine to do that the others can't?"

"Right now, Mr. Starks, advertisers make up only 30% of our revenues. However, we were still able to generate over 200,000 sales in the first quarter, growing by 20% during the next three quarters while opening markets in 20 new cities. The reason for our success is due to the quality of our product and the diversity of our articles. Unlike our competition we relate every aspect of what we do to relationships. Articles on topics such as exercise, sex, fashion, music, and books all deal with relationships. For example, when we do an article on music, it focuses on artists who perform romantic and relaxing music. Your company would fit in perfectly with this format because 25% of the recording artists that you represent are 30 and over and perform either contemporary jazz or love ballads."

"I can see you've done your homework, Derrick," Mr. Starks said. "I'm impressed. Please continue."

"With respect to the clothing manufacturers you represent, let me point out that women and men over 25 have increasingly become interested in lingerie and sex toys. And if I'm not mistaken, two of your largest contracts are with companies that manufacture and distribute underwear and other, how should I say, paraphernalia. What better way to advertise their products than with a publication that focuses on single, sexually active, adults?"

Mr. Starks put his hand on his chin and grinned slightly. Meanwhile his assistants sat stone-faced, taking notes. Derrick became a little nervous. He had delivered his knockout punch, and no one was saying a word. After a minute or so, Mr. Starks stood up with his hand still firmly pressed against his chin and walked around to the side of the table where Angela was sitting.

"Every company I represent has increased its advertising budgets by more than 20% over the last year in an effort to attract more female consumers," he said, glancing down at Angela. "Men, statistically speaking, spend money on automotive supplies, electronics, sporting goods, and music. So, when I make a decision to spend their hard-earned money on a particular form of advertising, I have to ask myself the all important question, will that form of media influence the female consumer? What do you think Angela?"

"Excuse me!" Angela said. She was caught totally off guard.

"I want your opinion of *Happily Single* magazine. Would a

woman such as yourself purchase and read it on a regular basis?"

"Mr. Starks."

"Calvin. Remember we're not being formal."

"Well, Calvin, I'm not qualified to speak on behalf of the magazine. Derrick and I are just friends, not business partners."

"I don't expect you to quote statistics," he said, placing his hand on her shoulder. "Just give me your honest opinion."

"Okay, here it goes."

Derrick wanted to cover his ears. There was no telling what Angela would say. Although she was very poised and professional, she could get ethnic at the drop of a hat. He sat down at the table and crossed his fingers. It was clear from the tone of Mr. Starks' voice that her response would probably determine the success or demise of the deal.

"First of all, I think Derrick is grossly underpricing his services. He should be charging you at least $1500 more for a full-page ad and $750 for a half."

Derrick slapped himself on the forehead worried about what she would say next.

"Furthermore," she added, "the other national publications may be well-established but they aren't attracting many new readers. *Happily Single* is fresh, exciting, and has a lot of momentum. And it's the only magazine on the market that focuses entirely on relationships, specifically single people. Just in case you haven't checked the statistics lately, most Americans are either single or well on their way, via separation or divorce court. As far as universal appeal is concerned, this magazine appeals to everyone, white, black, rich, poor, young, and old. If there's one thing generation X and baby boomers have in common it is that they can't find a date."

Mr. Starks and his associates stood up and applauded. Angela graciously took a bow and then walked over to Derrick and gave him a big hug.

"Thanks, baby. I needed that," Derrick said with a sigh of relief.

"Congratulations, Derrick. You've got the contract," Mr.

Starks said shaking his hand. "But under one condition."

The room all of a sudden got quiet.

"What's that?"

"That you hold on to this fantastic lady."

"You've got yourself a deal!"

The waiter came in and popped the cork on the champagne and they made a toast to a long and prosperous business relationship. Derrick could hardly wipe the grin off his face as he signed the one-year contact, which Mr. Starks promised to extend if things went well. For Derrick, this represented the first major step toward achieving his ultimate goal, to be number one.

"Good luck, Derrick," Mr. Starks said while handing him an advance of $50,000. "I'll be sure to tell my friends at Coke and Pepsi about you. I'm sure they'll be very interested in doing business with you."

Angela talked Derrick into going over to the Shark Bar on Amsterdam to unwind. Denise raved about their soul food ever since she visited New York last September and made Angela promise to check it out. This time her praises were not exaggerated. Even though they had already eaten, they shared a bowl of collard greens and blackened catfish. It was the bomb! Even Derrick, who was a big-time food critic, confessed that the macaroni and cheese tasted better than his mama's. But it was the laid back atmosphere that was most appealing. The restaurant was overflowing with casually dressed patrons sipping on cocktails and talking loud. And the sounds of R&B music filled the air. Derrick said it was the first time he ever ate dinner while listening to Tony Toni Tone' and R. Kelly.

Afterwards, they took a taxi over to Rockefeller Plaza to ice skate. It was cold as hell, but they hardly noticed. It was a special night and they wanted to savor it. By midnight Angela was beat. Derrick took her back to the hotel room and lay down with her until she fell asleep. At 1:00 she finally dozed off. He covered her up with the blanket and slowly got up, trying not to wake her. Once he was sure she was still asleep, Derrick went into his ritual. He lit one of the candles he always kept with him and cracked open the half pint of Hennessy he had stashed in his suitcase. Then he put in his favorite Sade CD, *Stronger than Pride*, and pushed the selector button to the #4 track called "Haunt Me." Derrick loved to listen to her music. She had a way of relaxing his mind and connecting with his inner soul. As the instrumental intro began to play, he looked out the window and celebrated within. This was the victory he had been waiting for his entire life.

The whole world seemed still as a light rain began to splash against the fogged window. He couldn't have written a better script if he tried. A million-dollar contract in his pocket, a beautiful woman in his bed, a hit of cognac, and Sade's smooth hypnotic voice to set it off. God is good, he thought to himself. It was pointless to try to fight back the tears. Watching the birth of a son couldn't have made him any more proud. In many ways this was his baby, his way of saying, "I am somebody!" While wiping his face with the sleeve of his shirt, he inconspicuously looked over his shoulder to see if Angela was watching, but she was still asleep. And even if she was awake, he made sure it was too dark for her to see him cry.

TENDER YOUNG THANG

Here I am freezing my ass off in Chicago and Derrick is down in Miami golfing and playing tennis in the 75-degree Florida sunshine. He had the nerve to call me on his cell phone yesterday while he was lounging outside at the hotel pool. I swear I wanted to reach through the phone and choke the shit out of him. But that's all right though, I'll be getting away from this cold weather myself right after Valentine's Day is over. I've been planning since last February 15 on how to make this year more prosperous than the previous ones.

Last year we sold over 500 dozen long-stem red and yellow roses; half of those sales came after three o'clock on Valentine's Day. Every year it's the same old thing. Men come rushing in at the last minute knocking each other over trying to buy whatever they can get their hands on.

The store seems more like the stock exchange with all the shoving, shouting, and plastic being flashed around. "Here, I'll take it!" they yell. "Charge it to my Visa!" It's funny watching them scrambling like chickens with their heads cut off for anything that resembles a Valentine's Day gift. Sometimes they purchase birthday and anniversary cards just to avoid going home to their wives and girlfriends empty-hand-ed. But all that excitement is two weeks away, thank goodness. All I want to do in the meantime is relax and continue to spend time with Nikki on the weekends. We still haven't had sex yet, but I'm sure I'll be getting some real soon.

The first to notice a change in my routine was Mark. We usually got together on Sundays to watch sports and drink beers. So when I started making excuses for not being able to get together, he knew what was up. At first he didn't get too upset, probably figuring it wouldn't last long. But after I can-celed for the third straight weekend he got on my case and warned me by saying, "Don't forget what happens every time you get involved with **those** types." His point was well taken. I have a horrible track record when it comes to dealing with beautiful young women. One look at those slender, sexy, firm young bodies and I'm hooked. I've tried dating women my own age who were probably more mature and financially sta-ble, but for whatever reason I couldn't get into them. They either had combative attitudes or their bodies were worn out from too much sex and not enough exercise.

Mark thinks it's a control thing. You know, the father fig-ure syndrome. And to a large degree, he's right! I mean, the younger women that I've experienced seemed more receptive to learning. And they were much better listeners, too. As long as I backed up my words with actions, my authority was never

challenged. On the other hand, the older and professional
women that I've tried to date would challenge me on everything. If I said the sky was blue, they would argue it was green
just for the sake of being contrary. I need a woman who is
open for education and inspiration, not one who is about trying
to prove she's my equal. But that argument never satisfied
Mark, who was very distrustful of black women, especially
young uneducated ones. He claims they always have hidden
agendas. We had plans to get together this Sunday afternoon,
and I knew he was going to pick up right where he left off. At
2:00 on the dot, I saw his white Blazer pull into my driveway.
I took a deep breath and prepared myself for his Montel
Williams lecture. Although Mark was three years younger
than me, he thought he was my daddy. When I heard the knock
at the door, I took my time getting there.

"If you're a Jehovah's Witness, there's nobody home," I
joked.

"O-o-open up, it's me."

When I opened the door, Mark fell onto the floor holding
his stomach and gasping for air.

"Are you all right?"

"Oh shit, oh shit!" he yelled.

"What's wrong, Mark?" I asked while stooping down to
see if he was shot. "Tell me where you're hit!"

"Oh my God," he said, sounding more like he was laughing. "I can't believe what I just saw."

"Man, ain't nuthin' wrong with you," I said. "Get your butt
up off my floor. You scared the shit out of me."

"I'm sorry, man, but I couldn't help myself."

"What's so damned funny?"

Mark wiped the tears out his eyes, took off his coat, and
walked over to the living room window.

"You know that crazy old man who lives across the street?"
Mark was peeking out the window from behind the curtains.

"Mr. Owens? What about him?"

"Wasn't he the one who was complaining about those kids

throwing rocks and snowballs at his house?"

"Yeah, and?"

"Well, as I was driving up to your house, those kids were making snowballs, getting ready to barrage his front window. Then all of a sudden the snowman in his yard got up and started chasing them. I've never seen anything so hilarious in my entire life. Those kids were knocking each other over trying to get away. One of them fell on the ground and started screaming for his mama."

It was easy to see why Mark almost pissed on himself. I had to laugh too. Mr. Owens had done some crazy things over the years, but disguising himself as a snowman, now that was an original. I should have known he'd find a way to get even. That crafty old bastard didn't have nuthin' better to do with his time but plot on how to terrorize little kids. Over the summer he kept every baseball, kite, and frisbee that landed in his yard. When the parents went over to ask for them back he called the police and threatened to have them arrested for trespassing.

This whole snowball and rock-throwing incident could have been avoided if he would have acted more neighborly. Last October, on Halloween, he put a big sign up in his front lawn that read, Trick or Treaters Beware, Poison Candy! That was asking for trouble. I mean, how much can a bag of M&M's and Snickers cost?

"Ok, that's enough," I said, trying to gain my composure. "Where are those videos I asked you to bring?"

"Damn, I was laughing so hard I forgot to get them out the car."

While Mark ran back outside, I put away the inventory sheets I was working on and got a couple of Miller Drafts out the fridge. I was hoping he didn't forget to buy some munchies. I hated drinking beer without chips or pretzels.

"Thank God," I said when I saw the cheddar and sour cream Ruffles under his arm.

"Thank God for what?"

"Never mind, just let me see what you got. Hopefully you

brought at least one decent movie this time."

"Hey, if you wanna be critical, you can take your cheap ass down to Blockbuster and pay three dollars a day."

Although I gave him a hard time, Mark was a connoisseur when it came to videos. He turned me on to movies that I never heard of before. Last month we watched, *By Dawn's Early Light*, with James Earl Jones. And another movie called, *Someone To Watch Over Me*, with Tom Berringer. Both were great!

"I hope you brought *The Long Kiss Goodnight*, with Samuel L. Jackson and Geena Davis," I said pulling the videos out the bag. "I've been dying to check that one out."

"It's in there, along with one of my special picks of the month."

"What in the hell is this movie, *The Fan*, with Wesley Snipes about? I never heard of it."

"When are you ever going to learn to trust me?" Mark said, getting up to go to use the bathroom. "I review movies better than Siskel and Ebert."

I put in *The Long Kiss Goodnight* video, cracked the top to my brew, and kicked my feet up on the stool.

"What happened to Tony?" I asked.

"He had to babysit Erikah. Valarie didn't come by to pick her up on time."

"Again? She's really giving him a hard time."

"She sure is," Mark shouted from inside the bathroom. "To be honest with you, I don't know how he puts up with it."

"Me either."

"If she keeps this up, Tracie is going to go upside her head."

"I'd pay fifty bucks to see that one on pay per view."

When Mark came out of the bathroom he grabbed his beer and joined me on the sofa.

"So, where is Christie?"

"At home in bed, where I should be right now. Where's Nikki?"

"Her and Jason went home early this morning," I said without thinking.

That did it! Mark knew about the last two weekends that Nikki and Jason spent over at my place, but I kept this weekend a secret, not wanting to hear his mouth. Like I said, he thought he was my father.

"Why do you insist on spending so much time with this woman and her son? You haven't known her two months yet and you're already playing house."

"All I did was take them out a couple of times to Chuck E Cheese and The Discovery Zone, what's the big deal?"

"The big deal is, children get attached. You may think it's all fun and games, but for them it's a commitment. Next thing you know they're asking about you and depending on you to be around."

"Like I said, it's only been a couple of times."

"If you were Pinocchio, your nose would be dragging on the damn floor right now," Mark said. "Jason has probably been over here every weekend since New Year's. Which means Nikki has too. I thought you were going to give that situation a break?"

"Look, man. This is my life, ok!"

"Yeah, but I'm the one who has to listen to your ass whining on the phone when you get your feelings hurt. You don't call Tony and Derrick with the drama, only me. So as far as I'm concerned, it is my business. And besides, I'm only trying to look out for you."

"But Nikki is different!" I said confidently. "She's not anything like those other women I've dated."

"And what makes her so different, Ben? She's young, uneducated, and broker than a motherfucker. In my book, that puts her right up there with the rest of them. Not only that, but the father of her son is a big-time gang banger. I asked around about him. Even the thugs say he's nuthin' but trouble."

"People make mistakes, Mark. That was seven years ago."

"Maybe she got pregnant seven years ago, but you told me

yourself she was seeing this loser up until May of last year. Doesn't that tell you something about her character?"

"Why are you so hostile towards Nikki? She was polite and respectful towards you at the party on New Year's Eve."

"Because I'm your friend, that's why," Mark said forcefully, "and I know how conniving black women can be."

"Like I said, Nikki isn't like that."

"Ok, then. Explain to me why her personals are laying all around your house?"

"What are you talking about?"

"I can see her panties on your bedroom door knob from here. And there's a curling iron under your bathroom sink."

"When did you start snooping around my bathroom?"

"I wasn't snooping, you idiot. I was trying to find a bar of soap to wash my hands with."

"So, she left a few things by mistake. So what?"

"For a man who knows everything about business, you don't know shit when it comes to dealing with women," he said, shaking his head in disgust. "That woman is marking her territory. The curling iron is one thing, I might have let that slide. But how in the hell do you just happen to forget to take your *draws* home?"

"She was in a hurry."

"Oh yeah? Then I guess she must have forgotten to take that stuff over there home too," Mark said, pointing at the Nintendo cartridges and red Power Ranger on top of the entertainment center. "This place is starting to look like Sesame Street."

"Fuck you, Mark!" I said getting up from the sofa. "At least I'm not laying up with some uppity white bitch!"

Mark stood up, too, and got in my face. For the first time since grammar school, we were about to throw down. Both our fists were balled and the adrenaline was pumping. But neither of us wanted to take the first swing. After what seemed like an eternity, he stepped away, put on his coat, and stormed out the door without saying a word. But I didn't care about how upset he was. Mark was way out of line. Nikki was my concern, not his. If I wanted her to spend the night seven days a week, it was none of his damned business.

Nikki was supposed to be finished with her last client by four o'clock. It was four-fifteen and she still hadn't called. I hated the idea of going next door to get her but I was pressed for time because of an important five-thirty meeting I had with a city councilman. Naomi's Hair Salon was always crowded on Fridays, and I didn't want the attention. But Nikki loved for me to come over so she could make the other girls jealous, especially the owner, Mrs. Naomi Phillips, who has been trying to get me in bed for years. Last fourth of July she came over after closing, drunk as hell, wearing nothing under her trench coat but a pair of laced pink panties. I wanted to go for it, but I didn't. She was a married woman and I was too uncomfortable with the idea of sleeping with a business associate who worked right next door. That's a definite no-no. After building up enough courage, I took a deep breath, exhaled, and then walked next door into the den of lionesses.

Looking through the large tinted glass window I could see that the salon was jam-packed. My first thought was to turn and run, but I was desperate to see Nikki. When I opened the door, the smell of chemicals and burnt hair overwhelmed me. My eyes were stinging and I felt lightheaded. How in the hell can they stand it in here? Right away Naomi spotted me and put down the hot comb she was holding and excused herself.

"Well, well, well, if it isn't Mr. Big Shot from next door," she said while brushing up against me slightly with her fake 38 DD breasts.

"Hello Naomi. How's business?"

"Couldn't be better, and how are things with you?"

"This is my time of the year, you know that."

"That's right. Valentine's Day is next week. I hope you

have something special for me."

"You know I always look out for my favorite next door neighbor?."

"Yes, you do. But not as well as you should be," she said, seductively winking her eye.

"So, how is **Mr.** Phillips," I said trying to block.

"Oh, him. He's all right, I guess. Yesterday he left for Detroit on business. As a matter of fact he'll be out of town until next Sunday."

"Be sure to tell him I said hello. By the way, where is Nikki?"

When I asked that, I could hear the sound of her face crack. Naomi couldn't handle rejection, especially being as sexy as she was. Any other man would have taken her up on that offer in a heartbeat.

"She's in the back doing a manicure," she said with an attitude. Then she turned and walked back over to her client.

If it wasn't for the fact that Nikki was one of her best stylists, I'm sure Naomi would have fired her the day after we began dating. But being the smart businesswoman that she is, her pride took a back seat to cash money. I waved hello to a couple of the girls that I knew and made my way to the back room where Nikki was set up. She was in the middle of filing the nails of a very dark-complected woman when I surprised her.

"Hey, you!" I shouted. "I thought we had a date?"

"Hi sweetheart," she said, jumping up from the table to give me a kiss. "I've only got one more client and I'll be ready to go."

"Ok, come see me when you're done. I'll be next door."

"No, baby, don't go. Stay here and keep me company. Renee and I were in the middle of a conversation about your favorite topic. I'm sure you'll find it interesting."

Nikki pulled a chair out of the hallway for me to sit down on and went back to filing.

"So, what we're you saying, Renee, about men needing to

grow up?" Nikki asked.

"I was saying that men need to grow up and stop chasing after these young-minded little girls and get themselves a real woman!" Renee said.

"And what exactly qualifies a woman as being real?" I asked.

"You know, a woman who earns her own money, pays her own bills, and doesn't take any shit off of a man."

"Are you trying say that older women don't get played?"

"That's right! A woman with experience under her belt knows how to tell a man to go to hell!"

"Before I respond to that, do you mind if I ask you a question?"

"Go right ahead."

"Do you have a man?"

"What's that got to do with anything?"

"Is that a yes or no?"

"For your information I don't, not at this particular time. I'm taking time out to get myself together. And so are many of my strong, independent, career-minded girlfriends."

"And what are we men supposed to do while you and your strong, independent girlfriends are taking time out, buy plastic dolls?" I asked raising my voice. "Let me tell you something miss, I don't know you well enough to say what I really want to say, but I will say this, a woman is a woman. It doesn't matter how much money she makes or how old she is. It's all about being in touch with who you are and knowing what you want out of life. And by the way, I know just as many messed-up women over forty as I do under."

"You're just making excuses like the rest of these insecure men out here. The only reason you're dating this little girl is so you can train her to do what you want."

"Now wait one damn minute," Nikki said, releasing Renee's hand onto the table. "You train a dog!"

"If the shoe fits!"

"I believe I'm through with your nails, Renee," Nikki said,

trying to stay poised.

"Good, 'cause I'm tired of looking at your bony ass, anyway!" she said, getting loud.

"You're just jealous because nobody wants to be bothered with you. You old hag!"

Renee gave Nikki a dirty look, took ten dollars out her purse, and threw it onto the table.

"Here, take your damn money! It's the last time you'll get any of my business."

"That's fine by me. I didn't like rubbing those big, rusty hands of yours, anyway. You need to put some WD 40 on those rascals."

Nikki had a way of comically putting people in check. Renee couldn't do anything but put on her cheap leather coat and leave.

"Now you see why I'm so determined to get my education." Nikki said. "I don't want to deal with these ignorant people for the rest of my life."

"Speaking of school. We should both get going. I've got an appointment at five-thirty and you have class tonight."

"Before we go can I ask you for a small favor?"

"Sure baby, what is it?"

"This is a little awkward for me."

"Just come right out and say it."

"Well, I haven't been able to work much over the last couple of weeks because of all the homework I've had. And my rent is due next week, and..."

"Hold on, baby. Are you trying to tell me that you need a couple of dollars?"

"It would really help out a lot."

"Here, take this," I said putting two hundred dollars in her hand."

"Thanks, Ben," she said, giving me a hug and tongue kiss. "I'll pay you back as soon as I can, I promise."

"Don't sweat it, sweetheart. Just take care of your business."

"You're so good to me, baby," she said, reaching down and palming my penis through my pants. "What can I ever do to make this up to you."

"How about finding a baby sitter tonight."

"And?"

"And pack that black teddy and those garter belts you told me about."

"And then what?"

"And then come over to my place and give me what you can't get back."

"I've got a better idea," she said while provocatively licking her lips. "Why don't I skip class tonight and go over to your place now and be there waiting for you when you get back."

My dick got as hard as Chinese Calculus. It took me all of two seconds to whip the extra set of keys out of my pants pocket.

"Give me at least until seven before you come home," she said. "I want everything to be laid out just right."

"Are you sure about this, Nikki? I don't want you to feel that just because I gave you a few dollars that you owe me something."

"But I do owe you, Ben," she said in a pacifying tone. "You've been a good little boy and tonight mama's gonna give you a special reward."

We walked outside, exchanged goodbye kisses, and I left for my meeting feeling as light on my feet as Sammy Davis Jr. After two long months, ten dinner dates, and almost $500 in cash, I was finally going to get my hands on that tender young thang!

Valentine's Day morning, the phones were ringing off the hook. Floral arrangements were being shipped out at a rate of more than fifty dozen an hour. The boxes of assorted chocolates were selling by the hundreds, and the stuffed animals were moving faster than Tickle Me Elmo dolls. By one o'clock we had already broken our single day sales record of $45,000. And that didn't include the money from the contract for setting up the arrangement at The State of Illinois Building downtown or the sales from our vendors who were pulling down two hundred dollars an hour selling roses on the street corners and downtown in the subways. If it's one thing I learned growing up in the ghetto, it was how to hustle.

I wanted badly to pick up the phone and call somebody to brag to, but everybody was either out of town or unavailable. Nikki was busy next door at Naomi's putting in extension braids, Derrick was on the West Coast promoting the magazine, Tony was working on rehabbing another property, and Mark was on the Carnival Cruise with Christie. But even if he was in town, I probably wouldn't have called him anyway. He's stubborn as hell, and so am I. I'm not calling him until he agrees to stop dogging Nikki. Then maybe we can get on with our friendship.

But I really missed kickin' it with him on Sundays, drinking beer and checking out new flicks. But I've got to draw the line somewhere. My feelings for Nikki are very strong. He's got to learn to respect that. Hopefully, when he gets back we can sit down and work this out like *boys*, preferably without Derrick and Tony around. Not that I don't trust their opinion, but Mark and I have a special kind of relationship. We know things about one another that no one else knows. I could tell him my deepest secrets without it getting out. That's why I miss talking with him so much. I needed to tell him how much I loved Nikki and that I think she's the one. But what I really needed most was his advice, specifically about shacking. I've asked Nikki to move in with me at the end of the month.

DADDY'S LITTLE GIRL

"**E**rikah, get your behind in here and finish eating your breakfast!" Tony yelled.

"I'm finished, Daddy!"

"No you're not. You still have a half glass of milk and two strips of bacon on your plate. You know we don't waste food around here."

"But I'm right in the middle of watching my cartoons. I'll come get it during the commercial."

Erikah usually came running the second she heard Tony's

deep voice, but since Valarie has been dating this guy named Cedric, she had become very spoiled and undisciplined. I loved Erikah like she was my own daughter but when it came to discipline I stayed out the way. This was strictly between father and daughter.

"What did you say?" Tony said sounding angry. "If you don't get your butt in here right now I'm going to beat the black off of you."

Erikah quickly got up off the floor and ran into the kitchen.

"When I call you, I expect you to come immediately. Do you understand?" Tony asked with his finger in Erikah's face.

"Yes sir," Erikah said, with tears running down her cinnamon brown cheeks.

"Now, I don't know what's going on with you lately, but it had better stop."

"But Daddy, Mommy and Cedric don't make me eat everything on my plate."

I could practically see the steam rising from Tony's head. This was the second time she used Cedric's name to defend her behavior. The first time had something to do with her going to bed too early. This Cedric person was beginning to seriously interfere with Tony's ability to parent. But instead of taking it out on Erikah, he decided to call Valarie later that evening to find out what was going on.

"Ok, sweetheart, stop crying. Daddy didn't mean to raise his voice at you. I just need you to understand that when I ask you to do something, it's for your own good."

"I understand, Daddy. I'm sorry too." She gave him a hug as far up his waist as she could reach.

"Are you still my beautiful little princess?"

"Yes."

"Well, give me a kiss and finish eating your food like a good little girl."

Tony stooped down so she could give him a smack on the lips. Then she went over to the table and sat down and started eating. As he walked back toward the living room, she called for him.

"Daddy!"

"Yes, sweetheart."

"I love you."

"I love you too, Princess."

It was times like this that made me love Tony most. He was a shrewd businessman, and could be very tough in the streets. But when it came to the women in his life, he was a pussycat. I noticed that from the first time he took me over to meet his mother. Tony was very respectful, always responding to her by saying, "yes ma'am, and no ma'am." Never once did he curse or even use the word *dag*. When he was a kid his mother said it sounded too much like damn. It's amazing that more women don't take the man's relationship with his mother into consideration when they are dating and especially getting married. The way I figure it, if he doesn't respect the woman who brought him into the world, he's definitely not going to respect you.

Later on that evening while Erikah was next-door playing with Tevin and Kevin, Tony called Valarie to confront her about Cedric. I snuck into the bedroom, picked up the phone and waited for her to say something to get him upset. If she did, I was ready to curse her out.

"Hello Valarie? We need to talk," Tony said.

"What's the problem?"

"The problem is Erikah. I've been having some trouble dealing with her, lately."

"What's that have to do with me?"

"Well, when I ask her to do something like go to bed or to clean her plate, she responds with, but Cedric doesn't make me do this and Cedric doesn't make me do that."

"You're not jealous, are you, Tony?"

"I'm not joking around, Valarie, this is serious!"

"Look, Tony, I was going to tell you after Erikah's birthday party, but I may as well tell you now."

"Tell me what?" Tony said, sounding concerned.

"Cedric is going to be moving in on the first of April."

"Are you out of your mind? You don't even know this man. He could be a mass murderer for all you know."

"Cedric and I are old friends. We go way back to high school."

"If he's such a bosom buddy, where has he been for the last thirteen years? The first I ever heard his name mentioned was a month ago."

"Now you're getting a little too personal."

"I'm supposed to get personal!" Tony said, getting excited. "You're talking about bringing some strange man in to live under the same roof as my baby!"

"You just wait one minute!" She said snapped back. "I didn't take you through this kind of interrogation when you started seeing Tracie, now did I?"

"First of all, let's get something straight. Tracie didn't even meet Erikah until after we were dating for at least six months. Secondly, I went out of my way to get you two together so that you could get acquainted. We both agreed that this was the process new people had to go through."

"And you'll get that same opportunity at Erikah's birthday party in two weeks. So why don't you wait until then before you jump the gun." She was sounding uncharacteristically calm. "I'm sure everything is going to work out fine."

After hanging up the phone, I ran into the living room. Tony was sitting back on the sofa with his hand over his forehead, looking dejected.

"You know Valarie is getting *some*, don't you?"

"Yep, I could hear it in her voice," Tony said. "The last time she was that calm was two years ago when she was dating that stripper named Hurricane."

"So, what are you going to do?"

"To be honest with you, baby, I really don't know. She does have the right to see whomever she pleases. And even if I decided to take her to court, the judge would never give me custody, not without concrete proof of neglect."

"I guess we'll just have to wait it out until March 26 to see who or what we're dealing with."

"This is going to be the longest damn two weeks of my life." Tony said. "I hate going through this same old shit year after year."

"It'll be ok, sweetheart," I said, putting my hand on his shoulder to comfort him."

"It's not ok!" he said, walking away. "There are too many crazy bastards in this world for her to gamble the way she does. One of these days she's going to bring the wrong person home. All I know is I'm not tolerating one single inappropriate incident from this guy, not one! If Erikah tells me he even so much as brushes up against her the wrong way, I'll kill him. I mean it!"

Tony stormed out the door, got into his car, and sped off. I had never seen him so angry before, never! You always hear experts taking about how powerful the protective instincts are of a mother. But watching Tony over the last four years has shown me that the love of a true father can be more overwhelming than anything on earth.

THE CEDRIC SITUATION

It's a week before Erikah's birthday and I can already feel myself getting stressed out. Valarie and I had been gradually reaching a level of civility for eight years but now that this guy Cedric has come onto the scene, I know we're about to get back to feuding like never before. So, be it! I'm not about to stand by and allow them to play house with my daughter. Valarie is rushing into this thing way too fast. She's not giving me or herself an opportunity to thoroughly evaluate this move. Living with someone on a 24-hours-a-day basis is a big decision, especially when a child is involved. Hell, it took me and Tracie four years to get to that point, and we didn't even have kids in the house to consider.

But what really makes my blood boil is how this guy is handling, or not handling, his responsibility. I mean, what kind of man moves into a one-bedroom apartment with a woman and her child? That's trifling! If he was a **real man**, he would've had a plan to provide adequate living conditions up front instead of leeching off of Valarie's limited space. Two adults and a child living in a small one-bedroom apartment is just too damned crowded. And then there's the money issue. It's no secret that I own a successful construction company. I can't help thinking that Cedric is using Valarie's dumb ass to get into my pocket.

The stress was getting to me, I had to vent. Derrick couldn't have come back in town soon enough. We hadn't seen one another in over a month, so I suggested that he come by to visit and get me up to speed on how things were going with the magazine. But I also wanted his input on this Cedric situation. He always had all the right answers. When he and Angela drove up, I politely said my hellos and ushered him down into the basement. To give us some privacy, Tracie took Angela for a drive to see the house we were having built in Naperville. The ride was about 30 minutes, each way, more than enough time to talk things over with Derrick.

"So, where did you fly in from today?" I asked.

"Cleveland."

"How was it? One of my clients told me it was kinda tired."

"Actually, it was pretty nice!" Derrick said enthusiastically. "I went out to this night club called The Mirage, downtown on the Flats."

"Was it live?"

"Boy, was it live! The place was laid out very classy. It even had a dance floor outside near the water. We've all got to get together and go down there during the summer. The one thing I didn't like about Cleveland was the way their traffic lights were set up."

"Traffic lights?"

"Yeah, man. They have these high traffic signals that sit in the middle of the intersection; not on the side of the corners like here in Chicago. If you don't pay close attention you could run a red light and kill somebody."

"Actually I was more interested in how things were going with the magazine."

"The magazine is taking off like a rocket! As a matter of fact, I was taking Angela out to celebrate tonight."

"Celebrate what?"

"Well, I was going to wait until we all got together to play ball to make the big announcement," he said, standing up like he was about to say something important. "But I guess I can give you the privilege of being the first to know."

"What is it, fool?"

"As of four o'clock yesterday, Motif Publishing has secured three of our largest contracts ever."

"With whom?"

"Let's just say that all three are listed as Fortune 500 companies."

"Stop stalling," I said, wrapping my hands around his neck. "Just tell me which ones!"

"Ok, ok. The contracts are with Coke, American Express, and General Motors."

"Derrick, you hit the jackpot! Congratulations, man!"

"Thanks, partner. God knows it's been a long and hard battle to get to this point. Those recommendations from Mr. Starks really made the difference. Now it seems like I'm receiving one blessing after another. Everything is going my way."

"I wish I could say the same," I said, killing the moment.

"I had a strange feeling something was wrong. Are you and Tracie fighting again?"

"No, it's much worse than that."

"What is it!"

"Remember when I told you about a guy named Cedric that

Valarie was dating?"

"Yeah, what about him?"

"Well, I talked to Valarie today and she told me that he was moving in with her."

"Boy, there must be something in the water. First Ben, now Valarie."

"What do you mean, first Ben?"

"I guess I may as well tell you. Nikki moved in with him about three weeks ago. He and Mark had a big falling out over it from what I understand."

"No wonder he's been so short with me on the phone lately."

"It was supposed to be a secret between him and Mark, but Mark let it slip out when we got on the subject of shacking up. Just don't tell him I told you."

"I've got my own problems," I said. "At least Nikki is moving in with a man who has a steady job and his own house. This Cedric character is living with one of his friends named Geno out in Hazel Crest."

"How old is this bum, anyway?"

"Thirty-six. Same age as me."

"You mean to tell me this grown-ass man still doesn't have his own apartment? What in the world is Valarie thinking about?"

"That's not the worst of it. She doesn't even know where he works. Either that or she's too embarrassed to tell me."

"He sounds like that Tommy character on the TV show *Martin*."

"This is serious, Derrick. Exposing Erikah to the wrong type of man on a day-to-day basis can be extremely dangerous. Kids are sexually assaulted every day. Not to mention, coming up dead. I'm not going to let that happen to my little girl."

"I hear you, partner. I love her too. Tell me what you need me to do."

"First we need to find out who this clown is. Do you still have your contacts downtown at the police department?"

"I sure do."

"Good, we can do a background check to see if he has any priors."

"No problem, I'll get right on it. All I need is his full name."

"No, we've got to go further than that. I want to run his fingerprints."

"Damn, Tony. You must really have a bad feeling about this one."

"I do, Derrick, and it's seriously messing with my head." I said. "Valarie has been hanging out with a lot of shady characters lately, and there's no telling what she's getting herself into. As much as I hate her guts, I never want to see anything bad happen to her. Erikah needs both of us."

It was Saturday morning, March 26. Tracie got up bright and early to get Erikah's presents out of the car. The night before we took her to see the movie *Toy Story* and then out for Uno's Pizza to begin celebrating early. We intentionally kept her up late so that she would sleep through most of the morning. But like most kids on holidays and birthdays, Erikah was up at the crack of dawn. Before Tracie could sneak back in with her gifts, Erikah came running into the bedroom all pumped up and ready to go.

"It's my birthday, it's my birthday!" she sang.

"It is? Nobody told me," I said.

"Are you for real?"

"Get that frown off your face, I'm only kidding, Happy Birthday, sweetheart!"

"Thank you Daddy, where's Tracie?"

"She went out to the car to get your presents."

"No wonder I couldn't find them."

"We knew you'd be snooping around trying to spoil your surprise, that's why we hid them outside. But I promise you, you'll be happy when you see what we got you."

"What did you get me Daddy, tell me, please tell me!" Erikah shouted while jumping up and down on the king-sized canopy bed.

"You're just going to have to wait and see," I said, trying to hold her still. "Now settle down before you bust a vein."

Two seconds later Tracie comes walking in carrying six large boxes. Her arms were so full I could hardly see her big head. Normally we didn't splurge on non-education gifts, such as dolls and makeup kits, but this year we decided to go for it!. Besides, Erikah had received straight A's on her last two report cards and had been behaving much better. But it probably had more to do with my reaction to the Cedric situation. It made me much more protective and appreciative of my one and only child.

"Surprise, surprise! Happy Birthday, Erikah!"

"Oh Daddy, can I open them, please, please!"

"Not all of them, just one."

"Why not?" she said pouting.

"Because I want you to open them around all of your friends at your birthday party."

"Ok," she said after thinking over how much she wanted to show off. "Which box can I open?"

"Why don't you go open the big one in the living room? I think you'll like what you find inside."

Erikah jumped off the bed and took off running. A few seconds later we heard a loud thump, and then the sounds of her tiny feet running across the floor again.

"Don't worry, I'm all right," she shouted.

Tracie and I burst out laughing knowing she had slipped and fallen on the hallway rug and was trying to play it off. "That girl is gonna kill herself if she doesn't learn to slow down," I said. We sat and waited for her reaction to the most expensive gift of all, a Macintosh computer. Erikah was very computer-literate for an eight-year-old, and we wanted to make sure she didn't fall behind the other students at her school who had personal computers at home.

"Oh Daddy!" she screamed as she came flying back into the room and onto the bed. "Thank you, thank you, thank you! You're the best daddy in the whole wide world!"

"And you're the best daughter in the whole wide world," I said. "But aren't you going to thank Tracie? She helped pay for it."

"Thank you too, Tracie. You're the best second mommy in the whole wide world."

It was Erikah's day. I kicked things off by preparing her favorite breakfast, pancakes, bacon, boiled eggs, and hash browns with cheese. Then we all got together in the living room to watch her favorite cartoons, Spiderman, The X-Men, and the really silly one called The Tick. At 11:00 we began getting ready to head out to the south suburbs to Cedric's house, or should I say, his friend Geno's house. Although the party didn't start until three o'clock, we got an early start so that we could pick up Tevin and Kevin, and then stop by my mother's house so she could give Erikah her gifts before heading out to the party. When I called her earlier that morning to asked her if she changed her mind about going, she said, "Now, baby, I don't like long car rides. And **you know** I can't stand the sight of Valarie's conniving, nappy-headed behind!" Needless to say, those were my feelings exactly.

We arrived at Geno's house at 2:30. Right away I was uneasy. The house was very lavish and there were several expensive cars parked out front in the long driveway. Two Mercedes, a Cadillac, an Acura Legend, and a Porsche 911 with a personalized plate that read CEDRIC 1. As far as I knew, Valarie didn't know any entertainers or professional athletes. Hell, she didn't even know anyone with a college degree, which meant Cedric and his friend Geno were either born into wealthy families or they were drug dealers. Tracie and I didn't say a word, we just gave each other **that look** and stepped out of the car. While

Erikah and I got her gifts out the trunk, Tracie helped Tevin and Kevin out the back seat. They were both wearing plastic sunglasses and identical blue jean outfits, the style that kids wear backwards. I swear they looked like a miniature version of the rap group Kriss Kross. Once we got everything together, we walked up to the house and rang the bell. When the door swung open a beautiful young woman wearing a mini skirt invited us to come in.

"Hi, I'm Tonya. You must be here for the party!"

"Yes we are. My name is Tony Page. This is my fiancee, Tracie. These two handsome young men are Tevin and Kevin, and this is my daughter Erikah, the birthday girl."

"So this is Erikah?" she said enthusiastically. "I should have recognized you from the pictures your mother showed me. Happy Birthday! Come over here and give me a hug!"

Erikah looked up at me checking to see if it was ok. She was very leery of strangers, especially men. Which is exactly how I trained her.

"Come with me," Tonya said, leading Erikah by the hand. "Your mama is out back barbecuing."

Following her was no problem at all. That outfit she had on left nothing to the imagination. Even the twins were looking at her like a piece of meat. Tevin tried to reach out and touch her on the behind, but luckily Tracie intercepted his tiny hand. As close as I was walking, she probably would have thought it was me. After weaving our way through a crowd of rowdy children, Tonya led us out into the back yard. The first person I saw was Valarie. She was standing at the barbecue grill making a plate.

"Look who's here!" Tonya shouted.

"There's my little angel!" Valarie said. She put down the plate and extended her arms. "Come give Mommy a kiss."

From where we were standing I could see three men sitting at a card table laughing and drinking beer. One of them was a big husky guy about Ben's size, with a scar on his face. The other was was a skinny little weasel with an annoying gold tooth and wearing about ten pounds of jewelry. He seemed to be doing most of the talking. And the other was a tall athletic-look-ing brother with wavy hair. Not naturally wavy like mine. He had chemical assistance. Without even having to ask, I knew which one was Cedric. But I asked anyway, just for the hell of it.

"So, which one is Cedric?"

"Aren't we impatient!" Valarie said.

"Look, I'm not in the mood for games. I've waited look enough to meet this - **gentleman**," I hesitated to say.

"Why don't you get the kids situated first? I know they must be starving?"

"Honey, I'll take care of Erikah and the boys," Tracie said, taking Tevin and Kevin by the hand. "Go take care of your busi-ness."

"Thank you for being so considerate, Tracie," Valarie said in a phony tone. "By the way, how are you doing?"

"I'm doing just fine. Thanks for asking."

You could cut the tension in the air with a dull knife when those two were together. Putting them under the same roof was like lighting a match to a can of kerosene. It could explode any-time. After Valarie finished fixing her plate, she escorted me over to where the three men were sitting and introduced me.

"Excuse me everyone, I'd like for you to meet Tony, Erikah's father. Tony, this is Tiny and our host Geno."

"What's up, Tony?" they both said, as they stood up and gave me contemptuous stares and weak handshakes.

"And this is my man Cedric," Valarie said as she proudly put her arms around him.

Cedric paused for a moment, took a pull off his cigarette, and stood up slowly to shake my hand. I wanted to laugh in his face because I knew he was trying to play mind games. But what he ended up doing was showing me his insecurity.

"Hello, Tony. It's nice to finally meet you." He was standing as erect as he could trying to be intimidating. "Valarie has told me a lot about you."

"I wish I could say the same." I looked him dead in the eyes.

"She hasn't told me anything about you."

"A little mystery never hurt anybody."

"I don't like mysteries myself. There's always a big buildup of suspense and then a surprise ending, and I don't like surprises."

"Whether a person likes something or not doesn't necessarily make a difference," he said with a smirk on his face. "Sometimes shit just happens and you don't have any control."

"Well, Shitdric, I mean, Cedric, there's two things I do have control over, my business and my daughter. And if anything or **anybody** affects them negatively, in any way, I will personally see to it that those things or persons are eliminated."

When I said that, he wiped that silly grin off his face. We stared each other down waiting to see who would make the next move. I was praying he would take a swing so I could knock his ass out! But before anything could happen, Tonya shouted for us to come inside to sing Happy Birthday to Erikah. Cedric unballed his fist, put his arm around Valarie, and began walking toward the house with his boys close behind.

Damn, I wish at least one of my friends were here right now, I thought to myself. Any two of us could easily take out the three of those punks. But I was outnumbered with no back-up, except for Tracie. And judging by the looks of the rough-looking women I saw inside the house, they would probably all gang up on her. Too bad my friends had other obligations. Derrick cancelled at the last minute, saying he had to fly out to Baltimore, Mark volunteered to referee a karate tournament, and Ben said one of his managers called in sick. Their timing couldn't have been worse.

By five o'clock my patience had completely run out. Cedric had bumped into me twice without saying excuse me, and I wasn't about to let it slide the next time. I figured the best thing to do was to get out of there before I ended up ruining my daughter's birthday by getting into a fight. But Cedric was determined to push me over the edge. When I came back into the living room from getting our coats out the closet, he was sitting on the sofa next to Tracie with his arm resting closely behind her. My first impulse was to smack the taste out of his mouth but instead I laid back and trusted Tracie to handle it herself. She was a crafty woman with years of experience of dealing with nitwits.

"Excuse me, Tracie. I just wanted to tell you that you are a very beautiful and classy lady." He was trying to sound charming. "Tony is a very lucky man to have a woman like you in his corner."

"Why, thank you, Cedric. But I think I'm pretty lucky myself."

"And how is that?"

"Tony is a wonderful father, an incredible lover, very attractive, and to top it off, he's one hell of a businessman."

"He almost sounds like a carbon copy of me, except I'm better looking."

"A carbon copy, huh? I guess that means you have a job."

"Of course I do. I'm in the, ah, construction business."

"Oh, really?" Tracie said with her eyebrow raised. "I've worked with every major construction company in Chicago. Which one do you work for."

"Well, I ah, work for a company downstate. At least I did before I injured my back about three months ago."

"So, what kinds of construction did you specialize in? Was it road construction? Commercial or industrial building? Which one?"

Cedric was completely stunned. He didn't have the slightest idea of what she was talking about. He went over trying to run his weak game and Tracie flipped the script and had him looking stupid. He eased out of the conversation and headed towards the twins from hell, Kevin and Tevin, who were sitting on the floor playing video games. I know I should have warned him, but I didn't.

"So, who are you two shorties?" Cedric asked.

"My name isn't Shorty, it's Kevin."

"And I'm Tevin."

"Okay, Kevin and Tevin, tell me what's up?"

"Ain't nuthin' up but the sky," Kevin said, looking up at Cedric through his plastic shades. "Now leave us alone, we're busy."

"Don't be like that, little man," Cedric said, picking Kevin up and causing his glasses to fall to the floor. "I'm just trying to be friendly."

"Put me down!" Kevin yelled. "I don't want to be friends with you."

"Put my brother down, you big dummy!" Tevin shouted.

"What are you going to do if I don't?" Cedric said as he purposely stepped back and smashed Tevin's sunglasses.

"See what you did! Now you're really going to get it!"

Kevin gave the signal and Tevin kicked Cedric in the ankle, real hard! When he bent down to grab it, Kevin kicked him right in the nuts with his steel toe boots.

"Ouch!" Cedric yelled as he dropped Kevin and grabbed both his ankle and balls. "I-I-I'm going to get you!"

"That's what you get, you big bully!" Kevin laughed as he watched him roll around on the floor moaning. "Next time pick on somebody your own size."

The whole incident should have ended right then and there, but Cedric was embarrassed because all the women saw what happened. After he caught his breath he took off his belt and began chasing the twins around the house.

"Come here you little fuckers!" he yelled angrily. "I'll give you something to laugh about."

"You'd better not touch those kids!" I yelled chasing after them.

It was total chaos. Cedric was tripping and knocking furniture over trying to catch the agile twins. He chased them around the back yard, into the kitchen, and then upstairs. The other kids thought it was some kind of new game and they all joined in behind me.

"I wanna play! Chase me next!" they yelled.

But all the fun came to an abrupt end when Cedric slipped and fell against one of the bedroom doors, breaking the lock. When the door swung open everybody was shocked by what they saw. Tiny and Geno were sitting at a long marble table bagging cocaine and counting stacks of money. There had to be at least fifty grand in small bills. The kids just stood there staring at the white powder, some not realizing what it was.

"You kids get out of here, right now!" I shouted.

"I'm sorry Geno, it was an accident!" Cedric said sounding like a punk.

"Just get all these people out of my house. I knew it was a bad idea to have this kiddy party in the first place."

While Cedric went downstairs like a flunky to follow orders, I stood in the doorway looking at the two of them, shaking my head in disgust.

"So, now you know what the deal is," Geno said with an arrogant smile on his face. "But if I find out you told the cops, I'll hire somebody to kill you, your fiancee, and that beautiful little daughter of yours."

"Don't worry about me calling the law, I'm no snitch. But if you ever make the mistake of threatening my family again, I'll make you wish you were never born."

"Are you finished with your Jesse Jackson speech?"

"Yeah, I'm finished."

"Good," he said pulling a 9 millimeter pistol from underneath his shirt. "Now get the hell out of here before I bust a cap in your ass."

"That's exactly what I expected from a little punk like you, always pulling a gun to keep from takin' an ass whipping. You ain't nuthin' but a coward."

I stormed out the room feeling frustrated and powerless. When I got downstairs to the living room, I quickly put on the kids' coats, picked up Erikah's gifts, and headed for the door.

"Where do you think you're going?" Valarie asked while

blocking the front door.

"I'm going home."

"Not with Erikah you're not. She's staying here with me."

"Valarie you must be out of your mind! These men are drug dealers. Do you understand what that means? Do you? It means they sell poison to little kids and hurt people. And judging by the size of this house, they've probably had to kill a few."

"That's Geno's thing," she said. "Cedric isn't involved in all that stuff. He has a legitimate job working construction."

I slapped myself on the forehead in total disbelief. Lord, please don't let this woman be this damned stupid!

"Valarie, you need serious psychiatric help. Cedric is out there slinging dope like the rest of them. You're just too dumb to see it."

"Hold up, Tony!" Cedric said, stepping between me and the door. "You're not going anywhere with Erikah."

That was the last straw. I put down the boxes, snatched him by the collar, and punched his ass so hard his eyes rolled back in his head. He fell against the wall and onto the floor like a sack of flour.

"I knew you couldn't take a punch, you sissy." I stepped over him and opened the door. "Next time stay out of family business."

"Look what you did!" Valarie yelled as she walked over to wipe his bloody mouth. "You don't own me, I can see whoever I want!"

"You go right ahead and continue to see him if you want. But I promise you this. If I ever hear about this piece-of-shit dope dealer being anywhere near my little girl again, I'll take your ass to court so fast it'll make your head spin. I mean it!"

MY SKIN IS MY SIN

Christie is driving me crazy with this annoying habit she has of setting my bedroom clock ahead thirty minutes. The alarm was set for 10:15, but I didn't realize it was only 9:45 until I went into the kitchen and saw the clock on the microwave. That's a whole half hour of sleep I missed out on, and I felt it too. And if there's one thing I hate, it's playing basketball without being totally rested. Those guys at the gym are going to murder me on the court today. I tried my best to lay back down and go to sleep, but it was no use.

Once I'm up, I'm up. So, I decided to kill time by taking my old Buick Riviera down the street and running it through the car wash before heading out to the gym. We all agreed to meet up at 11:30 and I wanted to be on time, for a change.

When I walked outside I was shocked by how sunny and warm it was. There wasn't a single cloud in the sky, and the temperature had to be at least 75 degrees. That's practically a heatwave in Chicago, especially for early April. There was no way in hell I was going to drive that old Buick into the city, not on a day like this. I didn't give a damn what I promised Derrick about being more low-keyed and humble. If he has a problem with it, fuck him! So, without an ounce of guilt, I did an about-face and ran back inside to get the keys to the Mercedes off the key hook. As I watched the automatic garage door open, I felt like that kid in the Nissan commercial. The Benz was calling out to me, "Enjoy the ride!"

I threw my gym bag into the back seat, let down the convertible top, and headed for the Amoco station to fill up with premium unleaded. By eleven o'clock I was rolling down the highway feeling like a million bucks. I popped an old Roy Ayers tape Christie bought me and fast-forwarded to one of my favorite songs, "Everybody Loves The Sunshine." I turned up the volume, did a gangsta lean, and jammed all the way to the south side. The ride usually took about 20 minutes from where I lived, but I drove 45 in the right lane to make sure everybody saw me. I mean, what's the point of having a nice ride if you can't show off a little?

When I arrived at the gym, it was obvious that more than a few other guys had the same idea. Freshly waxed cars with jet black tires shining with Armoral lined both sides of the streets for three blocks. The parking lot looked like a preview of the Chicago Auto Show. Ben's white Lexus was parked right out front next to Tony's red Corvette. Even Derrick broke down and drove his Jag. After I finally found a parking space, I clicked the alarm button on my key ring to activate the security system and hurried into the gym. The first person I saw was

Ben. He was sipping on a bottle of Gatorade and talking on the pay phone, probably checking up on Nikki.

I thought about going over to say hello but I found myself feeling a little uneasy about approaching him. Although we had talked on the phone a few times since our fight in February, he never did apologize for calling Christie an uppity white bitch. I decided to go get changed first and address that issue later.

The locker room was funky as usual and packed with unfamiliar faces. The regular ball players were being ran out by rowdy little kids and overweight wannabe athletes. Usually all of the lazy people who made New Year's resolutions to get in shape had given up by now and were back home drinking beer and gulping down Hostess Twinkies. But the warm weather brought them out of the woodwork like roaches. Even a few of the oldtimers were lacing up ready to play. After looking around for about ten minutes or so, I finally saw someone I recognized.

"Hey, Terrance! Have you seen Derrick or Tony?" I shouted.

"Yeah, I saw them getting dressed over there." He pointed towards the back of the locker room.

"Thanks, junior. I'll see you out there on the court. I hope you're ready to play ball today."

"I could beat you old geezers with one hand tied behind my back, and with a blindfold on."

"When will you youngsters ever learn? Age and experience will beat youth and athleticism every time."

"We'll just have to test that theory, now won't we?"

Normally I would have placed a friendly wager on the game, but Terrance was one of the best players on the South Side, maybe in the whole city. He was a cocky 21-year-old kid, standing about 6' 5" with serious hops. We nicknamed him M.J. because he stuck his tongue out like Michael Jordan whenever he dunked. It was too bad he didn't have the discipline to hit the books in college. He would've made it to the

NBA for sure. After I maneuvered my way past a group of senior citizens I finally reached the back of the locker room. Ben had somehow managed to make his way back and was sitting on the bench waiting for Tony and Derrick. But instead of getting dressed, those two clowns were standing around in their drawers slap-boxing.

"Excuse me! Is this some kind of new method of male bonding?" I asked.

"No, smartass." Tony grabbed his crotch. "We're having a contest to see who has the most defined dick imprint!"

"You must be in the lightweight division," I said, reaching into my gym bag and pulling out a pair of sweat socks. "Here, use these if you really want to impress the judges."

We all laughed and gave each other high fives and hugs. It seemed like ages since we saw one another. The responsibilities of running our businesses was making it harder to find time to hook up.

"So, what were you two knuckleheads doing before I so rudely interrupted?" I asked.

" I was just showing Derrick how I knocked out Cedric last weekend at Erikah's birthday party."

"You got into a fight with that loser?"

"You damn right I did! He got in my business and I had to straighten him out."

"What about this business with him moving in?"

"Oh, that's no longer an issue. I told Valarie that if I find out he's been around Erikah again, I'm suing for custody."

"On what grounds?"

"On the grounds that he is a damned dope dealer, him and his punk roommate Geno."

"Geno?" I asked curiously. "Geno who?"

"His last name is dope dealer as far as I'm concerned."

"I hope you're not talking about the Geno who lives in a big white mansion out in Hazel Crest."

"That's the one. But how do you know him?"

"Hell, everybody in the south suburb knows him. He's one

of the biggest dope dealers in Chicago."

"Who, that little punk?"

"That little punk runs an organization that pulls down more than a million dollars a year, selling everything from crack cocaine to heroin. That's why they call his place the White House."

"If he's so big, why haven't they arrested him?"

"Because Geno isn't stupid, that's why. He handles all of his transactions through his boys and he hires grammar school kids and young women to do most of the transporting and selling. If they get busted, nobody can say he was involved."

"Well, I don't give a damn who he is," Tony said. "All I care about is Erikah. As long as Valarie keeps her word not to see Cedric again, I won't have to pull a Rambo."

"Now that we've gotten all of this New Jack City business out the way, let's play ball!" Derrick shouted as he slammed his locker shut. "I'll meet you guys on the court. The funk in this locker room is making me dizzy."

"Hold up, I'm going with you," Tony said. "You coming Ben?"

"I'll be there in a minute."

While I finished lacing up my sneakers, Ben opened his locker and pulled out a small plastic bag. I could tell he had something to say, but he was apprehensive and awkward.

"Here, this is for you," he said setting the bag next to me.

"What is it?"

"The two videotapes you brought over to my house back in February and a check for $120."

"What's the $120 for?"

"Late fee. Two dollars a day for sixty days. I figure they're overdue."

"Thanks for returning the tapes, but I don't want your money."

"Just take it. It's my way of saying I'm sorry. I was way out of line when I called Christie, you know, that name."

"Apology accepted," I said, giving him a handshake. "And

I'm sorry for coming down so hard on Nikki. I guess every-body deserves a chance."

"Now that we have that behind us, maybe we can start get-ting back together on Sundays to watch the games," Ben said. "As a matter of fact the Bulls are playing the Lakers tomorrow. Why don't you and Christie come over? Nikki loves playing hostess."

"We can't make it tomorrow. Christie's parents invited us over for dinner."

"Yeah right, and Ross Perot is running for chairman of the NAACP."

"I'm not kidding. Christie called me from work yesterday and told me they insisted."

"You mean to tell me Mr. and Mrs. White America invit-ed a black man over to their plantation?"

"I'm just as surprised as you are. Maybe they've finally accepted that Christie and I are really in love."

"I wouldn't get my hopes up too high if I were you," Ben said as we walked out towards the court. "People like that don't change overnight."

"I realize that," I said. "But at least it's a beginning."

At 7:00 o'clock Easter morning the warm sunlight came blast-ing through the bedroom window and right into my face. I tried to escape its glare by covering up with my blanket, but that only made me sweat more. I just said, "fuck it," and got up.

"Christie!" I shouted.

"I'm coming," she shouted back from the bathroom.

The door swung open and Christie came rushing in with her face covered with a yucky-looking white cream.

"You rang?" she said, trying to imitate Lurch on *The Addams Family.*

"Ooh, what's that on your face?"

"Estee Lauder skin cream," she said with her hands on her hips. "Looking beautiful is hard work, you know?"

"Getting some sleep around here is getting to be hard work too. Yesterday you set my clock ahead 30 minutes, and now you forget to pull down the shades. I swear, if you weren't a criminal lawyer I would strangle you to death!"

"I'm sorry, sweetheart, but the weather outside was so beautiful I had to open a window."

"I don't have a problem with you opening a window, just leave the shades down, okay?"

"Okay, grumpy."

As frustrated as I was, my whole attitude changed once I looked out the window. It was another gorgeous day. Two consecutive days of sunny 70-degree weather was a rarity, especially on the weekend. The weather in Chicago during the spring is frustrating and unpredictable. Even the weather forecasters can't get it right. They promise a sunny and pleasant weekend, but then it rains from Friday night until three o'clock Sunday afternoon. Just long enough to ruin your plans for a softball game or barbecue in the park. But that wasn't the case this time. The sun was shining bright, the birds were chirping, and the neighbors were out washing their cars with nothing on but shorts. No drug in the world could have made me feel as exhilarated as I did at that moment.

But I quickly came down off my natural high when I remembered that Christie's parent's were expecting us for dinner at five o'clock. Right in the middle of the second basketball game on NBC. Damn! With my luck her father will be watching boring-ass golf, or even worse, fishing. But there was no sense of torturing myself. I promised Christie I was going, and I always keep my word. The only upside was that we didn't have to leave until after four o'clock. Which meant I had the whole morning and most of the afternoon to chill. I decided to kick off my half day of relaxation with a long hot bath. My back was still a little sore from chasing Terrance around the court yesterday. Derrick and Tony talked me into sticking his hyper young ass, and like a fool I fell for it.

While my bath water ran, I carried one of my speakers into the bathroom, tuned the radio to V-103, and grabbed this book I've been meaning to read called *Never Satisfied: How & Why Men Cheat.* Derrick told me it was funny as hell and very accurate. "I could have wrote that book," he said. But I wanted to read it for myself to see what this "Player Hater" had to say. Men don't like it when another man tells all their secrets, especially if it's the truth. Once I had everything in place, I took off my drawers and slid into the steaming hot water. Aah, this almost feels better than sex. After soaking for about twenty minutes I could feel the Epsom salt doing its job as the pain in my lower back began to subside. I dried off my hands picked up my book, and laid my head back against my inflated bath pillow.

After reading the first chapter I could see why Derrick liked it so much. It was very direct and real. Maybe too real! Especially the part about cheating men expecting their mistresses to be completely loyal. Now, that's true! Men know damn well they don't like to share. But I had to set it down because the music on the radio was ruining my concentration. The DJ Herb Kent, the smooth gent, was playing cut after cut. I hadn't heard. "Let's get it on" by Marvin Gaye in a while. It sounded too good. I had to sing along.

"I've been really tryin' baby. Tryin' hold back the feelings for so—long. And if you feel, like I feel, baby. Come on, aw, come on. Ooh!"

Just as I was about to really start blowing, there was a knock at the door.

"Damn! Who is it!"

"Who else," Christie said.

"Come in."

"Are you all right?"

"What do you mean, am I all right?"

"Well, I heard you in here screaming, and I thought something was wrong."

"I wasn't screaming, I was singing."

"Oh, is that what you call it?" she said. "I thought you slipped on a bar of soap."

"That's very funny. You should try out for Def Jam Comedy on HBO."

"Yeah, I could be the first white girl to do the show."

"Now that you found out I'm okay, can I please have some privacy. This is my personal time."

"Actually I came in here to tell you that my father just called and said he wanted us to come over at three o'clock instead of five."

"I wish he would make up his mind." I was getting upset. "Doesn't he realize we have lives too?"

"Calm down honey, I know you wanted to relax today."

"I'll be ok," I said, splashing a handfull of water in my face. "Just let me soak for a few more minutes and I'll get dressed."

"Looks like you've been in there long enough, if you ask me." She walked over and sat on the edge of the tub. "Your skin is beginning to wrinkle."

"This wrinkled skin is the reason why your father can't accept our relationship."

"Don't worry about my father, his bark is worse than his bite. In fact, I'm willing to bet that once he gets to know you, he'll love you as much as I do."

"I'll take you up on that bet!" I said.

"Okay, what do you want to bet?"

I sat there for a minute trying to come up with something real good. Then it came to me.

"If you're wrong, you have to learn how to cook chicken and dumplings and red beans and rice."

"And if I'm right?" she asked.

"You tell me."

"If I'm right, you have to cook me a gourmet meal and then give me a sensual candlelight bath."

"A candlelight bath, huh. I've got your candlelight bath, all right!" I pulled her into the tub. "This is as close as you're ever going to get to any kind of bath, because this is a bet you'll never win!"

Damn! Why did I drive this white Ford Bronco. The last thing I needed was for Christie's father to start in about O.J. Simpson. White people have a bad habit of assuming that just because you're black you will speak out in his defense. Personally, I think he did it. Or at least had something to do with it. But until the judicial system, their judicial system, finds him guilty, he's innocent, end of story.

The ride out to Christie's parents house in Lake Forest took about 30 minutes. That was more than enough time for me to get myself all worked up and nervous. As we approached the huge gates to the estate, Christie reached over and held my hand.

"Are you going to be all right?"

"I'll be fine," I said. "I just hope your father is open-minded and willing to give me a fair chance."

"Don't worry. He's really very sweet once you get to know him. He's just a little old-fashioned and conservative."

"By the looks of this place he doesn't seem too conservative to me. It looks like something right out of *Lifestyles of the Rich and Famous.* What did you say he does for a living?"

"He owns Davenport Inc., an international marketing and consulting firm. But he practices law in his spare time."

"Like father, like daughter."

"I guess you could say that. My father was very insistent that I follow in his footsteps and become a lawyer. But I think I disappointed him somewhat when I chose criminal law over corporate."

"Christie, you told me your family was well off, but this is ridiculous." We were driving past the horse stables and outdoor pool. "Your father must be worth a fortune."

"About five million a year, give or take a few hundred thousand."

"I don't understand." I said, shaking my head. "Why are you hanging out on my side of town when you could have all this?"

"This is their money, not mine," she said, looking serious. "Since I finished college, I haven't asked him for anything, not one thin dime. In fact, I didn't even tell him the name of the law firm I was working for, because I knew he would use his influence to get me a partnership. Now, when I look at my name on the outside of that office building I know that I've earned it through hard work and dedication. That means more to me than anything."

"I know it does, sweetheart." I reached over and gave her a kiss. "And that's why I admire you so much."

We drove up the circular driveway and parked the car around back by the garage. Christie got her parents' late Christmas gifts out the back and I limped out to give her a hand.

"What's wrong with you?" she said, noticing that I was walking a little stiff.

"My leg is still sore from playing basketball yesterday. The long ride must have cut off my circulation. I hope your father doesn't think I'm trying to pimp."

"You are so silly," she laughed. "I'll just tell him you're sore from all the wild sex we're having."

"Don't even play like that. I'm nervous enough as it is."

We gathered up the gifts, walked back to the front door, and rang the bell. I swear, I felt like Sidney Poitier in *Guess Who's Coming to Dinner.* A few seconds later the door opened and Christie's mother rushed out and gave her a big hug.

"Christie! I can't tell you how much I've missed you."

"I've missed you too, Mom."

"Hello, Mrs. Davenport," I said, extending my hand. "I'm Mark. It's a pleasure to finally meet you."

"It's nice meeting you too, Mark," She gave me a firm hand-shake. "Come in and make yourself comfortable. My husband is upstairs changing clothes. He'll be down in a minute."

She escorted me into their living room, which was beautifully furnished with traditional oak and fine art. Everything was spaced out perfectly, and the room had balance. It was obvious where Christie got her great taste in interior decorating. But what I loved most about it was the 52-inch television set that was sitting right in the middle of the room, and it was tuned into the basketball game on NBC. Maybe coming out here to visit wasn't such a bad idea after all.

"Can I get you something to drink?" Mrs. Davenport asked.

"No thank you, ma'am. I've got everything I need right here."

"I hope you don't mind if I steal Christie away from you for a minute to the kitchen to give me a hand?"

"No problem. I know you two have a lot of catching up to do."

While they went and did their mother and daughter thing, I relaxed on the sofa and watched the tipoff of the Bulls and Lakers game. This was a matchup I had been waiting for all year. Now that the Lakers had Shaquille O'Neal they would make the game interesting. Not win, of course. Just keep it competitive. I was hoping that Mr. Davenport wouldn't come down and interrupt my groove until halftime. But no sooner than I had that thought, he came walking into the living room with a phony grin on his face and his hand out.

"Hello, Mark. How are you? I'm Christie's dad."

"Mr. Davenport, it's a pleasure to meet you." I stood up and shook his hand firmly. "I've been looking forward to this opportunity for quite some time."

"So have I, Mark. I'm hopeful that we can work out whatever differences we have, for Christie's sake. She is my only child, and I'm extremely protective of her. I'm sure you understand."

"Yes, sir, I do."

"Well, then you can also understand why I would be concerned about the choices she makes, both professionally and personally?"

"Excuse me?"

"What I'm trying to say is, Christie has the opportunity to go far in her career, maybe even run for political office, which has always been a dream of mine."

"And?"

"And, being involved in the wrong kind of relationship could make that difficult, if not impossible. I'm merely saying, it's not a good career move."

When he said that, I didn't even get upset. I just took a deep breath, sat back against the arm of the sofa, and proceeded to educate his closed-minded, racist, and controlling ass.

"Mr. Davenport, with all due respect. Christie has already achieved a great deal while we've been together. I'm sure you've heard that she was made a full partner at her law firm four months ago."

"Yes she told me but..."

"Please, if you don't mind, I'm not finished," I said, cutting him off. "Right now she is happy with where she is, and if she should decide to go into politics, which she has never communicated to me, I will be right there by her side helping her to make it happen."

"Mark if you don't mind my asking, what is it that you do for a living?"

I didn't understand what the significance of that was but I indulged him nevertheless.

"My family owns three businesses in the south suburbs. Three very successful businesses, I might add."

"And what are your plans for the future?"

"Right now, I'm in the middle of purchasing more space to expand our wholesale business so that we can handle the demand from our new accounts. When that's finished I'll be looking into adding to my overseas portfolio. South Africa has opened up a lot of investment opportunities for small business since Mandela became president."

That shut him up quick. I guess he thought I was some dumb nigga from the streets who didn't know *The Wall Street Journal* from the funny pages. Well, I guess that will teach his pompous ass not to stereotype. He sat there speechless for a few seconds with his hand on his chin. But I could tell by the look in his eyes that he wanted to get to the point.

"I'm glad to see that you're a man who's not afraid of taking risk. That's very important in being successful. But let's talk more specifically about your relationship with my daughter. She told me that you're thinking about marriage."

"Yes, sir. Hopefully by the end of next year. But we won't be having kids any time soon. That's at least two or three years down the road."

His face turned bright red. "Kids? Why in God's name would you want to put two innocent children through all the pain of growing up biracial in this racist society. It's tough enough for them as it is."

"Look, Mr. Davenport, I came over here to meet you and your wife and to have dinner, not to be interviewed for a job." I was looking him dead in his eyes. "Now, I know that you don't like me because I'm black, and that's fine. But don't think for one second that you can dictate to me about what to do with my life."

"It's not your life that I'm concerned about, it's Christie's."

"In that case, you should take the time out to ask her whether or not she's happy and stop concerning yourself with the color of a man's skin."

"Don't get the wrong idea, Mark, I'm no racist. In fact, some of my best friends are black. I'm only trying to keep both of you from making a terrible mistake."

"The only mistake we made was coming out here expecting you to understand." I got up from the sofa. "Now, if you will excuse me, I'm ready to leave."

At that moment Christie and her mother walked into the room carrying two bottles of beer and a bowl of pretzels.

"I thought you two might want a refreshments while you watched the game," her mom said.

"Christie, I'm sorry, but I've got to go!"

"Why, what happened?"

"Ask your father."

"What did you say to him, Daddy?"

"I just told him that you two should think about what you're getting yourselves into, that's all!"

Now Christie was red-faced too. She slammed the beer and pretzels on the cocktail table and walked over and got right in her father's face.

"Daddy, I've always done whatever you asked me to," she said, getting emotional. "When you asked me to run for president of the student council in high school, I did it. When you asked me to drop business as my major and practice law, I did it. And when you asked me to go to Harvard for grad school, I did that too. Now, it's my turn to ask you to do something for me, just one thing. Stop being so narrow-minded and accept my relationship with Mark."

"I can't do that, sweetheart, I'm sorry."

"I'm sorry too," she said taking me by the hand. "Let's go Mark, this is not my home anymore."

On the way out, I saw a King James bible sitting on the stand next to the door. I stopped, picked it up, and opened it.

"Mr. Davenport, are you a God-fearing man?"

"Yes, I am. I'm a Christian."

"A Christian, huh? It seems to me that the ultimate test of a white man's Christianity is whether or not he's willing to accept his white daughter's dating black men. Why don't you pray on that!"

The drive home was a quiet one. Christie stared aimlessly out of the window trying not to cry. I turned up the radio and kept my eyes straight ahead on the road. But what was there to say? Her father was both a hypocrite and a racist. Nothing I did or said was ever going to change that. What we needed to do was concentrate on our relationship and stop worrying about whether or not our families accepted it.

I finally broke the silence by reminding her that she owed me a plate of chicken and dumplings. I know it wasn't exactly the ideal time, but a bet is a bet!

CLEAN UP WOMAN

I could hardly keep from smiling as I boarded my plane at the National Airport in Washington DC for my flight home to Chicago. Monica and Tiffany called me at my hotel first thing this morning with wonderful news. According to the sales figures from the last quarter, *Happily Single* has become the fourth best-selling African American publication in the country, right behind *Essence*, *Ebony*, and *Jet*. Everything is going just as planned, better in fact. If we can continue to have the kind of overwhelming response we had in Washington DC, the magazine could easily become number one by the end of the year. I've never seen so many people turn out for a promotional event.

The key was the support of the local radio stations. Let's see, there was WPGC, WOL, WHUR, WINN, MAGIC 95, V103, 92Q with Frankski, and WKYS with Olivia Fox and crazy-ass Russ Parr, who reminds me a lot of Doug Banks who used to be on WGCI in Chicago. What a character! All it took was a quick five-minute interview on each station and the magazine began selling out all over town. Now, that's what I call reaching your target market. I was hoping that Monica and Tiffany got the orders out by the end of the day so we don't lose out on any sales. Momentum is everything in this business.

But although business was booming, my social life has begun to fizzle out. Angela hasn't been on her J-O-B in the bedroom. And let me tell you, Washington DC is the last place you want your man to go if he's unfulfilled. The city is full of beautiful, educated, and single black women. There must have been at least ten women for every one man. That is, if you leave out the men who are either broke as hell, bisexual, or just too damned ugly. The temptation was overwhelming. It took a hell of a lot of control to keep from cheating. Which is becoming more and more difficult because Angela and I are going through these periods of not having sex for two or three weeks at a time. Shit, I'm about to explode! She's been flying back and forth to Atlanta trying to close on a deal to buy back her three health spas. And I've been touring the east coast promoting the June issue of the magazine, which, ironically, focuses on monogamy and infidelity in the '90s.

We hired a marketing firm to take a survey of single men between the ages of 21 and 35. They were asked if it was possible for them to commit to having sex with only one woman for the rest of their lives. The results were interesting. 10% said maybe, 30% said yes, and 60% said, hell no! One gentleman they interviewed was very adamant about the fact that he thought monogamy was an unrealistic social concept. "It wasn't

intended for males to be sexually committed to just one female
for life," he said. "Men are driven by nature to venture out into
the world and conquer women." And I'm beginning to agree!
It's almost impossible to stay faithful when you're in a long-distance relationship, especially when you're constantly surround-
ed by beautiful women who are throwing the pussy at you.
Sometimes I have to get up in the middle of the night and go
work out in the gym to relieve stress. I've even tried meditation
and taking cold showers, but it's not working. For the last two
weeks I've gone to bed frustrated and horny as hell. Last night
my dick was so hard I thought I was going to punch a hole in
the mattress. Angela thinks being apart is healthy for the relationship. "Absence makes the heart grow fonder," she says.
But I believe too much absence can make a man wonder. I'm
getting fed up with putting sex on my calendar like a damned
dental appointment. I need a woman who is going to be around
to take care of my needs.

Ever since Angela has been in negotiations to reacquire her
businesses, her sexual drive has gone from ten to zero. Even the
head is getting weak. Back in the beginning of our relationship
she would spread my legs, prop a pillow under her head, and go
down on me for a half hour. It was like feeding a bottle to a
baby. Now I'm lucky if she even puts it in her mouth for five
minutes. When I asked her what the problem was, she said,
"I've got a lot of things on my mind right now, just be patient!"
Of course, I interpreted that to mean I would be getting a half
way decent blow job sometime in the near future. Now here it
is two months later and I'm still left hanging.

Once the plane took off and reached its cruising altitude, I
let down my tray table and spread out the fifteen phone numbers I had filed away in my briefcase. I collected five at my
speech at Howard University, seven from The Fox Trap night
club, and another three while I was waiting in the airport.
Women were coming at me left and right, flashing business
cards and scribbling their numbers down on napkins. At first I
thought about throwing them away, as I had been doing faith-

fully for the last six months. But after thinking back on how much Angela has been slippin', I stuffed those bad boys into my pocket and kept on steppin'. Now I'm picking through this pile of cards and napkins trying to decide who to call first. I pulled the air phone out of the middle seat and began dialing their numbers alphabetically. The flight to Chicago was approximately two hours. That was all the time I needed to eliminate the ones with no money, no enthusiasm, and no freak potential.

It was four o'clock when I made it home from the airport. I dropped my bags right at the front door and threw myself onto my king-size bed. "Aah" I sighed as I hit the soft and familiar mattress. "There's no place like home." The stress of being on the road was starting to get to me. Traveling the country, hopping around from city to city, may seem like a glamorous lifestyle but it's hard work, especially when you haven't had sex in over two weeks. What I needed was a little TLC. I looked over at my calendar to check to see when Angela was scheduled to be back from Atlanta. June 3 was circled in red marker. Damn! That's two whole days away. There's no way in hell I was sitting around my apartment alone on another warm spring weekend watching videos. Fuck that!

I sprung up out of bed and turned on the light to my walk-in closet. I grabbed my Bernini tie off the rack and pulled out the sharpest Armani suit I had. It was a beautiful spring night and a warm breeze was blowing off the lake. It was time to get my mack on! I decided to go hang out at The Cotton Club on Michigan Ave. It's was one of the few places I went to hang out when I was in town. They usually have a nice after-work set on Fridays and the crowd was 25 and over. Before I jumped in the shower I tuned the radio to WGCI and turned up the volume. It was five o'clock. Right on time to catch the tail end of the Crazy Howard McGee Show. I loved listening to him play the most requested songs of the day. It always helped fire me up and into the party mood.

By seven o'clock I was ready to roll. I sprayed my neck with a light mist of Jean-Paul Gaultier cologne, rubbed some Luster's pink moisturizer in my hair, and took a Mega Men vitamin. "Some mother's daughter is in trouble tonight!" I said as I admired myself in the bathroom mirror. On my way out the door, I paused and thought about calling one of the fellahs to ask them to meet me out, but I figured it was a waste of time. Mark isn't interested in socializing with black women, Nikki has Ben under house arrest, and Tony is on his best behavior because his wedding is in two weeks. "Oh, well," I said as I feathered the white handkerchief in my suit jacket pocket. "The Lone Ranger rides again!"

The Cotton Club was crowded as hell. A jazz band was performing in the front to a packed room of stuck-up brothers and sistahs wearing business attire, posturing with their drinks like mannequins. That's not my scene. The real party was in the back room where the DJ was spinning. As I walked into the dimly lit room, my heart began to race. The thumping bass in the music was exhilarating. It had been months since I had gone out to a nightclub for the sole purpose of partying and socializing. I felt a little awkward and out of practice. Everybody was moving and talking faster than I remembered and the music seemed louder. I needed a minute to get my bearings and plan a strategy. So, I did what most men do when they come into a club, I went over to the bar and ordered a drink. The bartender was a tall, dark-skinned sistah wearing a short haircut, almost bald. I swear she looked exactly like that pop singer Me'Shell N'degeocello.

"My name is Ashira, what can I get you to drink?" she politely asked.

"I'll have a double shot of Hennesy, Ashira, no ice."

"Don't I know you from somewhere?"

"I don't think so."

"Gosh, your face looks familiar."

Ordinarily I would have taken that opportunity to whip out an application and sign her up for a one-year subscription to the magazine. But I wanted to remain anonymous. No sales, no business cards, and no autographs. While I waited for my drink I looked around the bar to see if there were any good prospects. At the end of the bar was an attractive woman sitting alone. I tried to make eye contact with her to see if she wanted company, but she looked me off. I figured she was with a date and turned back around to keep from appearing disrespectful. When Ashira came back with my drink, I quickly handed her my money, hoping to get rid of her before she recognized me, but it was too late.

"Now I know who you are!" she said getting loud. "You're the guy who owns that new singles magazine. My roommate loves your relationship articles. What's it called again?"

"*Happily Single.*"

"Yeah, that's it!" she said getting even louder. "Do you have any copies to give away?"

"No, I'm sorry I don't. But you can pick up the June issue at any newsstand or bookstore."

"Aw, man. I can't believe it's really you! My roommate is going to trip when I tell her I met you. Can I have your autograph?"

"Under one condition."

"And what's that?"

"You have to promise not to tell anyone who I am. I don't want to attract any attention. Is it a deal?"

"It's a deal!"

She pulled out a note pad from underneath the bar and folded back to the first blank page.

"Here, use my pen," she insisted. "Sign it to 'My lifelong friend Ashira. One of the most beautiful, intelligent, and down-to-earth women I've ever met.' And then sign your name at the bottom and date it."

"You sure are specific, aren't you?"

"Hey, that's the only way to get what you want in the '90s."

"I heard that!" I said giving her high five.

The woman standing at the bar next to me was obviously dipping in our conversation because right after Ashira left, she tapped me on the shoulder and asked for an autograph too. I quickly signed her napkin and thanked her for supporting the magazine. But that wasn't the end of it. Next thing I know her girlfriends, who had just returned from the ladies' room, took out their pens and paper. One of them even ran down the street to the newsstand and bought a copy of the magazine for me to sign. I admit, I was flattered by all the attention, but things were beginning to get out of hand. Before you know it there was a small crowd of people standing in line, waiting to say hello and to congratulate me on the success of the magazine. I greeted everyone politely and signed a few autographs. Luckily they kept the conversation short and I was able to get back to my drink. I made sure not to turn around in my seat, hoping that would discourage anyone else from approaching me. And for a while it worked, until...

"Excuse me ladies and gentleman," the DJ announced over the loud speaker. "Can I please have your attention? I'd like to send a shout out to Mr. Derrick Reed. The publisher of one of the most exciting new magazines in the country today. Stand up and take a bow, Derrick. Stand up!"

There I was standing with the spotlight beaming down on me like Denzel Washington. Not exactly the low-keyed night out on the town I had in mind. Normally, I was a big ham for any kind of publicity, but not on this night. I spent the next hour shaking hands, signing autographs, and giving advice to aspiring writers. One young lady was so persistent that she went out to her car to get a copy of her work and insisted that I read it right there in the dimly lit club. I couldn't see shit. But I acted like I was interested just to get her off my back. It wasn't until ten o'clock that I got a break. But by then I was out of the party mood and ready to go home. I drank the last sip of my Hennesy and flagged down Ashira to give her a tip.

"Are you leaving already?"

"Yeah, baby. These people have completely worn me out."

"But you can't go now."

"And why is that?"

"Because there's a very nice lady who has been waiting for you all evening. She told me she was an admirer of yours and wants to buy you drink. She's cute too."

"Oh, really?"

It's not that often that a woman is bold enough to buy a man a drink, especially a man who is receiving so much attention from other women. I must admit, I was curious.

"Tell her I'll accept her offer under one condition."

"You sure have a lot of conditions."

"Like you said earlier, that's the only way to get what you want in the '90s."

"Okay, what is it?"

"Tell her that I'll accept only if she comes over and introduces herself first."

"I think she already had that in mind."

"And how would you know that?"

"Because she's standing right behind you."

I paused at first, thinking she was kidding. But when I saw the way she was making eye contact over my shoulder, I knew she wasn't. I took a deep breath, expecting the worst. You know, some gold-toothed, finger-wave-wearing, hoochie mama. Boy was I ever wrong. What I saw when turned around was one of the most desirable women I've ever laid eyes on. She was light-skinned, wearing a long black sheer dress. And she had the most beautiful hazel green eyes you ever want to see.

"Will you accept my drink, now?" she asked.

"Most definitely!" I said, not caring that I was sounding impressed. "Would you like to join me?"

"Don't mind if I do. Give me a gin and tonic," she said to Ashira. "On the rocks."

"Coming right up.

"So tell me, do you make a habit out of going to clubs and buying drinks for strange men?"

"No. Usually I just walk up to them and say, let's go to bed."

I choked on my drink and started coughing.

"Are you all right?" she asked handing me a napkin.

"I'm fine. I just wasn't expecting you to be so bold."

"I'm only kidding Mr. Reed. Or can I call you Derrick?"

"Derrick is fine."

"Well, Derrick, the answer to your question is, no. I'm just a woman who knows what she wants. When I'm interested in getting to know a particular man, I go for it! I'm not a firm believer in fate. My Mama always taught me to create my own opportunities. That goes for business as well as men. So, here I am."

"Wait a minute, did you know I would be here? I'm hardly ever in town on weekends."

"Angela told me this was one of your favorite spots."

I choked on my drink, again.

"Angela who?"

"Your girlfriend, Angela."

"How do you know Angela?"

"We met at the airport in Atlanta in January. The day she came to meet you in New York. I'm Vanessa."

"Vanessa, the flight attendant from Detroit?"

"That's me!"

"Well, it's nice to finally meet you, I think." I was looking around for a video camera. "This isn't some kind of setup, is it?"

"Calm down, Derrick. I'm not a female operative for a sleazy detective agency." She laughed. "You've been watching too many talk shows."

"So what are you doing here in Chicago?"

"Like I said, I came to meet you. I was on my way to Detroit to visit my family for a couple of days and I figured I could kill two birds with one stone."

"Does Angela know you're here?"

"No, she doesn't. Is that a problem?"

I took one look at her long thick lips and those hazel green eyes and thought to myself, "Hell naw, it's not a problem." We were attracted to one another, that was obvious. But most importantly, she didn't try to play games. She let me know up front what the deal was and left it to me to take it or leave it. I took it!

"I don't think there's anything wrong with us talking," I said. "We're two consenting adults."

"I'm glad to hear that," she said in a seductive tone. "So where do we go from here?"

"Good question." I didn't want to appear too desperate. "How about a dance, do you know how to step?"

"We call it ballroom dancing in Detroit."

"Is that a yes or no?"

"Sure, I'd love to. But what about our drinks?"

"Don't worry about that. I'm sure the bartender will hold them until I get back from giving you a quick lesson on how to step, Chicago style!"

"This I've got to see, let's go!"

When we got up to go to the dance floor I noticed the woman sitting at the end of the bar was staring. The same woman who I tried to flirt with earlier. Now that I had an attractive woman on my arm, she decides to become interested. Too late, you stuck-up heifer, I thought. You study long, you study wrong.

The dance floor was crowded with rookies who didn't know what the hell they were doing. I don't know why people who don't know how to step insist on taking up precious space. They should be standing on the sidelines taking notes. We pushed our way to the center of the floor and made a small place to dance. Vanessa was aggressive but light on her feet. I was impressed by how gracefully she moved. Her timing was perfect and she knew how to follow. That's the most important thing for a woman to know how to do. When the DJ played "The Big Payback" by James Brown, the floor began to clear and all eyes were on us. It was like a scene right out of a Fred Astaire movie. Our steps were sharp and we turned in perfect harmony. It almost seemed choreographed. Vanessa was smiling and eating it up. I've never seen a woman so comfortable being watched. She was obviously used to being the center of attention. When the song ended, some of the people who were watching began applauding. We both took a bow and went back to our seats.

"Look, I know this may sound kinda forward," I said. "But can we get out of here and go somewhere where we can talk? I don't want to sign any more autographs, and I know these people aren't going to leave us alone. Not after that performance."

"And where do you suggest we go?" She gave me a curious look with those gorgeous green eyes.

"Now, don't get the wrong idea. I just want an opportunity to get to know you better, that's all. You can even pick the place."

"How far is your place from here?"

"About ten minutes. I have a condo on Lake Shore Drive."

"Okay, let's go."

"Don't you want to tell your girlfriends you're leaving?"

"I came alone."

"You are bold, aren't you?"

"It's not about being bold. I'm just too old and too impatient to be waiting around for a bunch of moody women to decide if they want to do go out. When I'm ready to go, I go."

I was impressed. It's rare that you meet a woman who is secure enough within herself not to worry about what society says is appropriate and inappropriate. In many ways she reminded me of Angela. Maybe that's what attracted me to her. While I helped her on with her coat I glanced over to see if the woman sitting across the bar was still looking. She was. Vanessa saw her staring too, and stared back. Women are so catty. The woman then took a sip of her drink and mumbled the word, bitch! I thought for sure Vanessa would go over and slap the shit out of her, but instead she played it cool. As we walked toward the exit, which was in the direction of the woman, Vanessa stopped at the end of the bar, looked the woman straight in the eyes, and then childishly stuck out her tongue.

The elevator ride up to my apartment was a quiet one. Vanessa and I just stared into each other with that, "I'm going to fuck your brains out" look in our eyes. The moment we set foot through the door we were all over each other. There was no sense wasting time with small talk. We both knew what was up. I threw my suit jacket on the bed, undid my tie, and began unsnapping my pants. Vanessa was already out of her trench coat and was lifting her dress over her head. Before you knew it I had her naked body pinned against the wall and was grinding the shit out of her. I palmed her breasts with one hand and began caressing her between the legs with the other. I can't remembered the last time I felt a woman so wet. My hand was soaked.

"I've been waiting a long time for this moment," she said.

"I promise you, it will be worth the wait."

After sucking her breasts and licking her on the neck to get her hot, I guided her hand to my penis and gently pushed down on her shoulder to let her know what I wanted. She got the message and dropped to her knees. First she paused, as if to make sure it was clean, then she put me inside her mouth, all the way inside. Angela definitely couldn't do that. A few minutes later, she put her hands to work, masturbating with the left and using the right to firmly massaged my testicles. Just hard enough to put me on that threshold between pleasure and pain. I started twitching and screaming like a sissy. "Ooh, baby, ah, baby. Sssss!" Damn, it felt good. And it looked good too. Watching such a beautiful woman going down on me was a serious turn-on. Each time my penis disappeared into her mouth, I moaned. It was like a fantasy come true. The classic one-night stand. I've never experienced a woman with such an animalistic passion for giving head.

After twenty minutes, it was time for me to return the favor. I helped Vanessa up off the floor and led her into the bathroom. Then I turned the shower on and reached underneath the sink for my glass candles and a plastic shower cap for Vanessa. "I won't be needing that," she said. When the water was just right, I lit the candles, turned off the lights, and we stepped inside. While the warm water splashed against our bodies we embraced like we belonged to one another, if only for one night. As I tightened my grip around her back. I was amazed by how firm she was. For a woman in her mid thirties, she was in outstanding shape. Her arms and chest had definition, and her buttocks were tight, like a track runner's.

"Lean back against the wall," I told her, "and hold on to the towel hanger."

"What are you going to do?"

"Don't worry, baby. It's all good!"

While she laid back, I took my face towel and soaked it with soap and water. Then I began washing her vaginal area, slowly, gently, and sensually. Not surprisingly, she was well groomed. Her hair was shaved completely off, except for a heart shaped patch right above her clit. Once I was sure she was thoroughly clean, I lifted her leg up so I could get a better angle. Then I dove in. At first she moaned quietly, while rubbing her breasts. But after I spread her lips and began sucking more aggressively, she grabbed me by the head and began screaming, "Suck it baby, suck this pussy!" She was pulling me so hard against her pelvis that I thought she was going to bust my nose. But I liked it. I liked it a lot.

I knew it was time to get out of the shower when the skin on my finger tips began to wrinkle. Vanessa and I took turns toweling each other off. Then we went to lay down on the bed.

"Do you have condoms?" she said.

"Absolutely. Let me get one out of the drawers."

But when I looked, I didn't have any. Angela and I had both been tested for VD and HIV five months ago, and she was on the pill. And since I had been loyal up until this point, I didn't have any need to restock.

"Don't worry," Vanessa said. "I have some in my suitcase in the car. I never leave home without them."

"Well, give me the keys and I'll go get it."

"Not right now. Just lay here and hold me a minute."

While I laid there holding Vanessa's head against my chest, I couldn't help thinking about Angela. She was my woman and should have been the one laying on top of me. But a man has needs. Needs that can't constantly be ignored and set aside. Angela was slacking off and left the door wide open for another woman to walk into. And she was also getting careless. She had obviously discussed intimate details of our relationship with another woman. A woman who openly confessed to having a crush on me. That was stupid. Vanessa knew exactly where to find me, when to find me, and what Angela was lacking. It's almost as if she planned for us to get together. Oh, well, I guess she got what she wanted.

Ten minutes after we laid down, Vanessa fell asleep. At first, I thought about waking her up so I could get the condoms out of the car, but she was resting too peacefully. And it really didn't matter, anyway. She had already given me what I needed most, attention. And despite the fact that we didn't have intercourse that night, it was the most satisfying nonpenetrating sexual experience I've ever had. Just looking at her in my arms, I knew one thing for sure. We would one day finish what we started.

WEDDING DAZE

Tony was packing the last of his things when Derrick called from his car phone to tell him he was only ten minutes away. "I'll be ready by the time you get here," Tony said. "Just blow the horn when you're outside." It was 5:30 and he was supposed to be gone by the time Tracie got home at 6:00. They didn't want to see each other until the wedding. Tracie thought it would add a little spice to the honeymoon. Tony went along with it because he needed a break from her constant nagging over the wedding arrangements.

She was driving him crazy, worrying about every little detail from her dress being ready on time to the DJ having enough old school music for the reception. She was such a perfectionist.

After he got all of his things together, he took his bags downstairs and set them by the door. While he waited for Derrick, he walked over and grabbed his favorite picture of him and Tracie off the mantel. The one they took three years ago when they were vacationing in the Virgin Islands. The same place they were going for their honeymoon. He had seen the picture a million times, but he couldn't get over how beautiful Tracie looked in her bikini. Back then she was fifteen pounds lighter and her hair was longer. "Damn, she looked good!" he was thinking. And she was still beautiful in his eyes, fifteen extra pounds and all, especially since it all went to her buttocks and thighs. Tony liked his women thick and made her promise not to lose a single of pound of it.

A wide grin came across his face as he reminisced on how much fun they had basking in the warm tropical sun sipping on strawberry daiquiris and watching the sun set over the ocean. But on this next trip they would be more than just boyfriend and girlfriend. In less than 24 hours they would be Mr. and Mrs. Tony Page, husband and wife. Then it hit him! "Husband!" he said aloud. "Shit, I'm not ready to be anybody's *husband*." The mere sound of the word made him feel old and mortal. All of a sudden his wide grin turned into a frown. After four years and six months of knowing this date was inevitable, he was getting a case of cold feet. He stood up and started pacing the room. As he looked around his house, he didn't recognize it. Tracie had rearranged his entire living room and moved his Lazy Boy into the den. She even took his favorite silverware and plate set out of the kitchen cabinet and replaced them with hers. "Man, what's happening to me?" he wondered. "I'm losing myself." At that moment, Derrick drove up and blew the horn.

"Tony, let's go!"

"I'm coming! Hold your horses," he shouted out the window.

Tony took a deep breath to collect himself, shoved the picture into his shirt pocket, then carried his bags out to the car. Derrick gave him a dirty look, then popped the trunk to his Jaguar.

"It's about time. You're slower than molasses."

"Just shut up and drive, junior," Tony said as he got inside and playfully slapped Derrick upside the head.

During the hour-long ride out to Mark's house, Tony didn't say a word. He just staring at the picture with a blank look on his face. Derrick didn't press the issue, figuring he probably had a lot on his mind about the wedding. So, he turned up the music and sped through traffic like a madman. Tony was critical about his wild driving, always warning him to slow down and watch out for the cops. When he didn't complain about doing 100 mph, Derrick knew something was wrong. Something serious.

It was a little after seven when they arrived at Mark's place. Tony put the picture away and got out the car, still not talking. Derrick grabbed the bag of liquor out the trunk and put the alarm on.

"Man, what's your problem?

"Huh, what?"

"I said what's up with the silent treatment? You haven't said a word since we left your house."

"I'm just thinking."

"Well, think out loud," Derrick said. "We're supposed to be enjoying ourselves, remember?"

When they walked up onto the porch Tony peeped inside the small window on the door and noticed the curtains were drawn and all the lights were out.

"Hey, what's going on?"

"What are you talking about? We're just going to watch the Bulls' playoff game and have a couple of brews. That's what you wanted, right?"

"Yeah, but."

"But nothing. Now turn the knob. Mark said he would leave the door unlocked if he made a quick run to the store."

This was a setup, and Tony knew it. The moment he opened the door the lights flashed on, and a crowd of people jumped up yelling, "Happy Bachelor's Party!" All of his close friends were there. Mark, Ben, Derrick's father, and his partner, Mitch.

"I told you guys I didn't want a bachelor party."

"Shut up and enjoy it, you party pooper," Mark said. "I've been waiting a long time to throw one of these. Now let's get this party started! Music, maestro."

When Mark gave the signal, Ben turned on the music and two strippers emerged from the dining room. One wearing a biker's uniform and the other dressed like a construction worker. They thought that was a good touch, since Tony was in the construction business. The sofa and cocktail table were moved aside and a chair was placed in the middle of the floor. Tony was seated with his hands tied behind his back. While the pulsating music played, the women took turns doing a striptease. Once they were completely nude, the one dressed as the construction worker smeared whipped cream on her breasts and put them right in Tony's face. But Tony wasn't responding. He just sat there staring down at the floor, looking uninterested.

"Relax, baby," she said while moving her breasts in closer, almost touching his lips. "Open your mouth and taste me!"

"Come on, Tony!" Derrick yelled. "That's as close as you're going to get to another woman's breasts for a long time. You better enjoy it while you can."

"I'm sorry everybody. I'm just not in the mood tonight," Tony apologized. "Mark could you please come and untie my hands?"

"I think the party is over, ladies," Mitch said. "Thanks for coming anyway."

Mark untied Tony's hands and handed him a bottle of Miller draft. While the strippers put on their clothes, everybody was quiet. They were completely puzzled and disappointed with Tony's attitude. But nobody said a word, not until Mitch got back from escorting the ladies out to their car and closed the door. Then the fireworks began.

"Damn, man! What the fuck is your problem? You've been trippin' all day."

"Look, I told you I had a lot of shit on my mind," Tony said, getting in Derrick's face. "So, back off!"

"Man, you better get out of my face before I knock your ass out!"

"Go ahead nigga, take your best shot!"

"Okay, that's enough!" Derrick's father said, jumping in between them. "Ain't nobody knocking nobody out around here but me. And Tony, you know I don't like that N word. Now both of you sit down and cool off. Sit down I said!"

Like two obedient school boys, Derrick and Tony sat down and didn't say another word. They knew Mr. Reed didn't repeat himself. He had been like a father to all of them, and they knew not to try him. And at 56 he was still a very menacing figure. They had all seen him bench press 400 pounds in the gym without straining. But their compliance had more to do with respect than fear.

"I'm too old for all this yelling and screaming. I didn't teach any of you to conduct yourselves this way. If there..."

"But, Dad..."

"Don't interrupt me again, Junior. I'm not finished yet."

"Yes, sir."

"As I was saying, if there's something bothering you Tony, let's discuss it like men. We're all family here."

"You're right, Mr. Reed. And I apologize for snapping. It's just that I'm not so sure anymore about getting married tomorrow."

"Say, what!" Ben shouted out. "I paid 500 dollars to get my tuxedo made. Somebody better be getting married tomorrow."

"Ben, if you say another word I'm gonna toss your big ass out the window," Mr. Reed said. "Now, let Tony finish what he was saying."

"All I'm trying to say is, I don't think I'm ready for that kind of commitment. Marriage sounds so permanent."

"Two weeks ago you were looking forward to the wedding.

I've never seen you so excited," Mitch said. "What happened to make you so unsure?"

"I don't know, it kind of hit me today right before Derrick came to pick me up. I looked around at my place and I felt like I was losing my identity. Since Tracie moved in six moths ago I've had to deal with all kinds of awkward and uncomfortable situations. Like looking at tampon wrappers in the trash can, and unclogging her hair from the bathroom sink. But what really set me off is when she moved my Lazy Boy out of the living room to make room for her aquarium, and without asking me first. I just don't know if I can handle sharing my space with a female."

"Aw, man, is that what's bothering you? For a minute there I thought you were going to tell me you caught her fucking the milkman," Mitch said. "You're just coming down with a case of wedding day jitters."

"How can you be so sure?"

"Because I had them myself."

"Me too," Mr. Reed said while slapping five with Mitch. "I had those same feelings right before I married Derrick's mom. I second-guessed myself all the way up until the time I saw her walking down that aisle. Then I felt like the luckiest man alive."

"No offense, Mr. Reed, but that was back in your day. Women were a lot more submissive and compromising back then. These women today are a whole different breed. They'll take over the whole damn house if you let them."

"That's true, women are different. But love never changes."

"Love? Hell, I know a lot of men who started out in love. Now they're either having an affair because they can't get any pussy at home or going through a bitter divorce. And let me tell you, divorce ain't cheap in the '90s. An associate of mine who owns a roofing company was ordered to pay his wife $1500 a month in alimony, and they were only married two years. That's a hell of a lot of money just for saying I do."

"But that's just a few exceptions. What about the happily married men you know? Don't they have anything positive to say about married life?"

"Shit, I don't even know any happily married men. At least not any my age."

"Come to think of it, neither do I," Ben said.

"Me either," Mark said.

"Let's face it, Dad, things are different nowadays. It's hard to stay married to the same woman for thirty-plus years like you did with mom. Relationships today are all about the money."

"It's only hard because nobody wants to put in the hard work it takes to make the marriage work. Young couples today are too quick to throw in the towel at the first sign of trouble. You've got to be committed to working things out no matter what, and stay true to your wedding vows."

"I hear what you're saying, Mr. Reed, but it's hard to have faith in the institution of marriage when you don't see any of your peers practicing it successfully. I know that sounds like a copout, but it really makes you wonder if it's even feasible."

"That's nuthin' but a crock of shit! Do you think your peers are going to be there for you when you're sick? Are they going to be there to rub your sore back after a hard day's work? And what about when you're going through hard times? Are your peers going to put their arms around you and tell you, baby, everything is going to be all right? Huh, are they?"

"I guess not."

"You guess not?"

"I mean, no sir."

"That's what I thought. Look, Tony, marriage is not just a business, it's a spiritual union, at least that's what it's supposed to be. If you can remember that and use it as the foundation to build your marriage, you can make it work. So, forget about all this nonsense about seeing good examples. That's not as important as marrying the right woman, and Tracie is about as right as they come. So, if I were you, I would get my head together and go down to that church tomorrow and marry that beautiful young lady before some other guy comes along who appreciates what she has to offer. Now, I'm not saying it's going to be easy, not by a long shot, but nothing in life worth having ever is. Don't you agree?"

"Yes, sir, I do." Tony was looking overwhelmed. "And thanks for keeping me from making the biggest mistake of my life. I'm okay now."

"Good! Now that we've got that all straightened out, somebody holler out the window and tell those strippers it's okay to come back in. We've got a bachelor party to celebrate!"

The church was packed. There had to be at least 500 guests in attendance, including the local newspapers and television stations who were there to record the big event for the ten o'clock news. Tracie and Angela had sent out hundreds of press releases announcing that it would be one of the most fashionable weddings of the year. It was certainly one of the most expensive. Tony spent over $50,000 to make sure everything was just the way Tracie wanted it. Since it was the first time for both of them, he figured "What the hell," and shelled out a cool $10,000 for the dress alone. It was custom-designed by a Leslie Coombs out of New York. Tracie saw her work in *Signature Bride* magazine and was hooked. The gown was made out of a gold satin fabric that was cut off the shoulders with a sweetheart neckline, which showed off her sexy cleavage. The skirt ballooned out at the bottom and was trimmed in gold. But what really made it unique was the metallic-like ropes that ran around the neckline around the bosom area and then wrapped around the back. It was definitely one in a million.

The wedding coordinator, T.J. Smith of Uniquely "Y" weddings was brought all the way from Dallas to give the wedding an Afrocentric theme. Tracie was adamant about adding a little soul to the event, and T.J was the best. But the best didn't come cheap. Her unique services set him back another five G's. Then there was the business of finding just the right wedding cake. Something that made a statement but tasted good too. Once again Tracie chose to shop out of state to get, "just the right flavor," as she put it. Charmaine Jones of Outrageous Cakes in New Jersey was contracted to create the creamy five-foot masterpiece. She had designed the same five-tier style for a wedding scene on one of the soap operas and Tracie wanted an exact copy, only bigger. It cost $2,500 and took two days to prepare, but it was well worth it.

At three o'clock on the dot, the wedding began. People were rushing in from the parking lot trying to find a seat. Nobody expected it to start on time, because weddings hardly ever do. When the music began to play, Tony and the pastor, Rev. Jackson, came strolling down the aisle followed by the three bridesmaids escorted by the groomsmen. Angela with Derrick, Nikki with Ben, and Christie with Mark. At first the crowd's reaction to Christie was a little cool. She was, after all, the only white girl in the church. But she was wearing the hell out that silk dress and the men soon overlooked her complexion. Even the women had to give her her props.

Cameras were clicking and bulbs flashing as the guests took several pictures of the wedding party. The ladies looked stunning as they stood with perfect posture in their straight white sheath dresses. Angela's dress was more elaborate, since she was the maid of honor. It had thin metallic-gold satin ropes running across her chest, similar to Tracie's gown. The men sported jet black tuxedos with white silk vests, covered in authentic Nigerian embroidery. They were sharp. Kevin and Tevin marched down the aisle as the ring and broom bearers, looking like miniature bouncers in their black tuxedos. Tony was biting his nails, hoping they would make it smoothly through their part of the ceremony. The day before, Kevin had flushed a classmate's crayons down the toilet, and Tevin attacked the dinosaur Barney at Toys R Us. He knew they could snap at any moment.

Once everyone was in place, Erikah came walking nervously down the aisle in her pretty white dress, sprinkling the floor with rose petals. Not once did she look up and make eye contact with the guests. She just kept her head down until she reached Tony at the altar. Then it was time for the main event. The presentation of the bride. "Everytime I close my eyes" by Baby Face played as Uncle John took Tracie by the arm and began walking her slowly down the aisle.

She was a vision of beauty in her long, flowing metallic gown. It truly illuminated the room. Tracie's mom, Aunt Catherine, Tony's mom, and Tracie's brothers were seated in the front row, smiling from ear to ear. When she was halfway down the aisle Tony could see her crying through the sheer golden veil. He wanted to cry too, because she looked so regal in her Cleopatra crown, just like an African Queen. At that moment, all he could think about was the comment Mr. Reed made at the bachelor's party. "He was right," Tony thought. "I do feel like the luckiest man in the world."

WHIPPED

Things aren't working out quite the way I planned with Nikki. She didn't register for the summer semester like she promised, and Naomi told me she hasn't worked at the salon for over a month. This relationship is starting to become an annoyance, and it's embarrassing as hell. All of my friends know Nikki isn't working, because every time they call my house in the middle of the afternoon to leave a message, she answers the phone. Mark is trying hard not to say anything negative, but I know he wants to explode. He tried to tell me she was a liability, but like always I was determined to make it work. And that's exactly what my damned problem is, always trying to fix shit. What I need to do is cut up those credit cards I gave her and tell her to hit the road. Hell, it's not like she's contributing to the household. I have practically supported her and Jason for the last six months, and she doesn't even have the common courtesy to have dinner prepared when I come home from a hard day's work. The way I look at it, if you're going to lay around at home on your ass all day, the least you could do is make yourself useful.

It seems that as time goes by, the true Nikki is starting to come out. Last month I came home at seven o'clock in the evening and found a gallon of milk spoiling on the kitchen table. Nikki had been at home all day, but she was too lazy to take five seconds to clean up and put away the food. That showed a lack of respect for me, as well as my house. And things have only gotten worse. Two weeks ago I found a receipt in the bottom of her panty drawer for a $2500 fur coat. I knew she couldn't have paid for it with the credit cards I gave her, because the limits weren't that high. When I confronted her with it she said that she borrowed a thousand from a finance company and used the last of her savings for the rest. I just looked at her, thinking to myself, "Where in the fuck is your broke ass going to wear a fur coat in the middle of July? To The Taste Of Chicago?" That showed me right there that she had no financial discipline. If she spent her money so irresponsibly, she damn sure wouldn't care about how she spent mine.

It's amazing how quickly a person can change once they get comfortable in a relationship. When I first met Nikki, she was working seven days a week, going to school part time, and talking about all these plans she had for the future. Now all she does is shop at the mall, party on the weekends, and sit in front of that idiot box all day watching soap operas. I'm just thankful that I never bought her that car she wanted; otherwise I wouldn't see her as often as I do, which is only four days a week. She says she's had to spend more time over at her mother's house to look after her. But I know that's just a bunch of B.S., because she has two older sisters who live with her already. Personally, I don't know how she can stand being over there in all that filth. The plaster is falling off the ceiling and cockroaches are everywhere. It's a pigsty. There are four adults living in a three-bedroom apartment and they all have small children. There's probably 13 people cramped in that small place. Not to mention two dogs and a cat.

Tracie made a good point when she told me to consider a woman's background. All the women in Nikki's family are single parents and not one of them has ever been married. Not even her whorish mother, who had five kids by three different men. I don't know how I could have been so blind. Now I've got to find a way to get rid of her before she comes up pregnant on me. With the money I'm pulling down, she could get $5000 a month easy. I've been lucky so far, probably because I don't have sex with her without protection, at least not within two weeks of her period. You know, the old rhythm method. But now that I see how scandalous she really is, I can't take any chances. I've already seen all the stress and frustration Tony has gone through with Valarie, and there's no way I can deal with that kind of drama.

From now on, I'm going to take Derrick's advice when it comes to dating. If a woman doesn't have at least $1000 in the bank and is actively pursuing her goals, I'm not going anywhere near her. I don't give a damn how fine she is or how firm her body feels. It's all about having someone in your life who you can grow with. I'm tired of baby sitting and lecturing about life. It's time for me to find out what an adult relationship has to offer. Right now, I'm in the middle of opening two new locations and it's taking up all my time and energy. But as soon as everything is up and running, I'm going to sit down and have a long talk with Nikki about our future. Basically I'm going tell her that the free ride is over and that she can go back to where she came from, the gutter.

Summertime in Chicago is always a busy season for designing floral arrangements for funerals. The heat and humidity causes tempers to flare, an incidental bump or a stare that lasts too long can quickly escalate into gunshots. During the Fourth of July weekend, the violence hit close to home. The daughter of one of the most notorious gang bangers on the South Side was shot during a drive-by. Luckily, the bullet only grazed her on the forehead. But everybody knew her father would be out for revenge. The police know him as Big Red, a thief, an extortionist, and cold-blooded killer. But his real name is Julius Armstrong, the guy I grew up fighting in grammar school and one of my closest friends. We used to humbug almost every day over control of the basketball courts and playground. In fact, he's the reason why Derrick, Tony, and Mark befriended me. They needed my big ass to keep Julius from taking their bikes and stealing their lunch money.

Eventually we called a truce and began hanging out at the gym lifting weights together. I guess we both got tired of whipping on each other for so many years. Neither of us ever got the best of the other. And although our lives have gone in very different directions, we've always stayed in touch with one another. I could care less about what the police or the D.A. said about him on the ten o'clock news. He'll always be down with me. So, when I heard about what happened to his daughter, Ariel, I arranged a meeting at my shop on 63rd Street.

When he showed up in his black Hummer, I was shocked by all the security he had with him. His boys jumped out with their hands on their pistols and looked around cautiously like Secret Service agents. Once the coast was clear, they escorted him inside and stood guard by the door, like soldiers. It was a scene right out of the movies.

"Hey, man, since when did you need the National Guard to come see me?"

"Since we went and hit those fools who shot my daughter yesterday. Somebody had to pay. But don't worry, Big Ben, I would never have come here if I thought I was putting you in the line of fire."

"Yeah, right! That's exactly what you said at that rent party your sister threw back in high school. Next thing you know, bullets were flying everywhere and I got shot in the buttocks because your clumsy ass fell and blocked the door."

"You still remember that, huh?"

"I remember, all right. Every time I take down my pants, I think of you."

"That's very touching," he said while sniffing on a rose. "Just don't let anybody else hear you say that. They might get the wrong idea."

"Okay, enough of the small talk. Tell me what happened to Ariel."

"There isn't much to tell. She was jumping double dutch in front of Mama's house and two fools drove by and started blasting. It was amazing that none of the other kids got hit. But they won't be shooting at anybody else's kids," he said with that look in his eyes. "I took care of that personally."

"Damn, Julius. When are you going to get away from all of the drugs and violence. You're getting too old for this shit."

"When these fathers stop leaving their sons out on the streets for me to raise, that's when."

"Come on, man. That's just an excuse. You're a smart brother. Why don't you let me set you up in something legitimate."

"Like what, Ben? One of your florist shops? I'm not cut out for nine to five. I live like a vampire. I get up at sundown and go to bed at eight o'clock in the morning. That's my life."

"But, Julius...."

"Look, homie," he said cutting me off. "I didn't come down here for a sermon. I just wanted to tell you what happened to Ariel and to thank you for sending the flowers. Why don't we just leave it at that?"

"All right, Big Red, but you haven't heard the last of me. If it's the last thing I do, I'm going to change you from your evil ways."

"Good luck! The last person who tried to reform me ended up in a mental institution. I'm bad to the bone." He laughed. "Now, let me get out of here so I can go take care of my business. I've got an employee who needs motivating."

"All right Les, Brown. Just promise me you won't get yourself killed or locked up before I see you again."

"That's a promise," he said as he gave me a hug and then headed for the door. "Oh, by the way, tell Mark and Derrick I said what's up. And be sure to tell Tony I said congratulations."

"So, you heard about the wedding, huh?"

"Heard about it? He asked sarcastically. "I was there. How many times do I have to tell you? Don't nuthin' go down on the southside without me knowing about it."

"Man, you're worse than the CIA, always spying on somebody."

"Yeah, but the CIA never looked this good," he said as he modeled his custom-made suit. "I'm out like a scout! And thanks again for the flowers. Mama really appreciated them."

Right after Julius left, I closed the store early and headed home. I thought about calling Nikki to ask her if she wanted something for dinner, but I decided not to. She had been at home all day sitting on her behind doing absolutely nothing. If she was too lazy to cook herself something to eat, then she could starve to death as far as I was concerned. But I did stop at McDonald's to pick up a Happy Meal for Jason. There was no sense of making him suffer just because his mother was trifling.

When I drove up to the house, I saw an old white Nova sitting in the driveway. At first I didn't recognize it. But then I remembered that it belonged to Nikki's girlfriend, Jackie. She must have had it painted recently, because when I saw it last month, it was brown. I didn't even bother myself over why she was there. I just pulled into the garage, grabbed the bag of McDonald's, and put the alarm on. All I wanted was a nice quiet evening of rest and relaxation, which meant that Jackie had to go. She was one of the most kind-hearted women I've ever met, but she had a loud mouth and she talked too damn much. Always gossiping about other people's business.

Before I got up to the door, I started plotting on how to get rid of her. The last time she came over to visit, she stayed until six o'clock in the morning. Nothing I did worked. When I yawned noticeably, she offered to get me a pillow. When I started rattling around dishes in the kitchen acting as if I was cleaning up for the night, she asked if I needed help. And when I took a shower and put on my pajamas, she made a pot of coffee and took out her bottle of No Doz. "Don't you get the hint?" I was thinking. "Get a life!" But this time I was spared. Just as I was about to grab the knob, Jackie was opening the door on her way out. And she had Jason with her.

"Hey. Ben! How you doing?"

"I'm doing just fine," I said. "Where are you two going?"

"Jason is spending the night with me so you and Nikki can have some quality time together."

"Oh, really? And whose idea was that?"

"It's mine!" Nikki said in a seductive tone. She was peeking from behind the door wearing a black teddy and four-inch pumps. "Why don't you help Jackie to the car with Jason and hurry back so I can tell you all about it."

I paused at first, not knowing quite how to react. Then I looked inside the house and saw it was cleaned for a change. No toys laying around on the floor and no newspapers scattered all over the dining room table. Nikki had finally shown some initiative by cooking and creating a romantic atmosphere. There were long-stem candles lit throughout the house and the table was formally set. And the delicious aroma of pot roast baking in the oven filled the air. Nikki could throw down in the kitchen, but she hadn't cooked a decent meal in months. Whatever she was up to, it looked interesting. So, I did an about-face and rushed Jason to the car. I threw his bags in the trunk, tossed him his bag of McDonald's, and gave him a pat on the head. "See ya," I said. And quickly made my way back to the house to see what else Nikki had on, or should I say, what she didn't have on?

The house was dimly lit. Other than the two candles on the table, the only other light was coming from the kitchen. I walked in to see what was cooking, if you know what I mean.

"You need any help in there?" I shouted

"No, I've got everything under control, baby. Just hurry up and take your shower so we can eat and watch X-rated videos."

"Which ones did you get?"

"Just one. It's called Ben Does Nikki."

It wasn't until I went into the bedroom that I understood what she meant. Nikki had the room set up like a TV studio. There was a video camera sitting on a tripod at the foot of the bed, hooked up to my 52-inch television set. Where she got the money for all that expensive equipment, I don't know. And to be honest with you, I really didn't care. All I was thinking about was getting my freak on! Nikki knew that it had been my fantasy for years to record myself having sex. I guess it was her fantasy too.

After I finished my shower, I wrapped a towel around my waist and went into the dinning room where Nikki served me a dinner fit for a king. Pot roast with baked potatoes and gravy, steamed broccoli, corn on the cob, and homemade biscuits. When I finished the main course she ask me to stand up while she placed a towel underneath me.

"What's for dessert," I asked.

"You are," she said and then spread Cool Whip between my legs and went down on me.

It was cold as hell at first, and I trembled. But the warmth of her mouth quickly soothed my nerves. I tried to help her with the rhythm by grabbing her by the back of the head, but she moved my hands away.

"I'm doing **this**," she said. "Just sit back and enjoy it."

I took her advice and leaned my head back on the chair and chilled. For the next 30 minutes she sucked me like a lollipop, never coming up for air. The candlelight cast a shadow of her head moving up and down on the wall. What a turn-on! She was doing me with such intensity and passion that it seemed like she was enjoying the act more than I was. Oh, I felt so used. So, cheap. I laughed at the thought.

After she was done, Nikki took me by the hand and led me into the bedroom. While I anxiously got into bed, she turned on the television and tuned it to channel three so we could watch ourselves while the tape recorded. She switched on the video and then joined me.

"Ben, I want you to do me a favor."

"Anything for you, baby. What is it?"

"I know you think I'm fragile, but I need you to be a little rough with me. I can handle it."

"Are you sure?"

"Yes, I'm sure," she said as she guided me inside of her. "I may be a lady but I need to be treated like a whore every now and then."

Nikki was wild and adventurous in the bedroom. The classic freak. She was deep into the domination thing. Sometimes she would ask me to handcuff her wrists to the bedpost and slap her on the ass real hard. I accommodated her when I could, but that kind of freaky stuff is not in my character, especially the dirty talk. Calling your woman a bitch can be a degrading experience. It can seriously affect the way you look at her. Pretty soon you start thinking to yourself, "Maybe you are a bitch." But I put all those inhibitions, insecurities, or whatever you want to call them, aside just for one night. When she flipped over on top of me I palmed her ass tight and slammed her down with force. If she wanted rough, I was going to give her rough.

"That's it baby!" she screamed. "Fuck me, fuck me harder!"

"Is it good, baby? Huh, is it?"

"Oh, yes. it's good. It's the best I ever had."

I wanted to stop right there and say, "Yeah right, that's what they all say." But once my ego kicked in, it really didn't matter. I tightened up my grip and slammed her down even harder. Bam! I was stroking her so hard I thought I was going to split her in two. But like so many thin women, Nikki was deceptively deep.

"Whose is it?" I asked while I slapped her so hard her butt turned red. "Tell me it's mine!"

"It's yours daddy. It's yours!"

All that dirty talk was making me even more horny. And watching it live on television only enhanced the experience.

I moved Nikki over to the edge of the bed and positioned her right in front of the camera so I could see myself sliding in and out of her. But she was moving so fast the picture was blurred. I tried to slow her down but it was no use. She was in a zone. After a few more strokes I couldn't hold back any longer. I exploded inside of her then fell back onto the pillow like a sack of flour. Suddenly everything she did wrong during the last three months was forgiven. I held her firmly in my arms, kissed her on the forehead, and fell in love all over again.

HOTLANTA

"**S**o, how's the weather in Dallas?"

"It's hot as hell! Even the white folks had to come inside from tanning at the pool." Derrick was being his usual funny self. "And you know how much they love baking out in that hot sun trying to get brown like us."

"You need to quit," Angela replied.

"You know I'm telling the truth. Then they have the audacity to be racist. Society is so ass-backwards."

"Speaking of backwards, when are you coming back home? I really miss you."

"I should be getting in on Monday afternoon. I still have one more stop to make."

"And where is that?"

"Atlanta. I thought I told you."

"No. You didn't mention it. Otherwise I would have made plans to meet you there. As a matter of fact, I can still fly down. I've got an extra ticket from last month that I haven't used yet."

"Oh, no baby, don't bother!" he said, sounding as if he was hiding something. "I've got a thousand things to do. I won't have any spare time for socializing. Anyway, I'm going to get off this phone and head out to DFW airport. I'll give you a call from Atlanta when I get settled in at my hotel."

"Okay, sweetheart. Have a safe trip and remember that I love you."

"Yeah, me too baby," Derrick said, then hung up.

Angela knew something was up. Derrick had been traveling to Atlanta more frequently than usual, four times in the last two months. That was way too often, even for business. Coincidentally, her best friend Denise had been dating some guy named Darnell who she claimed was a sales rep for a computer software company. This all sounded fishy to Angela, because she had never seen or even talked to this man before, not once. She didn't want to start trippin' over the thought that something might be going on, but she couldn't help it. Denise was an attractive and intelligent woman who had it going on. No kids, a house that was paid for, and a great career, just Derrick's type. What bothered her most was that she had shared intimate details of her sexual relationship with Denise and a few of her other girlfriends. That was a big mistake, especially in a city like Atlanta were many women are desperate for a man and will stab you in the back in a minute.

"No way, not my girl Denise!" Angela told herself over and over again. "We go back too far." True enough they had known one another since their first year of college. That was 15 years of blood, sweat and tears. And they promised above all else never to allow a man to come between them. But Angela wasn't that naive.

She knew even the most loyal of friends could fall prey if a man caught her at just the right time in her life when she was lonely and horny as hell. And it only added to her insecurity that Derrick and Denise had gotten together on a couple of occasions for lunch when he visited Atlanta. And like a fool, Angela was the one who insisted that they get together. She figured Denise was someone she could trust to be a friend to Derrick and keep him out of trouble. Suddenly she wasn't feeling very trusting. Thoughts of Derrick holding Denise in his arms was driving her crazy. Her best friend and her man, getting busy.

"Hell naw!" she said aloud. "I'm not getting played like a fool!" Angela called the airport for the next departure to Atlanta, then frantically began packing her garment bag and cosmetic case. "Here I am flying my dumb ass back and forth to Atlanta trying to run my business long distance just to be with this man," she angrily thought. "If I find out he's fuckin' Denise I'm going to punch the shit out of her and cut his dick off."

Angela's flight to Atlanta was a real nightmare. The baby seated behind her wouldn't stop crying, the man next to her was sloppy drunk and kept trying to hit on her, and the flight attendants were a couple of rude bimbos. She had to ask for a pillow three times before they remembered to bring her one. And when she rang her bell for a glass of water, the skinny blond acted like she had an attitude. "These glorified waitresses have a lot of damn nerve trying to act uppity," she thought as she gave them both dirty looks. "All they do is serve drinks and make announcements. I could train a monkey to do that."

But once the plane landed, all of her anger and frustration

was quickly redirected to Derrick and Denise. During the two-hour flight Angela had worked herself into a silent rage and was anxious to get over to Denise's house to see if they were together. After renting a Ford Taurus, she headed straight for the nearest 7-Eleven to pick up a few supplies, a bag of Baked Lays potato chips, a six-pack of Dr Pepper, a flashlight, a pack of Energizer batteries, and the latest issue of *Heart and Soul* magazine for reading material. She was determined to be right there waiting when they came home all hugged up and lovie dovie. If that meant camping out until sunrise, she wanted to be well-stocked.

When she arrived at the house, all the lights were out. Angela peeked inside the garage to see if Denise's red BMW was gone. It was. So, she parked across the street behind a row of thick bushes, turned off her headlights, and settled in. "What in the world am I doing here?" she asked while looking at herself in the rear view mirror. "It can't be this serious." But it was. Angela was in love for the first time in her adult life and was way out of control. Once upon a time, she would quit a man at the drop of a hat if she even so much as suspected him of cheating. And she advised her girlfriends to do likewise. But this time she was having a hard time taking her own advice. There she was on a beautiful warm summer night staking out her girlfriend's house like Angela Lansbury trying to find closure to her relationship.

As the hours passed, she began to feel more and more awkward. The digital clock inside the car read ten o'clock, then eleven, then twelve. By one o'clock she was almost out of food and self-respect. As she looked at herself in the mirror again, she laughed uncomfortably, trying to disguise how ridiculous she felt. Then she was overwhelmed by a sense of utter humiliation. "My mother is probably rolling over in her grave right now," she thought as she began to cry. "I never thought loving a man could make me sink so low." Angela popped open her last can of soda and took a sip to clear her throat. Then she blew her nose with a Kleenex and wiped the tears from her eyes.

"This whole thing has gone far enough," she was thinking. "I'm outta here!" She tossed the empty soda cans over to the passenger's side and adjusted her seat. All she wanted was a good night's sleep and to be on the first plane back to Chicago in the morning. But right as she was about to turn on the ignition, a car pulled up to the house. It was Denise's red beamer. Angela couldn't make out exactly who was inside the car with her, but it was definitely a man.

She watched closely as they walked from the garage to the house, trying to make out anything that was familiar. The man was medium built, with a low-cut hairstyle, and about six feet tall, exactly Derrick's height. His arm was wrapped around Denise's shoulders and he was leaning against her as if he had too much to drink. "Look at that no-good cheating dog. We haven't been dating for seven months yet, and he's already screwing my best friend," Angela said with fire in her eyes. "But that's all right, though. I've got a surprise for both their asses."

After waiting ten minutes for the bedroom lights to go out, she put the batteries in the flashlight and walked up to the front door with the extra set of keys she had to Denise's house. When she tried to open the door slowly, it squeaked like hell. And the slower she pushed, the louder it squeaked. Once she was inside, she tiptoed upstairs to the bedroom where she could hear the unmistakable sound of lovemaking. And judging by how loud Denise was screaming and carrying on, it was good, real good! Angela stood outside the room for a second to build up her courage. She counted to ten, took a deep breath, then jumped out into the open and shined the flashlight right in their faces.

"Ah, huh!" she yelled.

"What the .....?" Denise screamed while trying to cover herself and her lover with the blanket. "Get out of here before I call the police!"

"Go right ahead and call the police!" Angela screamed back. "I'll have your ass arrested for being a back-stabbing tramp."

"Angie, is that you?"

"It's me all right, and you're cold busted."

"Busted? What are you talking about?"

"You know damn well what I'm talking about. You and Derrick are fooling around. Let go of the blanket so I can see his two-timing face."

When Denise let go of the covers, guess whose head pops up? "Hello, Angela, it's a pleasure to finally meet you," Darnell said. "I was hoping to make your acquaintance with at least my socks or draws on."

"Oh, my God. I'm so embarrassed."

"Well, you should be," Denise said. "Now get that flashlight out of my face and tell me what the hell is going on. And it better be good!"

Denise put on her robe and excused herself to go talk to Angela. When she made it downstairs Angela was sitting at the dining room table sipping on a glass of brandy and looking as pitiful as can be.

"Girl, what in the world has gotten into you? I can't believe you thought I was cheating with Derrick. He may be fine but he's not fine enough for me to ruin my friendship over."

"I'm sorry, Dee. It's just that he's been coming down here more frequently over the last few months and I thought...,"

"You thought he was laying up with me. That's really messed up," Denise said looking disappointed and hurt. "Why didn't you just come right out and ask me instead of trying to play detective?"

"Yeah, right. Like you would have told me the truth if you were cheating."

"I guess you've got a point there. But why me? There are a million attractive women in Atlanta he could be cheating with."

"Look, I really don't want to go into all that right now. I just need some time to chill out and get my head together. You mind if I stay here tonight?"

"Of course I don't mind. But it seems to me that you and

Derrick have some serious issues that need to be resolved. Why don't you give him a call and get it out into the open?"

"He's probably asleep by now."

"I doubt that. We just ran into him downtown at Jazzmin's night club. He said he was headed back to his hotel. Do you know which one he's staying at?"

"If I know Derrick, he's probably at the Marriott Marquis on Peachtree Center. He's very regimented when it comes to hotels."

"Well, what are you waiting for? Go handle your business."

"Thanks for being so understanding, soror. I don't know what I would do without you."

"What are friends for?" Denise said while rushing her to the door. "Now get your paranoid ass out of here so I can get back upstairs and handle **my** own business. I just hope Darnell can still get it up after that traumatic experience you put him through."

"Judging by the way you two were going at it, I don't think that will be much of a problem."

It was 2:00 a.m. and the temperature outside was still a muggy 82 degrees. Angela could feel the suffocating humidity in the air as she sped down I 75 Expressway. Even with the air conditioning running on high, sweat was pouring down her back. "They don't call it Hotlanta for nothing," she was thinking. When she saw the sign for the International Blvd. exit, she pulled out her cell phone to check her voice mail to make sure Derrick was where he was supposed to be. Sure enough, he left her a message saying he was at the Marriott in room 4201, like always.

Angela was incredibly aroused by the thought of being wrapped up in his arms again. It had been more than two weeks since she smelled the masculine aroma of his body or felt him inside of her. She needed a fix. When she arrived at the hotel she quickly pulled her bags out the trunk and parked the car with the valet, charging it to Derrick's room. She thought about calling from the lobby to let him know she was coming up, but she decided to surprise him instead. As the glass elevator moved slowly toward the forty-second floor, she tried to think of a good opening line when she saw his handsome face. But she was also worried that he might be upset by her unexpected appearance. "I'll cross that bridge when I come to it." she thought.

Not surprisingly, the "Do Not Disturb" sign was hanging on his doorknob. Derrick was the type of man that hibernated like a bear once he got settled in for the night, and he didn't like his peace interrupted. Angela pressed her ear against the door and checked to see if he was still awake. She could hear the television playing in the background and what sounded like the shower running. She adjusted her clothes, took a deep breath, then knocked, making sure to stand away from the peephole.

"Who is it?" Derrick asked in a disturbed tone.

"It's the bellman, sir," Angela said trying to disguise her voice to sound like a man. "We just received a fax for you marked urgent."

"A fax? I'm not expecting any faxes this late at night. Why didn't you call me from the front desk?"

"We tried but there was no answer."

Angela was praying that his message light was blinking to back up her story. Otherwise the gig was up. Judging by his response, it was.

"Look, I'm just getting out of the shower. Can you slide it under the door?"

"I tried that already, sir. It won't fit."

"Okay," he said. "Let me put on my shirt."

Angela was starting to get a bad feeling. Derrick wasn't the kind of man who cared about people seeing his chest, especially another man. A few seconds passed, then the door slowly swung open. But instead of being happy to see her, the expression on his face was one of total disgust.

"Surprise!" she shouted halfheartedly.

"What the hell are you doing here?"

"Is that all you have to say? At least you could have the common courtesy to invite me in."

"What about you having the common courtesy of calling before intruding on my privacy? How would you like it if I came by your house unannounced?"

"I probably wouldn't appreciate it," Angela said, feeling like a child being scolded by her father. "I just thought you might want to see me after being on the road for the last two weeks."

"Well, you thought wrong."

"Damn, Derrick, why are you being so cold?"

"Because you haven't been there for me when I needed you. You go out of town for two weeks at a time on business leaving me alone to play with myself. And when you finally do come home, you've got cramps or a fuckin' headache. Now you pop up here in the middle of the night and you think it's supposed to be some kind of a romantic reunion. I don't think so."

"You're right, baby. I know I haven't been taking care of you the way I should and I'm sorry. But can't we try to work things out?"

"Derrick who are you talking to this late at night!" a woman's voice said from inside the room.

"Don't worry about it," Derrick shouted. "Just finish taking your shower."

Angela gave Derrick a dirty look, then forced her way into the room.

"I should have known it was you, Vanessa."

"Well, now you know."

"I can't believe you would pretend to be my friend then go behind my back. What kind of woman are you?"

"The kind of woman who knows how to appreciate a good man," Vanessa said, getting in Angela's face. "And unlike you, I don't go around telling every Mary, Jane, and Sally about what's going on in my bedroom. You need to learn to keep your big mouth shut when it comes to your man."

"Fuck you, you hazel-eyed bitch!" Angela said, snatching her by the hair and throwing her to the floor. "You may be screwing my man, but I'll be damned if you're going to talk shit about it."

Angela was beating the hell out of Vanessa, dragging her across the floor like a ragdoll and punching her several times in the face. By the time Derrick was able to break it up, Vanessa had a busted lip and carpet burns all over her back.

"Maybe that'll teach you to think twice about stabbing another sistah in the back."

"Just get the hell out of here!" Derrick said pushing her out the door. "You haven't done anything but make a fool of yourself."

"Fuck you too, you arrogant bastard. If it wasn't for me, you wouldn't be where you are today. I made you!"

Derrick's face turned to stone. He never thought Angela would stoop so low as to take credit for his success. Sure, she helped influence Mr. Starks in New York back in January. But he was determined to make it with or without that contract. And Angela knew it. All he could do was look painfully into her eyes as he closed the door in her face. There was nothing left to say. It was over.

SOLE CUSTODY

I was so pissed I wanted to punch a hole in the wall. I don't know what gave me the idea that things were going to change after Tracie and I got married. Valarie is up to her old tricks again. This time she let her sister take Erikah to a birthday party when she knew damn well that I was on my way over to pick her up to go shopping. Then she lied and said she called her sister and told her to bring Erikah back home. I sat outside in my car for over an hour waiting for her to show up. Then I said to hell with it and came home. Later on that evening, I called Valarie to get this nonsense straightened out once and for all.

"All this game playing has got to stop," I told her. "I'm sick and tired of you using Erikah as a pawn to get back at me. If you've got a problem with either me or Tracie, we need to sit down and talk about it like adults."

"What in the world are you talking about?" she said, playing the dumb role.

"You know exactly what I'm talking about. This is my weekend for legal visitation and you knew Erikah and I had plans."

"You're the one who left before she got home. Maybe you should learn to be more patient."

"Maybe you should learn to grow up and stop making things so damned complicated. I mean, here it is almost nine years since we've dated and you still haven't accepted the fact that I'm with someone else. And I'm beginning to think you never will. It seems like your only mission in life is to make everybody miserable."

"That's right, misery loves company, so get used to it. You and that old bama wife of yours."

"At least Tracie has a college education and runs her own business. What do you have?"

"I've got $1500 a month of your hard-earned money in my pocket, smart ass. That's what! As a matter of fact, I'll be seeing you and your high-priced lawyer in court at the end of the year for my annual raise. I read the article in the *Sun Times* about that big contract you signed with the state. Congratulations!"

"Valarie you ain't nuthin' but a blood-sucking leech. Why don't you get up off your narrow behind and make your own money? Erikah needs a positive role model in her life. Someone she can see getting up in the morning and working hard for a living like everybody else."

"I beg your pardon," she said with an attitude. "I work hard too! I cook dinner three times a week, clean this apartment from top to bottom, wash and iron school clothes, and help Erikah with homework. That's more than most parents can say."

"You act like you've got a house full of kids. I know women with three kids who work full-time jobs and go to school. All you do is watch soap operas all day and talk on the phone with your lazy-ass girlfriends. Have you even thought about what you're going to do with your life when the child support is gone?"

"I'll worry about that eleven years from now." She laughed. "Until then I'm going to live it up! I've got a comfortable apartment, a refrigerator full of groceries, and a bag of weed to keep me company."

"Is that what I hear you puffing on?"

"That's right. I'm sitting here getting blasted while I listen to you whine like a baby."

"Where is Erikah? I know she's not in the house."

"She's in the living room watching videos."

"Didn't I tell you not to smoke that shit around my daughter? What in the hell is wrong with you?"

"Chill out, dad. You used to get high yourself back in college. So don't try to act like Mr. Rogers." She took another pull and then blew hard into the phone. "And don't even try to tell me you didn't inhale."

"That was a long time ago when I was young and dumb. And even when I did get high I sure as hell didn't do it under the same roof as a seven-year-old child. That's child abuse!"

"I've been getting high with my aunts and uncles ever since I was in the eighth grade and it didn't have any negative effects on me."

I had to pause for a second to give her an opportunity to think that one over for herself. Valarie is damn near 30 years old with a G.E.D. and no college. The only real jobs she ever had was working as a cashier for Jewel's grocery store and as a waitress at a raunchy nightclub. But after Erikah was born she quit both those jobs and decided to stay at home and play housewife. That was nine years ago and she's been living solely off my child support checks ever since. Now, if she isn't the perfect example of why kids should say no to drugs, I don't know who is.

"Valarie, I'm going to say this once and only once. If I **ever** find out that you've been using drugs around Erikah again, I will use all my influence to get custody. Any woman who drinks and gets high as often as you do is unfit to be a parent."

"I don't give a damn about how many fancy lawyers you hire!" she screamed. "Ain't nobody takin' my baby away from me! Nobody, you hear me?" Then she slammed the phone in my ear.

That was a week ago, and I haven't heard from her since, which is perfectly fine with me. I've had it up to here with her nasty attitude and mind games. It doesn't make sense for any man to have to go through this much drama to see his child. You would think I was one of those deadbeat dads who was trying to run away from my responsibility by the way she treats me. Here I am spending quality time and providing for my child financially and she still insists on being difficult. I swear, sometimes I look in the mirror and ask myself, "Is it worth it?"

But I made a promised to God and myself that I would never walk out on my children the way my father did me. It really left a void in my life not having him around. And it also made me feel guilty, as if I was the reason for him leaving. I don't want Erikah going through life with that kind of baggage. She has grown too accustomed to having me around and I can't just disappear and expect her to understand and get over it. And besides, there's no way I can trust Valarie to raise Erikah with strong morals. Without me she would probably end up as a teenage mother on welfare, like so many other young fatherless girls do.

But I've got to do something! I've seen too many marriages destroyed by ex-wives and girlfriends because the husband refused to put down his foot and take control. Next thing you know they're filing for divorce on the grounds of irreconcilable differences. That's not going to happen to Tracie and me. First thing Monday morning I'm calling my lawyer. Somehow, I've got to find a way to get sole custody of Erikah. For her sake and for the sake of my marriage.

It was 9:00 o'clock Saturday morning when the phone rang. My loud and obnoxious buddies were over at Derrick's place getting ready to do something. What? I don't know. But I wished they would calm down and stop yelling in my ear.

"Are you guys on speed or something?"

"We don't need drugs, we're high on life!" Derrick shouted. "Now get your lazy butt up out of bed. It's game time!"

"Yeah, old man, and don't forget to bring that aluminum bat and an extra glove," Mark said, getting on the other phone.

"Bat? Since when do you need a bat and gloves to play basketball?"

"Derrick bet me ten dollars that you would forget."

"Forget what?"

"About the softball tournament at Grant Park today."

"Aw, man!" I said slapping myself on the forehead. "My bag. Just give me a few minutes to get dressed. I'll be there by 9:30."

"Take your time, the game doesn't start until eleven."

"Now, is this going to be a men-only affair, or are the women invited?"

"Hi, Tony!" Christie yelled in the background. "Tell Tracie I said hello!"

"Well, that answers that question. I may as well go pick up Erikah and bring her with us."

"That's a great idea, I haven't seen her since the wedding." Mark said. "But whatever you do, please don't bring those terrible twins, Tevin and Kevin. They might put crazy glue inside my glove like they did last time."

"Don't worry, they're out of town. But speaking of sticky fingers, is that pickpocket Nikki over there?"

"Unfortunately." Derrick sounded disappointed.

I couldn't believe Ben was still holding on to that no-good tramp. She gave her pager number out to three different men at the wedding reception. One guy palmed her ass on the dance floor. Derrick and I thought about telling Ben about it but we knew he wouldn't have believed us. He's really letting her pretty face and that young pussy blind him. But he's a grown man, so we stayed out of his business and kept our mouths shut.

"Well, tell her I said hello," I said, trying not to throw up. "Now let me get dressed and I'll meet you guys at the park near Buckingham Fountain at a quarter to ten."

"You better make it eleven." Derrick laughed. "Ben might still be eating breakfast."

"Eleven it is. I'll see you then. Peace."

I was careful not to bring Angela's name up during the conversation. Derrick told me what happened in Atlanta, and I didn't think he would appreciate me trying to be funny. It's been difficult for him not having her around over the past few weeks.

She was always there for him when he needed support and encouragement. And she was a great listener too. Derrick always said she was a great person to bounce ideas off of. And although he says it's over between them, she's constantly on his mind. When he came by to visit the other night, he called Tracie by Angela's name three times. He won't admit it, but he loves her. I can see it in his eyes. Hopefully they'll get together one of these days and work things out. They complemented each other so well. In the meantime, I had my own problems to deal with. It'd been more than a week since I heard from Valarie. And Erikah hadn't called either. Something was wrong, I could feel it.

While Tracie finished getting dressed, I decided to give

Valarie a call to see if I could pick up Erikah to go to the park, and to make sure everything was all right. But when I dialed the number, the operator said it was disconnected. So, I tried again, this time dialing much slower, hoping it would somehow make a difference. Once again the automated operator's voice came on. "The number you've reached has been disconnected. If you think you've dialed the wrong number, please hang up and try your call again."

"Tracie, hurry up! We've got to go, right now!"

"What's wrong?"

"I'll tell you about it on the way."

We jumped in the Corvette and sped down the Eisenhower Expressway at 90 miles an hour, weaving in and out of traffic, and driving on the shoulder. Tracie didn't say a word because she was just as concerned as I was. Within 20 minutes we were at Valarie's apartment in Oak Park. She lived on the second floor of a three-flat, two blocks away from the Lake Street L station. She was always sure to live near public transportation so she wouldn't have to spend Erikah's child support check on a car. Valarie may have been lazy, but she wasn't stupid. I parked around the back, walked up onto the porch, and rang the bell. When nobody answered, I knocked again, this time much harder.

"Erikah, it's Daddy, come open the door!"

"They're gone," said the old guy who lived downstairs.

"What do you mean, they're gone? Gone where?"

"I don't know where. Three guys came by last night with a U-Haul and moved all her stuff out."

"What did these guys look like?"

"One of them was a big husky guy with a long scar on the left side of his face. The other was kinda skinny and was wearing a lot of expensive jewelry. The third man was light-skinned, about your height. Maybe a little taller."

"Besides the truck did you see any other cars?"

"Yeah, the light-skinned fellah was driving a black Porsche with a custom plate."

"Don't tell me, it read: CEDRIC 1, right?"

"That's it."

"Dammit! Something told me to come by here last night to check on Erikah. Thanks for the information, sir. I really appreciate it."

I got inside the car and burned rubber heading straight for the expressway. "That motherfucker must have a death wish," I said to Tracie. "Taking my baby was the biggest mistake of his life." While I maneuvered my way through traffic I called Derrick and told him what happened. Two seconds later they were all piled into Ben's Lexus headed south to meet me in the parking lot of the Jewel food store on 87th Street, right off the Dyan Ryan Expressway. They knew exactly where I planned to go, to Geno's house.

When I arrived at the parking lot, they were already there waiting. I quickly jumped out the Corvette and into the front seat of the Lexus. The expression on their faces said it all. They loved Erikah like she was their own and were anxious to bust some heads.

"What are you going to do?" Tracie shouted out the passenger window.

"You know exactly what I'm going to do."

"Don't stoop down to their level. Let the police handle it."

"The police can have his ass after I get through with him. Let's go Ben!"

The last thing I remember was hearing Tracie screaming for me not to leave. But after that, I went into a deep trance. All I could think about was killing that fucker.

We parked a block away from Geno's house and walked around the back. The only weapon we had was Ben's nine-millimeter pistol, but I wasn't expecting to use it. I wanted to choke that bastard with my bare hands. When we got closer to the house, I could see two cars parked in the driveway, a

Mercedes and a Cadillac. But no sign of Cedric's Porsche. I wanted to walk up to the front door and kick that sucker down, but I knew that was suicidal. So we, made our way over to the side of the house and set off their car alarms to get them to come outside, and it worked. Geno and Tiny came running out that house like it was on fire. Ben grabbed Tiny from behind and Mark chased Geno down and tackled him on the front lawn.

"Where is she?" I asked him.

"I don't know what you're talking about," he said with a smirk on his face.

Mark folded his arm behind his back and twisted it. Geno let out a scream like a little sissy. "Ahhh!"

"Now you wanna tell me where she is?"

"Hell naw!"

"Okay, Mark, you can let him up," I said.

Geno got up off the ground and brushed the grass stains off his expensive slacks, still wearing that stupid smirk on his face. I guess he thought it was over. Not hardly. I was just getting started.

"I'm going to ask you one more time, where is my daughter?"

"Like I said, I don't know what you're talking about."

Smack! I punched him right in the mouth and split his bottom lip. He came back at me trying to wrap my legs up but I moved aside and punched him in the back of the head, knocking him to the ground.

"I'm going to ask your skinny dope-dealing ass one more time, and if you don't tell me what I need to know, I'm going to break those bird legs of yours and your bony arms. Now for the last time, where is my daughter?"

"Fuck you, nigga. You don't know who you're dealing with. I ain't no punk off the streets, I'm Geno!"

"I ain't no punk? What is that, Ebonics?" I laughed.

"You won't be laughing so hard when I put your sweet little daughter out on the corner to sell my dope."

"Who knows, when she gets old enough we might even put her out on the corner to sell something else," Tiny said with a grin on his face.

Ben let go of Tiny's arm and asked him to repeat what he said. Like a fool, he did. Then he made the mistake of taking a swing. Ben ducked under the punch and gave Tiny a vicious uppercut. While he was dazed, Ben put him in a head lock and started beating the shit out of him. He was punching Tiny so hard that he started coughing up blood. If Mark hadn't gone over to stop him, I'm sure he would have killed him. While all this excitement was going on, the neighbors were out on their lawns applauding, probably glad to see someone finally doing something about the drug problem in their neighborhood.

A few minutes later the police arrived, with Tracie right behind them. I knew she would call the law to keep me from killing that piece of shit. Little did he know, she saved his life that day. I just wish they would have given me another ten minutes. I'm sure I could have made him tell me where Erikah was.

I couldn't believe the district attorney dropped the kidnapping charges against Geno. He said there wasn't enough evidence to hold him. After all the trouble I went through, he's back on the streets and I'm the one who ended up being charged with a crime: trespassing. Ain't that a bitch? Now here it is a month later and I still haven't heard from Erikah. Geno isn't talking and the police aren't making much progress. I hired a private investigator, hoping to speed up the process. The cost was a thousand dollars a day, not including expenses. But I would have gladly paid a million just to know that she was all right.

Mark and Ben are helping out by putting up posters in their stores and passing out flyers to all their customers. Derrick took it another step further and ran a full-page photo of Erikah on the back cover of the August issue of his magazine and

offered a ten-thousand-dollar reward. But so far all that publicity hasn't gotten us one solid lead. Not even a phone call.
The stress of not knowing where she is or how she's doing is
beginning to wear me down. I can't function at work and I've
lost almost ten pounds. My doctor told me to relax and try to
get some sleep, but I can't. Every time I close my eyes I
have these horrible nightmares about her being buried in a
shallow grave out in some damp and dreary forest preserve.
I wake up in a cold sweat screaming her name. It's driving
me crazy.

At night when Tricie is asleep, I stand in the doorway of
her bedroom and imagine that she's balled up in her warm bed,
holding her black Barbie doll. I smile and let out a laugh trying to convince myself she's really there. But once I realize it's
only a mirage, I fall to my knees and start crying like a baby. I
try to stop the tears from flowing, but I can't. All that pent-up
frustration and pains comes pouring out and I lose control. If
I don't see her again soon, I don't know if I'm going to make
it. I need to hold her in my arms again, hear her laughter, and
feel the touch of her tiny hands on my face. She's more than
just my child, she's a part of me.

It was September third, the day after Labor Day when we
received our first solid lead. A woman, who wanted to remain
anonymous, claimed that she saw Erikah at a barbecue at a
friend's house over the weekend. She had Erikah's manner-
isms down to a tee and she gave a perfect description of
Valarie.

"Ms., can you tell me where I can find her now?"

"She's probably still at my friend's house. I think her and
the mother live there."

"Where does your friend live?"

"Not so fast!" she said. "I want my ten-thousand-dollar
reward first."

"You'll get your money as soon as we get my daughter back. Now, please, tell us where we can find her!"

The address she gave me was in Gary, Indiana. That was an hour and half drive away. I called ahead to the local authorities and notified them that I was on my way. The detective that I spoke with promised me that he would do everything in his power to bring her back safe, "I've got a seven-year-old daughter of my own," he said. Those words were very reassuring. I just hoped they caught Cedric too. I wanted to get my hands on him so bad I could taste it.

By the time we reached the location, it was nightfall and the police already had five people in custody. Two men, and three women, one of them Valarie. They said that the apartment was a well-known dope house and that a raid was already planned at the end of the week. I can't tell you how good it felt to see her in handcuffs. I wanted to smack the shit out of her, but I was more concerned about where Erikah was. I didn't see her anywhere around and I began to panic. I was praying she wasn't with Cedric because he wasn't among the group of men who were arrested. Then a female officer signaled me to come over to her car and pointed down to the back seat. And there she was, looking a little dirty, but all in one piece. When she saw me, she leaped out of the car and ran into my arms. "Daddy, Daddy, Daddy!" I hugged her so tight I thought I was going to break her in two.

"I'll never let anybody take you away from me again, never!"

"Where is Mommy?"

"You can see Mommy later. Let's get you cleaned up first."

I asked the officer to keep an eye on her while Tracie and I went over to have a few words with Valarie before they carted her off to jail. Judging by the glassy look in her eyes, she was high off of something.

"You need help, Valarie," I said. "And I hope you get it wherever you're going."

"Kiss my ass, Tony. I don't need sympathy from you."

"He's right," Tracie said. "And we'll be right here for you if you need us."

"You can't do nuthin' for me, you countrified bitch!" ·

Tracie's face turned cold. She walked over to Valarie and slapped the shit out of her. "That's Mrs. Bitch to you," she said, holding up her flawless two-carat rock. "I'm a married woman now."

Then the police put Valarie inside the car and drove away.

PAYBACK

It was the first week of October. The leaves had already begun to turn bright orange and the temperature was dropping into the low forties at night. Summer seemed like a distant memory to Mark as he and Christie snuggled under a thick comforter watching *Our Voices* on BET. Less than a month ago he was relaxing out on his patio in shorts and a tank top. Now he had on a pair of long johns and a thick Malcolm X sweatshirt, trying to stay warm.

"That's Chicago for you," Mark said. "Three months of

summer and nine months of rain, snow, and cold."

"I love the cold weather." Christie said. "I get to shop at the mall for all kinds of neat winter stuff like cashmere jackets and leather boots."

"All you women ever think about is shopping."

"Well, all you men ever think about is dumb sports."

"And your point is?"

"My point is, some women use shopping to compensate for the lack of attention they're getting at home."

"Where did you read that nonsense, in one of those stupid women's magazines?"

"As a matter of fact, I read it in your friend Derrick's stupid magazine. See?" Christie said. She reached over to the nightstand and showed him the cover of the October issue of *Happily Single*.

Mark walked right into her trap. He sat there looking stupid, trying to think of a good comeback line. But he couldn't. So, he did what most men do when they get caught with their foot in their mouths. He changed the subject.

"How about those Bulls? Do you think they'll win another Championship this year?"

"What does that have to do with anything?"

At that moment the phone rang. Christie was closest to the handset so she picked up.

"Hello?"

"Hello? Christie this is Ben, is Mark there?"

"Hi, Ben. Yeah he's right here, hold on a second."

Saved by the bell, Mark was thinking. He got up from the bed and took the phone in the den where he could have some privacy. He figured something had to be wrong, because Ben hardly ever called before noon on Sundays.

"What's up, Ben?"

"Mark, I swear I'm going to kill that bitch!" he said angrily. "This was the last straw."

"Calm down and tell me what happened."

"About a week ago I started feeling a little stinging when I urinated. I didn't think much of it until Thursday when the pain got worse and started to have discharge. So, I went to see my doctor and got tested. He told me I had gonorrhea."

"I told you not to trust that nasty little tramp!" Mark shouted. "You're lucky she didn't give you AIDS."

"That's not the worst of it."

"Now what? Don't tell me she stole money out your wallet."

"It's even more humiliating then that," Ben said, sounding depressed. "Remember when I told you about the video camera she brought so we could record ourselves having sex?"

"Yeah, what about it?"

"While I was tossing her things out of my closet I found a video she had hidden inside one of her shoe boxes, marked Naughty Nikki. I thought it might be a tape of her masturbating, or something like that. So, I put it in the adapter and popped it into the VCR."

"And?

"It was a recording of her with two other men engaged in sex. And it's explicit! I'm talking XXX material."

"I hate to say this, Ben, but I'm not the least bit surprised. I tried to tell you she wasn't nuthin' but a low-life ho! But you wouldn't listen."

"The last thing I need right now is to have this thing rubbed in my face." Ben was sounding broke down. "I called you expecting a little sympathy and all you can say is, I told you so? Some kind of friend you are."

"You're right, partner. That was way out of line," Mark said, checking himself. "Why don't we just concentrate on getting this thing over with? Where is Nikki at now?"

"She's been staying over at her mother's house for the last two days. But she called a few minutes ago and said she would be coming home sometime this afternoon."

"Okay, I'll be there in twenty minutes. Just do me a favor and don't do anything foolish before I get there."

"After what she did to me, I'm not making any promises,"

Ben said. Then he hung up.

Mark hurried to his closet and put on the first thing he could get his hands on. After he ran the comb through his hair a couple of times, he grabbed his leather jacket out the closet and rushed out the door. But he wasn't going anywhere. Christie had his car keys.

"Christie, have you seen my car keys?" Mark yelled, coming back inside.

"Mark, what's going on?"

"I can't explain right now, I've got to go!"

"Go where?"

"Over to Ben's house, okay? Now have you seen my car keys or not?"

Christie balled the keys into her fist and hid them behind her back. "I'm not giving you anything until you tell me what's so urgent that you have to run out first thing in the morning."

"Ben is going through a situation with Nikki and he needs my help, okay?

"No it's not okay! First it was Derrick and Angela, then Tony almost gets you thrown into jail. Now it's Ben! When are you going to let your friends handle their own damned problems?"

Mark stopped dead in his tracks and looked at her like she was crazy.

"Don't you ever, **ever**, try to tell me what I can and can't do for my friends! You haven't known me for two solid years yet and you think you can just walk into my life and come between 26 years of friendship? You must be out of your damned mind!"

"What about me?" she shouted back with tears in her eyes. "Don't I count for anything? I thought you loved me!"

"I do love you, Christie, but I love them too. And if you really cared anything about me, you wouldn't ask me to make a choice."

Christie flung the car keys at him and marched back into

the bedroom and slammed the door. Mark didn't bother going after her. He got in his car and sped off toward Ben's house not knowing or caring if she would be there when he got back.

By the time Mark showed up at Ben's house, most of Nikki's belongings had already been thrown out onto the front lawn. A few minutes later Nikki drove up. But she wasn't alone. Her girlfriend Jackie was with her and so were the police. She had a feeling Ben was on to her game and decided to bring a little protection.

"Just be cool," Mark said. "Let me handle this."

"I don't have anything to say to Nikki or the police. I just want her out of here!"

While Nikki and Jackie began picking up her clothes off the wet lawn, one of the black officers walked up to the house and knocked on the door.

"What's the problem, officer Johnson?" Mark asked, noticing his name tag.

"There's no problem at all. The young lady just wants to get her things out the house without any trouble."

"Everything she owns is out there on the lawn," Mark said, trying not to laugh. "And if she's looking for her laced pink panties, tell her the neighbor's dog ate them."

Officer Johnson wanted to laugh too, because Nikki's clothes were scattered everywhere. One of her gym shoes was on top of the roof. Her cosmetic case was tossed out into the street. And her expensive fur coat was shredded to pieces lying in a puddle of mud. Ben intentionally left the sprinkler system running to make sure everything got soaked.

"You mind if I ask you a question?"

"No, go right ahead," Mark said.

"Why did your friend toss her clothes into the street instead of packing them in boxes?"

"Because she's a conniving tramp, that's why!" Mark said

loud enough for Nikki to hear. "Women like that don't deserve to be treated with respect. If it was left up to me I would have poured gasoline over that junk and burned it."

"It can't be that serious."

"Trust me, brother, it is!"

While Nikki and Jackie stuffed the last of her wet clothes into plastic garbage bags, Ben stood still in the window and watched. He wasn't sad, and he wasn't angry. He was just tired. Tired of all the games and tired of being taken advantage of. All his life he played the nice-guy role and each time he ended up on the short end of the stick. He thought about changing his approach to dating and becoming a dog. Women seemed to be attracted to men who treated them like shit. And the worse they treated them the more attracted they seemed to be. But Ben knew dogging women wasn't in his nature. He was a kind-hearted gentleman who couldn't help being generous.

After Nikki loaded the last of her things into the trunk she thanked the police for their help and drove away. "Goodbye and good riddance," Mark said. When he came back inside the house he was expecting to find Ben balled up in a corner ready to commit suicide. But to his surprise he was pouring two glasses of champagne and smiling from ear to ear.

"I want to propose a toast."

"What are we celebrating?" Mark asked while picking up his glass.

"We're celebrating the death of an old fool who had to learn the hard way that true beauty comes from within." Ben said tapping his glass with Mark's and taking a long sip. "From now on I'm leaving these young girls alone and sticking with the mature women who have their lives and their money together. I'm through raising kids"

"I'll drink to that."

When Mark's alarm clock went off at 7:30 Friday morning he

reached out to the other side of the bed for Christie, but once again she wasn't there. A week had passed since their heated argument and he was missing her more than ever. But Mark was too damned stubborn to call and say he was sorry. Every time he got ready to pick up the phone to dial her number, his foolish pride kicked in and he slammed down the handset determined to wait her out. "If anybody is going to apologize, it's going to be her," he thought. But this childish waiting game was beginning to take its toll. For 17 months he had grown accustomed to having Christie in his space. Her sudden absence was throwing his life off balance and out of rhythm. Not only was he reaching over into an empty bed but had begun to talk to himself in the middle of the night thinking she was there listening.

Mark decided enough was enough. He sprung up out of the bed and emptied out his briefcase looking for the number to Ben's floral shop downtown. He wanted to have a dozen red roses sent over to Christie's office along with a note saying he was sorry. Seven days without her was all he could bear. Once he found his phone book he reached for the handset. But before he could dial the number, the phone rang. He was hoping it was Christie.

"Hello?"

"Is this Mark?" a man's muffled voice asked.

"This is Mark, who is this?"

"You know damn well who this is, you honky lovin' nigga. It's payback time!"

"Look, you damned coward. I don't scare easily," Mark said angrily. "If you want some of me, you know where to find me."

"I know where to find that white bitch of yours too. Maybe I'll pay her a little visit and show her what it feels like to be with a real black man."

"You leave her out of it, you hear me?"

The phone went dead. That was the fifth crank call in the last three days and he knew exactly who was behind it: Geno.

Ben and Derrick had received them too, and so had Tony. But this was the first time they threatened to harm Christie. That pushed Mark over the edge. "Fuck this!" he said out loud. "If he wants to play gangster, I'll find somebody for him to play with." He called Ben at the shop and asked him to set up a meeting with Big Red as soon as possible. At first he felt a little uncomfortable about asking someone else to do his dirty work, but after he thought about Christie's safety and the safety of his friends, he put his pride aside. Geno had to be sent a message. And Big Red was a professional ass-kicker who would make sure he got it, loud and clear.

It was 12:45 a.m. when Mark arrived at the projects to meet Big Red. As he walked down the dimly lit hallway past all the burnt out apartments, it was hard to imagine this was the same building he and his friends grew up in for the first 13 years of their lives. The walls were covered with all kinds of graffiti and gang symbols. And the floor was blanketed with sharp glass from broken wine and malt liquor bottles. It was a depressing sight. Back when they were kids the projects weren't such a hell hole. The courtyards had thick green grass, swings, seesaws, and monkey bars. Now the only exercise that kids get is from dodging bullets. It's a damn shame, he was thinking. Black children can't even go across the street to school without worrying about getting killed.

Big Red's apartment was on the 15th floor. The elevator was out of order so he had to walk up the narrow stairway which reeked of urine. The smell was so bad he had to cover his mouth with a handkerchief to keep from throwing up. Once he made it to the 15th floor, he was met by two armed men who frisked him thoroughly and then escorted him into the apartment where Big Red was sitting behind a long glass table with a cigar in his hand. It was a scene right out of *New Jack City*.

"Well, Well, Well, look who's here." Big Red said smiling.

Ben told me you were coming to see me, but I didn't believe him."

"What's up Julius, long time no see. Or should I call you Big Red?"

"I prefer Big Red, but you can call me Julius since we go way back. What brings you down to the low end. It must be serious."

"As serious as a cancer!"

"Well, let's get right down to business," Big Red said, gesturing for him to have a seat. "What seems to be the problem?"

"The problem is Geno. Ever since Tony whipped his ass over that situation with his daughter there hasn't been any peace."

"Why didn't Tony come to me himself?"

"Because he's too damned proud, that's why. But this shit is getting out of hand. Now Geno is making threats towards our women too. You know Geno doesn't play by the rules."

"You're right about that," Big Red said. "That low-down son of a bitch would shoot his own mother in the back."

"So, can you help us out or what?"

Big Red reclined in his leather chair, lifted his size 15 1/2 alligator boots up onto the table, and lit his cigar.

"Okay, I'll take care of it."

"That's it?" Mark asked.

"What were you expecting, a typed contract? I told you I would take care of it and I will!"

"So, how much do I owe you?"

"Don't insult me like that!" Big Red said with a serious look on his face. "I'm doing this as a favor to a friend. We've got to stick together, right?"

"Right. But at least come out to the house for dinner. I'll have Christie cook whatever you want."

"Christie? Is that the white girl you're dating?"

"Yeah, and?"

"No offense, homie, but I'll have to take a pass on that!"

"Why? Don't tell me that you don't like white people."

"As a matter of fact, I don't. But the reason why I'm not coming is because white people can't season food worth shit."

Mark fell out laughing. He agreed with Big Red one hundred percent. The last time Christie tried to make black-eyed peas it turned out so bland he had to use half a bottle of hot sauce to give it flavor.

"No offense taken."

"If you really want to return the favor, how about sending me a copy of that new John Singleton movie?" Big Red asked. "I heard it's coming out on video next month."

"You mean, *Rosewood*?"

"Yeah, that's the one!"

"You've got yourself a deal!"

After they shook hands and exchanged manly hugs, Big Red escorted him to the door and then watched out for him until he made it safely to his car. But before he drove off, Mark decided to get something off his chest. Something that had been gnawing at him for years.

"Hey, Julius!" he yelled. "Whatever happened to that ten-speed Schwinn you stole from me back in eighth grade?"

"You really want to know?"

"Yeah, I want to know! I loved that bike!"

"I sold it to this freckle-faced kid for three White Castle hamburgers and a pack of Now and Laters."

"That bike cost $200!"

"What can I say, man? I was starvin'."

ALONE

I'm staring out of the window and listening to my Maxwell
CD wondering how I could have been so damned stupid.
Angela was the best thing that ever happened to me, and I
ruined it. If I had an ounce of sense I would have gone over to
her house the minute I got back to Chicago and begged for for-
giveness. But just like most stubborn and controlling men, I
tried to play the hard role. Now my hard ass is sitting here
alone on Thanksgiving Day getting drunk off tequila and eating
peanut butter and jelly sandwiches. Tony called earlier to invite

me over to his house for dinner, thinking it would cheer me up. But I told him the only thing that would make me feel better was getting Angela back. I tried calling her to apologize for what happened, but she didn't leave a forwarding number when she moved back to Atlanta. I even tried writing letters asking for another chance, but she won't respond. Not that I blame her. If I was in her shoes I wouldn't want to talk to my no-good ass either, not after what I put her through.

The worst part about this whole episode is that Vanessa wasn't even worth the trouble. She turned out to be very self-centered and shallow. In fact, all we had in common was sex. And even that wasn't strong enough to build on. It never is. Two weeks after that dramatic scene at the hotel, we stopped dating. It seemed like all the passion and excitement went out of the sex once Angela was no longer a part of the equation. That just makes me feel like an even bigger jackass. I ended up losing the most wonderful woman to ever come into my life over a piece of pussy, and a temporary piece at that. Sometimes I look at my reflection in the mirror and think to myself, "Your dumb ass didn't deserve her anyway."

Now I'm all alone. Alone to deal with my immaturity and alone to think about what might have been. Angela was my soul mate, I'm sure of it. She was the first woman I ever met who actually taught me something; like compassion, patience, and how to listen. I guess you could say she complemented me perfectly. After we broke up I tried to find someone to take her place, but they never measured up. They didn't even come close. Either they were too aggressive, too uppity, or just too damned combative. Angela had balance. She was a home girl with intellect and class. That's a rare combination to find in a woman. Now all I have are pictures and distant memories. And the hardest part to live with is that it was all my fault.

The more I thought about how badly I fucked up, the more I drank. And the more I drank, the more depressed I got. This was the first time in my life that I was alone on a major holiday with no one to talk to and no one to hold. I could have gone over to Tony's and had dinner with him and the rest of my friends, but I didn't have a date. Sure, I knew women who I could have called just to hang out, but I didn't feel comfortable bringing just anybody over to my best friend's house for Thanksgiving dinner. That's an event reserved exclusively for someone special. And that's exactly what I don't have in my life, someone special. Mark and Christie are back together and going strong. Tony and Tracie are enjoying married life and have recently moved into their new house. Even Ben has a new woman in his life. I think her name is Beverly, Barbara, or something like that. He met her when he was at Walgreens having his prescription filled for that venereal disease Nikki gave him. When he introduced us, I knew she was perfect for him. She was 38 years old, worked as a registered nurse, and didn't have any crumbsnatchers. And although she is a little on the chubby side, she is a hell of a lot better than what I have, which is nothing!

Without Angela in my life, I feel empty. All of the things that I thought were so important don't mean shit! Not my extravagant condo, not my $75,000 car, not even the magazine I worked so hard to create. It took me three months of being without her to realize that all the money and success in the world didn't mean a damn thing if I didn't have her in my life to share it with. It seemed like everything I had done wrong was finally coming back to haunt me. All of these feelings about Angela and about life, were knotting up in my stomach ready to explode. I tried to control it by turning off the music and splashing my face with cold water, but it was no use. And for the first time in my life I did something I thought I would never do, I cried over a woman.

AIN'T TOO PROUD TO BEG

It was a week before Christmas. Derrick was disappointed that Angela hadn't responded to any of his letters. He even resorted to calling her office but the receptionist kept giving him the run-around telling him she was unavailable. Derrick got fed up and decided to go to Atlanta and sort things out with Angela face-to-face. If there wasn't any chance of them getting back together, he wanted to hear it directly from her. While he waited for his taxi to arrive, he called his father to tell him what he was about to do and to ask for his advice. As usual, Derrick

Sr. was very direct.

"It's a bad idea!" he said without hesitating. "Sometimes a stunt like this can do more harm than good."

"I know I'm taking a big chance, Dad. But this is something I've got to do."

"Why not give it a little more time? You might even meet someone else. There are more fish in the sea, you know."

"The only fish I want is Angela," Derrick said adamantly. "There's no doubt in my mind about that!"

"If you feel that strongly about it, all I can do is wish you luck. But promise me you won't get your hopes up too high. Sometimes things don't work out the way we want them to, even when we have the best of intentions."

"Don't worry. I'm not going to commit suicide."

At that moment the phone rang. Derrick told his father goodbye then clicked over.

"Hello?"

"Mr. Reed, your taxi is here," the doorman said.

"Thank you, I'll be right down."

On the way to the airport Derrick began to think that maybe his father was right. Angela had not made any effort to contact him since late August. For all he knew she could be involved with another man. Or maybe she completely lost interest. But he put those doubts aside and stayed committed to his plan. Instead of barging into Angela's office like a lunatic, he decided on a more subtle and creative approach. The day before, he contacted Justin at the radio station and arranged an interview for 7:30 the next morning. The exact same time and almost a year to the date that he first spoke with Angela on the air. He kept his fingers crossed that she would be tuned in again.

Derrick was so nervous he couldn't fall asleep that night. He stayed awake looking out of his hotel room window thinking about Angela and praying that his plan worked. If it didn't, he made a promise to himself not to get overly dramatic and try to force the issue. He knew Angela was in the driver's seat and had every right to tell him to go to hell. When the sun began to rise at 6:15 he took a quick shower, got dressed, and went to pick up his car from the valet. As he drove down the expressway listening to the radio, he laughed out loud thinking about how lost he was the first he went to the station. "Damn, I was mad!" he thought. But this time he was enjoying the ride and snapping his fingers to the music. It was Old School Friday and Justin was playing some of his favorite cuts.

Derrick pulled over into the far right lane and slowed down to 50 mph. As he cruised down the highway he began singing along to songs like, "Pull up to the bumper," "Yearn'in for your love," and "Forgetmenots" by Patrice Rushen. A wide grin came across his face as he reminisced on his childhood days. Like the times when he and Tony were in high school and they would invite girls over to play strip poker and blackjack. They always cheated with a marked deck, but the girls never found out. Then there was the time he and his friends got busted ditching school at Ben's house. His mother must have known something was up, because she came home early from work and caught them drinking Old English 800 and smoking Kool-Milds. She took out her extension cord and whipped all their asses. But what really made him laugh the hardest was remembering the times when Mark would put pennies on the arm of his stereo needle to keep the records from scratching. Those were the good old days, he was thinking.

By the time Derrick arrived at the radio station he was feeling relaxed. The music was sounding so good he almost forgot what he came there to do. But once he got upstairs to the studio and had that microphone thrown in his face again, he quickly snapped back to reality.

"You know the routine," Justin said. "Are you ready?"

"I thought we weren't going to start until 7:30," Derrick said nervously. "It's only 7:15."

"Next time don't bring your ass in so early." Justin laughed.

The On Air light came on, and they were live. Derrick gave Justin a dirty look, hoping he wouldn't throw a bomb at him the way he did the last time. Of course he did.

"Joining us live in studio this morning is my old buddy Derrick Reed, editor in chief of *Happily Single* magazine. Nice to have you back."

"Nice to be back."

"Okay, Derrick let's get right down to business. The last time you were here we talked about why men cheat. I guess the best way to follow that up is to ask, Can a man ever stop cheating?"

Derrick's jaw damn near hit the floor. Of all the questions in the world, he had to ask that one. And the irony was that Justin didn't even know Derrick was doing the interview to get Angela back. Talk about fate.

"My answer is, yes. I think anybody can stop cheating."

"What about the old saying, Once a dog always a dog?"

"That's not true!" Derrick said getting defensive. "People can change!"

"Have you ever cheated?"

Derrick knew Angela was probably listening. She lived out in Marrietta and was usually in her car by 7:00 a.m. This was the opportunity he had been waiting for. "Don't blow it," he thought to himself.

"Yes, I have cheated. And it was the worst mistake I ever made in my life."

"And why is that?"

"Because I lost the most wonderful woman to ever come into my life, that's why. And it's going to be impossible to replace her."

"Why didn't you think about that when you were stroking this other woman?"

That must have been the million-dollar question because the phone lines lit up. Even the women from the office were gathered outside the studio, peeping in the window and waiting for his answer. It was showtime at the Apollo all over again.

"Because I was I fool, that's why," Derrick said seriously. "I allowed my little head do all the thinking. Now I may never see her again."

"Looks like we've got a hot topic here," Justin said trying to instigate. "Let's go to the phones to see what our listeners have to say. Hello, you're on the air. What's your question or comment?"

"I just have one comment, I'm glad she left your two-timing ass!" an angry young woman said. "I hope you catch a disease and your dick falls off."

"Okay, people, let's keep it clean. This is a family show," Justin said. "Next caller, you're on the air."

"Derrick, my name is Michelle," she said in a calm tone. "I'm not going to attack you the way that other woman did, but I would like to ask you a question. Why should this woman ever trust you again? I mean, how can she be sure that you won't go out and cheat on her again after you get her back?"

"Derrick will try to answer that question when we come back from our commercial break," Justin said, cutting in. "So don't touch that dial."

What a tease! Everybody in Atlanta was holding their breath waiting to hear his answer. Even white folks who didn't normally listen to the urban station were tuned in. But this was more than just entertainment for Derrick, it was life or death. Each answer was either bringing him and Angela closer together or pushing them further apart. He knew he was running out of time. This next break was his last chance to let it all hang out. And he did.

"We're back!" Justin shouted. "Let's pick up right where we left off. Caller are you still there?"

"Yes, I'm here. And I'm waiting for Derrick to answer my question. In fact every woman in my office is waiting."

"Well Derrick?" Justin asked.

"She can trust me because I've learned my lesson. I guess you could say, I had to lose a good thing before I truly appreciated what I had. Sometimes that's what it takes," Derrick said sincerely. "I also learned that a real man keeps his word. I never should have told her we were in a one-on-one relationship if I wasn't adult enough to handle it."

Justin got ready to cut in, but Derrick wasn't finished. He pulled the microphone closer to his mouth and laid all his cards on the table.

"But the most important lesson that I learned was the value of a good woman. And if you're out there listening, Angela, I want you to know that you were the best I ever had. I'm sorry that I didn't recognize that while you were still in my life. And I'm sorry for lying to you and for ruining the special relationship we had. That's why I'm begging you in front of all these people to give me another chance. I know it won't be easy to forgive me because of the circumstances. But I promise you, with all my heart, that I'll do whatever it takes to make it up to you."

The studio was so quiet you could hear a pin drop, even the phones stopped ringing. The only sound was sniffling coming from the women crying in the hallway. It was a real soap opera. Justin was about to go to a commercial break when one of the telephone lines lit up. He was hoping it was Angela.

"Hello, you're on the air. Do you have a question for Derrick?"

"Yes, I do," a familiar voice said.

"Okay, try to keep it short."

"Don't worry, this won't take long," she said with an attitude. "Now, Derrick, if you caught your woman cheating with one of your friends, would you forgive her and take her back?"

Derrick knew it was Angela. Her voice was unmistakable. At first he thought about giving her an answer that would sound good. But then he decided to be honest. He owed her that much.

"The truth is, I probably wouldn't."

"So, why in the hell would you expect me, I mean her, to react any differently?"

"To be honest with you, I didn't know what to expect,"

Derrick said. "I just wanted the opportunity to let her know that I loved her and that I miss having her in my life."

"Excuse me, caller," Justin said interrupting. "Do you mind if I ask you your name?"

"This is Madam X."

"Madam X, huh?" Justin said, giving Derrick a wink. "Do you mind if I call you Angela?"

"Whichever you prefer."

"Well, Angela, what's it going to be, yes or no? The man is pouring his heart out and we're almost out of time."

"Can I give him my answer off the air?" Angela asked.

"Hell, no!" Justin yelled. "We've got millions of nosy people out there who want to hear the end of this, including me!"

"Then my answer is no!" Angela said bluntly. "Derrick, you meant the world to me, and I'll probably always love you. But there is no way I could ever trust you again after what you did to me. And without trust there's nothing to build, not even friendship. So, I guess this is goodbye. And please don't try contacting me again. All we have in common is the past, and I'd like to leave it at that." (click)

Derrick was hurt and embarrassed. That was the first time in his adult life that he was ever dumped. He was accustomed to being the one to decide when the relationship was over. Not this time. Angela flipped the script and gave him The Boot. No sympathy and no second chances.

"Well, Derrick, I'm sorry things didn't work out," Justin said.

"Actually, it worked out just fine," Derrick said sounding relieved. "I needed a woman to come along and tell me to go to hell. Maybe that's what a lot of men need to grow up. And if you're still listening Angela, I want to thank you for demanding your respect. It has made me a better person and a better man."

ABOUT THE AUTHOR

Michael Baisden was born June 26, 1963 in Chicago, Illinois. After two years of college he joined the Air Force where he continued his education and became interested in literature. "Terry McMillan, Ralph Ellison, Napoleon Hill, and Jawanza Kunjufu were among my favorites," he says. "But I felt there was a void in the book industry. There were very few authors writing about relationships from the man's perspective." After being honorably discharged in 1988 he established Legacy Inc., a company specializing in the manufacture of leather products. But it wasn't until 1993 that he discovered his God-given talent was writing. In January 1995 he self-published his first book, *Never Satisfied: How & Why Men Cheat*, and his life hasn't been the same since.

Michael has established himself as one of the top authors in the country today. His electrifying personality has earned him repeated appearances on talk shows such as *Ricki Lake*, *Maury Povich*, *Sally Jesse*, *Maureen O'Boyle*, *Tempest*, *Rolonda*, and *Our Voices* on BET. Michael is also a charismatic speaker. He has performed in front of standing-room-only audiences at events all across the country. His relationship seminars have toured cities such as Philadelphia, Boston, Dallas, Houston, Charlotte, Chicago, St. Louis, Los Angeles, San Francisco, Oakland, Washington, Atlanta, and Cleveland, just to name a few. And each time the audiences were left speechless and enlightened by his candid style.

For more information about when the *Never Satisfied Tour* is coming to a city near you, log on to Legacy Publishing's web site at www.flash.net/~legpub. Or you may send a brief letter to request information on how to schedule a seminar for your organization, convention, or exposition to:

Legacy Publishing
P.O. Box 168685
Irving, Texas 75016

Or send e-mail to **legpub@flash.net**
The web site also offers valuable information to aspiring authors
on how to write and self-publish.
CHECK IT OUT!